REGENCY

Rakes & Reputations

Two irresistibly sinful Regency romances
from Gail Ranstrom and Dorothy Elbury

005053021 6

Gail Ranstrom was born and raised in Montana and grew up spending the long winters lost in the pages of books that took her to exotic locales and interesting times. The love of that 'inner voyage' eventually led to writing. She has three children, Natalie, Jay and Katie, who are her proudest accomplishment. Part of a truly bi-coastal family, she resides in Southern California with her two terriers, Piper and Ally, and has family spread from Alaska to Florida.

Dorothy Elbury lives in England in a quiet Lincolnshire village—an ideal atmosphere for writing her historical novels. She has been married to her husband for fifty years (it was love at first sight, of course!) and they have three children and four grandchildren. Her hobbies include visiting museums and historic houses, and handicrafts of various kinds.

REGENCY
Rakes & Reputations

Gail Ranstrom
and
Dorothy Elbury

Mills & Boon, an imprint of Harlequin (UK) Limited,
Eton House, 18-24 Paradise Road, Richmond, Surrey TW9 1SR

REGENCY: RAKES & REPUTATIONS
© Harlequin Enterprises II B.V./S.à.r.l 2012

The publisher acknowledges the copyright holder of the individual works as follows:

A Rake by Midnight © Gail Ranstrom 2010
The Rake's Final Conquest © Dorothy Elbury 2011

ISBN: 978 0 263 89753 1

052-0412

Harlequin (UK) policy is to use papers that are natural, renewable and recyclable products and made from wood grown in sustainable forests. The logging and manufacturing processes conform to the legal environmental regulations of the country of origin.

Printed and bound
by CPI Group (UK) Ltd, Croydon, CR0 4YY

A Rake by Midnight

Gail Ranstrom

Prologue

London, England
July 13, 1821

Her first awareness was of bone-chilling cold at her back, then the incessant cadence of muted voices. She blinked in the flickering red-hued darkness, but pungent smoke stung her eyes so she closed them again, waiting for the air to clear. Incense? No. Something acrid that clogged and burned the back of her throat. Something more intoxicating?

She tried to focus, to gain her bearings, but found the task impossible. Searching her mind for her last lucid memory, she had a vague notion of drinking a glass of wine—bitter wine—given to her by a handsome blondish man. Mr. Henley? Her stomach roiled and she feared she would vomit.

She ached. Every muscle, every part of her, screamed in outrage, but she did not know why. Time was shifting, blurring. She couldn't remember. Why couldn't she remember?

The chanting stopped and a single voice rose above her. Someone standing at her head. The shadows closed in, then leaned over her, becoming vague faces and outlines. Yes. She was elevated, lying on a stone slab. The man above her stopped talking and reached over her to open whatever was covering her.

Bare! She was being exposed to all those faces surrounding her. She tried to move, to cover herself, but her limbs did not respond. Why couldn't she move?

Nameless terror squeezed her chest, cutting off her breath. She tried to scream, but she could only utter a tiny squeak barely audible above the chanting of dozens of voices. Everything had gone dreadfully wrong, but she could not make sense of it.

Another man appeared, kneeling between her legs. Lifting his robes. She knew. Oh, now she knew. She was to suffer Cora's fate.

Now terror had a name. *The Brotherhood.*

"No!" a distant voice screamed. Her sister's voice? Dear Lord! All was lost if they had Bella, too.

But suddenly the night was chaos and nothing made sense to her muddled mind. The clash of blades, shouts, shrill whistles and, suddenly, a blade at her throat. Searing pain. The warm ooze of blood as it seeped from her wound. She turned her head and closed her eyes, waiting for the inevitable, praying it would be quick.

But death did not come. Instead she registered the sound of running feet and distant shouts. A warm cloak covered her nakedness as she was lifted from the stone altar and cradled in strong arms. The cloying smell of incense still heavy in the air permeated his robe, but there was an underlying scent of clean masculinity. Something heated and strong. She clung to him, her fingers digging into his shoulder and arm, terrified he'd let her go. Terrified, too, that he might not have come to save her. She opened her eyes, knowing it was too late to fight anyway.

James Hunter. Oh, why did it have to be *him?*

Chapter One

September 12, 1821

Night again. Darkened streets, shifting movements in the shadows, muffled sounds, whispers on the wind, the damp chill of a suffocating fog. And always, the impending threat of disaster at her back. Gina O'Rourke hated the night, though she had begun to live her life in the hours between dusk and dawn—as if nothing evil could happen to her if she kept watch.

She brimmed with relief as she watched the lamplighter touch his torch to the lamppost outside the sitting room window. She could have sworn there were shadows in the park across the way.

Turning away from the window, she picked up her embroidery and sat by the fire where the light was best. As she pushed the needle through the fine linen she tried to direct her thoughts to the future, something she had not been able to do since *that* night.

Tomorrow, perhaps, she would speak to her brother-in-law

about finding her and Mama a place of their own. Andrew and Bella should have a chance to be alone, and to nurture their marriage without Mama's interference. Nothing so far away as St. Albans, but perhaps a cottage in St. John's Woods would do nicely. There, Mama could complain and fuss to her heart's content with no one inconvenienced. Except Gina. But there was something…*safe* in that sort of life. Safe and comforting, as only the familiar could be.

Yes, a quiet life without drama or danger was just the thing. No one would ever have to know about her past—about *that* night. She could stop racking her brain, trying to remember the horrid bits and pieces that came before finding herself carried away from the altar, cradled in James Hunter's arms. Just his scent, woodsy and heated, had calmed her then. Now the memory of it unsettled her in a most troubling way.

The front bell rang, followed by the sound of boots and a muted voice speaking with Andrew's butler in the foyer. She glanced at the clock. Nearly midnight. Andrew's meeting had run quite late, and he was still closeted in the library with Lord Wycliffe, but who would call at midnight? She stood, ready to make a quick retreat, but she was not quick enough. James Hunter appeared in the doorway and removed his hat.

"I beg your pardon, Miss O'Rourke. I came to see my brother and Edwards asked me to wait while he informs Drew that I am here. He must not have known you were using the room."

Gina struggled to think of something to say but found herself tongue-tied. She sank back on the settee, her heart racing, and wondered if her mere thoughts had been enough to summon him. Stranger things than that had happened to her lately.

Leaving now would be obvious and rude. And revealing. She retrieved her needlework again and rested it on her lap, praying her fingers would not tremble when she took up her needle.

"I believe he is in some sort of late meeting, Mr. Hunter," she told him. "I doubt you will have long to wait."

"With such charming company, I shall pray he delays."

She met his gaze and realized he was just being mannerly, and only because her sister was married to his brother. All the Hunter brothers were polite to a fault. Still, she could never encounter him without reading the memory of that wretched night in the depths of his violet-blue eyes. She saw pity there, too, and abhorred the thought that she was pitied. She could not help but wonder if he still saw her as she'd been that night—naked until he had covered her with his cloak. Heat shot through her and she swallowed her tiny moan at the mere thought.

He dropped his hat on a chair and went to a console table to avail himself of the sherry bottle there. He glanced at her over his shoulder and raised an eyebrow by way of invitation.

"No, thank you," she murmured, looking toward the sitting room door. Where was Edwards? And why did James, of all people, have to find her alone?

"How have you been, Miss O'Rourke?"

"Well, thank you." She glanced down at her embroidery but her right hand went to a spot near the hollow of her throat and the livid gash of scar tissue there. She met his gaze, swallowed hard and dropped her hand quickly. Why did he have to be so devilishly handsome? She might be able to bear it if only he were old or ugly or boorish instead of tall and uncommonly good-looking!

"I am glad to hear it," he murmured.

She stood, gripping her embroidery hoop in her left hand. "I…I am a bit fatigued. If you will excuse me?" She took several steps toward the door.

His eyes narrowed and he moved to block her way. "No."

Surely she had not heard him correctly. "What?"

"No, I will not excuse you. I've had just enough to drink to not give a damn for social niceties. 'Tis past time we had a talk, Miss O'Rourke. We cannot keep on as we have been."

A slow chill seeped through her. Surely he did not mean to discuss that night? "I do not know what you mean."

"Yes, you do. We must come to an understanding for the sake of our families."

"We are not at odds."

He took a swallow of his sherry and studied her with darkened eyes. "Being at odds would require a misunderstanding. Alas, that would require conversation. And we, Miss O'Rourke, have had precious little of that. Mere niceties exchanged in public is our forte. This is the first time we have been alone since…well, ever, and I intend to make use of it. God only knows when the opportunity may arise again."

"And my wishes?"

He shook his head. "I have tiptoed around your wishes, Miss O'Rourke, and could continue to do so for the next millennium if left to you."

He was right. She would never have chosen to have this conversation. Never have spoken it aloud. And this was, perhaps, the worst count against the infamous Blood Wyvern Brotherhood—they had robbed her of self-respect and dignity. The men at that ritual had been cloaked and hooded. She had not seen their faces, but they had seen her. *All* of her. And now, when a man looked at her and smiled, she wondered if he had been one of them—one of the villains who had meant to rape and kill her that night.

"I…I really think…"

"Your sister is married to my brother. For that reason alone, there will be countless times in the future when we are in each other's company. It would be easier if we could come to an understanding instead of this awkwardness we now engage in."

Gina looked down at her slippers, just peeking from beneath the hem of her yellow gown. "That night…you…."

A full minute passed before James finally filled the void. "I can think of nothing I did that night to provoke your ire. I did everything I could to shield your modesty and to stop the bleeding.…"

She *was* grateful. Truly grateful. But why could he not understand that, in her weakest moment, with nothing to hide her modesty, he had witnessed her deepest humiliation. He would never forget it—she had seen that much in his eyes. Each time he looked at her or talked to her, he would recall her as she'd been that night.

Panic and now-familiar anger began to bubble upward. She needed to escape before she said or did something unforgivable.

He stood between her and the door, and she tried to skirt past him. He reached out to stop her with a hand on her arm. She gasped at the warmth of his touch and the queasy sensations it stirred in her middle.

He lowered his voice as he drew nearer, and the heat of his breath tickled her ear as he leaned toward her. "I thought you and Isabella were so brave that night, to hunt down your sister's killers. I felt nothing but admiration for you. And for that, you shun me?"

Not for that, but for the knowledge in his eyes and the hours before her rescue. Hours that were still a blank to her. She could not go forward until she knew what transpired during that time. Had she been assaulted? Was she still a maiden? She looked up into his questioning eyes and shivered, trying desperately to think of something to say.

"Despite any personal feelings, for the sake of our families, Miss O'Rourke, shall we declare a truce?"

Personal feelings? The notion that he might dread seeing her, too, had not occurred to her before. She managed a slight nod. She'd agree to anything if he'd just let her go.

"Mr. Hunter will see you now."

They spun to find Edwards standing in the doorway.

A muscle jumped along James's jaw. He released her arm without another word, stepped back and bowed. "Miss O'Rourke, a pleasure, as always."

Gina watched him depart, then went to the console table to pour sherry into a glass and nearly choked on it as she drank it in a single gulp. She had to find those answers. To fill in those lost hours. She could never really be herself again until she did. And she needed to know that those men would never hurt another woman.

She placed her empty glass beside Mr. Hunter's and squared her shoulders. No more cowering in the dark. She would reclaim her life if it was the last thing she did!

Jamie studied the fire through the deep red contents of his glass, finding it difficult to keep his mind on the conversation after his encounter with Miss Eugenia. The memory of her always lingered with him long after she did. Tonight, was it the bloodred color of his wine that triggered the memories? Was it frustration? Lust? Anger? Did it matter? From their first meeting in the park in early July to this very night, he could not shake the memory of her away. Waking, sleeping, in a crowded room or a solitary moment, the thought of her would rise in him like an unholy obsession, disquieting him, kindling a deep burn in his soul.

Her form, with its soft, lush curves, promised delight. Her hair, a deep brown, gleamed with multicolored strands of chocolate, chestnut, caramel and copper when the light touched it. Her eyes—a deep greenish-hazel reminiscent of summer forests—captivated him. Her mouth—ah, that mouth! Inviting, plump lips curved up at the corners as if a perpetual smile was lurking, waiting to bloom with the slightest provocation—and, by the heavens, how he wanted to provoke it. Kiss it. Explore the silken depths beyond those rosy petals. Lose himself in her.

But Miss Eugenia cared nothing for him. Or, at the very least, she was not comfortable in his presence. Worst of all was that she had singled him out for this dubious honor. Her manner with Drew and Charlie was quite cordial. Clearly it was James she disdained.

"So deep in thought, Jamie?"

He came back to the moment and looked at his older brother and Lord Marcus Wycliffe, his superior at the Home Office. "I've things aplenty to think about, not the least of which is why you sent for me tonight."

Drew settled back in his chair, a bland expression on his face, a sure sign he expected trouble in one form or another. Jamie took his glass to the fireplace, stood with his elbow propped on the mantel and glanced toward his younger brother, Charles, who was prowling the room with restless energy. "I think Charlie and Wycliffe's presence here gives you away. Something about the Brotherhood, is it not?"

The Blood Wyvern Brotherhood, they called themselves. As members of the ton, they had thought themselves above the laws of decency and God. Only a week or so had passed since the last attempt of the covert section of the Home Office had failed to round up the remaining members of the ritualistic cult. Well, partially failed. They'd brought in all but a few unimportant dabblers and the one man at the top—the most evil of them all—Cyril Henley.

Drew nodded his confirmation. "We wanted to wait until the women had retired for the evening."

Jamie thought of Miss Eugenia, ready to flee with her

embroidery in hand. But he would not expose her. If she could not sleep, at least they had that much in common.

"Wycliffe wants to send you both abroad," Drew told him.

"Abroad? Me and Charlie?" Jamie turned to his superior. Why would Wycliffe send them away in the middle of an investigation?

"There has been no sign of the Brotherhood," Wycliffe told them. "No whispers. No sightings. And no more women have gone missing. With his cohorts captured, the secretary suspects Henley has left the country. Or perhaps someone else has disposed of him for us."

In Jamie's experience, which was prodigious, the Home Office wouldn't be that lucky. Men like Cyril Henley were like cockroaches. They survived all attempts to eradicate them, then came back to infest the world with their own sort of filth.

Wycliffe interpreted Jamie's silence for skepticism and nodded. "I doubt it, too, Hunter. But the secretary is convinced he has left England. Gone to France, Germany, Italy or perhaps even the Americas. He is bound to find followers and victims enough wherever he goes, as long as he does not make the mistake of trifling with the ton again. But this mad dog is our responsibility." Wycliffe paused to take another drink from his glass. "And that is why I recommended you to the Foreign Office."

Jamie opened his mouth to speak, but Wycliffe held up one hand to halt him. "You want these curs caught as badly as I do, Jamie. You, Charlie and Andrew know more than anyone else about this case. Andrew is married and does not work for the Home Office. You and Charlie are all we have left of the men who have been on this case from the beginning. If Henley is gone and the Brotherhood crushed, who better to send after him?"

Charlie stopped his pacing. "Transfer to the Foreign Office? Now there's an intriguing notion. Another day, I might be tempted by the proposition. But not at the moment. There are too many loose ends here. And I've fallen behind on my paperwork."

Jamie almost laughed. When had Charlie ever cared about paperwork?

"What do you say, Jamie?" Wycliffe asked.

"I think it is highly unlikely that Henley has gone anywhere." No, he would be thinking himself impervious to the Home Office. It was far more likely he was biding his time, waiting for the Home Office to put the case aside in favor of more urgent matters. He met Wycliffe's dark gaze. "I think I'll pass."

Wycliffe sighed. "I believe the secretary is expecting your acceptance. He has made arrangements."

"Tell him to arrange someone else."

"I thought you wanted to advance."

"Not at the expense of this case. Henley has not gone anywhere." Jamie noted Drew's distress and the look on Wycliffe's face and realized there was more to this than they were telling. "Why are you so anxious to get us out of the country?"

Drew sighed and sat back in his chair. "There is a price on your head."

"Henley?"

Wycliffe finished his brandy and stood. "Him, or any of the other cases you've brought to justice recently. I thought you'd be better off out of reach for a while. Take time to think about it, Jamie. Make yourself scarce. I will stall the secretary while you reconsider."

Jamie was no coward, but the thought that someone wanted him dead badly enough to pay for it was sobering. Henley would be looking for any way to stop Jamie from coming after him. "Give me another week, Wycliffe. I'll make my decision then."

His superior nodded. "Take care in the meantime."

Charlie gave a low whistle as they watched Wycliffe take his leave. "I wonder just how many people want you dead, Jamie," he ventured.

Jamie chuckled. "I can envision a queue from parliament to St. Paul's. But I have no intention of leaving the country. The bastard is here. In London. I feel it in my bones. Henley would never abandon his hunting grounds. I'd wager everything I own that someone is hiding him. His family, perhaps, or friends. Each time we get a lead, or think we're closing in, he disappears in a puff of smoke."

Drew looked doubtful. "How *do* you propose to find him?"

"Draw him out. There's a bounty on my head? Good. I shall make myself visible. And when he comes after me..."

"Setting yourself up as a target is a rotten idea, Jamie. He won't come for you himself. He'll hire cutthroats. And I don't want you dead."

Charlie began to pace, his head down. "Can we talk you out of this?"

Jamie pointed to his ears. "Deaf."

"Talk to Lockwood about this, Jamie. He still has connections at the Home and Foreign Offices, and he may have insights or be privy to information—"

Jamie took a deep breath. He did not want to involve their eldest brother, Lord Lockwood, in this quagmire. He had a wife and new child to think about, not to mention the duties attached to his title. "Not unless we are desperate. But this has to end now. Two months ago we thought it was over but they rose again. Last week we got the rest, but not Henley. I swear, the man is as slippery as an eel. As sure as I'm sitting here, Henley will find other hearts as dark as his own and rebuild his cult. He has a taste for killing now." And pray God he did not come after Eugenia to finish the job.

Drew combed his fingers through his hair and sighed. "There is a bounty on your head. Go, Jamie. Transfer to the Foreign Office. Make it a holiday. Let someone else handle this."

Jamie looked down into his glass again. Good sense and reason told him Drew was right. However. "I've been on this case from the beginning, Drew. I intend to see it through to the end."

"'Pears to me it's more personal than that."

Jamie tossed the remainder of his wine down and stood. Damn Drew's perception! "I want that blasted scum dangling from a rope for what he's done, and justice for—" he stopped himself from saying *Eugenia* and substituted "—for all their victims. And I bloody well want an end to all the secrets and lies."

"It always comes down to that with you, does it not— needing to know every last detail, every last truth? Why, Jamie? What drives you to that?"

"Truth never fails. There is no argument against it. It is the only rampart that remains when all else is crumbling. Truth tames chaos. It is just, honest and right. You can stand by it unashamed, depend upon it. If I did not stand for truth, what else would matter?"

"I pity when you finally learn that some questions are better left unanswered, and that the truth does not always serve you best." Andrew pushed his glass away and shook his head. "The world is not as black and white as you think, brother, and the truth is a double-edged sword. If you chase after it, be damned sure you are prepared to get cut."

"Living with lies could never be better," he said with unshakable certainty. "C'mon, Charlie. It appears I am going to need you to watch my back."

Chapter Two

Gina had expected shock, perhaps even outraged protests, but not stunned silence. Apart from the heavy rain outside the windows and the decisive tick of the tall case clock on the wall opposite the fireplace, the library was silent. Not even the clink of a teacup being replaced in its saucer broke the spell.

She glanced around the circle at the faces of her friends. Her sister, Isabella, looked as if she were sitting atop a coiled spring, ready to catapult off the settee and restrain her. Lady Annica, a darkly beautiful woman, wore a puzzled frown; Lady Sarah's expression was curious with a tinge of sympathy in her violet eyes—eyes so like her brother's that it always caught Gina by surprise. Grace Hawthorne, whom she had just met today, was more difficult to read, but Gina thought there might be a small crack in her serene countenance.

Gina cleared her throat and prayed she could keep her voice steady. "I was given to believe this group might be of some help in the matter. If not, then I apologize for broaching the subject."

A collective sigh was expelled and Isabella rose. "Gina! Are you mad?" She hurried to the library door, tested the lock, and returned to her chair.

"Nearly so," Gina admitted. Indeed, there was very little difference between true madness and what she'd been feeling for the past two months. "But I have come to believe that finding Mr. Henley is the only way I can change that."

"How do you propose to do that, dear?" Grace Hawthorne asked as she set her teacup down and smoothed her sky-blue skirts.

"I do not know how much you may have heard about my family's recent problems, Mrs. Hawthorne, but they have been extraordinary. The dust has settled a bit, what with Isabella and Lilly marrying, but I am still..." Gina stopped to clear her throat again, which was frequently raw since Lord Daschel had nicked it with a knife. "Still at odds."

Grace, who had been out of the country with her husband, gave a little smile of encouragement and Isabella hastened to finish Gina's explanation. "Almost as soon as our family arrived in London in May, our oldest sister, Cora, was kidnapped and murdered. Gina and I undertook to find the killer when the authorities had given up. Cora lived long enough to tell us that her killer was a member of the ton. With that as our only clue, we sought out men who fit that description and who had an interest in...in dark rituals and self-indulgence. Gina came close enough to be kidnapped by Mr. Henley as the next ritual sacrifice. But there were complications."

Gina looked down at her hands, clenched tightly in her lap. "Most of the men were arrested, and Lord Daschel, the man who murdered Cora, was killed. Then a fortnight ago, all the others were found and arrested but for their leader, Cyril Henley. I have been feeling so...unsettled. So vulnerable. And worse—increasingly angry. When I leave the house, I cannot stop looking over my shoulder or settle the nausea in my stomach. I cannot bear the thought of going through the rest of my life like this. I *must* do something to bring an end to it. And I fear nothing will end it until the villain is caught." Through the thoughtful silence that followed her declaration, Gina heard Lady Annica sigh.

"We understand more than you might think, Eugenia. You have come to the right place. The Wednesday League is prepared to assist women in your circumstances. We have certain resources and can work in ways that the Home Office cannot. But tell us, as precisely as possible, what you want to accomplish."

"Immediately after that night, I recalled nothing. Within a few days, memories began to return, but some of it still eludes me. I doubt it will ever come back entirely, and perhaps that is a blessing. But I want…" She could not tell them that she wanted the answers to what had happened to her. That she wanted the truth—all of it—good or bad. They would tell her to leave well enough alone. But there was something else she wanted, too. "I want…justice."

Lady Annica smiled. "We shall see that you get it, Eugenia, one way or another."

"I must be a part of it," Gina told them quickly. "I cannot sit idly by, waiting for someone else to free me from this poisonous feeling. Twice, the authorities have failed to capture him. How can you help me succeed when others have not?"

Lady Sarah stood and came to rest her hand on Gina's shoulder. "Give us a chance, Gina. We've succeeded in equally difficult circumstances. And what would you do? Haunt the Whitechapel streets alone? Prowl the rookeries after dark? That would be far too dangerous. Of course you will be involved in every aspect of the investigation, but surely you see the sense in allowing someone else to go about in your place."

"Please, Gina," Bella entreated. "What if something happened to you, too?"

If something happened? A sharp pain pierced Gina's brain. *If?* Oh, why couldn't she remember? Small bits and pieces, fleeting fragments, were all she had. She took a deep breath and pushed the uncertainty of the past two months away. "I do not want to waste another moment feeling like this."

"Give us a reasonable length of time, Gina," Grace appealed. "If we are not successful within a month, we shall find some way to involve you further."

That was more than Gina had expected, though not as much as she intended to take. No, she intended to confront those men, and she intended to have her answers. She took a deep breath and nodded. At least she would be moving forward.

Lady Annica stood. "Excellent! Shall we adjourn to *La Meilleure Robe?* I shall send ahead to Madame Marie requesting that she ask Mr. Renquist to be there."

"We are going to a dressmaker?" Gina asked in disbelief.

Grace leaned over and patted her clenched hands. "Madame Marie's husband is a Bow Street runner, dear. Quite the best of the lot. If he cannot help us, no one can."

Madame Marie, the French émigré owner of *La Meilleure Robe,* had been known to turn down clients on a whim. One was considered very fortunate to have a gown fashioned by the modiste to the aristocracy. The O'Rourke girls had been privileged to have had a number of their gowns made by her when they'd first arrived in London—gowns that had been meant to launch them in society but remained unworn in their wardrobes.

Gina was treated to a vastly different experience on this visit. She and Bella were ushered into a comfortable back dressing room which almost resembled a parlor where the other ladies were waiting. There were side tables and comfortable chairs arranged in a semicircle facing a small dressmaker's platform with mirrors behind.

When they were seated, Madame Marie entered from a side door and spread her arms wide. "La! 'Ow long 'as it been, ladies? Many months, yes? I pray you 'ave not gotten into more trouble."

Lady Annica removed her gloves and bonnet. "Not us, Madame. A friend of ours needs help."

Marie's glance skipped across the gathered faces—Lady Sarah, Grace Hawthorne, Charity MacGregor, Lady Annica, Bella and Gina, herself. Madame's gaze settled on Gina, and she felt a blush rise to her cheeks. Was it so obvious?

"François will be 'ere in a moment. 'E will want to 'ave the story from the beginning, eh? Be comfortable, and I shall tell the girls to bring tea. We must chat afterwards, yes?" And with that, the handsome Frenchwoman disappeared through the side door again.

Gina sank into a chair beside Lady Sarah. She was having misgivings about recounting her story—or at least what she could remember of it—to a man. The tale was difficult enough to share with another woman.

Bella came to her and took her hand. "You are very brave to be doing this, Gina. Do not let that courage fail you now."

Brave? Thank heavens they did not know the fear she lived with daily. The fear that Henley would come after her again. But she would conquer that fear for her rough justice. "Mama mustn't suspect."

Bella laughed. "Oh, you may be certain of that. I cannot even imagine what she might do—after she recovered from her swoon, of course."

"You may trust us all," Lady Sarah told her, slipping one arm around Bella's waist as she leaned close. "Everything that transpires in this room is utterly confidential."

Lady Sarah was the sister of Lord Lockwood, Andrew, James and Charles, and she was reassured to know that none of what was revealed here would be repeated to any of them. Relief brought a smile to her lips.

"Furthermore," Lady Sarah continued, "since you have said that you wish to be involved, you will have to enter society, Gina. It is the only way to gain access to the information we seek. We shall arrange for you to attend all the best functions, the more extravagant balls and crushes, and whatever other events that seem appropriate."

"Oh, I…"

"You met the Thayer twins at my oldest brother's house before…well, before. They have just arrived back in town after their summer holiday. Hortense and Harriet are quite lively and they know simply everyone and everything that goes on. In their company, you would have entrée to anywhere you wish to go."

Gina also recalled that the Thayer twins were singularly beautiful with their combination of copper hair and startling green eyes. But were they discreet?

The thought of entering society left her short of breath, but she had no time to protest when the side door opened and a maid carrying a tea tray entered, followed by a pleasant-looking man of average height. This would be Francis Renquist, Madame Marie's husband. His hair was sandy brown and his blue eyes had crinkle lines at the corners. Instinctively, Gina knew she could trust him.

"Ladies," he greeted them with a small bow, and when he straightened he rubbed his hands together. "I understand you have something for me?"

The maid left the tray on a side table and closed the door behind her, after which Lady Annica spoke. "We need to find some men, Mr. Renquist. Some particularly elusive men."

His bushy eyebrows rose. "What have they done, my lady?"

"Have you heard of the Blood Wyvern Brotherhood, sir?"

The color drained from his face. "How are you involved with these men?"

"We are not involved," Lady Sarah soothed. "Nor do we wish to be. We merely wish to locate the last of them, after which we shall inform the authorities where to find him."

"Even so…"

Lady Annica busied herself pouring out cups of tea and bringing them to the ladies, speaking as she did so. "Miss O'Rourke—" she indicated Gina with an inclination of her head "—and her sister, Mrs. Hunter, had some dealings with them a few months back. They are aware of the dangers and do not intend to encounter or confront the man involved. They simply have an interest in seeing that the perpetrators are safely locked away."

Gina blinked and squelched a pang of guilt. She fully intended to confront Mr. Henley. How else would she get her answers? But she feared the ladies would withdraw their support if she told them as much.

Mr. Renquist looked doubtful. "What, exactly, do you hope to accomplish?"

"Location, Mr. Renquist. That is all that we shall require of you," Grace Hawthorne said. "We do not want you to apprehend him or even speak to him. Just find him."

"As you are aware, these matters are rarely so simple."

"This will be, Mr. Renquist," Lady Sarah assured him.

"The Home Office is expending every resource at their disposal to bring this man to justice. Why must you risk involving yourselves—"

Lady Annica lowered her voice. "It is a personal matter," she said with a note of finality.

Mr. Renquist turned to look at Gina for one long moment. She held her breath, seeing that he wanted to refuse and was measuring her resolve. He must have read the determination in her heart because he let out a long sigh and nodded. "I will look into it, ladies, but I cannot make any promises. I will meet you here to report my findings twice a week unless there is need for more urgency. If you will let my wife know the days and times most convenient for you, I shall arrange to be here."

"Excellent!" Lady Sarah smiled and touched Mr. Renquist's arm as he turned to go. "Would you please send Madame Marie to us? Miss O'Rourke will need to commission a gown to account for her frequent visits here."

A moment later, Madame Marie appeared in the doorway, one finger tapping her cheek thoughtfully as she studied Gina's form. "Hmm. Something low and provocative, eh? Guaranteed to bring a man to 'is knees, yes? They will be so distracted that when you ask the questions, *chéri,* they will be compelled to give you the truth."

Gina suspected she would wear sackcloth if it would get to the truth.

By the time she and Bella arrived home, Gina barely had time to freshen up for afternoon tea. She hurried down the stairs on her way to the parlor, but the sound of muffled voices from the library stopped her. *Brotherhood,* she heard, and *Henley.* Not given to eavesdropping, she nevertheless hesitated outside the door. The sound of Andrew's voice, and those of James and Charles, was more than she could resist. Was this the business that closeted the brothers together in the library so often? *Her* business?

"But the leads are drying up," Charles's voice carried to her.

"...looking in the wrong places," Andrew replied.

"Where would *you* look?" James asked. "Parlors and sitting rooms?"

A laugh, cut off in the middle, answered that question. "Go back to the hells and Whitefriar taverns. Farrell will help. He's family now."

Gina shivered. Her sister Lilly's new husband was a bit frightening to everyone but Lilly. Even though he was family now, she suspected it would not be a good thing to be in Devlin Farrell's debt. But James's next words disavowed her of that notion.

"He has offered to help, and I will likely find a use for his particular talents. With him covering that end of the inquiries, Charlie and I will look to other avenues. But, as Charlie said, the leads are drying up."

"I can see you have your own suspicions," Andrew said.

There was a long pause before James spoke again, almost as if he were weighing his words carefully. "The one source we haven't explored in depth is his family and close acquaintances. They've been reluctant to speak with us and have denied any knowledge of the affair. But, damn it all, Drew, they've got to be involved in some way. Henley is canny enough, but he could not elude us so nimbly without help from someone in society, and who more likely to help him than his family or friends? God knows, his family would want to keep the secret of his involvement as long as possible. Their own reputations are at stake. And a man like Henley would not hesitate to prevail upon friends."

Gina frowned. If Henley's family was wary of James and the Home Office, she wondered if Mr. Renquist would be able to get past their defenses. Oh! She recalled there had been a woman at one of the two tableaus to which Cyril Henley had taken her before that last fateful night who had been almost as horrified as she. The woman had been familiar with everyone there, but her sensibilities had been more kindred to Gina's. Both had blushed and studied the floor when one tableau featured a nude woman reclining on a backless couch with nothing but a light shawl draped across one hip and her nether regions. Was that woman Henley's family? Or a friend? Could she know Henley's whereabouts? Or was she somehow connected with one of the other men?

Oh, if only she could remember the woman's name!

The rattle of teacups and saucers warned Gina that someone was bringing the tea service, and she dashed toward the sitting room. It would never do to be caught lurking outside the library door.

Bella looked up from her reading and patted the settee beside her when Gina rushed in. "Mama took Nancy and went shopping. Come sit, Gina. We rarely have time alone together these days."

Gina retrieved her embroidery from a side table and sat beside her sister. "We shall have to hoard all the moments we can."

"I know. Mama has been sighing and fretting over letters from her friends until just recently. I worried that she might want to go home, but it seems she is over the worst of her homesickness."

"I pray we will find a place of our own nearby. I would adore to be close to you and Lilly."

"Even when Mama finally goes back to Ireland, you should stay with me. Or Lilly. There is a dearth of eligible men in Belfast."

Gina poked the needle through the fine linen. "You know how it will be, Bella. The die is cast. Cora is gone. You and Lilly are wed. I am the last of us, so it falls to me to become Mama's companion in her old age."

Bella put her book aside and studied Gina's face. "I always thought we would all marry and shuttle Mama between us. In another few years, she will not want to live alone, and between us all, we could take turns."

"Heaven forbid!" Gina managed a laugh. "Would Andrew have married you, or would Mr. Farrell have married Lilly, if they had known Mama came in the bargain?"

"Andrew has managed quite well," Bella chuckled. "He did not think you and Mama should be without protection. And I am certain Lilly's husband feels the same."

Gina bit her tongue to keep from reminding Bella that her husband, and Lilly's, were the sort they'd needed protection *from*. Instead, she shrugged and guided the needle and silk floss through the linen again.

The sitting room door opened and Edwards brought in the tea service, followed by Andrew and his brothers. She and Bella stood to greet them.

"May we join you? Seems like forever since we've done anything quite so domestic as having tea with the ladies."

"Please," Bella said, her gaze holding her husband's and a soft color suffusing her cheeks. The room had shrunk to the two of them.

Was that what love looked like? Gina looked away, feeling as if she were intruding and she noted that James, too, was watching them. His gaze shifted to her and she blinked. He gave her a lopsided grin, as if they shared some secret that had eluded the others. She returned his smile, feeling schoolgirl shy.

"I hope you do not mind our interruption, ladies," Charles said. "We ran into Edwards in the corridor and he advised that it was just the two of you."

"Not at all," Bella said. She gestured at a console table that held several carafes and glasses. "May I offer you stronger refreshment?"

Charles grinned and went to the table. "Don't mind if I do."

Gina sank back to the settee. She wondered if her guilt at eavesdropping could be read on her face. She retrieved her needlework and rested it on her lap in a pretended study of her work while Bella took charge of the teapot.

"Where is the lovely Mrs. O'Rourke?" James asked as he took a teacup from Bella.

"She is out shopping," Bella said. "I think she is up to something. She's been quite giddy the past few days."

Andrew raised one eyebrow and Gina stifled a giggle. Bella was right—he'd been very good-natured about the O'Rourke invasion, and he was, no doubt, trying to imagine Mama giddy. Shrill, perhaps, feigning helplessness or demanding. But giddy?

The conversation floated around her and she felt herself withdrawing again, as she had so often since that night. Though her eyes remained on her needlework, her right hand went to the scar near the hollow of her throat as she thought of how James had bandaged the gash. He had seen her at her worst. Had he not, perhaps she wouldn't mind being around him quite so much.

Bella's voice cut through her thoughts. "Gina!"

She started and glanced up again, the question in her eyes.

"James asked if you are well," Bella told her.

When she realized she was trying to cover the fading scar, she dropped her hand quickly and nodded. She met his gaze and swallowed hard. Remembering his offer of a truce, she gave him a weak smile. "Quite well, thank you."

The stiff set of his shoulders relaxed slightly. "Good," he murmured, as if he had expected her to give a different answer.

An awkward silence stretched out as Bella and Charles glanced between them. Was her discomfort so terribly obvious?

She was relieved when everyone turned toward the sitting room door at a clatter in the foyer accompanied by raised feminine voices. A moment later, Mama burst through the sitting room door with nary an acknowledgement, apology or explanation.

"Oh!" she exclaimed, removing her straw bonnet edged in black silk ribbon and fanning herself with the brim. "Public coachmen are so rude! Why, this one did not even want to help me with my packages! Nancy and I had to fetch them all."

Gina tried to imagine their poor maid, now carrying the entire lot up the stairs to Mama's room. "What did you purchase, Mama?"

"Quite a few things, dear. Several bolts of cloth, for when I am out of mourning—" she gestured at her black bombazine gown "—and some very nice Belgian lace, trims and notions. Then I went to Fortnum and Mason to purchase tins of dried fruits, exotic teas and preserves."

Bella frowned. "I am certain Cook has enough—"

"They are not for cook, silly girl." Mama sighed as she sank into a comfortable chair. "They are for us to take home. So difficult to find the finer things in Belfast, you know. Why, Belgian lace costs twice as much in the shops there! I confess, I delight in knowing I shall be the envy of all my friends."

Gina smiled. These were the sure signs that Mama was beginning to heal from Cora's death. "Surely there will be time enough to find everything you want."

"Time enough? Why, there's scarcely any time left at all! We shall be returning to Ireland within the fortnight."

Gina could only stare at her mother in disbelief. She'd said nothing about returning to Ireland so soon! Not even a hint!

Bella intervened. "I thought you'd stay longer. With Lilly just wed, she may need you."

Mama gave her a jaded look. "I believe the Farrells have no need for me at all. Mr. Farrell seems to have Lilly well in hand." She turned to spare Andrew a glimpse. "As does Mr. Hunter seem to suit you well. No, you and Lilly have no need of me. Eugenia and I shall leave within a fortnight."

Fortnight? She could not possibly be ready so soon! Mr. Renquist had indicated it could take *months* to find Mr. Henley. She stood in her agitation, acutely aware that James Hunter was watching her with marked curiosity. "Could we not stay until Christmas?"

"Christmas? Good heavens, Eugenia!" Mama put her hat aside and accepted a teacup from Bella. "Why, we cannot leave our house in Belfast unattended so long. Was it not always our intent to give you girls a season and leave for home afterward? You will recall I originally let the house in St. James until September. Just because we removed here and have been in mourning does not mean I changed our plans."

"Mrs. O'Rourke, you are welcome here as long as you wish to stay," Andrew told her. Gina wondered how much that offer had cost him.

"Kind of you, I am sure," Mama said. "But I've already made arrangements. I decided that traveling overland is far too tedious and booked our berths yesterday, and today I ordered crates to be delivered for our goods." She spread her arms wide as if she dared anyone to argue. "'Tis a *fait accompli.*"

"Excuse me." Gina prayed she could keep her composure until she exited the sitting room.

Chapter Three

Gina breathed deeply of the fresh air, her mind whirling with the news. So this is what Mama had been "giddy" about—the prospect of returning to Ireland! She needed to think. To plan. This new development changed everything.

If she was to have any chance of learning what happened in those lost hours, of finally being free of the past, she would have to act quickly. Indeed, she would not be able to wait for Mr. Renquist to make progress. As much as she dreaded mixing in society, she would have to enter the search herself, just as Lady Sarah had suggested.

She found a quiet spot in the garden and sat on a bench balanced between two stone lions. The late afternoon breeze made her shiver, a reminder of oncoming autumn, and she hugged herself as she focused on the toes of her slippers, trying to unravel the problem at hand.

Lady Sarah had already made arrangements to call for her tomorrow evening and accompany her to the Auberville Ball. The Thayer twins would be in attendance and, if all went well, Lady Sarah would arrange for more invitations, and Gina would join their circle.

She would not ask Mr. Renquist to investigate what she'd overheard in the library. She'd leave him to his sources and *she* would seek out Mr. Henley's family and friends in society. The only thing she could not do was return to Belfast with this matter unresolved. To never know the truth. Never feel safe again so long as Mr. Henley roamed the earth.

The toes of two highly polished Wellingtons appeared before her. "Chilly, Miss O'Rourke?"

She looked up to find James Hunter standing before her. The familiar uneasy heat rose in her but she controlled it with a deep breath before she spoke. "A bit, Mr. Hunter. I should not have come out without my shawl."

"Shall I fetch it?"

She shook her head. She did not intend to stay a moment longer than necessary.

He sat beside her, close enough for her to feel his heat, but not close enough to touch. "I gather your mother's announcement was a surprise to you?"

"Completely. I had no idea she wanted to leave so soon."

"And you do not?"

"Yes. No! I mean, I want to go home, but this is so sudden, and there were things that I still wanted to do."

"*Things,* Miss O'Rourke? For instance?"

"I…I have not been much out in society due to…well, circumstances. I would like to experience a bit of the excitement of London."

He gave a chortle that made her shiver. "I would think you'd have had enough excitement to last for one season."

She looked sideways at him. There was nothing sarcastic in his countenance, and nothing chiding. Just a simple statement of fact. "A different sort of excitement than being abducted, Mr. Hunter."

His eyes caught hers and held them. "I understand. I shall be sorry to see you go. I would have liked to waltz just once with you. Have you been to Vauxhall, or the museums?"

She shook her head. "Cora was killed not long after we arrived. And everything since then has conspired to keep us otherwise occupied."

He laughed outright this time. "That would be a bit of an understatement, Miss O'Rourke. Your family has been the talk of the town. I must say, the O'Rourkes have collided with London in a most forceful manner."

"And yet your sister has offered to sponsor me. At great risk to her reputation, I surmise."

"Has she?" He looked surprised, and Gina realized he was thinking such a sponsorship was risky. "Well, Sarah knows best. She is an excellent judge of character. With her as your sponsor, your success is assured."

She didn't care a whit for social success. She only wanted to meet the people who could lead her to Mr. Henley, but given the conversation she'd overheard earlier in the library, she imagined all the brothers would forbid such a thing. Thank heavens they would be too busy with their own business to meddle in hers.

She shivered again and Mr. Hunter shrugged out of his jacket to drape it over her shoulders. Still warm from his body, it smelled of lime shaving soap and something clean. Starch? Very comforting, yet provocative. And once again, it conjured memories of that night. "Thank you," she managed, suspecting she should have refused and gone inside.

"My pleasure, Miss O'Rourke." He stretched his legs out and crossed his ankles. "One never knows how to dress for the weather this time of year."

"Is…is there a reason you followed me, Mr. Hunter?"

"I wanted to thank you for not running the moment you

saw me, as is your custom. Indeed, I think our truce will work admirably well."

"My dislike of you has been nothing personal, Mr. Hunter."

"You dislike me?"

Mortified by her gaucherie, Gina winced. "Oh, forgive me. I did not mean that the way it sounded. What I meant to say is that you make me uncomfortable...I mean—"

"Please do not explain further, Miss O'Rourke. I do not think my tender ego is up to it." He grinned and her stomach did an odd little flip-flop.

The sound of laughter preceded the arrival of others, and Gina slipped James's jacket off her shoulders and shivered in the sudden chill. She gave it back and watched as he stood and shrugged it on moments before Bella and Charles appeared around the hedge. Why did she feel as if they had done something wrong?

Charles bowed to Gina before he turned to his brother. "Here you are, Jamie. We're late for our appointment, and we ought to leave these good people to their evening."

Bella shook her head in feigned disbelief. "I tried to persuade him that they were welcome to stay for dinner, but Charles would not hear of it."

"Quite right. We are expected elsewhere," James confirmed as he stepped away from the bench.

The men bowed, but before they departed, James looked at her, something unreadable in his eyes before he turned and disappeared along the garden path. A vague feeling of disappointment filled Gina at their departure.

Bella led her through the library doors and went to the console table to pour sherry into a glass and bring it to her. "I had no idea!"

Gina accepted the glass and took a healthy gulp. "Of what?"

"That you were in love with James."

She choked, the sherry burning her throat. Love? Oh, to the contrary. She could barely endure his company. "You are mistaken, Bella. I am not in love with Mr. Hunter. If I am awkward in his presence, it is because I do not like to keep his company. He…he…*saw* me." Indeed, he was a reminder of all she had endured. Of all she had lost. And that was what she'd been at a loss to explain to him mere moments ago.

Bella gave her a wise older-sister smile. "Perhaps that is why he is so drawn to you. 'Tis almost painful to watch him when you are in the same room. He cannot tear his eyes from you."

"Because he imagines me naked! It…it is lasciviousness, Bella, and nothing more."

"Truly?" But Bella looked doubtful. "He looked genuinely distraught when Mama announced she was taking you home to Ireland."

Because he would have liked to waltz with her? She caught her breath at the sudden pain in her chest at the realization that, had things been different, had that night never occurred, she would have liked to waltz with him, too.

That night at the Crown and Bear tavern, Jamie Hunter rolled his eyes in disgust. "Good Lord, Charlie, you haven't had that much to drink. Focus, man!"

Charlie grinned, a canny look on his face. "I'm not far gone, Jamie. I'm thinking of something else."

"Some*one* else, more likely. Who is it this time?"

"The sweet little thing you just cast off. Suzette."

"That was two months ago." Jamie leaned back in his chair and folded his arms over his chest. "But Suzette can make the blood boil, can she not? Alas, what will she do when you move on to another demirep? She's damned near made a career of the Hunter brothers. You're the lone holdout, Charlie."

"Well, I am not holding out any longer. Suzette was saving the best for last. She is fond of the tall, dark and handsome sort." He waggled his eyebrows at Jamie and chuckled. "I've seen the *congé* she has acquired from Lockwood, Drew and you. I'd be willing to wager she could retire if she sold those jewels."

"Why would she retire when she has yet another Hunter brother to fleece?"

"I daresay you all got your money's worth. I know I shall."

Jamie shrugged. He couldn't say why he'd tired of Suzette Lamont, only that he had. Though, when he thought about it, he'd reached that decision very soon after his family had become involved with the O'Rourkes.

He suppressed a shiver and came back to the conversation. "Just be a gentleman when you leave, Charlie. Suzette deserves that much."

"Aye, she was so devastated when *you* left that she took up with a German not a week later. Ah, but she's done with him now, and 'tis my turn."

"Made a pauper of him, more likely. Watch your purse strings, brother."

"Jealous?"

Was he? Perhaps just a touch. Suzette was skilled and had taught him much about pleasing a woman. And he was beginning to feel the effects of prolonged celibacy. The fleeting thought that perhaps he needed a woman to take the edge off his lust for Eugenia made him shake his head in disgust. He downed his whiskey in a single gulp.

This eschewing of mistresses was what came of being around his older brothers. They'd become domesticated so quickly that he could scarce believe it. Lockwood had taken to marriage like a duck to water. Andrew, a libertine to rival the worst, was now a happy house cat, curling by his fire with his favorite new toy—Bella.

Ah, yes, and here came the latest in a long line of newly domesticated tomcats. Devlin Farrell. A man whose slightest twitch had roused terror in seasoned criminals was now a well-contented newlywed who literally worshipped his wife.

"Gents," he greeted them. "I see you started without me."

Charlie laughed. "I have no doubt you'll catch up, Farrell."

Devlin signaled the barkeeper and a tankard of ale magically appeared. "I have no intention of catching up. Lilly is waiting at home. Wouldn't want to disappoint her."

Jamie snorted. He very much doubted Lilly would be disappointed tonight, or any other night if he was any judge at all. If there was no saint like a reformed sinner, Devlin Farrell would soon have his own niche at St. Paul's.

After a long drink, Devlin answered their unasked question. "No sign of them, but I've confirmed they are still in the vicinity. Tell the secretary his information is wrong."

"We suspected as much." Charlie sat a bit straighter, as if he had suddenly shaken off the effects of the whiskey. "And is there, indeed, a price on Jamie's head?"

"A rather large one."

Jamie grinned. "How much am I worth?"

"Ten thousand pounds."

Charlie whistled and rolled his eyes. "There should be at least a dozen takers at that price."

"At least," Devlin agreed. "But common cutthroats do not have the finesse to take our Jamie by surprise."

Ten thousand pounds was, nevertheless, a daunting sum. Jamie shifted uneasily in his chair, taking the threat seriously for the first time. Who would come after him first? He held Devlin's gaze. "Will it be the Gibbons brothers?"

The corners of Devlin's mouth quirked. "They're mean as snakes and will turn on you in a trice, but blast if they aren't sometimes useful. They'll do anything for money, though I don't know what they do with it once it's in their hands."

"Wish they'd get a bath," Charlie muttered. "Or buy some manners."

"It's a mystery." Devlin shrugged. "They live in a hovel, never invest in a bar of soap, pick their clothes out of rag piles, eat garbage and even share their whores so they only have to pay for one. They must have a fortune amassed somewhere."

"Two more pathetic creatures I've never seen."

"Oh, I don't know.…" Devlin's right eyebrow shot up as he glanced between Jamie and Charlie.

Jamie and Charlie burst out laughing and toasted each other as if to confirm Devlin's analysis.

Devlin sat back in his chair and his expression sobered. "In view of the risk to you, Jamie, I'd like you to accept a bodyguard or two. I know just the men, and—"

"They'd get in the way. Make me conspicuous. And do not think to set them on me without my knowledge. I'd mistake them for bounty hunters and have to kill them."

Devlin did not look happy. "I might have a lead for you. If you handle it with your usual skill, you could end this thing quickly."

Jamie sat forward and lowered his voice. "What do you have up your sleeve, Devlin?"

"That night, at the ritual, when the charleys arrived and the brotherhood scattered down the tunnels, I recognized a few men. Some, you already know about. But I haven't mentioned that I saw Stanley Metcalfe and Adam Booth. They looked confused and frightened and, unless I miss my guess, that was their first time at a ritual, and is the reason I did not pursue them. They've kept their noses clean since, though."

How like Devlin to keep that information to himself until it was needed. Until Metcalfe or Booth could prove useful. "And?"

"As the last men on the periphery of the brotherhood still free, they might be useful to you. Might have some information. One of them could be in touch with Henley. They might know his family and have knowledge of... Well, you can imagine how helpful they might be."

If they could be trusted. And if they were still alive.

Jamie dropped some coins on the table and stood. "Get home to Lilly. And thanks for the tip. I'll be looking for them tomorrow."

Massive crystal chandeliers glittered multicolored shards of light across the room, laughter was shrill and the wine was free-flowing. The evening promised to be a huge success. Alas, Lord Auberville hadn't been able to tell him who, precisely, had been invited to the ball, so Jamie concluded he'd just have to see for himself. Charlie left him at the door to find the card room and a game of whist, leaving Jamie free to wander the perimeter of the dance floor. With a nod here and a smile there, he acknowledged a few friends and acquaintances, but nary a sign of Stanley Metcalfe or Adam Booth. Had someone tipped them off?

He was thinking he'd take any Metcalfe at this point, and there, in answer to his prayer, was Stanley Metcalfe's sister, Missy. Dressed in deceptive white, she was holding court in a circle of men. He wondered if she realized her popularity was attributable to the poorly kept secret that she granted certain...liberties, if one could get her alone in a garden.

He advanced on the group, knowing that most of the men would depart when the music stopped. The rest...well, he would just have to be quicker. He greeted the men, took Missy's hand and bowed over it.

"Miss Metcalfe, you are looking especially lovely tonight."

She twinkled at him and giggled. "How kind of you to say, Mr. Hunter."

"Just giving you your due, Miss Metcalfe."

The orchestra finished the set and one young man stepped forward. "I say, Miss Metcalfe, would you do me the honor—"

Jamie smiled apologetically at the young man. "Taken. I shall return her to you directly after." He took Missy's hand and led her away as she muffled yet another giggle.

"How naughty of you, Mr. Hunter," she said as the next dance, a sedate reel, began. "I have no recollection of granting you a dance."

"Then I must thank you for not giving me away." There would be an unavoidable risk in carrying on their conversation as they met between steps, so he led her into the dance, waited until they met for a turn, and then tugged her toward the terrace doors.

"Oh!" She pressed one dainty hand against her chest when they were outside and the terrace door closed behind them. Her eyes widened in feigned innocence. "We really shouldn't…"

He really wouldn't. But Missy needn't know that. "You break a man's heart, my dear."

She gave him a pretty pout. "What else am I to do? You dance with a girl now and then, and ignore her the rest of the time. Is that fair?"

"Fair? Oh, my dear, more fair than you can know. If I were to subject myself to your charms too often, why there is no telling what I might do. Perhaps I ought to take my pleas to your brother."

"No need for that, Mr. Hunter. He would likely just refuse you."

"Or he could give me his blessing to call upon you. Is he here?"

"No. He...he is keeping to himself these days."

"Do you know where I might find him? His club, perhaps?"

"You'd do better to petition my father, sir, but he is ill at the moment, and not receiving."

How coincidental that all the males in her family were currently unavailable. And suspicious. Something was being covered up, of that he was sure. "Is there no recourse for me at all?"

She moved closer until her breasts were pressed against his chest, and looked up at him with a sloe-eyed heat. "You could take what you want. I like men who take what they want."

He groaned. What was the harm in taking what was freely offered? He spanned her waist with his hands and held her still as he tilted his head down to hers. "You are too tempting, Miss Metcalfe," he said against her lips. When he deepened the contact and she moaned, he waited for the excitement, the rush of pleasure and anticipation. In vain. All he could think was that the rosewater she had splashed on was rather overpowering, and not at all like the stirring scent of Miss O'Rourke's skin.

Fortunately, he already had what he needed from Missy— she did not know where her brother was. And she was not what he wanted.

He stepped back from her. "We must get you back inside before anyone notices you're gone. I would dislike people talking about you."

She stamped her foot in frustration and was about to protest when the terrace doors opened and her erstwhile swain appeared. Thank God they'd broken contact or Jamie suspected he'd be fighting a duel at dawn.

"Miss Metcalfe became overheated," he explained. "Do keep her company whilst she cools down."

He edged past the young man and into the ballroom. When he glanced back, Missy Metcalfe was watching him with consternation. He gave her a wink, thinking she could prove useful in the future.

Inside, he scanned the room before leaving, but stopped dead when he met deep hazel eyes at a distance. Could it be? Yes. Miss O'Rourke was standing between Hortense and Harriett Thayer, looking a bit bemused as one of the twins—he could not tell them apart—told a story. Eugenia was dressed in a pink confection that complemented her complexion perfectly. Her lustrous golden-brown hair was done up in a perfect cluster from which ringlets fell to dance below her shoulders. He tried to imagine how those ringlets would feel tangled between his fingers.

What the bloody hell was Miss O'Rourke doing here? Did she not realize she was at risk for as long as a single member of the brotherhood was on the loose? She was one of the few people left alive who could recognize them.

The sound of conversation was nearly deafening but Gina could barely hear it over the thundering of her own heartbeat. Even supported by the Thayer twins, she wondered what had ever made her think she was prepared for this.

Standing in the ballroom, she could not banish the thought that one of the men present may have been at the chapel that night. Someone who might have been a part of her abduction, had hoped to be a part of her ultimate shame and death.

She shuddered and forced the thoughts from her mind. She had known entering society would not be easy. She could not let that stop her. She was running out of time if she meant to have her justice.

Just as she squared her shoulders and lifted her chin, her fears materialized. She glimpsed James Hunter in a group of revelers. James, who *had* been there. Who had seen her as nature had made her. But he, at least, had not meant her ill.

"Oh, look! There's Missy Metcalfe." Hortense nudged Gina in the ribs as she leaned closer to her ear. "Quite the little flirt, that one."

Gina shook off her vague misgiving and chuckled as she thought of the pot and the kettle. Missy Metcalfe, whoever she was, would surely fall far short of Hortense's skills.

Harriett, though, was a bit more sedate. Only a bit. "She prefers the company of men, Hortense. That does not make her a flirt."

"No, Harri. It makes her a—"

"Hush! Do you want someone to hear?" Harriett pasted a smile on her pretty face and waved to the young lady in question.

"She is quite lovely," Gina allowed.

Hortense turned and swept Gina's form head to toe in an assessing gaze. "You needn't worry, Eugenia. She cannot hold a candle to you."

"Oh, but she is fair and lively while I am—"

"Dark and mysterious," Harriett finished. "I can well picture young men hanging on your every word. And that gown! Pink becomes you. You must make it your signature color."

Gina smoothed the pale pink watered silk over her hips. The gown had been made for her not long after her arrival in London, and she had lost weight since then. It did not hang on her, but it gapped slightly at the scooped décolletage and Nancy had pinned a posy of violets there to fill the gap and save her modesty.

Hortense pinched her arm. "Upon my word! There is Mr.

Hunter heading our way. Mr. *James* Hunter. Are you not somehow related, Eugenia?"

"His brother is married to my sister," she confessed, searching the crowd for a sign of him as she experienced a pang of panic.

"How divine," Hortense declared with a wink. "What I wouldn't give to have such a man going in and out of my house. Do you often manage to encounter him?"

"Rarely." As rarely as she could manage.

"Pity," Harriett ventured. "He has a reputation to be envied amongst the ladies of the ton. There is scarce one who has not contrived to elicit a walk in the gardens with him."

"Why?" she asked.

The twins giggled and Hortense answered. "You cannot have missed how handsome he is. Oh, those eyes make my knees weak! And I have heard it whispered—no, I will not tell you by whom—that he kisses like a fallen angel. Heavenly and naughty at the same time. How I would love to know how that feels."

Gina closed her eyes, remembering how she had felt when he had carried her from the altar. Comforted. Safe. Mortified. But what would it have been like to let him kiss her?

She raised her hand to her throat where her scar was hidden beneath a wide pink ribbon to which a cameo had been fastened. Heat flowed through her, warming her blood and firing her imagination.

"Ah, well," Harriett continued, "I would make the most of your connection. If you are seen on his arm, your reputation as a 'desirable' is made."

Gina shook her head, not wanting to disappoint the twins. "Mr. Hunter has far more important things to do than 'make' my reputation." Her stomach fluttered when a crooked smile quirked his mouth as he met her eyes.

He arrived before them, bowed to Hortense and Harriett,

then turned his attention to her as the music began. "Our first waltz, Miss O'Rourke," he murmured in a deep, intimate voice as he took her hand.

She was amazed that her knees did not give out as he led her onto the dance floor.

Chapter Four

She detected an angry undercurrent in the way James Hunter took her hand and led her onto the dance floor. Was it not she who should be indignant at the way he'd claimed her and given her no room to demur? With the slightest tug, he spun her around and pulled her against his chest just as the music began.

"Fancy meeting you here, Miss O'Rourke," he said as he led her into the first steps of the waltz.

Gina raised her eyebrows at his clipped tone. "I do not recall consenting to a dance, Mr. Hunter."

He looked at her through those violet-blue eyes, rather wintery now instead of holding their usual warmth. His entire demeanor had changed since leading her away from the twins. "I wasn't actually asking."

Disappointment washed through her. She had wondered, if they waltzed, how it would feel to be in his arms, but not like this. Now she only wanted to escape. What had she done to provoke him? As she moved to draw away, his hand tightened at her waist.

"Careful, Miss O'Rourke, or everyone will know our business."

She fought to keep her face impassive and her manner as cold as his, but his demeanor bothered her more than she dared let him know. "We have business? If so, I am unaware of it, sir. Indeed, I thought we had called a truce."

"We have. Correct me if I am wrong, but I do not recall recklessness being a part of it."

She collected her wits as he swung her in a wide circle. "I...reckless? I haven't the faintest notion what you mean."

"Have you not?" Their progress around the dance floor had brought them close to an open terrace door and he waltzed her outside without missing a step. "Then allow me to enlighten you."

He stopped suddenly and released her in the dim glow of a hanging lantern, leaving her to catch her own balance. She had never seen him like this before—angry and challenging—and she did not like it. She lifted her chin and glared at him, daring him to berate her for anything.

But that did not stop him. "There are people around who... who could wish you harm. And here you are, flaunting yourself for all the world to see. Are you daring Henley to come after you, Miss O'Rourke?"

She blinked. He was right, of course, but she could hardly tell him that finding Henley had, in fact, been her goal. In his present mood, he was likely to throw her over his shoulder and carry her home. She lifted her chin a bit higher. "I fail to see how that is any concern of yours, Mr. Hunter."

The expression on his face was stiff and brittle, as if it might crack at any moment and reveal his true feelings. "You don't? Then allow me to count the ways. One—" he held up one finger "—you are my brother's sister-in-law. Two—" another finger went up "—I have already pulled you from Henley's reach once. Three, I am currently working to see that Henley is punished, and four…" His voice trailed off, as if he had thought better of continuing.

"Four?" she challenged.

He laughed, but there was not the slightest hint of humor in it. "You would not want to hear that one, Miss O'Rourke, believe me. Shall we say that my reasons are legion, and that your presence is a distraction and a deterrent?"

What could be so dreadful she could not hear it? She took a deep breath and let it out slowly, regaining a small measure of composure. "Very well. But your reasons are not my concern. I am tired of being a prisoner in my home. I am tired of being punished for something that is not my fault. I have had enough of allowing fear to dictate my life. No more, Mr. Hunter. Do you hear me? No more."

He gripped her upper arms and leaned toward her. His scent weakened her knees and for a moment the possibility of a kiss hovered in the air between them. She was breathless, torn by hope and fear. Then, in a very low voice, he said, "I hear you clearly, Miss O'Rourke, and as much as I admire your courage and determination, I abhor your foolhardiness in taunting a dangerous man."

She finally inhaled, trying to find her voice. How could she tell him that she had doubts, too. At least a dozen times a day, and twice already tonight. "Nevertheless."

He looked completely flummoxed by her refusal to see the matter his way. And her promise of utter confidentiality prevented her from mentioning that she had gained courage and support from his own sister and several of the most important ladies in the ton, so she merely held her ground.

He released her and stepped back. "Very well, Miss O'Rourke. Have it your way, then. But you cannot stop me from shadowing your footsteps."

"You shall soon become very bored," she warned. "Unless you have a secret *tendresse* for one of the Thayer twins."

The hint of a smile twitched his lips. "Redheaded hoydens. Trouble, if ever there was any, and certainly incapable of keeping you out of it. That would be like setting the fox to guard the henhouse."

"I do not need anyone to keep me out of trouble. I am quite capable of that, myself."

His gaze swept her from head to toe. "Really?"

A flash of heat washed through her. Was he thinking of that night in the catacombs beneath the chapel? He was right—she had gotten herself in trouble before.

She drew herself up and spun on her heel to go back to the ballroom. *He will not humiliate me into doing as he wants, and he will not intimidate me, either!*

Jamie watched her go, half wanting to go after her, and half wanting to lock her away in some safe place until this business with Henley was finished. Why had he never noticed that stubborn streak?

He plucked a rose from a bush climbing the arbor he passed on his way to the stables and held it to his nose. Sweet and blossoming, like Miss Eugenia, herself. His body stirred with the thought of her soft heated flesh beneath him, her dark hair spread upon his pillow and those lush lips parted with a sigh as he entered her. He groaned and shook his head. He had no right to be thinking of her in that way. She'd made it plain that she disliked him.

Happily, there were many who did, and he was not adverse to settling when his first choice was not available. He'd find Devlin, see if there was any news, and then go look for female companionship. Perhaps that would take the edge off his adolescent yearning for Miss O'Rourke. And Charlie? Well, Charlie would catch up when he could. Aye, Charlie always knew where to find him—some sort of brotherly instinct.

He tossed a coin to the stable boy who brought his horse,

then mounted, turning southeast toward Whitefriars and the Crown and Bear. If Devlin was not there, Jamie would have a drink or two and go find ease at Alice's. Her girls were known for their enthusiasm and accommodating nature. God knows he could use a bit of that.

Clouds had gathered, obscuring the moon and bringing a chill. This was a night made for chicanery and it was early yet in Whitefriars. Anyone who made an honest living was home abed, and the others…well, the others never slept. As he arrived at the Crown and Bear, the place was alive with noise and laughter. Somewhere down an alley, voices raised in a quarrel carried to him as he left his horse in the stable yard behind the tavern and tossed another coin to Cox, the toothless and bald man who tended the stock.

A few faces turned to look when he entered, then went back to their tankards. A quick scan of the room told him that Farrell wasn't there. He crossed to the bar and waited while Mick Haddon, the barkeeper, poured a measure of his favorite rye whiskey and brought it to him. Haddon was a good man fallen on hard times, and a cut above the usual trade in the Crown and Bear.

"Farrell in back?" he asked.

"Home. Rarely see him these days," Haddon answered.

Jamie raised his glass. "To domestic bliss," he said before he swallowed the contents.

Mick snorted in reply. "Anything I can do for you?"

"What has Farrell told you?"

"To keep an eye out for Henley, and an ear to the ground."

"And?"

"Nothing, though this is the sort of place Henley would come if he were in a drinking mood. And had he not already crossed Farrell."

Silently, Jamie agreed. Henley wouldn't go to his club or

to any reputable tavern or gambling hell. He'd frequent only
the dregs of London. Places where he'd be unlikely to run
into any of his old friends or new enemies. But someone,
somewhere, knew where he was and was helping him. Sooner
or later, Jamie would find him. He was a very patient man.

"Any unusual activity? Rumors?" he asked.

"Just the usual sort," Haddon said as he poured another
measure for Jamie. "A woman turned up dead in an alley not
far from here last night. The charleys were asking around, but
it seems she and her husband had a row, and you can guess
the rest. I believe the husband has been taken away."

"Domestic bliss," Jamie repeated as he finished his
drink.

Haddon laughed this time and nodded.

Jamie left his glass on the bar and returned to the stable
yard. Old Cox handed him the reins and ducked his head, as
if avoiding Jamie's eyes. His horse danced sideways, skittish
about something. Rather than mount, he led his horse out of
the yard to the cobblestones, an uneasy feeling raising the
fine hairs on the back of his neck. Something wasn't right.

He bent down to slip the dagger from his boot just as the
report of a gunshot sounded close at hand. Brick and mortar
scattered in a wide pattern behind him and his horse reared,
frightened by the noise. He released the reins, knowing the
well-trained animal would not bolt. He rolled to the side,
coming up on his feet again near a doorway, his dagger in
hand.

Suddenly the price on his head was not quite so amusing.
He'd left his pocket pistol at home, not anticipating that he'd
be visiting the rookeries tonight. The sound of running footsteps down an adjacent alley told him that the assassin had
taken his best shot and was now making his escape.

He was in full pursuit down the alley, gaining on the culprit, when it occurred to him that this had all gone off too

smoothly. He knew these streets well enough to know the assassin was leading him toward a blind alley. An ambush? But who would be waiting for him? Henley? The Gibbons brothers? He was alone. Should he take the chance?

"Oh! I nearly swooned when I saw him waltz you out the terrace door!"

Gina gave Hortense a bland smile. "Nothing happened. He was merely inquiring as to my mother's health."

"Was he, indeed?" Harriett teased. "And why should your mother's health be a concern of his?"

Gina laughed. "My mother's health is everyone's concern. She makes it so at every encounter."

"Then you cannot confirm or deny the rumors concerning Mr. Hunter's...skills?"

"Alas." *Indeed.* The memory of that brief moment of promise brought a little smile to her lips.

"Ah! I see you are gaining confidence, Gina." Harriett squeezed her hand and winked at her sister. "Our little protégé is blooming."

Yes, she was gaining confidence but she was far from being at ease. She was acutely aware that there could be men present who had heard of her ordeal. Perhaps even a few who had been there, who had seen her. Though they were unlikely to mention it, she had felt the weight of clandestine eyes upon her.

She glanced around the ballroom as they strolled toward the punch bowl, wondering if James Hunter was still there, watching her. When her eye caught Miss Metcalfe dancing a lively reel with an eager young man, she was suddenly struck with a memory. Metcalfe! Was that not a name she'd heard before? A man who had been a friend of Mr. Henley and who had been at that scandalous tableau?

"Harriett, what can you tell me about Miss Metcalfe?" she asked. "Does she have family?"

"Goodness, yes! A handsome brother by the name of Stanley."

"Is he here tonight?"

Hortense craned her neck to look about in one direction while Harriett scanned the other. "I do not see him. Come to think of it, Harri, have we seen him at all in the last few weeks?"

Harriett chortled. "No, but it does not matter. I do not think he would suit you, Gina."

"Oh?"

"He is engaged to a dear friend of ours. Miss Christina Race. Have you met her?"

Gina shook her head. In truth, she'd met very few people since arriving in London.

"She and Missy have been almost inseparable since the engagement, have they not, Hortense?"

Hortense nodded. "Like peas in a pod. Would you like to meet them? The reel is almost over and I believe I saw Christina near the fireplace."

Her heart beating harder, Gina donned an airy smile. "That would be lovely. The more people I meet, the less you will have to coddle me."

"Pshaw!" Harriett laughed. "We adore coddling you, Gina. Why, introducing a pretty newcomer lends us a certain mystery and importance we do not possess on our own."

Gina laughed. She had noted how many heads the twins had turned, and not just because they were identical. They certainly did not need an unknown newcomer to gain attention.

The twins flanked her as they headed toward the fireplace at one end of the ballroom, nodding at acquaintances as they passed. Their progress was slow and perfectly timed to coincide with the end of the reel.

Gina had been watching the dancers and when they stopped she turned her attention back to the group at the fireplace. Surprise coupled with a twist of her stomach shot through her. There stood a lovely woman of average height with glossy black hair and eyes nearly as dark. Her fair complexion deepened with the pink of a blush as she recognized Gina's face. The woman from the tableau—and she was engaged to Mr. Metcalfe!

Hortense performed the introduction. "Miss Eugenia O'Rourke, I am pleased to present our dearest friend, Miss Christina Race. Miss Race, please meet Miss O'Rourke."

Gina noted the tiny plea in those eyes. Clearly the woman did not want to acknowledge their previous acquaintance. How could they ever explain that away? She took a deep breath. "Miss Race, how nice to make your acquaintance. I pray you will not hold these two against me," she said with a nod toward the twins.

The woman smiled and squeezed Gina's hand in gratitude. "If you will do the same, Miss O'Rourke."

Harriett arched one elegant eyebrow. "Come now. Our reputations are not quite that bad."

Laughing and jesting with a young man over her shoulder, Miss Metcalfe returned from the dance floor and was quickly introduced. "O'Rourke? Is your sister the one who finally tamed Lord Libertine?"

Gina frowned, unfamiliar with the title.

Hortense laughed. "She means Andrew Hunter, Gina. That was our pet name for him until your sister domesticated him."

She smiled. "Yes, then. Isabella married Mr. Hunter and they seem quite content."

Miss Metcalfe sighed as she fanned herself. "That gives the rest of us hope, then. If he succumbed to the parson's mousetrap, there can be hope that one of us might yet snare James or Charles Hunter."

"I…I wouldn't know, Miss Metcalfe."

"Yet I saw you dance with James," she said, almost like an accusation. "That is, until he sneaked you out to the garden."

Gina was taken aback by the woman's bluntness. "He was doing his duty to me, Miss Metcalfe. And reminding me to mind my manners."

Miss Metcalfe fell silent after Gina's rejoinder and Hortense introduced her companion. "Miss O'Rourke, may I present Mr. Adam Booth? Mr. Booth, please meet Miss O'Rourke."

The man bent over her hand and a flicker of something passed through his eyes as he straightened and met her gaze. "Have we met, Miss O'Rourke? I could swear I've seen those remarkable eyes before."

He'd been at the tableau. Had he been at the ritual? She slowly withdrew her hand from his and forced a smile. "You are too kind, Mr. Booth. I doubt we have met since I have not been much in society. In any case, I am certain I'd have remembered a gentleman as handsome as you."

He grinned and the tension went out of his posture. "Well, I shan't forget you again, Miss O'Rourke. Alas, I must be off to meet friends but I pray you will save me a dance 'til the next time we meet." He bowed over her hand.

She gave him a stiff smile. Had there been something familiar in his request, or was she being overly sensitive? "I shall look forward to it, Mr. Booth."

Alone now, the ladies proceeded to discuss Mr. Booth and his various attributes—the width of his shoulders, the color of his gray-blue eyes, the size of his…bank account. Gina relaxed, the conversation so similar to those she'd had with her sisters long before any of them married.

"And you, Miss O'Rourke? Who do you prefer?" Miss Race asked.

"I am far too new to the scene to have a preference," she said, though Jamie Hunter's face came to mind.

"My dear," Harriett said, "I know just what you mean. Why, if Miss Race hadn't already taken Mr. Metcalfe, I might cast my cap in that direction."

Gina seized that opportunity. "When am I to meet Mr. Metcalfe?"

Missy Metcalfe rolled her eyes heavenward. "I can't imagine where he's been keeping himself. Between his friends and his club, we scarcely see him at home anymore. Why, Christina sees him more than we."

They all turned to Miss Race for confirmation.

"I, uh, did see him earlier tonight. I believe he said he was gambling with a few of his friends."

"Men," Hortense said, as if that explained everything.

Miss Race drew herself up as if she'd made a sudden decision. "Accompany me to the ladies' retiring room, Miss O'Rourke? I'd love to hear about your native land. I've never been to Ireland, though Stanley and I have discussed taking our wedding trip there." She linked arms with Gina, leading her away from the group.

When they were out of hearing, Miss Race pulled Gina into a private corner. "I must thank you for not giving me away. I saw that you recognized me, too, and I prayed you would not mention it to the others."

Gina gave a self-deprecating laugh. "I'd have had to give myself away, Miss Race, and I was not about to do that."

"Call me Christina," she said before rushing on. "And I want to assure you that I do not frequent such places as the one where we first met. Stanley had been invited by some of his friends and did not understand the sort of…affair it was to be, or he swears he never would have taken me. And I…

well, I could see that you were not accustomed to such things either."

"I had never seen a complete stranger unclothed before. But to do so in such a public manner, and in such a pose, was a great surprise to me."

"Wicked London," Christina murmured. "There is quite a different world here than the one we inhabit, Miss O'Rourke."

She weighed the risk of mentioning Mr. Henley so soon, but she hadn't much time herself. "You must call me Gina, then. Meeting you has been quite fortuitous. You see, I am actually looking for some of the people in our group that night."

The woman shuddered. "Why?"

"I lost something that night, and I believe one of them might have it, or know where it is."

"I cannot recall anyone finding something that night. But I wish you luck of it, Gina, and I must say I admire your courage. For myself, I hope never to see any of them again."

"Oh. I understand." Gina turned away.

"I did not mean you!" Christina stayed her with a hand on her arm. "Is there anything I can do to help?"

"Did you know them all—the people in our group?"

She shook her head and looked down at the floor as if searching her mind. "That was the first time I stole away to go anywhere privately with Stanley. I did not know many of his friends, then, and I have not seen those particular ones since. Most were like you, complete strangers."

"Would you ask Mr. Metcalfe if he remembers that night, and who was there? If he would be willing to meet with me, perhaps I could persuade him to help."

Christina looked doubtful. "I shall ask him, of course, but I think he'd rather leave that night in the distant past."

"Tell him that I urgently and desperately need his help. Tell him that my entire future depends upon it."

Christina searched her face and then nodded. "My goodness! What did you lose?"

"Something irreplaceable. Something I must recover."

"But of course I shall tell him, my dear. The very next time I see him."

"Tomorrow?" she urged.

"I… Yes. Are you going to the Albermarle crush Tuesday next?"

She recalled seeing that name in the calendar and stack of invitations Lady Sarah had given her and nodded.

"I shall ask him to accompany me there."

"Thank you." Gina squeezed her arm in gratitude.

Chapter Five

Jamie seized the reins again and swung up into his saddle. He hadn't wanted to disturb Devlin Farrell tonight, but now it couldn't be helped. The brazen attack on his life had raised too many questions that only Farrell could answer.

The butler left Jamie to cool his heels in Farrell's study, so he helped himself to a small glass of sherry and took the liberty of pouring one for Devlin. His nerves needed steadying. The warmth from the alcohol had just begun to untwist the knots in his stomach when Devlin entered the study, barefooted, his hair tousled, and still securing his dressing robe.

Jamie was amused to note the lack of a nightshirt where the robe gaped. From the expression on Devlin's flushed face, he gathered he hadn't exactly been sleeping. "Sorry," he said as Devlin downed the contents of the waiting glass and glowered at him.

"I gather this is more important than what I was doing?"

Jamie grinned. "That would depend upon your priorities, I suppose. My life?"

Devlin looked him up and down. "You seem none the worse for wear."

"I was fortunate. Even so, I barely ducked in time."

"Ducked? A pistol?"

"One very good shot."

"Not good enough," Devlin said, filling Jamie's glass.

"Oh, it was good enough. But there was something not quite right that put me on my guard just in time."

"Thank God for your instincts," Devlin murmured.

"So, it seems your intelligence was right. There actually is a price on my head. Though I think we both know the answer, I'd like confirmation of who is behind it. And, if possible, who was foolhardy enough to attempt it."

"The Gibbons brothers?"

Jamie shook his head. "I didn't smell them." But he'd been uncertain enough not to follow the shooter down the alley where an accomplice might be waiting. Somewhere in the back of his mind, he must have suspected something of the sort.

Devlin was silent for a few moments, an expression of concentration on his face. "I can think of a few more who might take that chance, Hunter. But I doubt they'd own it. I know your principles, and I know you'd need proof before you'd take action, and proof will not exist for such a deed. If the man had a partner, we could…convince his partner to talk. But if he is acting alone…"

"Given the circumstances, I doubt anyone would act alone," Jamie growled. "Have a word with old Cox, will you? Someone has gotten to him. I don't know if it was a bribe or a threat, but I'd stake my life that he knew what was afoot."

"Cox?" Devlin had stiffened and Jamie knew he was angry. Cox was Devlin's employee, and he'd be furious that the man would compromise his position. "What makes you think so?"

"When I went for my horse, he was behaving strangely. Wouldn't meet my eyes. 'Twas one of the things that warned me that things were not what they should be."

Devlin gave a grim nod. "Rest assured, Cox and I will have a chat first thing in the morning. I am certain he will be pleased to share whatever information he has."

Jamie could guess how "pleased" Cox would be by the time Devlin was through with him. "And you, Dev? Have you heard anything?"

"Nothing helpful. One of the lads reported seeing Henley in the rookeries. Said he appeared to have money and was dressed like the fop he is. The lad lost him before he could find out where his quarters are."

"Not helpful? To the contrary. That information confirms my suspicions. Henley has not left the country, and he has someone helping him if he has access to money and is well groomed. That means he has decent accommodations somewhere. And if he can lose your 'lads,' he hasn't let his guard down." He hesitated on his way to the door. The next bit of business was delicate, to say the least. "Dev, if you had a sister…"

"For God's sake! Have you got some poor girl in trouble?"

Jamie laughed. "Never. But your wife has sisters, eh? And if you had reason to think one of them might be in danger, what would you do?"

He studied Jamie for one long moment. "Miss Eugenia?"

"Perhaps."

"Who else? Your only sister is married to a man more than capable of taking good care of her. Drew would slice the hands off anyone who'd touch Isabella, and I'd do much worse, believe me, to anyone who would raise a voice to Lilly. The only sister left is Eugenia."

"After months as a recluse, she has decided all of a sudden that it is time for her to enter society."

"Miss Eugenia? Timid little mouse?"

Jamie sighed. "You do not know her if that is what you think, Devlin. Before that night at the chapel, she was full of fire and sparkle. I gave thought to…well, never mind. Any chance of that is past. But now she is venturing out into the same society that Henley and the rest belonged. You mentioned Metcalfe and Booth. I pray you are right about them—that they were not a part of the Brotherhood, but had only been invited to the ritual that night. But I worry that someone else, someone we don't know, could recognize her."

"I see the problem. They'd want to put her out of the way so she couldn't identify them. Have you talked to her?"

"She is determined. She will not listen to reason. You've seen her, Dev. You know what a beauty she is. She cannot help but draw attention. There is, quite literally, no way to keep her contained."

"One way. But it falls to you or Charlie."

Jamie nodded, already knowing what he was going to say. He'd hoped Devlin would know of another way, a safer way.

"Dog her footsteps. Wherever she goes, be there, too. It should not delay you long. Lilly told me that her mother is going back to Belfast in a fortnight and Miss Eugenia with her."

"How can I keep her safe when someone is shooting at me?"

Devlin chortled. "I doubt you will be following her to the parts of London you were in tonight. And once she is safely abed, you'll be free to follow your leads. A few hours a night for a fortnight. That cannot be too much a chore."

"Perhaps I could trade off with Charlie to keep her from

getting suspicious. I do not like to think what she would do if she suspected we were watching her."

"Charlie?" Devlin laughed. "If you turn a woman like Miss Eugenia over to your brother, you're not the man I thought you were."

The next night, Jamie blessed his sister and her penchant for writing things down. Taking Devlin's suggestion to heart, all he'd had to do was call on her this afternoon, ask her for a cough tonic, and then take a quick look through the papers on her little desk while she was in the kitchen concocting the brew. His hunch had been right. Sarah was easing Eugenia's way into society, using the Thayer twins as her companions for meeting the "right" people.

Now, there in the midst of the Albermarle ballroom, shining brighter than any crystal chandelier, and right where his sister's notes said she would be, was Miss Eugenia. Despite the crush of people, he had spotted her within seconds of entering.

Yes, he had Eugenia's complete schedule for the next fortnight. Convenient. And it barely troubled his conscience at all. Sarah would never know. And it wasn't as if he wanted the information for nefarious purposes. Quite the opposite. He could not keep her at home, nor could he let her wander into disaster, so following her was the only way to safeguard her. And there was no sense in hiding it since she would soon suspect something of the sort. He might as well throw down the gauntlet.

As he approached her group, peopled by the crème de la crème of the ton, he noted that she was even more stunning tonight than last night. Her gown was of a deep violet watered silk. A row of tiny leaves had been embroidered at the hem and décolletage. A matching neck band displaying a perfect oval amethyst hid her scar, and she looked as untouched and serene as a Madonna. How was it possible that she grew lovelier each time he saw her?

As if she could feel the weight of his eyes, she turned to him. A fleeting smile curved her lips, then died as if she had remembered something unpleasant. He hid his disappointment as he approached the group.

Harriett Thayer was the first to acknowledge him. "Mr. Hunter! How delightful. We so rarely see you, and here, two nights in a row, we are fortunate enough to encounter you. To what do we owe this rare pleasure?" Her smile was coy and her eyes slid toward Miss Eugenia. Harriett, at least, suspected the real reason for his being there.

He smiled as a few of the young men bowed and wandered away, unsure which of his varied reputations was responsible. "Why, to your charming company, ladies. What else could lure a gentleman out on a cold night?"

"Then we shall require you to warm yourself by dancing with all of us," Hortense teased. "There is a scandalous lack of eligible men here tonight."

"Then you first, Miss…Hortense?"

She took his offered hand. "How very clever of you, Mr. Hunter. Most people cannot tell us apart."

"I am observant, m'dear. Under ordinary circumstances, I cannot tell you apart, but I know, for instance, that you have a charming little quirk of raising your right eyebrow. When Miss Harriett attempts it, her left eyebrow raises."

"The mirror effect," she said with a little laugh. "Drat! We have been found out, Harri."

He led her to the dance floor where a lively reel was in progress. Both Misses Thayer were excellent partners, quick, supple and skilled. The pace kept them apart quite a bit and spared him the necessity of making mundane conversation. When he returned her to her friends, he claimed Miss Harriett for a stately march.

"I conceive you have an interest in our Miss O'Rourke, do you not?" she asked when they met for a bow.

"I own it. She is family now, you know."

"I mean beyond that, Mr. Hunter. You do not look at her as a brother would."

Denial was useless, but perhaps he could manage her suspicions of his reasons. "Your perception astounds me, Miss Harriett. Will you expose me?"

"Tout au contraire!" She gave him a saucy wink. "I shall do all I can to encourage her. Not for your sake, Mr. Hunter, but for the good of all womankind."

"How would such a suit serve the good of all womankind?"

"Cupid's arrow has already brought your brothers Lockwood and Andrew down. Should you follow, I vow that women of the ton would be vastly encouraged. Yes, women everywhere would take heart that *any* man can be caught."

He laughed at her outrageous analysis of the situation, though he realized there was a grain of truth in it. He and his brothers had all been single far too long, and he was apt to remain so for a good deal longer than Miss Harriett suspected.

When he returned Miss Harriett to her companions, there was another young lady he had not met. Miss Hortense performed the introduction to Miss Christina Race. She was a darkly ethereal woman, as quiet and composed as the deep green gown she wore. When he bowed over her hand, she returned his smile.

He watched Miss Eugenia from the corner of his eye, noting that she looked anxious. Was she concerned that he would not mind his manners? No. She knew him well enough by now to know he would not embarrass Miss Race.

He led her onto the dance floor for a quadrille and attempted polite conversation as they met, parted and met again. "I believe we have been previously introduced, Miss Race?"

"I do not think so, Mr. Hunter. I am certain I would have remembered."

"Then how is your face familiar?"

"'Twould not be so odd, sir, as we frequent the same events. Perhaps you have seen me across a room? Perhaps at the punch bowl? Or perhaps we have passed in the street?"

He conceded the point, though he still suspected they knew each other in some manner or another. "How have you fallen into such bad company as the Thayers and Miss O'Rourke?"

She laughed softly and he was enchanted by the sound. "I have known Hortense and Harriett for quite some time. Our families are connected. I have only just met Miss O'Rourke."

"Tell me what you think of her."

He sensed a slight stiffening in her frame as he passed her beneath his arm. "She is quite agreeable. In fact, she has requested that I join their group tonight. I think we shall get along famously."

Miss Eugenia requested? An innocent enough way to meet and become acquainted with new people, though he could not help but think she was up to something. Miss Eugenia was not random in her actions.

The dance ended and Jamie's anger rose when he returned Miss Race only to find that Miss Eugenia had disappeared. She'd known she was next and had tried to subvert him. How little she knew of his determination! It would take more than she was capable of to keep him from his purpose.

"Miss O'Rourke offers her apologies, but she was…ah, fatigued and has gone to the ladies' retiring room," Miss Harriett explained.

Harriett Thayer was not a good liar. He smiled, offered a

bow, and excused himself to take up station at the corridor leading to the ladies' retiring room.

Before long, and thinking she was now safe, Miss Eugenia rounded the corner on her way back to her friends. He fell into step beside her and took her arm, guiding her back toward the ballroom. "Ah, my patience has rewarded me. How could I possibly leave without our dance?"

Gina covered her astonishment as best she could. She'd been so sure she'd evaded him. He was more patient than she had thought. "I confess to a certain curiosity, Mr. Hunter. Have you always been quite this…social? Or is this a new habit?"

He laughed. "You have me there, although I do tend to be more social than my brothers. And, when there is something to interest me, I am positively unshakable."

"Hmm. So then am I to gather that you are testing the boundaries of our truce? Or are you sweet on someone here?"

"Both, if I am to be honest. And, since it is my fate to dote upon someone who hates me, if you refuse me I shall be quite inconsolable."

He led her into the strains of a waltz and Gina sighed. She was glad he had saved their dance for last. Oh, she had dreaded it, and had even tried to avoid it, but now that the inevitable had happened, she found her excitement rising. James Hunter always made her feel as if she were about to embark on an exciting adventure.

"So thoughtful, Miss O'Rourke? Or are you anxious to return to your friends?"

"They are quite diverting," she allowed, but she was more concerned with keeping him away from Miss Race. If he made the connection between the girl and the Brotherhood, he would instantly know what she was doing. And yet, she could not help but ask, "Had you not met Miss Race before?"

A brief look of uncertainty passed over his features. "I had not had that pleasure. I must say she is quite lovely. I find it difficult to believe I managed to miss her before."

"Connoisseur of lovely women that you are?"

He laughed and swung her in a wide circle. "Are you calling me conceited, Miss O'Rourke?"

"Heaven forbid! Fickle, perhaps…"

"For what it is worth, I rank you among the loveliest to grace the ton, Miss O'Rourke. And by my reckoning, you are generating a good deal of interest."

The hair raised on the back of Gina's neck. She had felt the stares, but she suspected they were for a different reason, and likely from men who had seen her naked on a stone altar. And interest was not what she wanted to generate. She'd rather blend into the background—the better to overhear snippets of conversation that could be of help to her.

"There is that look again," Mr. Hunter said. "The one that tells me I've said something wrong."

"Not wrong, Mr. Hunter. It is just that…well, I do not want to generate interest."

"Then why have you come out in society?"

"I…I thought I should experience London before returning to Ireland."

His eyes narrowed and he drew her off the dance floor. "That is a bare-faced lie, Miss O'Rourke. It was a lie the first time you told it, and it is now. I would hazard you have experienced more than enough of London."

She gasped at his sudden fierceness. "The wrong London. I wanted to take a happier memory home with me."

He took her hand and led her into the famed Albermarle gardens among dozens of strolling couples. Still, it was more private than the ballroom. He found them a bench surrounded by sculpted evergreens and gestured for her to sit. As much as she would have liked to return to the ballroom, she followed his direction.

"Now, Miss O'Rourke," he began as he stood in front of her, one foot propped on the bench next to her hip, as if to keep her from bolting. "I know you are up to something. Do not bother to deny it."

"Really, sir. I needn't explain myself to you."

"You are going to explain to someone. Me or Andrew. Or better yet, your mother."

Gina shuddered. Her mother would have hysterics followed by locking Gina in her room until their return to Ireland. "I've told you the truth before. I am tired of hiding in fear. I will not live the rest of my life locked away or shunning society. I've done nothing wrong."

"Apart from sneaking out and joining in fast company to go places no decently brought-up young woman should ever go? Apart from keeping company with the likes of Henley? Apart, even, from nearly getting yourself killed?"

She had underestimated his anger. And he had misjudged hers. He had backed her into a corner, and he was going to pay the consequences of that. "Are you saying that I am to blame for what happened to me?"

"Only in that you made a series of wrong decisions for all the right reasons. But you cannot ignore the fact that you are a female, with all the vulnerabilities of that sex."

"I am not ignoring it, but I will not allow it to prevent me from doing what I must."

"And what is that, Miss O'Rourke?"

"Talk to people, discover if anyone knows what has become of Mr. Henley. See to it that he is captured and punished."

"Even if that means exposing your…"

Gina's stomach turned. Exposing her shame? The fact that she had been splayed on a stone altar? That she was to have been raped and killed for the titillation of dissolute men? No! Dear Lord, no. She did not want any of it made public. But if she was not willing to risk that, Henley was sure to get away with what he'd done to her and countless others. "Even then," she confirmed, keeping her voice steady and determined.

He looked into her eyes, measuring her determination. "Miss O'Rourke, the Home Office is doing all it can. How can you think you will succeed where they have not?"

"For precisely that reason. They have *not* succeeded. How can I possibly do worse? And how can I return to Ireland knowing that vile man is still free? Free to come after me. Free to debauch other innocent women."

"You think we failed you." Anger coupled with something darker crossed his handsome features. "Then surely you can see the folly in putting yourself in harm's way."

"Mr. Henley is in hiding. He is no threat to me as long as I am in society because he will not risk being seen. I only want to discover if anyone knows where he can be found. I promise you, Mr. Hunter, I will give you that information the moment I have it."

"You will…" He looked at her in disbelief and raked his fingers through his dark hair. "Damn it, the only thing you should do is go home to Ireland!"

She stood and turned toward the terrace doors and the ballroom. She hadn't taken more than a single step when he seized her arm and spun her around as he stepped forward. The momentum landed her squarely against his chest and she was forced to look up to see his expression—fury and frustration. "I don't give a fig where you think I should go!" she exclaimed.

"Don't you see the danger? Don't you know what the mere sight of you does to a man?"

She opened her mouth to ask what he meant, but it was too late. His left arm went around her to hold her captive while his right hand cupped the back of her head, preventing her from turning away.

His mouth came down on hers with desperation she could feel in every line of his body. His lips were challenging, not punishing. They were firm, warm and tinged with sweet wine. His tongue slipped along the seam of her lips, urging hers to open. Not knowing why, she did, and his moan was the answer. She brought her fists up, intending to push him away, but her hands opened and slipped around his neck. She had never felt anything as exciting as this before and she was dizzy with the heady sensation.

Surer now, more confident, he softened his assault to coax an answering moan from her. She scarcely recognized her own voice in that sigh. He pulled her closer, pressing her along the length of him until she could feel something as firm and unyielding as his chest pressing against her lower abdomen. Oh, how she wanted more of that feeling! Encouraged, he deepened the kiss and Gina knew she was being branded, claimed, owned entirely by this man. Only James Hunter could have robbed her of the will to resist.

Heavenly and wicked at the same time. Now she understood. She couldn't move, couldn't break the spell of his arms, and she didn't want to. No, she never wanted this kiss to end. She was breathless at the way her breasts tingled as they pressed against his chest and at the way a needful ache bloomed where his erection burned into her. She wanted him. She needed him.

He released her with a choked groan and stepped back, leaving her to stagger without his support. "You…you have my apologies, Miss O'Rourke."

She spun around and ran for the terrace door. He must never know what that kiss had done to her. Never see it in her eyes or read it on her face. She'd been ready to surrender everything to him when he'd only kissed her to shut her up or teach her a lesson. Well, he'd never have that opportunity again!

Chapter Six

Gina was certain there was some trace of that kiss visible to the guests in the ballroom. She was changed somehow, and there would have to be a sign of that. She glanced toward Hortense and Harriett, who were laughing and fanning themselves flirtatiously while engaged in conversation with at least five young men. How could she join them when her heart was still racing so?

She glanced around for a familiar face, someone she could talk to. Where had Miss Race gone? She'd promised to bring Mr. Metcalfe. A quick glance around the ballroom revealed that the girl was not dancing. In fact, she could find no trace of her. Surely she wouldn't have left without a word?

A flash of green caught her attention and she watched as Miss Race entered the ballroom from a terrace door. She paused to pat her hair into place and sweep a gaze about the room. When she saw Gina, she gave a small smile and a nod as she came toward her.

She was flushed when she took Gina's hand and led her

into the corridor. "I looked for you, Gina, but you disappeared. Stanley was here, but he could not stay."

She tried to hide her dismay. "I...I have missed him?"

"He said he knew who you were and was willing to help you, but he does not like to stay too long in any place."

"Has he always been like that, Christina?"

The girl frowned. "Only since...the middle of summer. It is as if he is afraid something will happen if he stays too long."

Could Mr. Metcalfe be trying to avoid Mr. Henley, too? But Mr. Henley would never attend a ball—too brazen, and too many people knew him. Or did Mr. Metcalfe fear the authorities were after him? What a hopeless muddle.

Gina squeezed Christina's hands. "Did he say how he could help me?"

"Oh, yes." She rummaged in her little beaded reticule, pulled a small object out and pressed it into Gina's hand. "I was to give you this, and tell you that he will find you at a more opportune time. I took the liberty of telling him I have been invited to attend the Morris masquerade three days hence, and that you will be there with Hortense and Harriett. He said we should look for a leper."

Leper? That would mean a black hooded robe and bell about his neck. He should be easy enough to find. "Three days? Could I not speak to him sooner?"

"I am afraid not. He said he had much to do. Now, you must excuse me. I should return to my party."

Gina tried to hide her impatience as Christina hurried away to join a group of young people who were preparing to leave. Almost forgotten in her disappointment, she looked down and opened her hand. A key? Pray, what did it open?

Throw down the gauntlet? What a bloody good idea that turned out to be! Instead of basking in triumph with little

Miss Eugenia packing for home, Jamie was the one who'd been defeated with a kiss and at the mercy of a sweet-smelling nymph who gave as good as she got. Gave better, actually. And the accusation that the Home Office—*he*—had failed her ripped through his heart. It was bad enough to fear it himself, but to hear her say it was a confirmation of all his worst fears.

He riffled through the papers on his desk at the Home Office looking for his notes, certain there would be something to either bolster his case or tell him where Henley was hiding. Fast. He had to end this before Henley came after Eugenia. There had to be something he had overlooked. Something so subtle that it had escaped him.

"Good Lord! You take to abandoning me at balls and I find you working into the wee hours! What has happened to you, Jamie? All work and no play is not like you."

He glanced up to see Charlie leaning against the doorjamb, his arms folded over his chest and looking for all the world as if he'd just slept twelve hours. "Not like *you*," Jamie corrected. "What are *you* are doing here—and do not tell me you were trying to find me."

Charlie shrugged and came to sit in the chair across the desk from him. "My mind wanders. You know how easily bored I am. And I'm looking for company. I hate to carouse alone."

Jamie finally pushed his papers aside and gave his brother his attention. "You haven't been carousing, Charlie. You're far too fresh for that. Come clean."

He grinned. "Not precisely carousing. But I've certainly been in that part of town. I met Devlin at the Crown and Bear."

"Lilly will not thank you for leading him astray."

"Me? Perish the thought. I am merely learning from the master."

"Master of what? Are you taking up a life of crime?"

His grin faded as he sat forward in his chair. "I am trying to decipher Devlin's sources, his network of informants. Alas, I lack his reputation to give strength to my requests, but I am gaining ground there."

"I wonder if I should ask what is required to become credible to that lot of scoundrels."

"I wouldn't. Not for the squeamish." Charlie quirked an eyebrow.

"I should also warn you to be prepared for rumors concerning Miss O'Rourke and me."

Charlie blinked, then shook his head. "You had me there for a minute. I almost thought you, of all people, had found the 'one.' Well, never mind. So you want society to *think* you're courting? Is Miss O'Rourke going along with this?"

"She will likely be quite distressed when she learns of it. But my requests that she stay at home and be protected have fallen on deaf ears. She intends to ask her own questions and meddle in Home Office business. Henley will be looking for a way to get at her. She is one of the last who could testify against him—that he drugged and kidnapped her."

"So you intend to hang on her every word? Discourage any other suitors? Make it impossible for her to locate Henley?"

"Precisely."

"And if she sends you away?"

"I shall stand fast."

"You know what society will say about this affair, do you not? That you are beyond smitten, and that the O'Rourke girl has made a jackanapes of you."

Jamie laughed. "Not to my face, they won't."

"Ah," Charlie said, "and this will work well into your usual scheme, will it not? In seasons to come, it will be whispered that your heart is broken and no marriage-minded chit should set her cap for you. Damn clever."

"My usual scheme?"

"Your reputation in the ton, Jamie. Nary an ingenue nor a courtesan has held your attention long. 'Tis just a matter of time before you move along to the next entertainment."

He forced a grin and a shrug. "You will not give me away?"

"Never! Furthermore, I shall join you in your game. I do not intend to let you go about alone at night again. Whoever wants you dead will not have an easy time of it."

"Or Henley will get two Hunters for the price of one."

"I am so pleased that you let the gentlemen go off to their club after church," Mama announced as they sat down to the table and shook her napkin out to lay it across her lap. "Now it is just me and all my girls. Well, the ones I have left." She sniffled and touched her handkerchief to the corners of her eyes.

Gina shot a quick glance at her sisters and noted that both Bella and Lilly did the same. By their tense expressions, she realized they all feared that Mama was winding up for a bout of hysteria.

"But enough of that," Mama continued, laying their fears to rest. "We all miss Cora dreadfully, but we must accept God's will. I am simply grateful for the opportunity to have my little family all to myself. There are things we must discuss. Plans to form and decisions to be made."

"There is time for that, Mama," Bella said as a maid served a platter of cold sliced meat.

"Not much time at all, dear. Less than a fortnight. 'Twould be sooner if I could arrange it."

Ten days, by Gina's reckoning, counting this one. Yes, she was painfully aware of the ticking of the clock. Ten days to find Henley. Ten days to avenge Cora and reclaim her own future.

"And we must look to the future. I will scarce be settled at home when I will have to come back here. March, will it not be, Bella?"

"M-March?" Her sister colored a most interesting shade of fuchsia.

"Oh, do not deny it," their mother smirked. "I know my daughters. Your husband did not waste much time getting an heir on you. You shall have an early spring babe. And I know a girl wants her mother at such a time. Never fear, Bella. I shall be here for you."

Bella looked at Gina and Lilly for help, but as Bella did not deny their mother's conclusion, there was nothing they could say.

"And Lilly, you shall not be far behind, I think. From the look of that strapping husband of yours, I would not be surprised to welcome twins by summer."

"Mother, we have been married little more than a week!"

"Aye, it does not take long. My girls will be no less fertile than I. And your husband looks no less virile than Bella's. Boys, I'd warrant. A great pity your father will not be here to see it. He always wanted sons."

"Then perhaps you should stay rather than go and have to return so soon," Bella offered. "Andrew has often said you are welcome to stay as long as you please."

"Aye, but we cannot leave our home in Belfast vacant so long. The servants will be stealing us blind. No, we must return as soon as may be, and Gina will have to stay there when I return in the spring. Someone must watch over the house."

Lilly raised her eyebrows and leaned forward as she spoke. "But you cannot leave Gina alone, Mama. A single woman…"

"Faugh! Gina is a spinster now. Both older and younger

sisters are married. No one is like to offer for her now. She may as well make herself useful."

Gina was astonished. It had never occurred to her that her own mother would consider her little better than an unpaid companion.

"And she is scarred, besides," Mama continued. She turned to look at Gina with a frown. "You were never clumsy before, child. Falling on the stairs and cutting yourself with a broken glass—why, I never heard of such a thing happening before to any of my girls. And now you must cover it whenever you go about in public. I am certain you would much rather not leave the house. Yes, you will be more comfortable at home. In Belfast."

Gina's hand went to her throat as it always did at any mention of her scar. The story they'd told their mother about how it had happened was a bit flimsy, but she had believed it, nonetheless.

"Mama!" Lilly protested. "Gina is in her prime, and the physician said the scar will fade with time."

Bella nodded. "Lady Sarah has said that Gina is a great success in society. Why, a few young men have asked after her. If you must return to Belfast, you should leave Gina here with us."

She was warmed by her sisters' defense, though she doubted Bella's veracity. Who would have asked after her? She'd only danced with a handful of young men.

Mama shrugged. "What? Leave her with *you?* And no one to guide her? Why, Mr. Hunter and Mr. Farrell are hardly the sort to look after a young girl."

A young girl? Moments ago she'd been a spinster. Gina sighed as the simple truth dawned on her. Mama did not want to be alone. She did not want the last of her daughters to be out of reach. And Mama was likely to do anything she could to keep Gina by her side and at her beck and call.

"Mama—" Lilly began.

"Gina is coming home with me, and that is an end to it." Mama waved one hand in dismissal of the subject.

The remainder of lunch was punctuated with sighs and awkward spurts of bland conversation while Gina felt as if she might jump out of her skin. The future her mother had mapped out for her was never one she would have chosen. One, in fact, she found abhorrent and, in its own way, terrifying. But given her circumstances, and if she could not find the answers she sought, it would be the only course open to her.

She wouldn't give up yet, though. She still had ten days and she would make the most of them. Regardless of Mr. Renquist and the Home Office, she would just have to take matters into her own hands.

Her mother excused herself, declaring that she was quite fatigued and needed a nap. The table fell silent until they heard a door close somewhere above them.

"Gina, did you know what she planned?" Lilly asked.

She shook her head, still a bit stunned.

"We must find some way to divert her," Bella mumbled.

"It is hopeless, and you know it. When Mama has made up her mind, nothing can change it. Nothing will do but that she have her way."

"But you have not…"

"Escaped?" Gina smiled and looked down at her plate, largely untouched. "Perhaps I could learn to bear that, but I cannot resign myself to the thought that Mr. Henley will not pay for what he has done. That is the one task I cannot leave undone."

Bella's eyes darkened as she sat forward. "I've seen that look before. What are you planning, Gina?"

"I hardly know. I have made some headway amongst the ton, but progress is slow. I am to meet with Mr. Renquist tomorrow for his report. And…" she hesitated, reluctant to tell them about the little key "…and there has to be more I can do. Other ways to learn what I need."

Lilly dropped her napkin on her plate and glanced over her shoulder before lowering her voice to a whisper. "If you are game, Gina, I may have an idea. There were some street urchins—lads, Devlin called them—who helped find the evidence against the Brotherhood. They are quite engaging little pickpockets and, for a few coins, they could discover anything."

"I vow I am not going to turn any source away."

Lilly nodded and stood, determination in her voice. "I know just where to find them on a Sunday afternoon. Bella, you stay here and if the men return, tell them Gina and I have gone for a stroll through the park and shall be back presently. Gina, fetch your bonnet and shawl."

Gina glanced around the square at Covent Garden, almost as busy as Hyde Park on a summer afternoon, unable to shake the feeling that she was being watched. "How will we ever find them?" she asked Lilly.

"Just dangle your reticule from your wrist and they will come along. Walk slowly and smile as if you have nothing more on your mind than meeting friends. Ned will find us."

"What will your husband say?"

Lilly laughed. "He would likely ask how much we paid them, and then tell me it was too much."

"He will not be angry?"

"Not in the least. But I do not intend to tell him."

"Why?"

"Because I do not know if I can trust him not to tell Andrew or Jamie. Am I correct in thinking you would not want them to know?"

Gina grinned. "Oh, yes. Andrew would take his duty as

my closest male relative to heart and forbid me to do more than drink tea and embroider. I thought Devlin might be the same."

Lilly's eyes twinkled. "Devlin is far too protective, but he admires women who can think for themselves. Still, he would not want you to endanger yourself. Ah, but how can hiring a few lads endanger you? No, I think we are safe in this."

Gina was not nearly as worried about what Andrew or Devlin would do as she was about another man. "M-most importantly, I do not want James Hunter to know. He told me last night that, if he had his way, I would return to Belfast at once."

Lilly's eyebrows shot up. "No! He would not be so ungentlemanly."

"He was not in a gentlemanly mood. I am afraid he knows I am looking for Mr. Henley. And I might have suggested that I could hardly do worse than the Home Office."

"Oh, my!" Lilly did her best to contain her laughter. "I can imagine how he took that. Whatever possessed you to make that charge?"

"I cannot recall. Our conversations tend to deteriorate after a moment or two. It would be best if we simply avoided one another as much as possible, but he has decided to take my safety upon himself. Quite aggravating."

"I wish you luck, Gina. Knowing the Hunter men, you will need it."

Gina felt a tug on her arm and turned in time to see a ragged child trying to cut her purse strings. "Here now!"

Lilly peered around her. "Let loose, Ned."

"Mrs. Lilly! This a friend of yers?"

"My sister."

The lad released his hold on Gina's reticule, removed his cap and swept an exaggerated bow. "At yer service, Miss Sister."

"Miss Eugenia," Lilly corrected. "And we were looking for you, Ned, and some of your mates."

"Got a job fer us, Mrs. Lilly?"

"Indeed we have. But I shall let my sister tell you what she needs. Whatever she pays you, Ned, I shall double it if you deliver."

The boy grinned ear to ear. "You know I will, missus." He turned to Gina. "What do y' need, Miss Eugenia?"

"The location of a man named Cyril Henley."

"Gor! 'E's the one we looked fer before, missus."

"He escaped the net we cast, Ned. But his mates were brought in. He's the last of them."

Ned nodded. "I already knowed he got away, missus. I spotted 'im a couple days ago and told Mr. Farrell. 'E's lookin' for the gent, but I didn't know anyone else was lookin' fer him, too."

Gina held her breath. "Do you know where he is?"

"'E lost me, Miss Eugenia. Never knowed a gent so slippery. I recognized 'im from last time, but 'e got away before I could follow 'im back to 'is 'ole. Can I work fer both of ye?"

"I do not object to Mr. Farrell having the information, Ned, but he must not know I have hired you, too."

Ned seemed to consider this for a moment. "Well, since ye ain't askin' me to keep information from 'im, I s'pose there's no 'arm. Mum's the word, miss."

Ignorant of what a pickpocket would charge for such a service, she withdrew a crown from her reticule and pressed it into the grubby hand. "And another when you bring me the information."

The lad looked down at his palm and grinned. "Aye, miss. An' where'll I find ye?"

"You mustn't come to my home. I shall meet you daily at St. Mary's."

Ned glanced at the church on one side of the square and nodded. "Noon too early fer ye?"

"Not in the least."

He tipped his worn cap and gave an awkward bow. "Don't ye worry, miss. We know the warrens like nobody else. We'll 'ave yer gent soon enough. Oh, an' did ye know ye was bein' followed?"

A deep cold invaded her vitals. She scanned the crowd, looking for some sign of someone watching, but nothing appeared amiss. No one betrayed the least interest in her or her sister. Could Ned be wrong?

Chapter Seven

Jamie sipped his wine and allowed the conversation to drift over him as he watched the ladies across the drawing room. Earlier at the dinner table, sitting opposite Miss Eugenia had been a sweet agony of yearning. Each time she brought a spoon to those luscious lips, he remembered how they'd tasted, how they'd felted crushed beneath his own. Though it pained him to admit his own lack of self-control, he knew he'd do it again, given half a chance. And knew, too, that kiss had been the biggest mistake he'd ever made. He'd have been better to imagine it than experience it and yearn for it the rest of his life.

The ladies laughed at something Bella said, and then Miss Eugenia glanced in his direction. Their eyes met for a moment and he held back a groan. He wanted her in a way he'd never wanted any other woman, and with an intensity that left him breathless.

Upon reflection, he realized it was true—what Charlie had said. He had spent his adult life avoiding serious entanglements. He had gone so far as to shun the company of women who would expect more of him. But Miss Eugenia...no, she would be no different. Even as he watched her now, her hand went to her throat, and he knew she was remembering that night. He was a reminder of all she had suffered, of her pain and humiliation. There could never be a future with her.

Ah, but there was the next week or so, until she was whisked back to Ireland. And, torture though it would be, he would avail himself of every opportunity to be near her until then.

"...Cox."

Jamie returned his attention to his own conversation at the mention of that name. "Cox?"

Charlie grinned, as if he knew where Jamie's mind had been. "Were you not paying attention, Jamie? Devlin just told us that his stableman, old Cox, is dead."

"Dead?" Jamie frowned. "Accident?"

"Murder. We found him in a stall. He'd been covered over with hay, but the smell gave him away."

Jamie studied Devlin's face. Had Devlin avenged the attempt on Jamie's life? As usual, Devlin was inscrutable. "Coincidence? Or do you think it had something to do with the other night?"

Devlin's lips twitched, as if he might smile. "It wasn't me, if that's what you're thinking, Hunter. Were I a betting man, I'd wager he was silenced for whatever role he played in that debacle. If he had been paid to help an assassin, it wasn't by me. He'd been carved up like a Christmas goose. It wasn't pretty."

Knife, not a pistol? A pistol was more likely to be a hired killer, but a knife was more...personal. More familiar. Henley was quite proficient with a dagger. But then so were the Gibbons brothers.

He glanced back at Miss Eugenia and a vision of her suffering Cox's fate chilled him to the bone. She could identify

Henley. She could testify against him. Would she be next? Or would he?

Damnation! She had refused to stay safe at home, and he could not let her wander through society indifferent to the danger to her. No simple mooning after her would do. He would have to dog her every footstep. He would have to play the role of her most ardent suitor to keep her close. He would not let her die as Cox had.

It was time to pay the Gibbons brothers a visit. Gina would be safe enough tonight, since Mrs. O'Rourke forbade her girls from entertainments on Sunday nights.

The Gibbons brothers did not have a known address. When Devlin wanted to see them, he merely put the word out and, sooner or later, the brothers turned up at the Crown and Bear. Considering what Jamie suspected, they were not likely to respond this time.

Luckily, he had learned they were known to frequent a flea-infested gin house off Petticoat Lane by the name of the Cat's Paw. He elbowed the door open and eased in, giving his eyes a moment to adjust to the gloom. The odor of unwashed bodies and years of spilled ale and gin was noxious. Behind him, Charlie coughed to cover his disgust and they moved to a section of the bar nearest the door.

"What the bloody hell are we going to order?" Charlie muttered under his breath.

Jamie shook his head. The gin would strike them blind and the ale was likely the poorest to be had and diluted with filthy rain water. The tavern keeper, a man with one good eye and another that wandered, asked, "What'll it be, gents?"

"Bottle of whiskey," Jamie said. "Bring it unopened."

He noted they were drawing attention and was undecided if that was good or bad. The Cat's Paw did not attract men of Hunter's ilk, but most of the bully boys in the place would think twice before assaulting a gent in public. Once he and Charlie departed and entered a darkened street, however…

When the tavern keeper brought the whiskey, Jamie held it to the light. It was sealed and looked clear, not cloudy with the foul water hereabouts. He nodded at the tavern keeper, who opened the bottle and handed it to him. Jamie raised an eyebrow, took a swig and winced as the cheap rotgut burned a path down his throat. He passed the bottle to Charlie, who did the same.

Jamie tossed the tavern keeper a few coins and waved the unwashed tin cups away.

Charlie grinned as the tavern keeper turned to attend other customers. "I wondered what we could possibly order in here that wouldn't poison us."

"We'll see how big our heads are in the morning."

A tall figure emerged from the shadows at the back of the room. A shorter figure followed on his heels. They approached Jamie cautiously.

"I knows you," the taller man said. "One o' Farrell's friends, ain't ye?"

"Hunter's the name." Jamie inclined his head toward Charlie. "And this is my brother, Charlie."

"You th' gents askin' fer us?"

"Aye." He grabbed the whiskey bottle around the neck. "We want a private talk."

Richard "Dick" Gibbons, the taller and older of the brothers, led the way to a table in a far corner. He and his silent brother, Artie, sat against the wall, leaving Jamie and Charlie to sit with their backs to the room—a dangerous position in this sort of place. Jamie tilted his chair to one side, facing the room, and Charlie did the same, forming a rough semicircle. Artie grinned at their ploy.

Dick Gibbons held out his tin cup and Jamie obliged by

pouring a measure of whiskey into it, then did the same with Artie's cup.

"You remember what we wanted last time?" Jamie asked.

Dick nodded.

"I want it again."

The eldest Gibbons's grin made Jamie wary, and he suspected that Henley might have escaped the authorities a few weeks ago because the Gibbons brothers had warned him off. Selling that information to two parties, both Devlin Farrell and Henley, made for double profit. The Gibbonses were treacherous enough for such a move and greedy enough to risk Devlin's anger.

"Thought ye got 'em all."

"You know we didn't," Jamie countered, running his own bluff. "And you know who I want."

Dick seemed to contemplate denial and decide against it. "Henley, is it?"

Charlie took a swig from the bottle and eyed the Gibbons brothers warily. His glance at Jamie warned of caution, but Jamie was beyond that. There was only one way to deal with men like these—plainly. "Henley," he confirmed.

"'E's a dangerous one," Dick said. "'E offered a bounty fer ye, didn't 'e?"

"You know he did," Jamie confirmed. "Was it you who took a shot at me two nights ago?"

Artie's shoulders shook, but his laugh sounded more like a wheeze. His grin split to reveal two rows of rotten teeth. Dick shrugged, but did not answer Jamie's question.

"I thought a knife was more to your liking," Charlie said. "Was it you who carved up old Cox?"

"A smart man'd use whatever'd get the job done. We hears th' Hunters is dangerous, too. Wouldn't pay ta get too close."

"I didn't know that mattered to you and your brother."

"Don't." Dick sat back in his chair and took Jamie's measure. "If there's enough money in it."

Here was the confirmation that the Gibbons brothers would play a double game without the least compunction. "Name your price."

The Gibbons brothers put their heads together and communicated in whatever way they were able given Artie's reluctance or inability to speak. When Dick faced him again, he laughed, expelling a cloud of foul breath that nearly sickened Jamie.

"Considerin' the risk, hundred pounds," he said.

Jamie kept his expression neutral. The sum was enough to keep a small family for a year. The Home Office would never pay so much, but Jamie could muster that much from his personal accounts. And capturing Henley had become a very personal matter. "Done," he said. "On delivery."

"Ain't our usual way o' doin' business," Dick said, his dull eyes narrowing.

"If you know the Hunters' reputations, you know we honor our debts. And you know it would not be wise to cross us. You're already living on borrowed time as far as Devlin Farrell is concerned."

Both the Gibbons brothers looked nervous for the first time. Whether due to Devlin's wrath or the Hunters', it did not matter. All that mattered was that the Gibbons brothers would be unlikely to double-cross them again.

"How'll we find ye when we gots the information?"

"The Crown and Bear after midnight. If I am not there, leave a message with Mick Haddon and I'll find you."

"How lovely Vauxhall is this time of year," Lady Annica sighed, gesturing at the roses as the ladies strolled along one of the paths. She glanced over her shoulder and the vapid smile faded from her lips. "At last we are alone. Now, tell us what Mr. Renquist reported to you this afternoon, Eugenia."

The day had been warm and the sun was just dipping below the horizon as their group halted and gathered in a circle to hear the news. Gina took a deep breath before she began.

"He is not particularly hopeful. He says he has made inquiries in all the most likely places, all to no avail. He has not given up, however, and informs me there are still a number of sources he has not yet tapped."

Grace Hawthorne squeezed her hand. "You look discouraged, dear. But Mr. Renquist has proven his worth ten times over. We have a great deal of faith in him."

"Yes, but my mother has said she is looking into ways whereupon we can leave for Ireland sooner. I do not know how much more time I may have."

"Never fear." Lady Sarah's violet eyes narrowed, reminding Gina of her brother's eyes and causing a little tingle to race up her spine. "Should it be necessary for you to leave before we have found the scoundrel, we shall continue. Nary a man has eluded us for long."

The assurance was comforting, but Gina wanted to be present herself for Henley's capture. She wanted to witness *his* humiliation. "Thank you, Lady Sarah. I appreciate all the Wednesday League has done for me."

She hesitated and glanced at her sister, Lilly. Would the ladies be angry? Chastise her? Even so, they had been forthright with her, and she could be no less with them. "I have also employed some street urchins to keep watch for any sign of Mr. Henley. And to gather whatever information they can."

They fell silent for a moment as the lamplighters came by, illuminating the pathways for the evening. Lady Annica's husband, Lord Auberville, had arranged for their entire party to stay for supper and to see the fireworks, one of the last of the season.

Lady Sarah resumed the conversation as if it had never been interrupted. "Excellent. I employed two, myself, when it became necessary. I could give you their names and perhaps they could be pressed into service, as well."

Gina exhaled a long breath. "Thank you."

Lady Annica closed her parasol. "Ah, here come the gentlemen. I vow, Sarah, your brothers make a merry group. I would have thought they'd be carousing or scaring up a card game. What do you think could account for their devoted attention to us of late?"

Lady Sarah laughed and shot Gina a teasing wink. "I cannot imagine, though it has been suggested that one of my brothers might be smitten."

Gina stopped herself from turning around to see who was coming and Lilly gave her a nudge. "There, you see?" she whispered. "James or Charles Hunter is taken by you. Perhaps both. And either of them would do nicely for a husband."

Husband? Dear heavens! Lilly really had no idea of the nature of her relationship with James. Even if she were able and inclined to marry, he was the last man she would consider.

"Ladies," Lord Auberville greeted them. "You look as if you are hatching some scheme or surprise. Is it a game we can all play?"

Lady Annica smiled as she took his arm. "It is for ladies only, Auberville. I assure you, you would not want to be a part of this conversation."

He looked down at her and his smile was only slightly suspicious. "Ah, I see. Ladies' business, is it?" He turned to the others and quirked an eyebrow. "I have learned not to ask too many questions lest I become privy to information no man should know."

James Hunter was studying Gina rather too closely. A sardonic smile hovered at the corners of his mouth, telling her that he suspected what the conversation had really been about. She glanced away, afraid she might reveal too much.

Lord Auberville and Lady Annica led the way back toward the pavilion. "We have come to fetch you as our table is ready for us. I shall apologize in advance for the food, but the wine is tolerable."

Laughter dispelled the tension and they proceeded to the supper box. Dining for such a large party, more than a dozen, took several hours and the evening had grown chill by the time they were finished.

As they exited the dining area, Andrew glanced at his pocket watch. "It is still more than an hour before the fireworks. Shall we take in the musical performance?"

Agreement was quick, but before they'd gone far, Gina found James at her elbow. "Would you consent to stroll down to the river with me, Miss O'Rourke?"

"I…"

"The lights reflected off the water are quite lovely this time of evening."

"Go on, then," Lady Sarah said. "But be back for the fireworks. And mind your manners, Jamie."

He took her arm and turned her toward one of the promenades leading to the Thames. Gina looked up at him and sighed. "I would have thought your sister, of all people, would know that you haven't any."

"Manners?" He laughed. "Aye, you'd think she would. Alas, she thinks her brothers are perfect—a myth we tend to perpetuate. Will you give us away?"

"That would depend, Mr. Hunter."

"Upon what, Miss O'Rourke?"

"Upon how you choose to deal with me."

"I cannot foresee any changes in the near future."

"Then your reputation is in jeopardy."

"Are you still disgruntled about the kiss? I would say I

regret it and ask your pardon, but I don't regret it in the least. In fact, I count it among my most memorable moments."

She shivered, remembering the bittersweet yearning for something more, and glanced down at the pebbled path rather than betray herself. Unfortunately her little shiver had given her away and he chuckled knowingly as he leaned closer to her ear.

"I think you will not soon forget it either."

"Did you ask me to walk with you for the express purpose of taunting me, Mr. Hunter?"

He sighed deeply and turned her down a path that branched to their right. "We are a bit past formalities, Eugenia. When we are alone, at least, would you call me Jamie? Or James, if you'd like."

He had made her name sound like a caress or a sigh. She'd never really cared for her name until that moment. "If...if you'd prefer. But if you did not want to talk to me about what happened in the Albermarle gardens, why did you ask to walk with me? Now your sister thinks..."

"That I am courting you? Precisely. As will everyone else in our party. And, with luck, the news will spread like wildfire throughout the ton."

"You...you *want* people to think that? But why?"

"You have refused to stay at home and avoid places and situations where you might encounter trouble. Since I cannot stop you, this is my best chance of protecting you."

She halted beneath a lantern at a fork in the path and withdrew her hand from his arm. "I do not recall asking for your protection, Mr. Hunter. And, had you asked, I would have refused."

His voice carried a slight chill when he answered. "Not an option, Eugenia."

He had put himself directly in her path. Would people talk as freely to her now if they thought she was intimately connected to James Hunter? She rather thought not. This little charade of his would render her completely ineffective. "We must halt this ridiculous rumor at once!"

She turned back the way they'd come but had not gone more than a few steps when he caught her by the arm and pulled her down an unlighted path to the right. When they were quite alone and could not possibly be overheard, he halted and turned to face her.

"We will do no such thing, Eugenia. To the contrary, you will support the fable. There is no escape from it. I intend to dog your every footstep until you are gone back to Belfast."

"You have no right!"

His handsome face settled into hard lines. "Would you rather I take this matter to someone who does have the right? I believe my brother Andrew and perhaps Devlin Farrell are your nearest male relatives. Do you really think they would look more kindly on your activities than I do?"

"You wouldn't!"

"Care to make a wager on that, Eugenia?"

Good heavens—he would! From the look on his face, argument would be useless. She took a deep breath and calmed herself. A show of defiance would gain her nothing, but perhaps they could reach a compromise. "I shall do nothing to contradict you, then, but when you are not present—"

"You, Eugenia, will not contradict me. I will always be present."

"What are you saying?"

"That I intend to be at every function you attend. Furthermore, I shall escort you and your party home each night."

"Are you mad? People will be expecting a marriage. At the very least, an announcement. One of us will look a jilt when I return to Ireland."

"I shall take the blame. I have no intention of causing you or your reputation harm. But you must see that you have left me no other recourse to keep you safe from your own recklessness."

Trapped. She was trapped and she would be hard-pressed to make any progress finding Mr. Henley now. With James at her elbow every time she left the house, who would confide in her? Why, how would she even meet with Miss Race and Mr. Metcalfe at the Morris masquerade? This was intolerable.

She looked up at him in the moonlight, aware for the first time that they had ventured down one of the "dark walks." Somewhere in the distance, she could hear the strains of an orchestra playing a waltz. Nearer, the call of a bird disturbed from its nest startled her. If James had meant to find privacy, he'd succeeded.

He looked down at her and slipped his arm around her waist. "Eugenia, it will not be so bad. I promise."

How could she ever make him understand? Frustration surfaced as she looked into his eyes and her deepest fear slipped out unbidden. "Perhaps it is already too late to save me...."

"Not while you still breathe, Gina." His lips were soft and beseeching as they touched hers, as if making a request or waiting for permission to do more.

She responded in a way she hadn't known she could, and she realized just how badly she'd wanted this—this closeness, this intimacy, this deep and poignant longing. She surrendered to it, sinking against him with a little moan.

His arms tightened around her, one hand winding through her hair and making a fist, holding her immobile and unable to turn away. Unnecessary, since she'd lost the will for resistance long ago. She wanted to find what lay at the end of this.

Chapter Eight

God help him, Jamie knew better. Gina wanted nothing to do with him, she'd made that clear enough. But when she looked at him with those doe eyes, when he saw the spark—half question, half plea—in her eyes, he had responded without thinking. When she'd fit herself against his body, his own had hardened with his long-suppressed need.

Her lips parted with a sigh and he teased her tongue, relishing her boldness mingled with timidity in the way she tasted him and in the sweetness of her moan. He'd been afraid she would turn away so he held her tight, preventing her from slipping away from him. He needn't have worried.

From the moment he'd seen her tonight in her ivory gown with the daring décolletage, he'd been longing to do this very thing.

His fingers were tangled in her hair and he pulled her head back, the better to kiss her. The better to nuzzle his way from her earlobe to the hollow of her throat. He nudged the ivory ribbon around her neck aside and kissed the little line of thickened tissue where she'd been nicked by Daschel's dagger. He could not see that scar without remembering that horrible moment before he'd swept her from the altar when he'd feared she was dead.

He was afraid she would protest at his recognition of her wound, but the sweet vibration of her sigh against his lips nearly drove him wild with desire. Where? Where could he take her? He could not soil her gown on the grass and return her to the fireworks. Nor could he whisk her from the gardens and take her to a private inn, no matter how much he wanted to. But he couldn't let her go without tasting just a bit more because, when she came to her senses, she would never let anything like this happen again.

He edged his kisses lower, this time nudging the lace of her bodice out of his way and freeing one rose-peaked bud. She shivered, but he did not take pity on her yet. Instead he captured that little bud between his lips and circled it with his tongue. It hardened and formed a taut bead that tasted vaguely of sugared cream and made him hunger for more.

She made a whimpering sound and cupped the back of his head, pressing him closer and whispering something that sounded like his name. What wild music that made in his mind. He nipped gently in response and her hand tightened through his hair.

He relished her unpracticed responses, knowing she'd never done anything like this before. Whatever had been done to her the night of the ritual, whatever she had felt that night, could have been nothing like this. She was too surprised. Too caught up in the madness that possessed them both.

Her chest rose and fell rapidly and her heartbeat hammered against his lips. He knew the signs. She was his for the taking, and he was painfully capable of doing just that. Desperate to do it, in fact. But this was Eugenia. Stunning, brave and principled Eugenia. How could he disregard her wishes or sate himself at her expense? How could he risk loving her, *knowing* her, only to have her leave him?

A chill went through him and he slowly separated himself from her, straightening and steadying her until she could support herself again. "I…I apologize, Eugenia. I shouldn't have done that. I know I've said that before, but you have my oath it will not happen again."

She blinked, as if trying to recall where she was or what they'd done, blissfully unaware that the deepened pink of one areola still peeked above her décolletage—a temptation that nearly undid his good intentions. She winced as he sighed and reached out to tug the fabric upward.

Even through the deepened twilight he could see the stain of a blush rise to her cheeks as she turned away from him and struggled to put herself to rights. "You should not start something you do not intend to finish, Mr. Hunter."

Finish? Everything inside him begged to finish what he'd started. But her accusation…was it a rebuke for stopping? Or for beginning? He wanted to reassure her, and he touched her shoulder in what he hoped she would interpret as support. "Eugenia, my concern was for you. You cannot know what a man—"

She shrugged his hand away and turned to face him, her eyes burning like dark coals. "This is precisely the point, is it not? I cannot, but I should."

"What—"

"Never mind, Mr. Hunter. It is my problem and has nothing to do with you." She smoothed the hair he'd tangled and tucked it back into the ribbons.

He wanted to tell her that anything to do with her was his concern, but he knew that would only make her angrier. He was saved the necessity of a reply by a reverberating boom, the first of the fireworks.

She jumped, startled by the sound. "We should be getting back before your sister comes looking for us."

"Eugenia, about the matter we discussed…"

She took several steps back toward the path. "Our 'court-ship,' Mr. Hunter?"

"Yes. Perhaps I should have asked you if you are husband hunting." He followed close on her heels, barely daring to breathe until he had the answer to that question.

She laughed. "That is the last thing on my mind at the minute."

He exhaled with relief. "Then I cannot see what objection you could have regarding our charade."

"*Your* charade," she corrected as she took the arm he offered.

"You can make this as difficult as you please, Eugenia, or you can cooperate. What you cannot do is stop me. My course is set. And you might want to consider the benefits."

"There are benefits? For whom?"

"If society thinks I am near to making an offer for you, my name may lend you some measure of protection."

She looked up at him through the deepening twilight. "Why are you so determined to carry out this scheme…James?"

"I am responsible for you. Had I succeeded in capturing Henley…"

She considered this as they entered the clearing and heeded a wave from Lady Sarah. "You most certainly are not respon-sible for me, but I…I suppose there can be no harm in pre-tending if you will try to use a bit of discretion. The less you flaunt it, the less there will be to explain when it ends."

"Agreed."

Gina glanced down at her décolletage to be certain every-thing had been put back in place. She was already humiliated enough and she did not want to rejoin their party betraying any sign of impropriety.

That kiss, more seductive than the last, warned her not to become entangled any further with James Hunter. Indeed, how would she manage to coax information from young men if James was always lurking? How could she trace the only clue she had?

She dropped her hand from his arm to smooth the fabric of her gown, trying to brush away any remaining trace of their indiscretion. Her fingers skimmed a small lump of metal dangling from the corset strings beneath her gown. The shape seemed to burn its impression into her skin. Thank heavens James had gone no further or he might have found the key Christina Race had given her. She *must* find the lock it fit.

Standing on the steps of St. Mary's Church as the bell rang the hour of twelve, Gina scanned the crowd for any sign of the street urchins Lilly had introduced to her. In the distance, she could see Nancy amongst the stalls of vegetable vendors. Soon she would rejoin Gina, and they would walk home.

She felt conspicuous and realized meeting so openly with a street child would be noted by any of the family's friends and acquaintances. She would have to think of a different place. Somewhere more private and less open.

A small head sporting a dirty blue cap bobbed through the crowd in a direct line for her. As he drew closer, he waved and finally joined her on the steps. "Mornin', Miss Eugenia."

"Good morning, Ned. Do you have anything for me?"

"Not yet, miss. I been lookin' though. I rounded up some o' the lads and told 'em to keep a look out. Promised a shilling to whoever brought the news."

Ned was a clever lad. The more eyes on the watch, the more likely Henley would be sighted. "Thank you, Ned. Is there some way you could send to me immediately when you have news?"

"Instead o' waiting until noon, y' mean? I dunno. Could knock on yer kitchen door, I suppose."

"No!" Gina could just imagine the questions she'd face if a street child turned up asking for her. "I…I could meet you twice a day."

The boy removed his cap and swiped his forehead with the back of his arm. "Naw. Shouldn't take us long to spot 'im, but that Henley is a wily one. If 'e catches us… An' we gots bigger problems than that, miss. If you wants him real quick-like, I'm gonna need 'elp. One of me mates thinks 'e saw the gent goin' into a gamblin' 'ell. I can't get in some o' the places 'e goes. I know 'e's one fer the ladies, an' I can't get in those places either."

Gina's mind whirled. She could not ask any of Henley's peers without alerting James. And he was likely pursuing that angle himself. Aside from that, she could not know if they'd been in league with Henley, which would only land her squarely in more trouble. And she dare not hire a woman for fear of the danger that might befall her.

No, apart from her own inquiries, her best chance of finding Henley lay with Mr. Renquist and this savvy urchin. But the threat of James watching her every minute would keep her from pursuing the matter. Unless she could find a way around him.

He'd declared his intention to escort her home every night. But what if she did not stay at home? What if she met with Ned, instead? She'd sneaked out at night before and managed quite well before she'd run afoul of Mr. Henley. And she'd learned her lesson there—never again would she go anywhere with someone she did not know very, very well.

"Ned, how late are you about at nights?"

"Don't usually sleep until dawn, miss. Some o' my best pickin's are in the wee hours when the gents are deep in their cups and not payin' attention."

"Then would you meet me after midnight? I could help you. Perhaps I could disguise myself and gain entry to the places you cannot. I will reimburse you for your losses and also pay anyone else you think may help. But we mustn't involve too many people. The more who know, the more likely our secret will get out."

He seemed to consider the matter for a moment, then brightened. "Aye. There's a few I know 'oo could 'elp. An' they won't tell, neither. When do y' wanna start, miss?"

The Morris masquerade was tonight. She was attending with the Thayer twins, but she could beg a headache just before midnight, allow James to escort her home, then sneak away as soon as his carriage disappeared around the corner. But tonight she had important business. If fortune favored her, once she spoke with Mr. Metcalfe, she would have no need of Ned's services. She would have all the answers she needed.

But Gina had learned nothing if not to be cautious. "Tomorrow night, Ned? Quarter past midnight?" Wherever she found herself tomorrow, she would be sure to be home by then.

"Aye, miss. I'll wait for ye down the street."

"Stay hidden, Ned. The neighbors are a bit nosy."

The atmosphere in the Morris ballroom—indeed, in all the rooms the masquerade spilled into—was lively and gay. More than half the attendees wore elaborate costumes. Others, like Gina, wore bright colors in lieu of a costume and merely sported a mask or a domino. Her mask was crafted from silk sewn with yellow feathers and sparkling jewels to complement her bright yellow gown and she dangled a yellow feathered fan from her left wrist. Hortense had dressed as a shepherdess while Harriett wore a nun's habit. And James, who had arrived to escort them true to his threat, wore a domino with his usual evening attire. When he had delivered them safely to the ballroom, he'd excused himself to greet some of his friends in the billiards room.

Under the protection of disguise, and relieved of the usual restraint of propriety, the gathering was rife with hilarity and spontaneity. And, unless Gina missed her guess, all were imbibing more than the usual amount of punch laced with alcohol, along with wine and ale.

She wondered how she might find Miss Race in the crush, but removed her mask often enough to make certain Christina could find her. But, so far, not a single trace of a leper. Surely Mr. Metcalfe would not fail to come. Christina had told her how anxious he was to speak with her. She felt the key hidden in her bodice and said a quick silent prayer that her long nightmare would end tonight.

"I do so love masques," Hortense said, shifting her hooked staff to her other hand. "Though I do wonder how I shall dance with this thing."

Mr. Booth, another guest who had deigned to wear a domino rather than full costume, approached them with a rakish smile. "I have always had fantasies about dancing with a nun. You must have pity on me, Miss Thayer, and fulfill my dreams at last."

Harriett laughed in a way no nun would ever laugh, both seductive and pleased. "Granted, Mr. Booth. But mind your manners, sir. I have friends in high places."

Hortense chuckled as Mr. Booth led her sister away. "And Harri has always had fantasies about Mr. Booth. Two wishes satisfied with one dance."

"Let us hope that everyone's wish comes true tonight."

"Whatever do you mean, Gina? What do you wish for?"

Answers. The truth. "Happy endings," she murmured.

"Amen," Hortense agreed. "And sooner would be better. But I think you need not worry over that. James Hunter has very obviously set his intentions on you. Any girl would be mad to refuse him. Charm, looks, wealth. What more could you ask?"

What more indeed? "He has not proposed yet, Hortense, and may not. And should he, I have not decided what my answer will be." There. That should cut short the wagging tongues of the ton and not raise any unrealistic expectations.

"Mark me, he will be back to claim a waltz. You will see him often before it is time to go and he calls for his carriage."

"I hope he will not hover," she said. She did not want Mr. Metcalfe to be hesitant to approach her.

She caught sight of Christina, in an elaborate peacock mask, just entering the ballroom. She was on the arm of a man Gina hadn't met and she wondered if this was the elusive Mr. Metcalfe. But where was his leper disguise? She waved and caught Christina's eye.

Hortense followed her glance and grinned widely. "Oh! 'Tis Christina and her cousin, Mr. Marley. He knows every dance ever and has the most devilish wit. Almost as devilish as Charles Hunter's. How lovely, they are coming our way."

The man in question bowed deeply to them as Christina made the introductions and then he promptly swept Hortense into the rollicking reel, leaving Gina to hold her staff. When they were alone, she asked, "Where is Mr. Metcalfe?"

"He said he would meet us here," Christina told her.

Mr. Metcalfe was clearly afraid of something. Even his costume had likely been chosen to veil his identity. She took a sip of punch, wondering what could cause him to be so cautious.

When the dance ended, Mr. Marley returned Hortense and claimed Christina with a promise that Gina would be next. A quick glance toward the punch bowl told her that Harriett was still occupied with Mr. Booth. When a figure dressed in a long black robe with a cowl pulled low over his face and a small bell around his neck approached her, her heartbeat sped. Mr. Metcalfe, at last!

He held his hand out to her without speaking and she returned Hortense's staff. Once on the dance floor, the leper turned and lifted his cowl just enough that she could see his face. Yes, this was the man who had been at the tableau with Christina. The dance was a waltz, which would allow them to talk without the interruptions of a reel. Very wise of Mr. Metcalfe.

"Miss O'Rourke, I implore you to drop this matter at once."

Whatever she'd expected to hear, it was not this earnest plea. "I cannot, sir. I am committed."

"You are ill prepared for what lies ahead. You cannot succeed."

"You do not even know what I plan, sir. How can you presume—"

"Because I know Henley. Far too well."

Gina almost panicked when she noted James on the sidelines, watching her. Had he come to dance with her? Or had someone alerted him?

"I cannot let him get away with what he's done to my family."

"And to you, Miss O'Rourke?"

Her cheeks burned. "You were there…that night?"

"To my shame."

She tried to pull away and caused him to stumble, but he held tight and resumed the step. "You must believe me, Miss O'Rourke. That was the first night I attended one of Daschel and Henley's 'passion plays.' I was appalled when I realized what was going to happen. But…there were so many there that I could not expose myself by going against them."

"Yet you were willing to allow them to defile and murder me?"

"Murder? I did not know about the murders until the

following day, when the news spread like wildfire through the clubs and hells of town."

Oh, how she dreaded the answer, but she could not stop herself from asking. "How many? How many 'postulants' knew who I was?"

"Perhaps a handful. Perhaps less. I was not certain until I saw you here tonight. Most of them were so far gone in their cups and with the hashish Daschel had burning in the incense bowls that they wouldn't have known their own mothers. Henley laced the wine with opium, you know."

Opium—enough of it—would explain her drugged state and her inability to remember what had happened to her in the hours before the ritual began. That, at least, could be the answer to one of her questions.

"Still, I cannot let him get away with it," she murmured more to herself than to Mr. Metcalfe.

"Believe me, I understand. But you must leave this for others. Others more ruthless."

"I can be as ruthless as I must, Mr. Metcalfe."

He shook his head in disbelief. "You are not a match for a man of Henley's ilk. You have no idea—"

"Then, pray, enlighten me so that I will not go into battle unprepared."

There was a long hesitation while Mr. Metcalfe evidently struggled with his conscience, then continued in a lowered voice. "Henley is a patient man. He has been waiting. Waiting for an opportunity to finish off his enemies. I am one of his loose ends. I know too much. I know who—" He stopped as if afraid he'd said too much. But when he continued, his words surprised her.

"And you, Miss O'Rourke, are top of his list. London is not safe for either of us unless, or until, Henley has been dealt with."

"By whom? Who is left to deal with him, Mr. Metcalfe?

The Home Office has failed twice. If not me, if not you, then who?"

He shook his head as if to deny her words. "I am merely trying to stay alive until he has been caught. I'd advise you to do the same."

She squeezed his arm to make her point. "I need your help, Mr. Metcalfe. Tell me what you know that makes you fear for your life. Tell me anything you know that could bring him down. Tell me what lock your little key fits and what I will find there."

"I've already said too much."

The dance ended and Mr. Metcalfe released her, glancing over his shoulder with a harried look. Before she could form a protest, he was gone, disappearing into the crowd almost instantly.

At least she finally had an answer to one of her questions. Now she knew *why* she couldn't remember the events of that night. But there was still so much more she needed to know. If she could not remember herself, surely there was someone, somewhere, who could fill in those lost hours.

Her head whirled with the implications of Mr. Metcalfe's warnings. She needed a moment to think, to gather her composure and plan what she should do next. As the next dance began, she crossed the dance floor to the wide terrace doors and slipped through, ignoring the couples gathered there and others strolling along the paths. She needed to find just a single moment in a quiet place.

She stopped at an ivy-covered arbor and gripped the lattice-work until her knuckles were white. Gradually she became aware that she'd punctured her thumb on a hidden thorn. She shook her hand. "Ouch!"

Mr. Metcalfe appeared out of the shadows and came to her side. Had he decided to tell her about the key?

He took her hand and lifted it to his mouth. He licked the

little droplet of blood. Shocked, she pulled her hand away. "Sir!"

He produced a handkerchief from the folds of his black robe and she accepted it reluctantly.

"Delicious," he said.

A chill spiraled up her spine. That was not Mr. Metcalfe's voice! Instinctively, she spun around to make a dash for the terrace doors, but the leper's hand clamped over her mouth and she was yanked back against a hard chest.

"How nice to see you again, my dear. You look just like a pretty little canary. I wonder if your neck will be as easy to break."

Henley! Dear God!

He began dragging her backward. "But you and I are like the phoenix, m'dear. We have both risen from the ashes, eh? Though I shall rise and soar whilst you shall burn again. Poor little bird."

A sound, half moan, half muted scream, rose from her throat and he clamped his hand tighter, mashing her lips against her teeth and closing her nostrils.

Henley's breath was hot and foul against her cheek. "Ah, and here comes your erstwhile savior. How fortunate for me. Now, if I only had a pistol. My, my. Yes, a knife will have to do again."

James was looking for her, turning in every direction, but he could not see them in the shadows of the arbor. Henley could slash him when he walked past! "Eugenia? Miss O'Rourke?"

Henley chortled. "So proper? Are you not his whore yet?" he asked in a raspy voice.

She brought her heel down sharply on his instep and pulled away at the same time. "Jamie!" she screamed.

He turned toward her voice and came running at full

speed. Henley uttered a foul curse and ran in the opposite direction.

Jamie reached her and gripped both her arms as he looked into her eyes. "Are you all right?"

She forced her tears back as she nodded and pointed in the opposite direction, her throat raw. *"Henley!"*

"Run to the house. Do not stop until you are there. Find Charlie and tell him what's happened." He took off in pursuit and she thought she heard him utter an equally foul curse.

Chapter Nine

The gardens were empty near the back mews. No sign of Henley, damn it all! The man could not have doubled back or Jamie would have seen him. He arrived at a scene of confusion at the stables.

"…just took his lordship's stallion and rode off," one groom was saying to another.

Jamie could still hear the hoofbeats in the distance. "Who?" he shouted.

The stable hands turned to him. "A leper, sir. Dressed like a leper. I was just saddling Lord Grenleigh's stallion when the man ran up, knocked me on my arse, took the reins and rode away. What'll I tell his lordship, sir?"

Jamie couldn't think of that now. Only that Henley had gotten away again and by the time his coach was made ready Henley would be enjoying a pint in whatever hole he hid in. "Have my driver ready my carriage and bring it around front. I'll give Grenleigh the news."

"Thank ye, sir." The stable master tipped his cap with a look of profound relief.

Damn Henley, that misbegotten son of Satan! Jamie strode back through the gardens, his head down, hoping to find some clue, some hint of Henley's presence or an indication of where he'd been. In the shadows of the arbor, the toe of his shoe skimmed something soft and pliable. He looked down, startled to see something that looked suspiciously like a hand.

He knelt and parted the shrubbery. A man's body, covered partially by the foliage, had been hidden beneath the branches. Dreading what he might find, he rolled the body over. *Bloody hell*…Stanley Metcalfe. The very man Jamie had been searching for this past week. Henley had gotten to him first.

Metcalfe's pale blue eyes were still open and his mouth gaped in a silent scream. A quick inspection of the still-warm body revealed that the crimson-stained vest had a clean cut through to the flesh. Metcalfe's death had not been easy. Had Eugenia seen the body?

"Holy Mother of God," Charlie whispered over Jamie's shoulder. "What happened?"

Icy cold pierced Jamie's heart. "Where is Eugenia?"

"Inside. I calmed her, told her to say nothing, and took her to the Thayers with instructions not to leave the ballroom. Then I came to find you."

"She told you Henley—"

Charlie nodded and knelt beside him. "Shall I assume he melted into the night as is his wont?"

He gave his brother a rueful smile. "Not quite. He stole Grenleigh's prize stallion."

"Not very sporting of him, was it?"

He ignored the attempt at levity. "He had her, Charlie. God only knows what would have happened.…" He looked down at Metcalfe's body again, knowing that Henley had planned something of the same sort for her.

"But he doesn't have her now," Charlie said in a deadly calm voice. "And we shall see to it that he never has that chance again. Meantime, we will have to inform Wycliffe and our erstwhile host. 'Twould seem the party is over."

"Not yet." Jamie passed his hand over Metcalfe's face to close his eyes before he stood. "Let me take Eugenia and the Thayer girls away first. I need to talk to her before the Home Office interrogates her. And the Thayers do not need to be a part of this. My carriage should be waiting around front. Once I have them home, I will come back and we shall handle this as discreetly as possible. Oh, and tell Grenleigh he'll have to find other transportation tonight, will you?"

Charlie helped him arrange the branches again to shield Metcalfe's body from immediate discovery. "You know what this means, do you not?"

"That Henley is growing bolder. And that boldness must be a measure of his desperation."

"He will only escalate from here. He'll get careless and, sooner or later, we will catch him."

Jamie clenched his fists. "He'll come after Eugenia again."

"And you, Jamie. He has already tried to stop you, and he won't quit now."

Gina hid behind her vivid yellow mask, careful to betray no outward sign of distress, though she'd been seething with suppressed anxiety. Where was James? Had Henley used his knife? Was James dead in an alley somewhere? And how had Henley known where to find her?

Hortense and Harriett had been teeming with questions when they'd seen how shaken she was. She'd settled for a version of the truth, telling them only that she'd been accosted in the gardens by a man in a costume. They had steadfastly flanked her since that moment, refusing dances and making inconsequential conversation to cover Gina's lack of attention.

She could only watch the terrace doors and pray that James was safe.

She nearly collapsed with relief when she saw him come through the terrace doors and scan the ballroom until he caught sight of her. But the look on his face was not reassuring as he came directly to their little group. She managed a smile as he approached, certain he would not want her to give their business away.

Hortense sighed when he offered a slight bow. "Oh, here you are! Did you catch him?"

He glanced at Gina and she knew he was wondering how much she had told them. "I told Hortense and Harriett about the stranger who accosted me in the gardens before you arrived in time to rout him."

"To be accosted in such a manner by a complete stranger!" Harriett said with an indignant look on her pretty face. "I told Gina we should report the incident to Mr. Morris at once, but she would not hear of it until you came back."

He gave Gina a slight nod of approval, clearly relieved that she'd prevented the twins from spreading alarm though the gathering. "I will take care of that presently," he told them. "But first I think I should take you home. I would be remiss in my duty as your escort to allow you to be present if there should be any problems."

"Do you really think there will be problems? Could that dreadful man yet be lurking in the gardens?" Hortense asked.

"I believe I frightened him off." He cast a reassuring glance in Gina's direction. "But we should not take any chances. I've had my carriage brought round."

Harriett sighed, whether in relief or disappointment, she could not guess. "You are too kind, sir," she said.

They made a quiet exit and were safely on their way before any fuss could be made. The Thayer home was their first stop, and James handed the twins down from the carriage with a courtly flourish. Both girls thanked him graciously and quickly promised him dances the following night.

He settled himself beside Gina as the carriage started off again. Before she could ask, he posed a question of his own.

"Did he hurt you?"

She removed her mask and sighed. Where she had once been uncomfortable with James, she was now relieved to be alone with him. She hadn't realized the strain she'd been under to keep her composure until that very moment.

"He was going to break my neck. When he saw you, he said he had a knife. What happened when you went after him? I was so afraid you'd fought and that he…" She began to shiver, unwilling to even entertain the notion that James might not have returned to her. That Henley could have killed him.

He took her hand between his to stop her trembling. "He'd stolen a horse and gotten away before I got to the stables."

She frowned. "But you were gone so long."

"There's more, Eugenia. I have been searching for a man who could have helped us find Henley. Stanley Metcalfe. I found him dead beneath some bushes when I was returning to the house."

Dead? But she'd just danced with him. There must be some mistake. "Are you certain it was Mr. Metcalfe?"

"He'd been knifed. I wanted you safely away before anyone could question you. Should anyone ask, you know nothing about the entire affair."

Her eyes burned with unshed tears. "I danced with him. He warned me that Henley wanted to kill me."

"Metcalfe?" he asked, a note of disbelief in his voice. "Was this something to do with your search for Henley?"

"I…I was to meet him tonight. To persuade him to help

me. He'd been hiding from Mr. Henley, afraid to appear in public. Oh, I wish he'd never come to meet me."

"I didn't see you dance with him, Eugenia."

The tone of his voice should have warned her. "He was dressed as a leper. But he disappeared so quickly after our dance that I was unable to question him further."

"Leper? Was that not the costume Henley was wearing when he attacked you?"

She nodded. "I thought he was Mr. Metcalfe. I thought he'd come back to tell me…"

James groaned. "Blast it all! Henley killed Metcalfe and stole his costume to get close to you before you discovered who he was. But what did Metcalfe have to tell you?"

The hidden key burned its impression into the soft flesh of her bosom. If she told James about it, he would take it from her. He was so stubbornly determined to protect her from herself that she could not trust him. "Something more," she improvised. "Perhaps where to find Mr. Henley. Or where he is living."

"How did you draw him out of hiding?"

"Miss Race. His fiancée. She interceded for me. He was dreadfully afraid of Mr. Henley. He said he knew something that Mr. Henley would kill him for." Suddenly the horror of the situation struck her. "Oh! Miss Race! She will be devastated. I should go to her. Be with her when she hears the awful news."

"Did she come with him?"

"She came with friends. Mr. Metcalfe was in the habit of meeting her wherever she went."

"Then she would best hear it tomorrow in the privacy of her own home. But think carefully, Eugenia. Did Metcalfe say what he knew?"

"That is not the sort of thing I'd be likely to forget, sir. No. He did not tell me what it was."

He cupped her cheek and turned her face to his. "Now I've made you angry. That wasn't my intention."

She flinched at his touch. "I dislike being interrogated as if I've done something wrong."

"Wrong? No, Eugenia. But you've done something reckless and dangerous. You've put yourself at risk when you've promised you wouldn't. Ask questions. That's what you said you were going to do."

Gina's conscience tweaked her. That was all she'd done. So far. But she'd made plans to do more with Ned. She would have to meet him tomorrow night and beg off. The incident with Henley had shaken her more than she'd wanted to admit.

James ran his thumb over her lower lip, his voice deadly calm. "'Tis swollen, Eugenia. Did Henley steal a kiss?"

"He had his hand over my mouth. He was dragging me away from the arbor." To kill her and leave her body beside Mr. Metcalfe's, no doubt.

He leaned forward slowly, giving her time to turn away. But she couldn't. His mouth was soft and gentle as he cherished her lower lip before took her whole mouth in a kiss no less exciting than those that had come before, but somehow more comforting, reassuring.

The carriage stopped in front of Andrew's house, jolting her out of the hypnotic hold James had over her. Slowly, and with a heavy sigh, he released her scant moments before the driver opened the door. He got out and offered his hand to help her down.

"Are you returning to the masque?"

"Yes. Charlie is waiting and we will need to inform Mr. Morris that there is a dead body in his garden. He has likely sent for Wycliffe already."

"You will let me know what happens?"

"Tomorrow." He took her arm, walked her to the door and waited while she rummaged for her key in her reticule.

He took it from her and unlocked the door. "Good evening, Eugenia," he said as he opened the door.

She stepped into the foyer and stopped. At least eight crates were stacked floor to ceiling just inside the door. Suddenly she could not breathe. Had Mama found early passage?

"Eugenia? What…"

Alerted by her sudden halt, he followed her into the foyer. "You did not mention you were leaving," he said after a moment.

"I did not know." She turned and looked at him. "Mama must have found an earlier departure."

"When?"

She shook her head. "She did not say a word to me. Passage must have become available suddenly."

He looked at her and she knew there was something he wanted to say, but he merely bowed, turned on his heel, and closed the door behind him as he departed.

The thought of Mr. Henley escaping justice haunted her, but the realization that she might never see James again tore at her heart. How had she let things go so far? How had she let herself love James?

She could not change one, but she could do something about the other. There was no more time for fear or hesitation. Tomorrow she would meet Ned as planned, and she would do whatever she must to bring Henley's reign of terror to an end.

As he climbed back in his carriage and gave his driver instructions to return to the masquerade, cold fury gripped Jamie's viscera. Once again, Henley had damaged Eugenia. Once again, Jamie had failed to protect her. But any qualms he'd had about killing Henley to prevent a public trial had disappeared the instant he'd seen her swollen lip and the tiny bruise on one side of her throat. The knowledge that Eugenia had been so close to death horrified and angered him. Henley would pay for that.

Even more unsettling was the realization that his time with Eugenia was over. She would be gone from London and from his life. And the emptiness would return—the mindless, meaningless affairs, the endless days and nights, the soul-deep loneliness that no amount of friends or family could fill. Since he'd met her, the emptiness had receded and been filled with memories of her voice, her eyes, the warmth of her skin, the lushness of her mouth and the sweetness of her sighs.

No doubt it was for the best. He'd take that post with the Foreign Office. He'd lose himself in service to the king. Somewhere, he'd find a meaning for his hitherto wasted life.

On his arrival back at the masquerade, Lord Marcus Wycliffe was waiting for him in the foyer. "Charlie is with Mr. Morris in his private study. I said we'd join them as soon as you arrived."

Jamie nodded, noting that the orchestra still played and that guests were still strolling the rooms. "Has he told you what's afoot?"

Wycliffe rolled his eyes heavenward as he led Jamie down a corridor to Morris's study. "Just that there is a body in the garden."

Jamie nodded as Wycliffe knocked and opened the study door. Charlie and Mr. Morris turned to them, and Jamie noted the strained look on Morris's face. Without asking, Charlie went to a sideboard and a bottle of brandy to pour two more glasses.

"Now that we're all here, someone damn well better tell me what is going on here," Morris said.

Jamie took a glass from his brother. "I suppose Charlie told you there'd been an incident in the gardens?"

"And that's all he'd say until you and Wycliffe arrived. I thought I saw you earlier."

"I took the young woman in question home. I thought you'd want to keep this as quiet as possible."

"*What,* damn it all? What should I keep quiet?"

"One of your guests was assaulted."

"What? Who?"

"Miss O'Rourke. Rest assured, she is well and safely home. I cannot say the same for one of your other guests."

"Damn cryptic of you, Hunter."

"First, I wanted to see your guest list and ask if you spoke with Cyril Henley tonight?"

Morris reluctantly riffled through his desk drawer, brought forth a list of names three pages long. "Henley? I haven't seen him for months. I do not think he was invited tonight."

Since Morris did not seem willing to turn the guest list over, Jamie leaned forward and took it. He scanned the names until he found one he was looking for. Oddly, Henley had been invited, but so had Metcalfe. And that raised the question, why had Morris lied? He would have been the one to provide his wife with the specific names of friends he wanted invited.

"I encountered Henley in the garden," he said. "He was the man who assaulted Miss O'Rourke."

"Henley..." Morris flushed with a look half angry, half disbelieving. "Why would he assault Miss O'Rourke?"

Morris had to be aware of Henley's reputation with women. "His reasons aside, Miss O'Rourke recognized him. He wore a leper's costume to mask his identity. What of Stanley Metcalfe?"

"Er, yes. I believe Metcalfe was invited."

"He, too, wore a leper's costume. Miss O'Rourke danced with him. When Henley approached her in the garden, she thought it was Metcalfe."

"But what has that to do with anything?"

"I chased Henley to the stables where he stole Grenleigh's stallion and got away."

"Grenleigh? Hell and damnation! He'll have my hide."

Charlie gave a grim laugh. "He is not too pleased, but I lent him mine. I warrant the horse will turn up in a day or two. Henley will not keep anything that would give his identity or location away."

Morris drank the entire contents of his glass in a single gulp. "So this is it, then? Henley assaulted a girl who is safely home and took Grenleigh's prize stallion which will turn up in a day or two?"

"Alas, there's more to it than that. When I came back through the garden after chasing Henley, I stumbled across Mr. Metcalfe. He'd been stabbed in the chest and hidden in the bushes behind the arbor."

"Is he all right?"

"Afraid not, Morris. He's dead. The question is, how shall we handle this unfortunate event?"

Morris's mouth moved but did not form any intelligible words.

Wycliffe finished his brandy and slammed his glass down on the sideboard with a resounding thud. "Metcalfe. Damnation! Another lead silenced."

"So my question is this," Jamie continued, determined to get to the bottom of the matter. "Where did you send Henley's invitation, and when did you last talk to him?"

"I...I... He came to me. Here. He'd heard about the masquerade and wanted to attend. 'Twas he who asked me to put Stanley Metcalfe on the guest list. I did not see him tonight."

So Henley had devised this plan to get at Metcalfe. Poor bastard. He'd never had a chance. But there was still another question. "Why would you oblige a man like Henley? Surely you've heard the rumors."

If Morris had looked uncomfortable before, he now looked as if he were about to flee. "He was blackmailing me. I...I was present at Daschel's passion play. Or that's what I thought it was. It was actually a—"

"We know what it was," Wycliffe interrupted. "So he was threatening to expose you if you did not do as he asked?"

Morris acknowledged with a curt nod.

"There's more," Jamie guessed.

"I've been paying him. Large sums of money."

"How?"

"He waits outside my club. Demands cash."

Cash. Large sums of it. Why would Henley need large sums of money when he was living in Whitefriars? And was Morris the only one from whom he was extorting funds?

Morris was a member of Brooks's, an elegant establishment in St. James Street. Henley would have to lurk in the shadows to avoid being recognized, but it could be useful to set a watch on the place. A glance at Wycliffe and Charlie told him that they were thinking the same thing.

"Are you going to arrest me?" Morris asked Wycliffe.

"If you were no more involved with the Brotherhood than you say, Morris, you needn't worry. If you were…we'll be back. At the moment we need to deal with the damage done tonight.

"The guests are beginning to leave. We will keep this quiet until tomorrow. Charlie, go to the arbor and make certain no one stumbles across Metcalfe meanwhile. Morris, encourage the guests not to linger. Remove the punch bowl and cork the wine bottles."

"They will think I am penurious!" Morris blustered.

"Would you rather they panic when they learn there's a dead body in your garden or sneer when they learn that you've been paying blackmail, and why?"

The man sank heavily into his chair.

"We have use for you, Morris. Keep your mouth shut and your head down and you may yet get out of this untainted."

Chapter Ten

Gina stood still, rooted to the little stool while Madame Marie pinned the hem of her new gown. But it was not the hem with its little train that concerned her. It was the provocative décolletage. True to her word, Madame Marie had crafted a gown that was sure to draw attention. Styles were changing, but Gina had not yet worn a gown with a neckline that curved over her breasts and dipped to a point midway between them.

She traced the curve of the blue French silk with one finger, studying her reflection in the looking glass. "Are...are you certain I will not cause a scandal?"

"*Mais non!* The style is perfection for your figure, *chéri*. Smaller bosoms and there would be no point. Larger, and it would make you look like a demirep, eh? Ah, but this much will tease the senses and disarm your suitors. The men—they will appreciate the titillation, yes? They will tell you anything you ask."

"You...you're certain I will not be banished from polite society?"

Marie, a lovely woman, gave a full-throated laugh. "You must tell me when you plan to wear this gown, *chéri*. The ladies of the ton will be crowding at my door the next morning, demanding a gown of the same cut."

"If you are certain," she conceded, not at all certain herself. She was glad that Nancy, waiting in the outer room for her, could not see the gown. If the maid told Mama, that would be the end of it.

Madame Marie called entry at a soft knock on the private door and Mr. Renquist entered, then halted in his tracks, blinking several times. Madame had been correct. His eyes went directly to her décolletage. Oddly, after a moment of embarrassment, Gina felt empowered, as if she were in control of the situation.

"Have I interrupted?"

"*Mais non, m'amour.* What do you think of our little Gina now?"

"That it is a good thing she has the protection of the Hunter family."

"Ah, you appreciate the nuance?" Madame asked, tongue in cheek.

"Perhaps a bit too much nuance?" he ventured.

"Oh, la! You are such a proper one, François. Little Gina will 'ave the ton eating from 'er 'and."

Gina smiled, suspecting the modiste had been quite experienced before her marriage to Mr. Renquist.

"The male half," Mr. Renquist muttered as he sat on a small chair in one corner while Madame continued to pin her hem.

"Have you discovered anything, sir?" she asked.

"Progress is slow, Miss O'Rourke. I've learned that, until recently, Mr. Henley occupied rooms above a public house in Whitefriars. But for sleeping, he was rarely there. Following the raid two weeks ago, he disappeared, taking most of his belongings with him.

"Since then, he has been spotted from time to time at various establishments in Whitefriars, never staying one place very long. I gather that is the reason for his success in evading capture. Speculation has it that he has found quarters in more desirable environs but that he still frequents the pubs of Whitefriars.

"My sources were less forthcoming when I inquired as to Mr. Henley's companions. Apart from various prosti—soiled doves, he has occasionally been seen with the worst scum Whitefriars has to offer, the Gibbons brothers among them. On rare occasions, he has been seen with gents, and rarer still, genteel ladies.

"I am devising a plan whereby I may be able to cross his path, Miss O'Rourke. Should that be the case, I shall follow him and send to you of his location immediately, but you should know that I am bound to notify the Home Office, as well."

She nodded. She had no objection to the Home Office benefiting from Mr. Renquist's investigations. In fact, if they could manage it on their own, she would not have become involved. But, should she find him first...

Mr. Renquist cleared his throat and went on. "Mr. Henley departed his last accommodations rather quickly, and the proprietor has a small box of items he left behind. If you are inclined, I shall purchase it from him for the unpaid portion of the rent."

"Did you see what it contained?"

"The proprietor wished me to pay for that pleasure."

"Then yes, please. Acquire it by any means. If it contains even the smallest clue..."

"Aye, Miss O'Rourke. Consider it done."

* * *

Nancy tugged her sleeve, wanting to leave. "Oh, miss, should we really be here? Like as not, she isn't receiving."

Gina held her ground on the stoop of the Race home in Russell Square. "Then I shall leave my card. How can I not offer my condolences? Christina was very good to me when I had few friends in the ton."

"Yes, miss, but—"

The door opened and a maid in a starched white apron answered.

"Is Miss Race at home?" Gina asked.

"She is, but she is not receiving this afternoon, miss."

Gina took a card from her reticule and passed it to the maid. "Will you please tell her that Miss O'Rourke is here? I think she may wish to see me."

The maid nodded and hurried away, leaving the door open but no invitation to step in.

Nancy tugged her sleeve again and whispered, "T'ain't a good time, miss."

"She may only have been a fiancée, but she is nonetheless bereaved." James had not given her details of what had happened last night and Gina was desperate to assure herself of Christina's safety. Pray she had not been present for the awful deed, or that Henley had not gone after her when his attack on Gina failed.

The maid was back and opened the door wider to admit them. Nancy looked down at the floor and went to sit on a small chair in the foyer, where servants were accustomed to waiting, while Gina followed the maid up a flight of stairs and down a corridor.

After a soft knock, the maid opened the door to admit Gina and closed it after her. The draperies had been drawn and the room was cast in gloom. She blinked to adjust to the darkness. "Christina?"

A deep and melancholy sigh answered her. "Thank you for coming, Gina. I wondered if you would."

She followed the sound of the voice and found Cristina, still in her wrapper, curled up in a chair, at least a dozen handkerchiefs abandoned on the floor near her. She knelt beside the chair and took one of Christina's hands.

"I am so sorry, Christina. I blame myself. Had I not asked for his help…"

"It would have happened anyway." The girl looked down at her with infinite sadness in her hollow eyes. Her face was flushed and puffy from crying.

"But I forced him out of hiding. Had he stayed away—"

"Stanley has been hiding for weeks now, Gina. Mr. Henley was blackmailing him. It did not begin with you."

"Blackmail? But what could Mr. Henley have held over Mr. Metcalfe's head?"

"I cannot say. Other than his attendance at an event that went horribly wrong, Stanley was not the sort to engage in wrongdoing. I believe he felt complicit for something, though he swore he did not know the full measure of the consequences."

The Brotherhood. Of course. Mr. Metcalfe had said as much to her in their short meeting. Had Mr. Henley been threatening to turn him over to the authorities if he did not pay hush money? But there had to be more. Mr. Metcalfe had readily admitted his involvement with the Brotherhood to her. He'd said he *knew* things. Things Mr. Henley would kill for.

"Did he ever talk about that night, Christina? Did he ever tell you anything that might damage Mr. Henley?"

She nodded, and her unbound dark hair fell over her face, shielding her as she began to weep again. "I cannot tell you without damaging Stanley's reputation."

"Did he tell you what the key opened? He hurried away before he could—"

"He only told me to give it to you, and that you would know what it opened."

But she didn't. Unless this, too, was something she had forgotten that night. But she could only press Christina for the one thing that might save her life. "Please reconsider, Christina. If Mr. Henley killed Mr. Metcalfe over the knowledge you hold, and then suspects you might know, too, he might want to silence you, as well."

She gasped and pushed the hair away from her face to look at Gina. "Surely not!"

"I cannot be certain, but can we put anything past the man at this point? All I know for certain is that Mr. Henley must be stopped, by whatever means possible. Stanley would not want you dead, and your best protection is to tell the authorities, the Home Office and whoever else will listen. The more people who know the secret, the less reason Mr. Henley would have to kill for it."

"I will not be leaving the house for several months, Gina. Can I be safe in my own home?"

Gina wished she could reassure her. Wished none of this had ever happened. Wished, too, that she'd never enlisted Christina's help. She shrugged. "I do not know."

Christina sniffed. "It would feel like a betrayal if I told now." A fresh storm of weeping shook Christina's shoulders. She buried her face in her hands and Gina could not imagine the depth of Christina's sorrow until she thought of losing James. Oh, she was prepared to leave for Ireland and never see him again. But to know that he no longer breathed, no longer smiled? Intolerable, unbearable.

"If I could turn back time, I would rather die myself than be the cause of Mr. Metcalfe's death or your grief. And, though I would never ask it again, I cannot ever thank you enough for your help, and everything you've done. I will leave you now, but should you change your mind and decide to tell me Mr. Metcalfe's secret, send to me and I shall come at once."

Gina closed the door after herself, catching one last glimpse of Christina, her dark head still bowed over her hands.

A heavy mist descended, obscuring the light from the single lamppost at the end of the street. A dense fog would follow, and Gina shivered.

She'd begged off the affair she was slated to attend earlier, pleading a crushing headache. James had feigned disappointment, though she had read the relief in his deep violet eyes. And when the household had retired for the evening, she'd crept downstairs to "borrow" some clothing from the laundry tub. Now dressed in a gray woolen dress, brown boots a size too large and a frayed brown shawl over her head, she was virtually unrecognizable.

"Miss Gina?"

Or so she'd thought. "Is that you, Ned?"

The boy stepped out of the mist and pulled his cap off his tousled head. "Aye, miss. I thought it was you, but I couldn't be sure."

"I did not know how to dress. Will this be suitable?"

He grinned. "I 'spose so, miss. Wasn't takin' you anywhere fancy tonight. One o' the lads said 'e saw Mr. H go in the Cat's Paw. That's a gin house near Petticoat Lane." He stood back and squinted at her through the gloom. "They won't let me in there, miss. Say I gotta shave first. But y'look like you belong there, miss. Won't no one bother you if you keeps yer head down."

"What shall I do?"

"Listen, miss." He put his cap on and pulled the brim low over his forehead. "You orders somethin' to drink, and then you just disappears into the walls and listen, if y'know what

I mean. Maybe you'll see Mr. H, maybe not. Maybe you'll 'ear something about where 'e is."

Yes, she thought she could do that much. But what did one order in a gin house? She pondered that as Ned started off at a fast pace, leading her farther and farther from familiar surroundings. She wondered if she'd ever be able to find her own way home. "Will you wait for me, Ned?"

"Aye, miss. Outside."

She took comfort from that much, at least, as her environs became poorer and more dismal. They passed taverns and public houses where raucous conversations carried into the streets and drunks lay where they'd been tossed. The women she'd seen were surely disreputable, since all women with a mind to their reputations would be safely home after dark in this area.

"Where are we, Ned?"

"Whitechapel, miss. Just around the corner."

And, true to his word, he halted at a sign with a painted black cat raising one paw. Beneath it was a low door with a stone stoop to step over, and she wondered if that was to keep sewage out during a heavy rain. A dim light cast a yellow glow in a window just above the door. She was relieved the rising fog kept her from seeing more clearly. The stench was bad enough without having to see what caused it.

She took a sixpence from her boot. Would that be enough? Should she take off the boot and shake out a shilling? Sensing her hesitancy, Ned gave her a little push over the threshold.

Gina had never been in an establishment like this one. It was dirty, foul smelling and dark; she had to stop just inside the door to brace herself and take her bearings. A long counter against one wall served as the bar and had shelves behind it with bottles of various sizes and colors. Were they all gin? At least ten tables were scattered to each side of the door but only a few were occupied this late at night. Another door opposite the one she'd entered was closed, and she wondered if it led to the privy or apartments where the light had shone just above the tavern door.

A man sitting at a table was staring at her and she quickly went to the bar and placed the sixpence on the grimy surface. The barkeeper, an unshaven man with few teeth and dirty hands, shuffled toward her, looked down at her coin, took a tin cup from the counter behind him and went to a barrel. He pulled the tap, seemed to measure the amount with one squinted eye and brought the cup to Gina.

She kept her head down and neither of them spoke. As he walked away, she breathed with relief and took her cup to a table near the door. She had passed the first test. Now, according to Ned, all she had to do was make herself inconspicuous.

After a moment, all interest in her ceased and the low tones of conversation resumed. Once she became accustomed to the drone of voices, she could distinguish a few words. Her eyes adjusted to the meager light of the few candles and the dirty oil lamp on the bar, and she noticed four men at a back table. Though she could not make them out, or catch their conversation, there was something hauntingly familiar in the tone.

As she strained to hear, she lifted her cup to her mouth and took a sip. She nearly choked. Struggling to catch her breath and not spit the swill back into the cup, she forced the liquid down her throat.

Gin? *This* was gin? Dreadful! How could anyone drink it? She coughed and took another swallow to force the first down. Her eyes watered and she wiped them with the back of her sleeve.

When she looked up again, she was startled to see that attention was again focused on her. Too late, she remembered to keep her head down. The brown shawl she'd kept over her head had fallen back when she coughed and she hurried to pull it back into place.

An argument erupted at the back table and Gina froze. She knew that voice now. And she could never forget the inflection of his voice when he swore. James Hunter. But what was he doing here? Looking for Mr. Henley?

She pulled the shawl even lower over her head, took another swallow of the gin and stood. She had to get out of there before she was recognized. Three steps and she was out the door, scarcely pausing to catch her breath. The fog had thickened and disoriented her, but she turned in the direction she thought they'd come and took several steps.

A hand seized her elbow and spun her around. "Good God! It *is* you! What the bloody hell do you think you're doing?"

Ned appeared out of the fog, his eyes wide and his mouth gaping. She waved him off quickly, knowing that, no matter how angry Jamie might be, he would not harm her. The boy disappeared into the fog before James noticed him.

To make matters worse, Charles was fast behind James, a look of pure astonishment on his face. "Miss Eugenia! How... What possessed you to..."

James turned her toward Whitechapel Street and took long strides in that direction, pushing her roughly ahead of him, as if he were afraid she'd bolt if he didn't keep her within sight every second. Rightly so.

"Charlie, run ahead and signal a coach. I'm taking Miss Eugenia home."

Charles disappeared into the fog without further questions.

"You had better have a remarkable explanation for this, Eugenia. Apart from your reputation, you have risked life and limb coming to this part of town at night. Night? Hell, any time of day."

"I...I..." But she couldn't answer. She was so breathless

from the pace he set that she could not say two words together.

"I cannot even imagine what your mother and Andrew will say when we tell them how out of hand you've become."

"No! You cannot!"

"Oh, can I not? I rather think I can, Eugenia. In fact, I consider it to be my moral obligation to you and my duty to your family."

"Moral obligation to me? And where, pray tell, was that mere days ago in Vauxhall Gardens?"

James shot her a dark look but pressed his lips together as they arrived on the wide High Street. Charlie had summoned a passing coach and the door was flung open, waiting for them. James wasted no time lifting her and placing her on the seat.

He turned back to his brother. "I will catch up to you at the Crown, Charlie." He turned to her again, climbed into the coach and called her address to the driver.

Alone in the dark interior, Gina could only stare at James, sitting across from her and regarding her with such fury that she couldn't think what to say. Was there no way to appease him?

He crossed his arms over his chest and stretched his long legs out in front of him. "Well, Eugenia?"

It occurred to her that he really had no rights where she was concerned, and decided to take that position with him. "I must say that I resent your high-handed treatment, sir."

He laughed, though she could detect no humor there. "High-handed? Well, take a good look, Eugenia. What you see is me acting with all the restraint I can muster. But if you'd like to see high-handed, I'd be only too happy to oblige."

She mirrored his action and crossed her own arms over her chest. "Furthermore, you will say nothing to your brother or my mother. Do you understand?"

"Me? Understand?" A look of astonishment passed over his face. "You cannot seriously think you will get away with this?"

"Oh, I shall. Have no doubt of that."

"You are mad to challenge me, Eugenia. I am not in my usual accommodating state of mind."

"Accommodating?" She sniffed. "All I have ever heard from you is 'no.' I cannot think of a single time you have accommodated me. From our mock of a courtship to… to…"

"I accommodated you when you confessed that you were going into society with the express purpose of asking questions and trying to ferret out Cyril Henley. I have kept my mouth shut and allowed your little subterfuge, and where has it got me? Here! Finding you in a Whitechapel gin house dressed like a…a…" He gestured at her woolen dress and shabby shawl.

"Servant?" she supplied.

"I was going to say a washerwoman, but if you bared a bit of breast—"

Her cheeks burned at that comparison and she glared at him. "I imagine that is a subject about which you know a great deal."

He was suddenly on the seat beside her, turning her face to his and bending close. "I have never purchased the services of a common whore, Eugenia."

Chapter Eleven

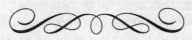

Eugenia drove him to such extremes that he could scarcely comprehend his own reactions. Had it been any other woman, he would have walked away. Hell, any other woman and he would have left her in that tavern to fend for herself. But Eugenia? He looked into her eyes and saw not fear or confusion, but anger and a heavy dose of desperation.

He released her chin and leaned back against the squabs. "What is it you are not telling me, Eugenia?"

Her sigh nearly made him relent. "I do not know what you are asking."

"Why? Why must you push yourself to such lengths? What drives you to such foolhardy endeavors? I think you are bent on self-destruction, and I do not know how to stop you."

She dropped her gaze to her hands, twisting the gray woolen fabric of her dress. "You cannot stop me, James. It would be better for us both if you would stop trying."

"You know we will catch Henley eventually. You know Cora's death was avenged that night when Daschel was killed in the catacombs beneath the chapel. And yet you press on with an almost crazed determination—against all good sense, against all reasonable care for your safety. There has to be more that drives you. What is it, Eugenia? Why can you not leave this to me?"

For the first time, he saw a flash of fear in Eugenia's eyes and he recalled the night at Vauxhall Gardens, when she'd hinted that it was already too late to save her. "Answers," she said so softly he barely heard her above the rattle of wheels and harness.

"To what?"

"That night. That night in the catacombs."

"You know the answers. You know who killed Cora, and who kidnapped you. If you are looking for an answer to why… well, there is no answer to that but for the darkness in some men's souls."

"I cannot go on without the answers. There is no future for me without them."

"Gina—"

"My entire life hinges on the answers, and there *is* no life without them."

A tiny seed of doubt began to take root. Had Eugenia told them everything that happened that night? Had they left any question unasked? Any truth untold? Or, God help her, had she lied? Had she been more involved with the Brotherhood than she'd admitted? Had she lied about what happened?

He gripped her shoulders and forced her to look into his eyes. "What have you withheld, Eugenia?"

Those glorious dark eyes welled with unspilled tears. "That I do not know."

"What, damn it?"

"What happened to me. I cannot remember most of it. Mr. Henley gave me opium, and my mind is a blur."

"But…what can you recall?"

"Nothing until the ritual, when I was lying upon that altar.

I remember Mr. Henley bending over me, and I thought he was going to…to…"

"He was. But I still—"

"And then you covered me and carried me from the altar. Someone asked me later if I was unharmed. Bella, I think. And I told her yes. But the truth is, I cannot remember. Only hurting. Aching in all my muscles. And my head pounding." The waiting tears began to trickle down her cheeks.

"You do not know if you were unharmed? But here you are, Eugenia, whole and well."

"Not that.…"

Jamie groaned as understanding dawned on him. "You think that…things…might have been done to you while you were unconscious."

She nodded and he realized she was holding on to her composure by a slim thread.

"Why didn't you tell us?"

The anger was back, refining her grief and uncertainty. "And have everyone look at me with pity? Have Mama shut me away in a spinster's room? Listen to whispers behind my back? I couldn't bear that."

"But what did you mean to do? Find Henley and simply ask him?"

"Yes! What other course do I have? Yes, I want him to tell me the truth—everything about those lost hours."

"Good God! And you think he'd actually tell you the truth? Don't be naive, Eugenia. He'd lie just to see the pain on your face. Hell, he'd lie on principle."

"What other choice do I have? Who else can answer that question? How can I ever build a future or a family without knowing if…if…"

He wanted to feel compassion for her, but all he felt was anger that she'd endangered herself for such an inconsequential thing. "What earthly difference does it make? I'd venture to say that a good portion of brides are not virgin on their wedding night."

Her eyes widened and she regarded him with astonishment. "*I* must know! Before I could marry, my husband has a right to know if I am whole."

He was still gripping her shoulders and he shook her roughly, as if that would rattle some sense into her muddled thinking. "Any man who loves you would take you as you are, without questions or guarantees. Any man who wouldn't is not worth your consideration."

"I cannot bear that I have lost that part of my life. I cannot tolerate the thought that I could go through life never knowing."

God help him, he could think of nothing to persuade her, nothing to comfort her, but to kiss her. To show her what his words could never say without disgusting her. He lowered his lips to hers, cherishing the salt of her tears mingling with the gin she'd had at the Cat's Paw—a potent brew, drawing up his suppressed longing, his denied needs.

Fear that he was taking advantage of her vulnerable state made him lift his head to mutter an apology, but she raised her arms to circle his neck and offered those rosy petals again.

"Yes," she whispered in a longing sigh. "Yes, Jamie."

It would have taken a stronger man than he to refuse that invitation. He deepened the kiss. And she did. Her heat, her taste, the sweetly innocent way she met his tongue, swept him into a tide of desire.

He moved his hand to her breast and she moaned deep in her throat. Even through the rough woolen dress, he could feel the taut bud of her breast against his palm. Now the moan was his.

This was madness. Insanity. He pulled away again. "Gina, you cannot mean—"

"Don't stop, Jamie. Not this time."

But the coach lurched as it drew up at the end of the street. Her eyes cleared as if she'd been sleeping and she seized the handle of the door. "Do not tell my family, Jamie. I beg you."

And she was gone, running up the steps and disappearing through the door. He sat there for a moment, waiting until he saw a light in an upper window. Pray she was safe for the night. Until he could decide what to do next.

Charlie was waiting for him at the Crown and Bear. He'd already claimed a back table and had a bottle of Devlin's private stock and two glasses. And God knew, Jamie needed a drink.

"Still no trace of the Gibbons brothers," he reported as Jamie sat down.

"Blast! Where can they have gotten to?"

"Just know where they're not. Not at the Cat's Paw, and not finagling free ale here," Charlie stated the obvious.

"I need to talk to them. I'd swear Henley killed Metcalfe and stole his costume to assault Miss O'Rourke, but there is always the possibility that he paid to have it done. Old Cox is dead and there's been an attempt on my life. I'd wager a fortune that there will be others. If anyone knows anything about it, I'd guess it would be Dick Gibbons."

"Aye," Charlie agreed. "If he's not behind it, he'll know who is. But I'm of a mind that we should simply put that vermin out of the way."

"Kill them?"

"Assassinate," Charlie corrected. "Though *exterminate* might be more fit for the Gibbons clan. Some men are in need of dying. They tried to kill you, and tonight after I put you and Bella in the coach, someone took a shot at me. Two someones, by the sound of the footsteps. It's a coward's method, and neither Gibbons would risk a direct attack on anyone remotely their size."

Jamie quickly looked Charlie over, reassuring himself of his brother's well being. "One shot?"

"Cowards. Had they stopped to reload, I'd have been on them."

There'd only been one shot the night he'd been attacked. Had he pursued the shooter, likely the brothers would have been waiting at the end of the blind alley armed to the teeth.

He suspected the idea to eliminate the Gibbons brothers had come from Marcus Wycliffe, but he knew his brother was not above such a thing. "The flaw in your plan to improve London by eliminating Dick and Artie is that we'd never get the truth from them then. But I must say I admire that you are not hindered by such lofty principles as proof. If you know in your gut that someone has tried to kill you, that is enough for you."

Charlie laughed. "Aye, well, we cannot all fit on that small patch of high moral ground you stand on, Jamie."

"Not so high, Charlie. I'd kill Henley if I could lay hands on him," he admitted.

Charlie sighed and sat back in his chair. "I am sick to death of that subject. Just for a moment, could we talk about more pleasant things? Miss O'Rourke, for instance?"

"She is safely home, if that is what you are asking."

"Only half of what I am asking. The other half is what the hell she was doing in a cesspit like the Cat's Paw."

"Looking for Henley, or for information about him."

"Good God," Charlie muttered under his breath. Then, "You put an end to that, did you not?"

"I thought I'd put an end to it a week ago. Since then, we'd reached a compromise. I'd keep an eye on her, and she'd confine her inquiries to the ton—mothers, sisters, friends of the bastard. Then I'd escort her home to be certain she was safely tucked up for the night.

"Now she had found herself a guide to London's underbelly. She thinks I did not see that boy waiting for her in the shadows, but I simply did not have time to deal with him tonight. But I will. Believe me, I will. Meantime, you can see how well our agreement worked?"

"Exceedingly." Grinning, Charlie leaned forward and placed his forearms on the table in an attitude of confidentiality. "Which confirms my suspicion."

Certain he'd regret it, he asked anyway. "What suspicion?"

"That Miss Eugenia is a match for you. Though you have most of the eligible heiresses of the ton eating from your hand, she resists your charms and you cannot abide that. I collect it is more than a matter of pride. More than a matter of protecting our brother's sister-in-law. You care for her, do you not?"

"Charlie, do not tweak me with this. I am not in a mood to indulge you."

"I would not mention it now but that she is part of our family. You would not dally with her, would you?"

Dally? No. He suspected it was rather more than that. "If you are asking if I am trying to seduce Eugenia, I am not."

"You've always kept your dalliances within the demi-monde. Very discreet of you. Very safe. But I thought I saw something different happening with Miss Eugenia. Something a bit more dangerous."

"Dangerous? What the hell are you talking about, Charlie. How could she be a danger to me?"

"You've only been with women you could never love, Jamie. The demimonde, courtesans, mistresses. The moment some likely miss gets close, you back away. Our little Suzette is an excellent example. Did she ask too much? Surely she did not suggest marriage?"

He shook his head. "Suzette is too wise for that. But I sensed that she was growing rather fonder of me than she should. In her profession—and mine—close attachments are not a good idea."

"Your profession has nothing to do with it."

Jamie tossed down the rest of his drink and started to stand. His bed was calling. The last thing he needed on a night like this was a lecture from his younger brother.

"You need a good woman, Jamie."

"I've had a good woman. Several, in fact. Some were good. Some were *very* good. And some were…well, downright—"

"Enough, then. But be warned—Eugenia is different than your usual interests. She is not adept at the little games that so amuse our set. Despite her foolhardiness tonight, she is too vulnerable to trifle with."

He settled back in his chair. There was nothing trifling about Eugenia, and he suspected Charlie was right—Jamie was acutely aware of her vulnerability. He felt differently about her than he had any other woman. Stronger. More… possessive? And he had more than a passing desire for her.

Charlie downed the remainder of his glass and lowered his voice as he continued. "I've watched you my whole life, Jamie. You've always kept yourself removed from close attachments and safe from disappointments and rejection. For whatever reason, you set your course for bachelorhood long ago. If you cannot offer her more, leave Miss Eugenia alone. She deserves better."

She did. He'd known that from the beginning, but he'd returned time and time again, craving her smile, the softness of her voice, the feel of her in his arms. He wished, now, that he'd left Charlie or Devlin to sweep her from that altar. Had he never known the feel of her in his arms, her sweet smell, her sighs, it wouldn't trouble him so much now.

A few more days. Surely he could endure a few more days.

"She should be safe enough from me. They will be leaving London quite soon anyway. Her mother has crates already packed. And, with a bit of luck, we shall find Henley and deal with him, hence there will be nothing left to throw us together."

Charlie nodded his understanding. "I think that is best for our families. An unfortunate affair would make gatherings quite awkward."

Jamie reached for the bottle. On his way home moments ago, he now felt like getting quietly, blissfully drunk.

Sitting between Hortense and Harriett, Gina trained her eyes on the stage where actors were posturing as they said their lines, but her mind whirled with the events of last night. If she were to be honest, she was relieved James had found her at that tawdry little gin house. She'd felt conspicuous and terrified. And she wouldn't have known what to do if someone had talked to her. Had Ned really thought she'd hear something about Mr. Henley there?

By their very presence at the same establishment, James and Charles Hunter had confirmed that they were on the same track, so she hadn't really been needed there. She shivered.

"Are you cold, Gina?" Harriett whispered, leaning closer.

"I just felt a little breeze on the back of my neck." As if the Devil had walked across her grave.

"Shh," Hortense warned them.

Standing behind them near the curtain of their box, James stirred and crossed his arms, as if impatient and ready to leave. He'd fetched the Thayer girls before he'd come for her, obviously not wishing to be alone with her. The twins were enjoying the attention of being squired about town by the elusive James Hunter, and Gina had kept the real reason to herself. It was much more flattering to think he craved their company than that he wanted to keep Gina out of trouble.

Ironically, the gravest danger to Gina was James himself. Her virtue would be forfeit with very little fuss if he but crooked his finger. Heat washed through her as she recalled the way she'd pleaded with him not to stop in the coach last night. And, just for a moment, she had thought that if she made love to James, it would wash away whatever Mr. Henley had done to her. As the moment had drawn out, she realized she'd been foolish to expose herself, her deepest fears, to him. And her only excuse was that, if he had made love to her, at least she would know, for better or worse, if she'd been defiled.

She'd do anything—*anything*—for the answer to that question. She'd ask questions, put herself in danger, pose as a lightskirt in a Whitechapel gin house, and more. And she suspected that the key to the answers to all her questions dangled at the end of her corset strings—if only she could find what it opened.

The music rose to a crescendo and Gina blinked. She'd been so lost in her own thoughts that she had missed the entire first act of the play. If pressed, she would not have been able to say what it was about. She clapped with the audience as the lights came up, guttering as the wicks were raised.

Charlie pushed the curtain aside and entered their box. "I say, did you notice that all eyes were upon this particular box? The excess of beauty here has charmed the audience. I would not be surprised if the actors ask you to leave so they may get their fair share of attention."

Hortense laughed and waved her fan furiously. Harriett

and Gina merely smiled at his ridiculous flattery while James lifted an eyebrow in amusement.

"What accounts for your interest in the theatre this evening, Charlie?" he asked.

Charlie grinned and shot a glance at the ladies.

Gina wondered what James had told him about her presence in the Cat's Paw last night. The truth, no doubt, but how much of it?

"Oranges!" came a cry from below.

She looked down and saw a girl with a basket of fruit, holding one perfect orange aloft for all to see.

"Mary!" Charlie tossed the girl a sixpence and laughed when she snatched it out of the air.

"She did not throw you the orange, Mr. Hunter," Harriett said.

He turned to them and explained. "Mary supports her mother and crippled brother. I always throw her a coin but never take the orange."

Harriett glanced at the pretty girl again, and back at Charlie. "That is very kind of you, Mr. Hunter. Not many are as charitable."

Charles looked embarrassed and shrugged. "'Tis little enough—a shilling here, a sixpence there."

Gina looked back at the girl in time to see her blow Charles a kiss. The incident spoke well for a man whose modesty prevented him from speaking well of himself. Mary turned away and began crying her goods again.

As Gina watched the girl weave a path through the audience, she noted a man approach her and say something in her ear. Mary appeared to shrink in size and began walking with the man toward the stage. Before they disappeared behind the curtain, he turned and looked directly at their box. Mr. Henley!

James had seen him, too. "Charlie, will you see the ladies home, please. I have sudden business to attend."

'E's one fer the ladies.... Ned's words rang in Gina's ears. Would Mr. Henley harm Mary in any way? Surely he would not dare with every charley and runner in London looking for him. The Brotherhood was disbanded. There were no more followers.

And yet her desperation for answers and the shortness of time overshadowed the lingering fear. So much so that she had once again dressed in the rough woolen dress and shawl, and had gone out to meet Ned. All she had now was the little key clutched in her hand and an idea nagging at the back of her mind.

Knowing, now, where she was and that she was not far from home, she'd dismissed Ned and stood in the shadows of a tree across the street from an abandoned estate on the outskirts of Mayfair. The gate stood open to an overgrown lawn and the house was partially obscured by trees that stirred in a chilling breeze. Behind the house, the spire of a small chapel rose above the trees—the place that had changed her life forever.

Gina shivered and drew her shawl closer. What secrets did this eerie estate hold? What had happened there that night, and all the nights before? Teasing dancing flicks of memory appeared and disappeared before her, leaving her with only vague impressions. Mr. Henley forcing bitter wine down her throat. Being carried somewhere and unable to fight. Hands plucking at her clothing. Then…then nothing.

The wind soughed through the trees, moaning like a lost child, and Gina sank deeper into the shadows, frozen in time—at that very moment in the catacombs beneath the chapel. Locked in an eternal cold. She wanted to feel again, to reclaim whatever remained of herself. And the only way she could do that was to find out, to finally know, what had happened to her during those lost hours.

She fingered the little key stashed in the slash pocket of her dress. Would it open a door here? Which door? And what would she find? Answers? More questions? Peace?

She reached into her mind, almost as if she could grasp and pluck out the memories that escaped her. And again the elusive memories teased her as if they were near, then flitted away, afraid to expose themselves to her scrutiny.

Her back straightened as she screwed her courage up to the sticking-place and her hand fisted around the key. She would not shirk, no matter how frightened she was. She took one determined step forward, then another.

A hand clamped over her mouth and an arm slipped around her to drag her backward, once more into the darkness.

Chapter Twelve

Gina twisted and fought like a dervish, trying to loosen herself from the unforgiving hold and clawing at the hand over her mouth. Dear Lord! Not again.

"Are you mad?" a familiar voice whispered.

She went limp with relief.

"Dare I release you?"

She nodded and breathed deep as he eased his hold on her. He still held her to steady her and she turned in the circle of his arms. "You nearly scared me to death," she whispered.

"No less a fright than you gave me," James said, a sardonic smile twisting the corners of his mouth.

"How did you find me?"

His mouth was mere inches from hers. "Coincidence."

"But—"

"It was a trap. Henley drew me away deliberately. He had cast Mary off by the time I got backstage. I gave chase, but he had already disappeared. He has set traps for me before, and I suspected he had done so again when a coach nearly ran me down. A clumsy attempt, to be sure, but one that put me on my guard. 'Twould appear half of London is looking to collect the bounty on my head. I will be lunging from runaway coaches, watching for falling objects and dodging bullets until this thing is over. All unnecessary since *you* will be the death of me."

Gina sighed. Though she'd listened to him carefully, her mind was overwhelmed with other things—the clean, spicy scent of his cologne, the way a faint dimple appeared in one cheek when he grinned, the warmth of his arms around her. She found she could only nod her understanding.

"I had a report earlier tonight that someone had seen a light in one of the upper windows here, so I came to investigate. I found nothing. But that still doesn't explain your presence here, Eugenia."

"A light?" She looked over her shoulder at the eerie deserted house.

"You're going nowhere but home, Miss O'Rourke."

"Directly after we search the house."

He looked astonished and angry at the same time. "I already have. You have sorely underestimated me. When I took you home after your ill-conceived foray into Whitechapel last night, I thought you would know enough to abandon such foolish tricks. If you do not, you leave me no recourse but to act as your missing conscience. I am taking you home, Eugenia, and we shall waken Drew and tell him what you are about."

Panic sent gooseflesh up her spine. "You would not dare!"

"Convince me not to, Eugenia. Give me a reason—just one—to hold my tongue. But be warned, it had better be good."

In her heart, she knew he was right. She knew she'd been foolhardy even though Mayfair was not Whitechapel, and that desperation had driven her to absurd lengths. She knew, too, that she'd put herself in danger akin to the sort that had landed her in trouble in the first place. She was ill at ease all the time, but she couldn't help herself.

Lacking a sane reason to convince him, she rose on her tiptoes and placed her lips against his. She felt him stiffen in shock, then soften to her insistence. His arms tightened around her as he deepened the kiss, invading her mouth with his tongue, testing her resolve. Did he think she'd relent? Beg off? Run home?

Oh, he'd sorely underestimated her.

Eugenia's sweet persistence took Jamie by surprise, though his body responded in the most primitive way. For the briefest of moments he'd been angry at her ploy, but then he'd understood her desperation. Understood it and knew he could never use it to take what he'd wanted for so long.

Ah, but what could a kiss or two hurt? Something to carry with him after she'd gone back to Ireland. Something to warm him in the long, cold days to come.

He lifted her slightly to fit her against him, to feel the hollow of her femininity. She moaned and clung tighter as he pressed her back against the tree that had sheltered them from vision. She tangled her fingers through his hair and held him close, as if she were afraid he'd withdraw. Oh, but not in this life.

She was breathing hard, her chest rising and falling rapidly. Giving her time to catch her breath, he lifted her a few inches more and trailed kisses down her throat to the little dip at the base. The scent of ambergris and moss rose to him as he ran his tongue over the vulnerable spot.

He could feel her trying to deepen the contact of their hips, but her skirts would not allow it. He began to hitch them higher, to wrap those graceful limbs around his waist, but he caught himself. He had not lost that last shred of his decency.

"No," she gasped. "Find a place. Now, Jamie. Now."

He could not mistake her intent. She wanted to finish this, to make love fully rather than their usual interrupted attempts. "You cannot know…"

"I want to, Jamie. I need to know."

He knew a public house very near. The proprietor would not ask questions this time of night. He draped the brown shawl over her head, took her hand and led her away from the deserted house and around a corner, but he balked. His sensibilities would not allow him to take Eugenia to a common public house. His flat was less than a mile away and he'd sent his valet on a fortnight holiday to have him out of the way should any attempts to murder him extend to his home. Now on the busier street, he flagged a coach, shouted his address and lifted Eugenia in, wondering if she would change her mind and if the moment of madness had passed.

He need not have worried. The coach was scarcely in motion before she was in his arms again, kissing him with a fervent desperation. He'd never sensed such honest and overwhelming passion before.

She fumbled with the buttons of his waistcoat, slipped her hands inside and awakened a rising anticipation in his too-responsive body. He needed her, craved her like no other. And he was well past embarrassment when the coach door opened and the driver gave him a wink.

"Shilling, sixpence, sir."

Jamie tossed him a few coins without looking and was met with a pleased, "Obliged, sir."

Shielding her from the driver's view, he escorted her up the steps to his rented flat, fumbled with the key and had her safely inside by the time the coach drew away.

Her shawl fell to the foyer floor as she reached up to him

again, her eyes already heavy-lidded in anticipation of another kiss. He complied, almost laughing as she pushed his jacket off his shoulders. He lifted her in his arms and carried her to his bedroom, knowing there was still a chance for her to change her mind. Pray for her sake that she did, because he could not.

The room was darkened but for the glow of banked coals in the fireplace. He placed her on her feet beside the bedpost and went to open a window to the summer night, and by the time he turned back, Eugenia was fumbling with the fasteners at the front of her gown. He watched her for a moment, feeling his libido riot with good sense.

She was not practiced in the art of undressing for a man, as his mistresses had been, but there was something very endearing in her innocent haste. Then she looked up from her task and her eyes met his. A blush spread across her cheeks even as her lips lifted at the corners in a shy smile.

He went to her and held her shoulders. "Are you certain, Eugenia?"

She nodded, a universe of promise in her eyes.

He slid his hands down to cover hers and take their place. One lace at a time he undid her gown, revealing fine silk beneath the rough homespun. Like Eugenia herself, the deeper he went, the finer the fabric. By the time her gown slid to the floor and he sighed at her lack of a corset, he was burning with his need to feel her beneath him, fitting herself to him, closing around him.

The sheer silk of her chemise and stockings taunted him, revealing, and yet not revealing her. He was uncertain how to continue without ripping the delicate fabric when she took matters into her own hands. Or, rather, took *him* into her own hands.

She quickly slipped the knot of his cravat, discarded the length of cloth and unbuttoned the neck of his shirt. She'd forgotten his waistcoat and had to push it off his arms. He smiled at her eagerness. She was new territory for him. He'd never made love to an innocent girl before, and he wanted this to be memorable for her. With that thought came another.

Leave Miss Eugenia alone. She deserves better.

Charlie's words sobered him. How could he do this to Eugenia? How could he take the incredible gift she offered and ask no more?

"No, Eugenia. I cannot do this. It was a mistake. I am so sorry for—"

She blinked and her eyes narrowed. "You *can*not? Or *will* not?" She pushed him in anger and, unprepared, he staggered backward, landing against the wall. "Is it because you have already seen me naked and did not like it?"

By all the saints! How could she ever think such a thing? She had haunted his nights ever since, but not with disgust— with longing and desire. "Eugenia, you will thank me when the passion clears. How could I take advantage—"

She threw herself against him, and bunched the fabric of his shirt in her fists as she shook him. "You cannot stop now, Jamie. You cannot. You owe this much to me."

The violence of her passion, the raw emotion in her voice, reached him and he understood what she wanted, what she needed. Though he suspected he'd regret it the rest of his life, he surrendered his conscience.

Lost. He was lost. All his lofty principles about leaving the ladies of the ton alone, of restricting his amorous activities to the demimonde, to women who had no power over him, went out that window on the late summer breeze.

"Easy, Eugenia," Jamie cooed.

Caught up in her own need, she pulled his shirttails over his head and he lifted his arms to help her. She swayed slightly at the sight of his bare chest. She'd never seen this much of a man exposed before. Her breath hitched and she realized she'd stopped breathing for a moment.

He steadied her and waited while she looked down at his remaining clothing. She skimmed her trembling fingers along the warm flesh above his breeches, seeking the button to the flap that covered him. Could she go so far as to... She slipped her fingers beneath the band but he stopped her and backed toward the bed to sit.

Toe to heel, he wedged his boots off, dragging his stockings with them, then lifted her in his arms and placed her on his lap. He traced the line of her hip beneath the fluid silk and sighed. "I am afraid I will rip your underpinnings, Gina."

He'd called her Gina. Oh, he could leave her underpinnings in shreds for all she cared.

With a little sigh, he pinched one corner of her chemise and eased it from under her to glide it up her sides and over her head. As she was exposed, she shivered and her nipples grew taut. She had thought it would be easier once she was undressed, as if the deed were almost done, but as Jamie dropped his gaze to her breasts she held her breath in fear. Oh, pray he did not think her inadequate. But his next move dispelled her worry.

He nuzzled her neck, stopping to worship her scar with his kisses, and half turned to ease her back against pillows that smelled of his cologne and his uniquely masculine musk. Something tingled deep inside her and she was suddenly impatient to have this done with. Despite the vague memories, despite the ever-present fear, to know, once and for all...

Leaving a trail of kisses in his wake, he lowered his head farther, drawing one firm areola into his mouth and teasing it with his tongue, nipping gently with his teeth. Oh! She had never felt anything half so delightful! She bent one knee to rest against him and he groaned deep in his throat.

He stood quickly, but before she could form a protest,

he had undone his breeches, dropped them to the floor and turned back to her. He was glorious. He was terrifying. Her heartbeat sped and she fought her rising anxiety.

Jamie was beside her again, kissing her with a fierceness that took her breath away and left no doubt that he wanted her. At least for this moment. For this small space of time.

She tangled her fingers through his hair, wishing she could hold him there forever. He was doing such wondrous things to her, such unspeakably pleasurable things, that she could not remain still. Again she raised her knee to glide along his bare hip, reveling in his heat and strength.

He groaned and moved lower, taking one breast into his mouth, and nibbled, gently drawing forth an answering heat in her middle. She felt as if she were straining for something as yet unknown, but she knew Jamie would reveal it to her in the fullness of time.

He slid his hand lower, to the juncture of her legs, and her raised knee made her vulnerable to his touch. He began a seductive rhythmic stroking at the top of her cleft that had her lifting her hips to meet him.

"Ah, that's it, Gina. Open for me. Let me in."

His praise warmed her and she was ready when he moved his hand just a bit lower and entered her with one long finger. She stiffened at that foreign invasion and caught her breath, then expelled it slowly as the rhythmic stroking began again.

Heavenly and naughty at the same time.... That could be said of more than Jamie's kisses.

"Like molten silk, Gina. So soft, so snug."

The pad of his thumb continued to stroke that sensitive little nub as he slipped one finger steadily in and out. Within moments she was arching to his hand, craving more, hungering to have him deeper inside her.

Unthinkingly, she reached for him, for that part of him that was uniquely male, wanting to know how he felt, and if she could give him the pleasure he was giving her. As her hand closed around his shaft, he groaned and jerked as if she'd hurt him, but she knew she hadn't by the deep sigh he gave her.

"Yes, Gina. Yes. Touch me."

She smiled, delighted that she'd pleasured him. As she rose to his hand, she tightened her hand around him, following the rhythm he'd set, finding it so insanely sensual that she shuddered.

Suddenly Jamie pulled away and moved down her body, stopping to explore her navel along the way, then dipping lower to where his hand had been. The first stroke of his tongue drew a shocked gasp from her, but then the sheer pleasure of it blanketed her in heat and had her incapable of thinking of anything but the next stroke of his tongue, and the next.

His hands bit into her hips to raise her slightly and give him freer access, but the building tension inside her made it impossible for her to remain still for long. She thought she would die with the insistent need. Little frissons of delight burst at her center and raced along her nerve endings.

"Jamie," she keened.

He rose between her thighs and the look on his face was raw and strained. "Steady, Gina. Do not fail me now."

Fail him? How could she ever fail him?

The staff she had so recently held had changed. Swollen to an even greater size, it looked red and angry, as if it would burst. Fear, primal and vivid, gnawed at the back of her mind but she fought it, knowing now that he would not hurt her.

Jamie lowered himself, hovering only slightly above her. The hard probe of his shaft at her entrance discomforted her and she had the first inkling of how different this would be than the welcome invasion of his strong fingers.

She looked up at him and he nodded, as if reading her

mind, then covered her mouth with his as he probed again, his tongue mimicking his shaft. She wanted to protest, tell him he would never fit, but she found her arms going around him, pulling him closer as she raised her knees and hips to meet him.

And then he was inside her, thick and strong, but shallow still. He withdrew just a bit, then thrust again, going deeper, ever deeper with each thrust. Pleasure mingled with pain, and back to pleasure again until he had buried himself inside her, rocking against her and awakening that sleeping bud to full blossom. The strokes of his shaft coupled with the deepened contact sent her into a spiral of pleasure and need. She wanted more, and more and more.

Her breathless moans shocked her and she marveled that they had come from her. But then, she'd never felt pleasure so powerful, so insistent, building to an explosive burst of rapture so intense that it racked her entire body.

"Yes," Jamie whispered, his breath hot in her ear. "God, yes. Come, Gina. Come with me."

Anywhere. Always. Forever.

Jamie stood at the window and watched the first tinge of violet stain the horizon. He would need to waken Gina soon if he was to have her home before the house was stirring, but not a moment sooner. Gina needed rest.

After they'd made love, she'd fallen asleep in his arms, her cheek and one hand resting on his chest and her leg crooked over his. He'd only been able to watch her, touch her—the curve of her cheek; her lips, dusky and swollen with his kisses; the violet shadows of sated fatigue beneath her eyes; the silken mass of gold and brown hair scattered across his pillow and the velvet warmth of her skin as he stroked her hip. She was the most glorious creature he'd ever known.

And when she'd stirred an hour later, he'd kissed her and

they'd made love again. Slower, sweeter, with all the wonder of first love and filled with all the power, all the ecstasy of their first time, but suffering none of the angst. More than anything, he wanted to believe that she had not been seduced by the moment, and that she desired him half as much as he desired her. But he was a man of the world, experienced in the art of seduction, and he knew that he'd caught her unaware and used her own passionate nature against her.

He turned and went back to his bed to study her, to burn the vision of her there on his memory. He did not deceive himself that she had fallen helplessly in love with him or that they could ever build a future given what he represented to her. No, he had served a purpose. Gina had wanted to know what making love was like, wanted that answer, and he'd been only too eager to give it to her, and flattered that she'd chosen him. But he should never have given in to her pleas. Should have been strong enough to give her up and preserve her virtue. He had failed her, but he would not do so again.

He reached out and touched her cheek, brushed a lock of silken hair out of her eyes. Leaning close, he kissed her forehead and whispered in her ear. "Arise, Eugenia. The night is done and the day awaits."

Chapter Thirteen

The afternoon was half gone by the time Gina was dressed and made her way downstairs in an agony of suspense. Had Jamie given her away when he'd brought her home before dawn? Or had he managed to escape unnoticed? She'd tried to make him leave her at the end of the street, but he insisted upon seeing her to the door with a promise to come later in the day, and there was no arguing with him.

She found her mother and sister in the parlor, conversing in perfectly normal tones. She breathed a sigh of relief. If Mama knew where she had been last night, and what she'd done, she would be in shrill high dudgeon.

Mama scarcely glanced up at her. "Good heavens, Eugenia! You look as if you have not slept in weeks! You really must stay in tonight and get some rest."

Bella came to her rescue. "Really, Mama, there will be time enough for rest when you have gone back to Belfast. Let Gina enjoy London while she can."

"Well! I do not need advice from you, Bella. Once you have children of your own, you will know how I feel."

Gina rolled her eyes and sighed. She was tired of her mother's endless nagging—never mind that she was right. Gina actually did need sleep rather badly. She'd been barely coherent last night when Jamie had gotten her home. Exhaustion and satiation had mixed in a powerful brew, muddling her mind so that all she could think was that she never wanted to leave Jamie's bed.

"I shall take a nap if that will reassure you, Mama."

Her mother contrived to look satisfied. "Nap? You are scarcely up, girl. The day is most gone. I do not think a nap will serve you now, Eugenia. I would prefer that you cancel your evening plans and stay in. Those Thayer girls are far too…too…"

"Too engaging? Interesting? Pleasant? Diverting?" Bella stood and went to the teapot to pour a cup for Gina. "Really, Mama. You complained when Gina had not yet made friends, and now you complain that she has. Give her a slack rein for the next few days, will you?"

Bella brought her the cup as she sat on the sofa and gave her a sharp warning look, as if she suspected that Gina had been sneaking out at night. "Thank you," she said in a soft tone, hoping Bella would realize it was for keeping silent and for supporting her as much as it was for the cup of tea.

Her sister gave her a quick nod that said she would be seeking Gina out later for some answers.

"Well," Mama sighed, leaning back against the cushions of her chair, "I really do not see why Gina should bother to go about in society. Three days hence, we shall be bound for Ireland. What point is there, really, in socializing now?"

Three days? Gina sat up straighter, her mind in turmoil. She could not possibly be ready to leave in three days' time. Mr. Henley, Jamie…

Bella answered to cover Gina's shock. "To make friends, Mama. To make connections that may serve her in the future.

How pleasant it will be to correspond with Hortense and Harriett to have all the *on dit*."

"And what good will that do her, I ask? Once we are back to Ireland, Eugenia is unlikely to leave again. What earthly use will she have for friends in England?"

"You should not map out Gina's life, Mama. Many things could happen. She had gentlemen callers in Belfast before we left, who will likely be awaiting her return. Should they have connections in London..."

"Pshaw! With both older and younger sisters married, Eugenia is quite upon the shelf. Who will have her now, even with the inducement of her not inconsiderable dowry?"

Gina cleared her throat and smiled. "Have you forgotten that I am in the room, Mama?"

"Oh, well..." Mama had the good grace to look a bit confused. "I was only stating the truth, my dear. You know I did not intend any insult."

Oddly, Gina believed her. "None taken, Mama." Her mother never intended insult, but she had no idea how high-handed she was. She had planned Gina's life to her own advantage and did not see any reason to consult Gina in regard to her preferences or to the details.

Mama stood and waved one hand airily. "Eugenia, I hope you will not be needing Nancy. I have some shopping to do and wish her to attend me."

To carry the parcels, no doubt. "I am quite at leisure today, Mama. Do go, and have a lovely time."

Bella expelled a long sigh when Mama departed, leaving them alone at last. "Gina, you are a saint if you can picture a life at Mama's beck and call."

"To tell the truth, Bella, I cannot picture it. Perhaps that is the only thing that keeps me calm."

Bella giggled and placed one hand over her stomach. "I

pray you will thump me over the head if I treat my children thus."

"I shall. That is a promise, Bella."

"As for you, Gina, I shall be glad to stand in for Mama. At least today." She stood and came to stand beside Gina's chair to give her a gentle thump on her head. "What were you thinking, Gina?"

"I do not know what you mean," she temporized.

"Do not come over all coy with me, Gina O'Rourke. You kept quiet when I was slipping out at night. I shall do no less for you. But you must see the danger in not telling anyone what you are about. Mary—the washwoman Mary, not the scullery Mary—reported that her spare gown was missing. Then Nancy brought it to me early this morning. She said she found it in your room when she was straightening up. What are you about?"

Heavens! She'd been so exhausted when she'd gotten home that she'd simply dropped the gown where she stood instead of hiding it in the clothes press. "Did she tell Mama?"

"She came to me, Gina, so she could avoid Mama's hysterics. I repeat, why did you need a washwoman's dress?"

"I wanted to go out anonymously. I took Mary's shawl, too, to cover my head. You know that no one notices servants, Gina. I thought I could go places inappropriate for a young woman, perhaps hear things I would not otherwise be privy to."

"No wonder you are exhausted. But you must stop, of course."

"Of course. Just as you did."

"I am not amused, Gina."

"Neither am I. Three days, Bella. That is all I have left before Mama whisks me back to Belfast. Three days to find those missing hours of my life."

Bella frowned and sat beside her. "I cannot imagine how

difficult that must be for you, Gina. You know I will help you in any way I can, but I cannot condone you prowling the London streets after midnight and putting yourself in danger. If I lost you…I could not imagine such a thing."

"You will not lose me, Bella. James has taken it upon himself to look out for me." Heat crept into her cheeks with the thought of just how well Jamie had looked out for her last night.

"Jamie is courting you, Gina. I have been hoping he would speak for you soon, and that you would marry and stay in London with Lilly and me."

"Oh, poor Bella. Had I known you were thinking in that direction, I would have told you sooner. Jamie is merely trying to keep me out of trouble. He is watching out for me. Ever since Mr. Henley accosted me in the Morris's garden—"

"What?"

"Mr. Henley came to me in disguise. He spoke to me, and he was dragging me into the shadows when Jamie came looking for me. And since then, he scarcely lets me out of his sight. I tried to discourage him, but he will not relent. Society might think we are courting, but his real purpose is to watch me. That is why I've been sneaking out. I cannot have him hovering all the time. People will not speak freely with him glowering like some looming gorilla."

Bella sighed and her shoulders drooped. "I was so certain…even Drew thought you were courting."

"No. The furthest thing from it." Though he'd done a fair imitation of it last night, after she'd begged him.

Bella squeezed her hand. "Very well, Gina. Since I know Jamie is looking after you, I shall hold my peace. *Three days,*" she repeated. "If there is anything I can do to help, you must tell me. Now run up and change. We are meeting the ladies and Mr. Renquist at *La Meilleure Robe* in half an hour."

* * *

The little dressing room was hushed when Gina came around from behind the dressing screen and stepped onto the platform in front of the mirror. She smoothed the curve of the fabric over her breasts and turned in a full circle.

Bella was the first to speak. "Stunning. Simply stunning, Madame. You have made our Gina look like a goddess."

Lady Sarah stood and touched the fabric. "Silk. Of course. The drape is magnificent, Madame."

Lady Annica smiled her approval. "I have little to add to *stunning* and *magnificent,* but perhaps *provocative* would do. You are going to drop jaws, Miss O'Rourke."

Madame Marie preened. "I cannot take all the credit, eh? Miss O'Rourke contributes to my creation in some small part, does she not?" The ladies laughed at Marie's joke as the modiste knelt to adjust a flounce.

"Pearls, I think," Grace Hawthorne contributed. "The luster will complement the color without detracting attention from the wearer."

"I think I shall have to commission a similar gown," Sarah mused, a teasing sparkle in her violet-blue eyes. "Though I would like it done in willow-green. It is Ethan's favorite color."

Madame Marie stood and adjusted the small puffed sleeves. "*Mais oui.* I shall 'ave to order fabric in every color at once. And you, Miss Gina, shall take this 'ome with you today."

A soft knock at the side door interrupted their laughter. "La! That François, 'e 'as the good timing, no? Now we shall see what a man thinks of our Gina. *Entrer,* François!"

True to Lady Annica's prediction, Mr. Renquist, holding a small carved wooden box, stopped short and his mouth dropped open when he saw Gina. Madame Marie went to him and gently lifted his chin with her forefinger. "Careful, *mon amour.* You will make me jealous."

He blinked and focused his attention on his wife. "No need, dearest. No one can hold a candle to you."

Marie laughed and headed for the door. "You see 'ow well I 'ave 'im trained?" She closed the door behind her.

Mr. Renquist nodded at the ladies and offered Gina his hand to step down from the platform and take a seat with the others. "I have several things to report, ladies. Shall we begin with the box?"

At their nods, he continued. "I have picked the lock and found several items." He opened the lid and gave it to Gina.

This, then, was the box she had asked him to purchase from Mr. Henley's former landlord. She rested the box on her lap and poked through the contents.

Mr. Renquist continued as she examined each item. "There is a cravat pin in the form of a dragon with small ruby eyes, a broken watch, a pocket knife, a list of household items and a small packet of unsigned letters."

"What sort of list?" Lady Annica asked.

Gina ran her finger down the list. "Candles, tinderbox, blanket, wine—"

"He was setting up new quarters, or a hiding place," Lady Sarah guessed.

Gina skipped over the cravat pin, unwilling to touch the wyvern from which the Brotherhood had taken their name, and lifted the packet of letters. She untied the ribbon that held them together and picked one random letter from the middle of the stack of ten.

It began without salutation and concluded without signature. Gina read it aloud for the rest of the group. "'I concur, dear Henley, that your position is untenable. I am working on a solution and beg that you be patient. I shall meet you Tuesday next at the usual place and time.' The writing looks feminine. But how can that be?"

Mr. Renquist nodded. "I thought the same thing, Miss

O'Rourke, and that would fit with another piece of information I've gleaned. One of the boys I employ from time to time reports that he spotted Henley with a woman. A woman of quality, according to him. That would confirm our suspicion that Henley has help from the ton."

"Blackmail?" Gina asked, thinking of Mr. Morris.

Mr. Renquist gave a philosophical shrug. "Or affection."

"Where were they seen?"

"At the Bucket and Well in Whitechapel. The place is a bit better than the usual Whitechapel taproom."

"Tuesday next," Bella mused. "Is the letter dated?"

"None of them are. Since the letters have been in the box for a week or more, I believe that meeting has come and gone. Nevertheless, since it appears to be their usual place and time, I shall be at the Bucket and Well this coming Tuesday. All day and night, if I must."

Tuesday next… Gina would be en route to Belfast. A quick sharp pain gripped her stomach. There had to be some way to conclude this matter by then. She covered her panic by unfolding a single sheet of paper and pretending to study it.

"Ah, yes. The ledger sheet. As you will see, Miss O'Rourke, that is a list of receipts and payments made to various individuals by initials, with the exception of the notations for 'Gibbons.' I would like to turn that particular item over to the Home Office, if you do not mind. Perhaps they will have the resources to match the initials and payment to certain individuals and events. I suspect this is a record of Mr. Henley's blackmail and murder attempts."

Gina nodded and scanned the list quickly, committing as much as possible to memory before she refolded it and handed it back to Mr. Renquist. "Should they be able to identify anyone from their initials, I would like those names. I conceive it could be quite useful to know who might have pertinent information, and who I should avoid."

"Of course, Miss O'Rourke. Forewarned is forearmed." He cleared his throat and finished his report. "The last item is a list of notorious criminals who have been known to kill for hire. I believe Henley has either hired them, or intends to hire them. It is possible he used these individuals to procure women for their…entertainments. What we lack is an explicit list of men he is blackmailing."

She handed him the list. "I have no use for this, Mr. Renquist. I would not know any of these people, nor would I wish to interview them. Perhaps the Home Office would find this useful, as well." She closed the lid on the little box, unwilling to give up anything more.

"Thank you, Miss O'Rourke, for not putting me in a difficult position. I am certain the Home Office will make good use of this information."

She glanced around at the group and sighed. "I do not know when, or if, I shall be seeing any of you again. My mother and I shall depart for Belfast three days hence. If the matter is not concluded by then, I hope I may prevail upon you to follow it to its end."

"But of course!" Lady Annica frowned thoughtfully and tapped one finger against her cheek. "Do not despair, dear Gina. We shall devote ourselves to a solution."

Jamie had gone early to the ball at Duchess House, leaving Charlie to escort Gina and the Thayers a bit later. He hoped Gina realized he was not deliberately avoiding her. He'd wanted to talk to Lord Marcus Wycliffe before he focused his attention on her.

Wycliffe always arrived early at such events, preferring to watch arrivals and thus know who was in attendance, a habit he acquired after an uninvited guest at a soiree had attempted to slip a knife between his ribs. Wycliffe never made the same mistake twice.

They stood alone with a glass of wine, watching the wide foyer as guests trickled in, most choosing to be fashionably late. Jamie did not meet his gaze as he made his request.

"I had the news today that Mrs. O'Rourke and her daughter are leaving London soon. Monday, if my information is correct."

"Really? Well, I cannot say I am sorry. The daughters have been somewhat of a distraction—the eldest murdered, Isabella cutting her way through the ton in her search for the killer, Lillian abducted by a scoundrel, and now Eugenia interfering in Home Office business and distracting you from your duties. Yes, I think it will be quite peaceful come Tuesday."

"In point of fact, I am here to tell you that there are some matters I need to settle with Miss O'Rourke before she returns to Ireland."

"Has she done something to compromise our investigation?"

Jamie sighed, ignoring the question for a different admission. "Actually, I fear I may have compromised Miss O'Rourke."

Wycliffe grinned. "*May* have? What did you do? Kiss her behind the hedgerow?"

Jamie bristled. He was not about to give details. "What I did or did not do is not the issue. What I do next is."

"I see. And what are you going to do next?"

"I intend to ask her to marry me."

Wycliffe choked on his wine and Jamie thumped him on the back. "What? You? Marry? Is this some perverted joke?"

"Not in the least. In fact, I believe it is the only solution. For both of us."

Wycliffe glanced around to be certain they could not be overheard. "I pray you are not swayed by excessive sympathy for her and her family. Or that you have not overreacted to some imagined impropriety. Truthfully, Jamie, I cannot see you doing anything to risk such dire consequences. Of all my acquaintances, I thought you least likely to commit any such offense. Or to marry, for that matter."

"You needn't worry overmuch. I fully expect that she will refuse me."

"You… Why?"

"She does not care for me."

Wycliffe cleared his throat and Jamie thought he heard a surreptitious rumble of laughter. "I've yet to meet the woman immune to your charms. What have you done to make her dislike you?"

"I carried her from the altar. I am a reminder of her deepest humiliation. Indeed, the worst day of her life."

Sobering, Wycliffe's expression turned grave. "If she will not marry you, why ask her?"

"I hope to persuade her. Apart from that, I fear for her. The communications we received from Francis Renquist today lead me to believe she would not be safe even in Ireland. If Henley wants her dead… You have sent men to bring in the blackguards on that list," Jamie said. "But there may be more whose names we do not have, and how can I protect her against that? I need her closer to hand."

"Can you control her?"

Could anyone? "I have as good a chance as her mother, and I'm more unlikely to relax my vigilance."

A large party arrived, turning the foyer into a cacophony of laughter and shouted greetings. On the wide steps outside, he could see Charlie arriving with his charges. Though he could only see the top of her head, his stomach lurched. He'd never been so nervous. He felt like a schoolboy in the throes of his first crush.

He should have called on her earlier in the day. Surely

leaving her alone to fret had not been a good move. She was, no doubt, furious with him once she regained her senses. How would he ever woo her back to trusting him?

Chapter Fourteen

Gina was in agony with suspense. When Charles had called for her instead of Jamie, he'd only said that Jamie would meet with them at Duchess House. Not so much as a personal word. Nor had he sent her a message or an explanation. In view of her behavior last night he would, no doubt, wish to distance himself from her as far as possible.

All she could do was to maintain as much dignity as possible. If he feared that she would weep, hurl accusations, make demands, or denounce him, he would be quite pleasantly surprised. She had only one question, and then he'd be free to go his own way. No matter that it would break her heart.

When they entered the foyer at Duchess House, she saw him in deep conversation with Lord Wycliffe. Charles called a greeting and she took a deep breath and cast him a bright, cheery smile. He blinked, then smiled in return. So he *had* been expecting trouble.

"Here comes my brother. I pray I will not be banished now that I've served my purpose," Charlie said.

"Never!" Hortense vowed. "So long as you dance."

"I shall dance until your toes tingle, dear Miss Thayer."

She giggled and fanned herself feverishly, and Gina suspected Hortense might have a secret tendress for Charlie. But Charles Hunter was an odd one—always open and charming though she sensed an underlying darkness.

Jamie bowed deeply to them. "My apologies, ladies. Alas, I had some pesky business to attend, but now that you are here, I shall devote myself to you entirely. Miss Harriett, will you consent to dance with me?"

Harriett glanced sideways at Gina, as if embarrassed that he had asked her to dance before asking Gina. "I should be delighted, Mr. Hunter."

Charlie frowned, watching Jamie as he led Harriett onto to the dance floor. "Shall we find the punch bowl, ladies?"

They stopped to share pleasantries with acquaintances, and before they arrived at the punch bowl, Jamie and Harriett had rejoined them. When Jamie asked Hortense to dance, Gina suspected that he had a plan. Having done his duties to the twins, he could then leave without having to talk to her. Or, more worrisome, he would then have time to deal with her. That thought disconcerted her since it suggested that he had rather more to say to her than she'd like to hear.

And when, at last, he returned Harriett and extended his hand to her, she was not at all certain she wanted to dance. But she could not refuse without raising eyebrows, so she placed her hand in his and followed to the dance floor. As the waltz began, he pulled her into his arms and smiled.

"I trust you slept well?"

She trained her eyes on a point just over his right shoulder. "Tolerably."

He chortled. "You were sleeping well enough in my bed. Perhaps I should have left you there."

"Ten minutes more and the entire household would have known where I'd been."

"We came that close to discovery, eh?"

"Yes." But she wouldn't have cared.

"I need to talk to you, Gina. Everything has changed now, and we need to sort it out."

She nodded, a cold feeling settling in the pit of her stomach. Why did that sound so ominous? All she wanted was the answer to her question.

He glanced outside the terrace windows and muttered a curse. "Rain. We shall have to find a private room."

"Can it wait?"

"There is too much at stake."

He led her from the dance floor and toward the central passageway from the foyer. He opened each door and peeked in until he found one suitable then swept her into the darkened room. By the light from the streetlamp outside, it appeared to be a small parlor.

"Perhaps we should not—"

But his decisive closing of the door assured her Jamie meant to have this talk immediately. She perched on the edge of a small settee covered in deep blue brocade. At least they would have privacy.

He came to sit beside her and took her hand in his. "Gina, last night was…was…"

"A mistake," she finished. "I regret putting you in that position. I regret taking advantage—"

"Advantage? You?"

"I…I distinctly remember asking you to find some-place."

"So that I would not take you against a tree in public. Good God, Gina! I am amazed that you are even speaking to me."

Confused, she met his gaze for the first time since they'd entered the room and was struck dumb by the depth of passion there.

He squeezed her hand as he continued. "I think we both know we have been moving toward this for quite some time. You cannot deny the physical attraction between us. Given the strength of it, last night was inevitable."

"Inevitable," she agreed, "but regrettable."

"I do not regret it, Gina, though I am sorry to learn that you do. I have never known anything quite like it."

He seemed to expect some sort of reply, but she was so humiliated that she could not think what precisely. "It…it was lovely," she said for lack of better words.

"Lovely?" He arched one eyebrow at her as if she'd delivered an insult.

Heat swept over her as she recalled just how *lovely* it had been. "Ah, *quite* lovely?"

He stiffened. "I see. Well, I gather I shall have to do better in the future. Which, of course, brings me to the point of this conversation."

"Yes, please. What is the point?"

"Be my wife, Gina. Marry me as soon as it can be arranged."

"Marry? You cannot be serious."

Jamie seemed to lose patience with her reply. He stood and threw his hands up in surrender. "I have never been so serious, nor have I ever had such a difficult time convincing anyone of it. Marriage, Gina, is the logical culmination of our impetuousness last night. It is the most prudent way to solve the attendant problems."

She shook her head in disbelief. "Do you think I begged you so that I could trap you into marriage?"

He paced to the window and back. "Gina, I thought we'd both been swept away in the moment, judgment clouded by passion, as it were. But I begin to think I was the one swept away and that you had some other purpose."

"I doubt I could have stopped had I the chance. But when it began, when you first kissed me, I wondered…"

"Wondered what? If I had fallen in love with you? If I would make a fool of myself by proposing?"

Oh, she had muddled this whole affair beyond repair. He'd mentioned passion, and being swept away, but he'd never used the words she needed to hear. In the absence of that, the only thing she could give him was the truth. "I was desperate to know if I was a virgin. And I thought I could find out if I just—"

"Just let me make love to you? That's it? That's why you asked me to find somewhere private? To find out if you were virgin?"

He looked outraged, as if she'd done something unspeakable. In the face of his anger, she was afraid to speak. She only dared a nod.

He threw his hands in the air again and stalked to the window. "I cannot believe this. Did you ever stop to think that your little experiment would *cost* you your virtue if you were still intact?"

She nodded again, trying not to think how badly she'd wanted him, how she'd have made the same decision if she hadn't had that question, or how she'd thought she'd die if he stopped.

Or how deeply she loved him.

"Well, Miss O'Rourke, you are certainly no virgin now. You have been quite thoroughly introduced into the erotic arts. And you have demonstrated an aptitude for it, by the way." He went to the door as if he were finished with her, then turned around and fixed her with a glare so intense it made her squirm. "Was it worth it?"

She looked down at her feet. How could she answer that? That it had been worth everything she ever hoped to possess in this lifetime to have the memory of him for the rest of her life? That she was glad she would have that little piece of him to take back to Belfast with her? That, if she never married, never had children, she would at least know what it was like to have been loved by Jamie Hunter for the space of an hour?

But what was his answer? Had she been virgin? Or had Mr. Henley defiled her? Dare she ask again? She quietly cleared her throat and clasped her hands together in her lap to still their trembling. "Yes. It was worth it. Whatever your answer, it was worth it."

"Answer? You want *me* to tell you if you were a virgin? You do not know?"

Tears sprang to her eyes but she blinked them back quickly. Jamie would think her silly and would not want to see her weakness now. "If you would, please."

A myriad of emotions passed over his face so quickly that she could not read them all. But the final one, evident as he came toward her, was one of desire. He stopped before her and lifted her chin with his forefinger. "Gina, none of that matters. Can't you see that? Henley and the others—what they saw, what they did or didn't do—doesn't matter. You are who you are, not what someone may or may not have done to you. And you, my dear, are the most beautiful woman I've ever known."

"Jamie, that is not an answer."

"This is the only answer you need." He leaned forward and fit his lips to hers, cherishing them softly. She responded in the most primitive way, pulling him closer, astounded by the need that single kiss awoke in her. He came down on one knee to meet her on her level and deepen the kiss. She savored his intoxicating heat, losing herself to his passion and her own need.

He pressed her back against the cushioned seat even as he swept one hand down to free one of her breasts from the curve of her bodice and the filmy lawn of her chemise. When he dropped his head to take her into his mouth, she thought she would swoon with the sheer pleasure of it.

She tangled her fingers through his hair and pressed him harder against her, arching to him, desperate for the feel of him there. He did not pause in his ministration as he slipped one hand down to edge beneath her gown and sweep up her thigh.

Her breathing deepened as his bare hand found the soft flesh above her garter and beneath her chemise. His knowing hand found its destination—the small firmed bundle of nerves he had discovered only last night. She gasped and opened her legs to give him better access.

"Jamie…"

"I love the way you say my name when you are about to—"

"Oh!"

He chortled. "That's it, Gina. Just a little more and…"

She reached for him, wanting to give as much pleasure as she took, but he caught her hand and stayed her.

"Not here, Gina. Not now. Later."

Then he turned his attention back to her gratification, as if that was all that mattered to him now, and she accepted greedily, wanting even more as he slipped two fingers into her sheath, stroking, curving slightly to find a spot so exquisitely delightful that she nearly fainted with pleasure.

"Stay with me," he urged, as if he feared she would slip away from him.

"Please," she sighed, not even knowing what she pleaded for.

But Jamie understood what she did not, quickening his stroke and deepening the pressure until she uttered a soft scream of delight as the world narrowed to her center and then ruptured outward again in radiant heat and light.

"Yes," he praised. "Burn for me, Gina. Only for me."

Her breathing evened slowly and her mind cleared of the overwhelming passion. Oh, how could he do this to her? How could he know her body better than she knew it herself and give her such unspeakable pleasure? How could she let him go two days hence, and never know this joy again?

Jamie's own breathing slowed and he withdrew his hand, smoothing her skirts and nuzzling her ear. "You're like fire, my love. I've never known any woman to burn as bright."

Gina tried to make sense of his words, but all she could think was that he had not found the same release she had. "But you…you did not."

He smiled and kissed her cheek. "Were we truly private, my love, we would not be finished for hours. As it is, we've risked more than we should."

Heavens! They were at Duchess House. Behind an unlocked door! She stared at the door, fearing it would open any moment and expose their indiscretion. How had she so forgotten herself that she could allow Jamie such intimacies? How could she ever explain such a thing if discovered?

He laughed again, as if reading her mind. "I fear there is no such thing as good sense where passions are concerned. We shall have to be more careful. After we are—"

"We must return to the ballroom before they come looking for us." She patted her hair into place and smoothed her bodice, knowing there was nothing she could do about the blush that must surely be scarlet by the heat she felt.

"Ah, yes. We would not want them asking questions. At least until I have asked one of my own."

"Oh! Yes, questions. I completely forgot. I have not had your answer."

The warm reassuring look on his face faded as if he remembered their earlier argument. "After…*that?* Your answer is all you care about? That is all you want from me?"

"I…yes." Did he think she would ask more of him? She only wanted what he would willingly give.

He gave a joyless laugh. "'Twould serve you right to keep that information to myself."

"Jamie…."

He held up one hand, palm toward her in a gesture of denial. "No, Gina. Suddenly I am not in an indulgent mood. I'm likely to say nearly anything just to cut you as deeply as you've cut me."

"But—"

"You used me to your own purposes, Gina. Can you blame me if I take a bit of revenge against you?"

"You cannot withhold that information from me. I risked everything to know—"

"I risked more, Eugenia, but I cannot expect you to understand that." And the parlor door closed behind him.

Jamie stalked back to the ballroom, torn between anger and sympathy. The proposal had not gone even remotely as he'd planned. He'd hoped for a sweetly uttered acceptance, and had been poised to acquire a license to wed at once. He'd even been prepared for refusal and had devised an argument to counter it. But he could never have predicted Gina's admission that she'd only wanted to test whether she was virgin or not. What utter twaddle! She would not have him? Well and good. He would not trouble her further.

He spied Hortense and Harriett surrounded by beaux, and signaled Charlie to him. "Can you escort the ladies home tonight, Charlie? I find I have other pursuits."

His brother studied him, then laughed. "Our Miss Eugenia is responsible for this sudden dark mood, is she not?"

"Do not tweak me, Charlie. I am not in a mood for it." In fact, his body was still throbbing with unrequited lust and his head was filled with the memory of Gina, flushed and dewy from his lovemaking.

Charlie grinned, as if he guessed the reason for Jamie's ill temper. "Go on to your 'other pursuits' then, but leave Suzette alone. She has just warmed up to me, and I do not want her confused in her affections."

"Suzette is yours," he growled. "But mind that you do not neglect your duty where Eugenia is concerned. She is still in grave danger."

"Where did you leave her?"

He pointed down the corridor. "The small parlor."

Taking the front steps two at a time, he gained the street and hailed one of the hackneys that always waited outside large events such as the one at Duchess House tonight.

As the carriage turned onto Oxford Road, he caught a glimpse of a familiar figure, revealed through the clinging rain-soaked cape she wore. Missy Metcalfe? Should she not be home in mourning? "Ho, there, driver!" he called.

The carriage stopped and he hopped down with instructions to follow. He caught up to Missy just as she was rounding a corner.

She gasped as he took her elbow and turned her around. "Miss Metcalfe. Are you alone?"

Her eyes widened. "I am going home, Mr. Hunter. I beg you will not tell anyone you saw me."

"I shan't. I have a carriage. May I offer you a ride?"

She glanced over her shoulder toward the following carriage. "I do not think so, sir."

"You should not be out alone after dark, Miss Metcalfe. There are dangers for an unprotected woman."

A sardonic smile curved her full lips. "Would you be one of them, Mr. Hunter?"

He could scarcely miss that she was flirting with him. Or

that he found himself responding after Eugenia's stinging rebuff. "If encouraged."

"Then perhaps we should take that carriage."

Jamie signaled the hackney forward, handed Miss Metcalfe in and followed her, settling himself beside her.

She loosened the strings of the cape around her neck. "Would you mind terribly if we took a turn or two through Hyde Park, Mr. Hunter. I cannot go home too early as my parents might still be up, and they think I have already retired for the night."

"You pled a headache?" he guessed.

"Mourning," she replied with a little smirk.

Something about her answer set him on edge. He could not imagine his own sister behaving in such a manner if one of her brothers had been killed less than a week previously. According to the rules of mourning, Missy Metcalfe should not be seen in public for three months, and she should be clothed in dark or drab colors instead of the vivid persimmon she wore now.

"And are you not in mourning, Miss Metcalfe?"

"I am devastated, Mr. Hunter. Simply devastated."

Clearly an exaggeration if ever he'd heard one. Had there been no love lost between the siblings?

He leaned out the window and called to the driver. "Hyde Park, please, and keep driving until I tell you otherwise."

"Aye, sir." The driver laughed and Jamie knew he was thinking that he and Miss Metcalfe would be making the two-backed beast.

"Tell me, Miss Metcalfe, were you and your brother close?"

"As close as some," she demurred.

"Then I wonder at your being abroad so soon after his death."

"What good will grieving do Stanley now? If there was a time to help him, it has passed."

"Help him? Was he in trouble?"

She gave another little smirk as she nestled closer to him. "Enough trouble to get him killed."

She was a cold little piece. "Do you know who did it?"

"Now why would you ask such a question? If I knew, would I not have told the authorities?"

That would very much depend upon what Missy had to gain. "Unless you were frightened of the consequences," he suggested.

"I do not frighten easily, Mr. Hunter."

"I can see that, Miss Metcalfe. I confess to wondering what could have been so important as to bring you out to this particular place at this time."

She settled back against the cushions and gave him a sultry look. "Perhaps I was looking for excitement."

She'd been looking for something, or someone, of that he was sure. "At Duchess House?"

She shrugged, allowing her cape to slip open and reveal a very naughty décolletage. He was man enough to avail himself of the view, even if he was not inclined to take advantage of it. Her corset had pushed her breasts high enough that the rosy rims of her areolae were peaking above the lace ruching. An invitation?

"I thought I might recognize someone. Truly, I have been longing to see friends, and craving human contact." She heaved a sigh and the sleeve of her gown slipped down over her shoulder. She gave him a coy sideways glance from beneath her lowered lashes.

What a coquette! Human contact? Just how much contact did Missy Metcalfe crave? No stranger to flirtation, Jamie was nonetheless at a loss. He'd never been as expertly seduced by courtesans or demireps.

With great difficulty, he forced his mind back to his query. "Looking for anyone in particular, Miss Metcalfe?"

She shrugged again, allowing her sleeve to slip even lower and reveal a small beauty mark above one areola. Artifice? Or natural? "I thought I might find Mr. Booth. Did you see him there, sir?"

Adam Booth? He and Metcalfe had been friends. Wouldn't Booth be as surprised as Jamie to discover Missy about town alone? Or did Adam have more intimate knowledge of Missy's true nature?

He smiled down at the pretty girl, so unlike Gina in almost every way that the contrast was startling—and not particularly flattering to Missy. Ah, but Missy appeared to want him, and Gina did not. "I believe I saw him, but I did not have time to talk to him. Did you have business with him?"

"Business?" She gave another of those coy smiles that made him think she was enjoying a personal jest. "I suppose you might call it business. Though my motive was more that I am quite lonely."

She wiggled closer to him, rubbing her soft breasts against his side and placing her hand on his knee. Very brazen for a girl of Missy's class. He wondered how much further she'd go with even the tiniest encouragement. "Are you still lonely, Miss Metcalfe?"

She lifted her mouth to him as she slid the hand on his knee upward to cup his erection. Her voice was a purr as she answered. "Oh, I do not think so, Mr. Hunter. No, I think I am about to be quite thoroughly amused."

The patter of rain against the hackney roof muffled her soft moan.

Chapter Fifteen

The guests laughed at some witticism of Mr. Booth's and Gina smiled, trying to put the memory of her confrontation with Jamie from her mind. He'd been so angry he'd abandoned their group to Charlie and then disappeared. The mere thought of such a thing caused her to sigh.

"But I see our Miss O'Rourke is not much amused," Mr. Booth said with a sardonic smile. "I admit my wit is not a universal taste, but I am rarely met with such indifference."

Gina blinked as attention was shifted to her. "I am sorry, Mr. Booth. My mind was wandering."

"Indeed?" He pushed a shock of blond hair back from his forehead and regarded her somberly. "But I have been entertaining your group with the sole purpose of gaining your attention. It appears I will have to try harder. I hear a waltz, Miss O'Rourke. May I have this dance?"

With all eyes upon her, Gina could do little else but accept. She had been meaning to talk to Mr. Booth anyway. "Delighted," she said, taking his outstretched hand.

They had scarcely entered the dance when the music ended,

but instead of returning her to her friends, he kept her there awaiting the next dance. "Are you enjoying London, Miss O'Rourke?"

"As much as I've been able. My family has had no small amount of problems since arriving here."

"I have heard, Miss O'Rourke. You have my sympathies."

She believed him. His manner and speech were so warm that he was hard to doubt. "Thank you."

He hesitated before he spoke again, obviously choosing his words carefully. "Am I correct in thinking matters have eased for you, and that you and your sisters are well?"

For Bella and Lilly, matters were much improved. As for herself, she had certainly regained a healthy measure of courage and self-confidence. "Very well, thank you."

She fancied that he looked somehow relieved. But why would that be the case, unless he felt somehow responsible?

"I have heard whispers that you are leaving soon for Ireland. Is that so?"

She laughed. "I should not be surprised at the amount of information shared over teacups, yet I confess I am. Yes, it is true. My mother and I have berths aboard a ship departing on Monday."

"I am sorry to hear that, Miss O'Rourke. I should very much have enjoyed getting to know you better."

Warmth crept into her cheeks at his apparent sincerity. "No matter how much time we have to explore new possibilities, it is never enough, is it, sir?"

His smile was his answer. He looked around the ballroom and the expression on his face tightened, as if it had frozen in place.

Fear prickled the back of her neck and she turned in the direction of his stare. Dancers whirled past, obscuring her view. What could Mr. Booth have seen to cause such a reaction? "Are you all right, Mr. Booth?"

He blinked and came back to himself. "Quite. I collect the orchestra will be taking an intermission. Would you consent to stroll with me in the garden?"

A request, that if made moments ago she would have accepted, she now refused. "Thank you, but the paths must be wet from the rain. I'd prefer to stay inside."

"Oh. Yes, certainly. But I am loath to return you to your friends just yet."

As harmless as he seemed, she knew she dared not trust him, but she desperately wanted to question him. "Shall we find a quiet spot?"

He nodded and she followed him down the same corridor she and Jamie had taken barely an hour ago. Knowing the room would be vacant, she went directly to the small parlor and went inside, leaving Mr. Booth to follow and close the door.

She no longer had the luxury of time. Only bluntness would serve her now. She turned and tilted her head to one side. "We have met previously, have we not, Mr. Booth?"

He bowed his head. "We have, Miss O'Rourke, but I gather you do not recall the particulars."

"Enlighten me, sir."

"'Twas about two months ago. An estate on the outskirts of Mayfair."

"You were there that night?"

"To my shame."

"And mine," she whispered to herself. She sat and folded her hands in her lap to gain her composure before she dared look at him again. "I have always wondered what sort of man would attend such an affair. I would not have thought it of a man of your ilk, Mr. Booth."

"'Twas my first attendance at such an affair. I had been

led to believe it was voluntary by all the participants and for salacious purposes rather than the debacle it turned out to be. But then, I gather that was Daschel and Henley's method of recruiting postulants into their 'brotherhood.' I've heard from others that one attendance was enough to be drawn in, and that it was impossible to leave. Blackmail, you see. Dash was determined to convert us all to elemental base practices, while Henley merely wanted us to sink to his level. To control us."

Gina breathed deeply. As ugly as Mr. Booth's words were to hear, at least they had the ring of truth.

"I realized, after the chalice was passed and we all drank, and once I saw you, that you'd been drugged as the postulants had been. I am not mistaken in that, am I, Miss O'Rourke? You did not volunteer to be a virgin sacrifice?"

A gurgle of hysterical laughter erupted from somewhere deep inside her. Volunteer? "Never."

"Then I am glad to see you so well, and pleased that it ended the way it did, even though it had quite grim consequences for some of us."

In her own self absorption it had never occurred to her that others might have been affected. "What, prithee, were the consequence to you and your friends?"

"We've been blackmailed, Miss O'Rourke. Half our fortunes have lined Henley's pockets. We cannot denounce him without exposing our complicity. And we cannot expose our complicity without utter ruin to our families and loved ones."

A small tingle of sympathy worried the back of her mind. Impossible! Sympathy for her tormentors, albeit unwitting ones?

"And I furthermore collect that you have been seeking us out, one by one, and disposing of us?"

"Disposing? You mean…no! I want Henley caught and

punished, as much for my sister Cora as for myself. I want the authorities to lock him away forever, but I have not taken the law into my own hands."

"You did not kill Stanley Metcalfe?"

"No! I think he was trying to help me."

"You were the last person to be seen with him alive."

"Moments after he left me, I was assaulted by Mr. Henley."

"Christ! If Henley was there that night…"

"He killed Mr. Metcalfe. Perhaps to prevent him from giving me information."

Mr. Booth sank to the settee beside her. "He is a madman."

"Will you help me, Mr. Booth? Will you tell me where to find him so that I can inform the Home Office?"

"I do not know where he is hiding. He comes to us with his demands in public places, where we cannot attack him without drawing attention. He is a marked man, Miss O'Rourke. Leave his demise to others. It is far too dangerous for you."

"I cannot. I shall be taken back to Ireland soon, and I am desperate to have the matter concluded before then."

He took her hand and squeezed it. "Yes, then. I will help you. A day—two at most—and I will find information for you."

The door was thrown open and Charlie stood there, looking as outraged as a cuckolded husband. "Damn me, Miss O'Rourke! There you are! You gave me a bad turn. Come along now. 'Tis time I took you home."

"One moment she was dancing with Booth, and the next she'd disappeared completely. I swear, Jamie, that girl takes perverse pleasure in giving me apoplexy."

Jamie smiled and tipped his chair back on the hind legs. Perverse pleasure is precisely what he'd had with Missy

Metcalfe. Well, a form of it, at any rate. He hadn't taken her, even when she'd opened her legs in an invitation. Nor had he taken her up on those lush, full breasts so enticingly offered when she'd pushed her gown lower to reveal them in their full glory.

She'd been completely nonplussed that he'd refused her and had gone even further to tempt him, pinching and teasing those taut rosy buds herself until they'd tilted up to beg his mouth. Had it been Gina to do those things, he'd have found the scene insanely erotic. But Miss Metcalfe was so practiced, so contrived, that she'd been no more interesting to him than Suzette. And he suspected the rumors about her were kinder than the actual truth.

He suspected, in fact, that Missy might have been sent to distract him. He'd called her address to the driver and dropped her in front of her house a few minutes later, leaving her to adjust her own clothing.

Now, well past midnight and safely tucked away in a corner of the Crown and Bear, he merely sighed and nodded to Charlie's complaints. Gina was, undoubtedly, elusive. And perverse.

"She was with Adam Booth, by God. The two of them sitting there in the dark, her hand in his. I thought she was sweet on you, Jamie. I'd have sworn there was something powerful between you two."

Booth? Could she prefer Booth to him? The notion angered him. She'd given herself to him and, virgin or not, he damn well knew she hadn't given that up to anyone before last night. No, there had to be another explanation for their meeting.

"Calm yourself, Charlie. We had a rather nasty argument before I left the ball. Perhaps she was just trying to prick my pride." As he'd tried to prick hers with Missy Metcalfe?

"Must be a new experience for you, eh? A woman who does

not fall all over you? But I still think you should not amuse yourself with her. Keep your carousing to the demimonde."

Jamie merely ignored Charlie, it being far too late for such warnings now. Still, the thought of Gina's hand in Adam Booth's caused him a bad turn. He would have to have a word with the man.

"Ah, here they are," Charlie murmured. "Are you sure you want to do this?"

Jamie watched as Dick and Artie Gibbons sidled through the door, both scanning the room with a quick sweep of dull eyes. "They are utter strangers to truth and honor, Charlie. I really don't know why we bother. If we weren't so damned desperate…"

When Dick saw them he nudged his brother and they headed for Jamie's table. "Hear you was lookin' fer us t'other night at the Cat's Paw," Dick said.

"Aye, we were."

"Y'gots somethin' fer us?"

"We were hoping you'd have something for us."

"Like what?"

"Information. Have you found Henley's hiding place?"

Artie licked his lips, indicating he'd like a drink, and Dick eyed Charlie's glass. Jamie signaled Mick to bring two more glasses and a bottle of whiskey.

The brothers dragged chairs from a nearby table and sat, staring at Jamie as if they could unnerve him. Jamie leaned back in his chair again and crossed his arms over his chest.

Dick broke eye contact when Mick brought the bottle and glasses. Two quick shots later, he seemed ready to talk.

"Found it, but he'd gone." Dick rubbed the stubble that lined his dirty jaw. "Ain't found 'is new hole yet. Y' want more, yer gonna have t' pay fer it."

Jamie ignored the clear extortion and addressed the other

subject that had been on his mind. "Did you hear that Stanley Metcalfe was killed a few days back?"

Artie gave one of his wheezing laughs while Dick merely grinned. "Well, now. Ain't that interestin'."

"Do you know anything about that, Dick?"

"Maybe I got my suspicions."

"I've got mine, too. Want to compare?"

"You first."

"Henley, himself. Someone saw him at the masquerade."

Dick looked surprised. "So y' knows about that, eh?"

"Why do you suppose anyone would want him dead?" Charlie asked.

"Got in somebody's way, I'd say."

"How so?"

"Dunno. Askin' too many questions, 'd be my guess. Kinda like you an' yer brother."

Was that a none too subtle warning for him and Charlie? "Metcalfe aside, there have been an extraordinary number of attacks of late. For instance, someone took a shot at Charlie the night after Metcalfe's murder. I don't take kindly to that."

A shrug was Dick's only answer, but he looked down into his glass and would not meet Jamie's eyes nor look at Charlie. The hair stood up on the back of his neck. Every instinct he had pointed to the Gibbons brothers for that attempt. And here they were, sitting across the table drinking their whiskey. His fingers itched to tighten around Dick's throat and go for Artie after. Instead, he took a deep breath and gave Charlie a sharp warning look.

"Seems like London is getting dangerous for certain men of the ton."

"I don't give a ha'penny for nabobs," Dick said. "They c'n all go to hell, an' I wouldn't care."

"Who would you blackmail then, Dick? Where would you get your money?"

He gave a sideways grin. "We'd find a way. Right, Artie?"

Artie chuckled and bobbed his head.

Charlie narrowed his eyes. "Good idea, Dick. Because I'm thinking jobs might get pretty scarce for you. Hope you've put some money away for a rainy day."

"Never you mind what we gots," Dick snarled. Even Artie turned somber at the mention of money.

Jamie wondered again what these men did with their blood money and how much they'd be paid for killing Charlie and him. One thing had become evident—the Gibbons brothers were not their allies. Either Henley had something on the or he was paying more, and nothing Jamie could say would sway them.

Suddenly, Jamie was done with them. The price to his soul for dealing with such scum was too great and nothing but treachery could come from it. He pushed his chair back and stood, and Charlie followed suit.

"I'm out, lads. No more games. No more bribes. You'd do best to stay out of my sight."

A look of such anger passed over Dick's face that Jamie suspected he was planning revenge. "You sure you wants to make enemies o' us?" he asked.

"Never surer of anything in my life."

Dick and Artie stood together and measured themselves against Jamie and Charlie. The decision made, they backed toward the door and faded into the night.

From the bar, Mick Haddon grinned and raised a glass to them.

By the time Charlie arrived at the Argyle Rooms with his charges the next night, Jamie was waiting anxiously. After what Charlie had told him last night about Eugenia and Adam Booth being closeted together in a darkened room, he'd been ready to call the man out. Never mind that he was one of Charlie's best friends.

He stood in conversation with their host, Lord Geoffrey Morgan, and watched as a footman lifted Gina's cloak from her shoulders. When she turned toward the room, he broke off in the middle of his sentence. Gina wore a gown of French blue fashioned with a bodice that dipped to a low point between her breasts, revealing only the lush curves to each side. Oh, but it hinted at so much more. A white mother-of-pearl cameo fastened to a matching blue ribbon circled her throat. The gown was tenfold more seductive than Missy Metcalfe's bold gown of last night.

Behind him, he heard a man whisper to his companion. "Good Lord! Who is that breathtaking creature in blue? And what would I have to do to gain an introduction?"

"I believe that is Miss Eugenia O'Rourke. She is the sister of Andrew Hunter's bride, and the chit who was betrothed to the Marquess of Olney but ran off with Devlin Farrell."

"Wild blood, then? All the better. Here's Morgan. Shall we maneuver that introduction?"

As the men moved from behind to face them, Jamie was ready. He'd be damned if he'd allow another man to taste what he'd tasted. Gina was his.

That thought astonished him. *His.* Gina was *his.* Damned if he didn't love her. Why had he never realized that before? Oh, the mere thought of her, the memory of her, had haunted him since they'd met. He'd wanted her for as long as he had known her. He'd been saddened by the realization that she could never love him because he was a memory of everything loathsome to her, but he'd never stopped to realize that he *loved* her. Yesterday he had *proposed* to her. But he'd never recognized his own feelings for what they were. Love had happened to him at last, and it was undiluted Hell.

"'Lo, Morgan," one of the men said.

Geoff Morgan nodded. "Hoppes," he acknowledged. "Worick."

"Excellent diversion," Hoppes said by way of pleasantries. "Worick and I were wondering if you could introduce us to that comely creature who just arrived with the Thayer twins."

"Afraid he couldn't," Jamie answered for Geoff.

Geoff covered his surprise and regarded Jamie with an appraising eye. "Uh, yes. My good friend Hunter, here, has laid claim."

Hoppes and Worick regarded Jamie with a jaundiced eye. "Declared yourself, have you?" Worick asked.

He nodded.

"Haven't heard any announcements," Hoppe added.

Jamie gave them a cold smile. "You will."

"If she should change her mind, tell her I am waiting."

Change her mind? She hadn't the least notion yet that she would say yes. But she would. He'd do whatever he had to do to make that happen. "She won't."

Both men gave a quick bow to Geoff and backed away.

"Congratulations?" Geoff ventured.

"She hasn't said yes."

"Will she?"

Jamie shrugged. "I may have some persuading to do."

"Just made up your mind, eh? From the interest she is garnering, I'd make my intentions clear very soon, Jamie."

Excellent idea. "Thanks for the advice," he said, handing his wineglass to Geoff and heading for Gina's group.

Charlie saw him coming, glanced between him and Gina, and took a single step back to make room for Jamie at Gina's side. She was engrossed in conversation with Harriett Thayer and she hadn't seen him.

"Miss Eugenia," he greeted her with a bow.

She turned to him and his heart stood still for a moment, then resumed beating in a rapid measure. She was dazzling and conjured memories of their night together. Her lips curved in a smile, then dropped into a straight line as she evidently recalled their last conversation. He'd been boorish and bad-tempered, but she'd tweaked his pride rather badly. He'd apologize and find some way to make it up to her.

He extended his hand in a silent invitation, then held his breath at her hesitation as she stared at a point over his shoulder.

"Miss O'Rourke! How fortuitous. I have been looking for you. Might I beg this dance?"

"I was… Of course, Mr. Booth."

Chapter Sixteen

Gina glanced over her shoulder at Jamie. He was staring after her with such a thunderous look that she suspected she would answer for it later. But she could not depend upon finding a moment with Mr. Booth later.

"Did I interrupt something, Miss O'Rourke?"

"Not precisely, sir. I collect Mr. Hunter was about to ask me for a dance, but I wanted to talk to you."

He grinned, clearly pleased to have been chosen over Jamie. "I am gratified. As it happens, I have been able to uncover a bit of information for you. 'Twill be difficult to discuss this over a dance. Shall we take a turn about the room, instead?"

She took his arm as he led her to the perimeter of the dance floor. Her excitement built when he laid one hand over hers as they walked slowly. "I wish there were someplace we could be private, Miss O'Rourke. This is not the sort of thing one would wish to be overheard."

"I have not been here before, Mr. Booth. I do not know if there are any private venues."

"There are some private rooms, but I believe that would cause a bit of a scandal, would it not?"

She laughed. If Mr. Booth knew just how accustomed she was to scandal, there would be no denying him. She gestured to the niches with upholstered benches along the far wall, which provided quiet, private opportunities for conversation.

He led her to one near the back of the room, and therefore away from the light of the chandeliers and the sound of the orchestra. He waited for her to be seated, then sat quite close to her and tilted his head toward her. "There, quite cozy, are we not?"

She smiled and folded her hands in her lap. Mr. Booth was flirting and she did not want to give him an opportunity to touch her in a familiar manner. "Quite," she agreed.

He took a deep breath and fastened his attention on the toes of his shoes. "After we talked last night, I spent a great deal of time wrestling with my conscience. Though I had no complicity in what was done to you, Miss O'Rourke, I still bear a measure of responsibility and guilt for my presence there, and that is why I have agreed to help you.

"I was not the only one to be drawn into the promise of entertainment of a salacious sort. Metcalfe was another. I can see now that Henley and Daschel were slowly accustoming us to experiencing ever increasing debasements. He took us on an excursion to Bedlam, then to those tableaus with nak—unclothed females in provocative poses. At each turn, he increased the titillation, likely believing that we would join him in his 'brotherhood.' Please believe me when I say that I had no knowledge of his true purpose that night."

Gina sighed deeply, wondering just how many men present that night would make Mr. Booth's claim. And were they true? Or merely an excuse? She glanced at him from the corner of her eye and thought he appeared sincere. She had learned nothing if not that appearances could be deceiving. But he hadn't asked for forgiveness, so she remained silent.

"And because I feel a need to atone, I have begun asking questions. There are very few of us left—those who were there that night. It ruined a good many lives, you know."

A polite way of saying Mr. Henley was blackmailing them? Yes, he'd already told her this. "How much have you paid, Mr. Booth?"

He gave her a quick appreciative glance. "To date? At least a quarter of my fortune, Miss O'Rourke. And I have heard by the grapevine that I am not the only one. Henley has made quite a fortune on this, and I've begun to wonder if it wasn't the whole purpose from the beginning. He and Daschel were both living beyond their means. What better plan to improve their fortunes than to draw the ton's wealthiest men into a scandal, and then bleed them to keep quiet?"

"You will not make me see you and the others as victims, sir. You could have refused Mr. Henley at each step."

"I am painfully aware of that. He played on our basest instincts and won, to our everlasting shame. Henley must be put down like the rabid dog he is."

"Quite an advantage to you and the others if he were. I cannot help seeing your motives as being rather self-serving."

For the first time, Mr. Booth looked angry. "What would you have me and the others do, Miss O'Rourke? Pay with our entire fortunes and allow Henley to go scot-free? Why, I have come to think Henley continues the blackmail to enrich himself in preparation for an escape."

She fell silent. Perhaps enlisting Mr. Booth's aid had been a mistake. Could she ever join forces with anyone who'd been there that night? Could she ever trust him?

"I doubt it will make much difference in the end," Mr. Booth continued in a lowered voice. "Henley is determined to ruin us all. And he has more than money as a motive for some of us."

"Because you can testify against him?"

"I do not believe he is much worried over that. How could we testify without exposing and implicating ourselves?"

Gina had thought that same thing. Self-interest was a powerful emotion. She could not expect anyone to step forward if they would suffer in any way for doing so.

"Nevertheless, Miss O'Rourke, I have been able to determine a few things. First, I believe that Henley killed Metcalfe."

She was certain of it, but one question remained. "Why? If he was extorting money from Mr. Metcalfe, would killing him not run counter to his purpose?"

"I believe there was some sort of personal grudge. And in such cases, it tends to be a woman."

How could it be possible that Mr. Henley would have tender feelings for any woman and still do the things he'd done? And yet, Mr. Renquist had reported that Mr. Henley had met with a woman, and Gina had seen the proof of that in the letters.

"I believe there may be a chance to trap him through her, but I have not been able to find out who she is. I am still looking. I hope I shall have a name soon."

"I shall pray for it, Mr. Booth. The poor thing needs to be warned what sort of man he is."

Mr. Booth nodded in agreement. "I shall keep looking, Miss O'Rourke, but I do not see him frequently. Only when he wants money."

"When was the last time you saw him, sir?"

"The night of the Morris masquerade. He was collecting from me, but he was obsessing over something he said he'd misplaced in his last move."

Gina turned to him. "When was that?"

"Very recently, I believe. He said he'd gone back to his

previous rooms but that the landlord told him everything he hadn't taken had been disposed of."

Could this *something* be the box Mr. Renquist had purchased for her? But she couldn't recall anything of particular value except for the dragon cravat pin. Had she missed some clue in the items? Mr. Renquist had turned the list and letters over to the Home Office, but she still had the box.

"Miss O'Rourke?"

She came back to the conversation with a start. "Yes?"

"There is one more thing."

She met his gaze and waited.

"The last time I spoke with Stanley Metcalfe, he was very nervous. He mentioned that he knew something, or had learned something, that Henley would kill for. Whether he meant that figuratively or literally, I cannot say."

Yes, Mr. Metcalfe had been quite nervous when they'd met at the masquerade, and moments later he was dead. She sighed. There had been altogether too many deaths.

"Do you wish me to continue asking questions?"

"Please, Mr. Booth. Anything might help. Most especially, if you could find out where he lodges…but be careful."

He nodded as he stood, and offered her his hand. "I should take you back to your friends, Miss O'Rourke. We have been gone longer than a dance or two."

Heavens! She had lost track of time.

But she needed a moment to think about the things Mr. Booth had told her. She shook her head. "Go on without me, sir. I need a moment to collect my thoughts. And thank you so much for your help."

He bowed and backed away from her, a puzzling expression on his face.

Her head spun. What had he said? That he suspected Mr. Henley had killed Mr. Metcalfe over a woman? But what women might Mr. Henley and Mr. Metcalfe have had in common? Christina Race? Surely not! Christina had been hopelessly in love with Mr. Metcalfe. Then, Miss Metcalfe? Ridiculous. Unless…Mr. Henley had somehow wronged the girl, as he'd wronged Gina.

Suddenly she wanted to go home and examine the contents of Mr. Henley's wooden box. Was there some damning clue in the tiny cravat pin with its ruby eyes? Something that would betray where he could be found?

Jamie studied Gina from across the dance floor. She had shaken her head and Booth had left her there alone, retreating with an air of extreme nervousness. Now she looked down and a dark ringlet fell over her shoulder. She brushed it back and continued deep in thought. What could cause her utter distraction? An indecent proposal?

He shifted his attention to the retreating Booth. He should go after the bounder and beat him within an inch of his life. If he had hurt Gina in any way, had caused her the least distress, he would pay for it.

But Gina stood and began walking toward him and he put Booth from his mind. They had matters to discuss. Things to settle between them. She came directly for him and he was gratified that she did not attempt to avoid him further.

"I think we need to talk, Mr. Hunter."

He raised an eyebrow. "Ah, I am—Mr. Hunter? So you are still angry with me?"

Her lush lips twitched. "A bit. You were not quite a gentleman last night."

"You were not quite a lady," he reminded her.

"But you left me unfulfilled."

"Really? Hmm. I do not recall it quite that way. I believe I was the one to leave unfulfilled."

She flushed but bravely met his gaze. "I am referring to the fact that you did not answer my question."

God. How could he give her an answer that would satisfy her? The truth was so…blasted unsatisfactory. Lie? But that was not in his nature. She tilted her head to one side, and still he did not answer.

She took a deep breath and exhaled slowly. "Very well. I shall wait for you to get over your pique. Meantime, there are other matters we must discuss. I have information regarding Mr. Henley, and—"

He took her arm and turned her about. "And we should not discuss this where we could be overheard."

He guided her down a corridor to a salon, ushered her through the door and gestured for her to sit on a small settee, leaving the door ajar for the sake of propriety, and to preclude any repeat of last night in the sitting room at Duchess House.

When he turned back to her, she appeared so proper that he almost sighed. "Now, Miss O'Rourke, I would like to hear any news you might have of Mr. Henley or any of his cronies."

"Last night I enlisted Mr. Booth to assist my inquiries, and he has brought me news."

"How in the world did you persuade him to take that risk?"

"I asked him if we had met, and he seemed embarrassed. He was beneath the chapel that night, and confessed that he was ashamed to have been even a small part of that. I used his guilt to gain his consent."

Ah, then he could let Booth live. Fortunate for them both since a duel at dawn could draw all manner of unwelcome attention.

Gina smiled at him, evidently proud of her machinations. "Tonight he brought me news. According to Mr. Booth, Mr. Henley has been blackmailing a good many people. I believe he may be putting money aside for an escape. A rather grand one, from the sums I gather he's been collecting."

Jamie nodded as he paced with his hands behind his back. He knew all this from Mr. Morris, but he did not want to stop Gina when she'd finally trusted him enough to bring him such news.

"I have also come to believe that Mr. Henley is involved somehow with a woman. Perhaps one who meets with him frequently."

This was new information. "Do you know who she is?"

"I fear not. Though surely there cannot be too many who would be willing to trust him."

"If they knew his true nature," he appended. "Society at large does not know of the events that night, or before. Everyone has been quite close-mouthed. Husbands would not want their wives to know, nor would unmarried bucks want such news spoiling their chances to land an heiress."

"There is more. Mr. Booth suspects the woman is from the ton. He thinks that Mr. Henley killed Mr. Metcalfe over her. Nothing else makes sense, since killing Mr. Metcalfe would dry up the funds he was extorting. Do you know of anyone Mr. Henley might have been close to before he was exposed?"

He tried to think of the women he'd seen with Henley. Since he'd been friends with Metcalfe, he'd been seen in the company of Missy, and also Miss Race. Apart from that… Wait! That was why he had recognized Miss Race—he'd seen her in the company of both Metcalfe and Henley on a few occasions: the theatre, soirees and a few more questionable events. Could she—surely not. An unknown woman, then. Someone who traveled in their circles, but had not been previously connected with Henley. Yes, it made sense. A personal grievance was the missing motive for Henley to kill a friend—especially one who was paying him for his silence. He would inform Wycliffe at once of this new avenue to investigate.

He thought aloud. "We could find Henley through this woman."

She looked uncertain, as if she wanted to say more, then she shrugged and the moment was gone. "I am glad I could help. I would do more, you know. Whatever is necessary."

He admired her bravery and determination. "I wish you would do less, Gina. I do not like you putting yourself in harm's way."

"You will be getting your wish very soon now. Mother and I are leaving in two days. Meantime, I intend to do everything I can to bring an end to this."

"Two days…" Jamie's gut twisted. Two days, and Gina would be gone from his life. Two days, and life would return to its dull sameness.

He reached out to touch her cheek when the unmistakable report of a pistol being fired reached them. The sound had come from the street and he crossed the little room to look out the window.

Almost directly beneath them, a body lay facedown on the cobblestone. By the manner of the man's dress, he had been in attendance at one of the events at the Argyle Rooms that night. As he watched, people began to gather around the body. Jamie recognized Geoff Morgan and Charlie among them.

"Charlie?" he called.

His brother, kneeling by his friend, looked up, an expression of grave concern on his face. "Booth," he mouthed.

Beside him, Gina struggled to catch her breath. "No…"

"Find the twins and stay with them until I come for you," he told her.

"But—"

He dashed down the corridor to the servant's steps, the quickest path to the street below. He did not realize Gina had followed him until he was beside his brother.

"What the hell happened?"

Charles looked furious. "We were just talking."

He turned Booth over to reveal a bloodstain oozing over the crisp white linen of his shirt and a look of utter surprise on his face, frozen at the moment of his death. Charlie closed the man's eyes.

There was a soft moan, a hand gripping his sleeve. He turned to find Gina's attention riveted on the dead man. "Because of me. He was killed because he was helping me."

She was near hysteria. He needed to give her something to focus on, and he needed her to be safely inside, away from this debacle.

"Go inside, Gina. Find the Thayers, and stay with them."

She took a step back, then another, her attention never leaving Booth's body. Worried that she was in shock, he reached out to her, intending to take her to her friends to have them calm her while he and Charlie got to the bottom of this tragedy.

Another loud report reverberated in the narrow street and Jamie spun Gina behind him, shielding her from harm. In the confusion, the gathered men shouted and began to scramble away from Booth's body. But Charlie, face up, lay motionless on the cobbles, a terrifying crimson stain spreading across his left shoulder.

Geoff Morgan and a few others sprinted in the direction the shot had come from.

Jamie gave Gina a quick shake to startle her from her shock. "Run, Gina. Find a doctor, and send him to us. *Hurry.*"

He knelt by his brother, relieved to hear Gina's retreating footsteps as she ran to do as he asked. He unfastened his cravat and pressed it to Charlie's wound, trying to stem the flow of blood.

"Charlie? Charlie, wake up. Stay with us, man. Come on. Open your eyes, Charlie. Fight, damn it!"

His brother's eyes fluttered open. "Christ…where'd that come from?"

"Shut up. Save your breath. Gina's gone for a doctor."

Charlie gave a faint nod. "Don't think it's too bad. Barely hurts."

"You're in shock, you idiot."

Charlie's chuckle turned into a gasp for breath. "I'm fine. Go after…killer."

"I'm staying with you until help arrives. Did you see who it was?"

"Think…Gibbons."

"Did you see them?"

"Smelled them."

"Who were they after? You or Booth?"

"Both. Second shot came…from a second pistol. Not… enough time to reload."

That was good enough for Jamie. He'd get word to Wycliffe immediately. And his brothers.

Morgan and the others who had chased after the shooter returned and Morgan shook his head, his lips pressed into a grim line. "Gone," was his only comment.

The Gibbons brothers knew every alley and hiding place in the city. It would not be difficult for them to simply disappear. But now Jamie knew their favorite places, and knew the brothers were not wily enough to realize that every Hunter, every runner and every agent of the Home Office would be after them.

A moment later Gina was back, a doctor who had been in attendance in her wake. Jamie stood as the doctor began to cut Charlie's jacket away from the wound to assess the extent of the damage. There was so much blood. Could Charlie survive?

Gina came to stand beside him. "He will recover, Jamie. God would not be that cruel."

He slipped his arm around her, pulling her close, wanting to believe her and grateful for the comfort she offered. Comfort she'd been denied when her sister had been murdered and she'd been placed on an altar.

He kissed the top of her head as a crowd gathered behind them, not caring who might see or gossip. "Gina," he whispered for her ears only, "I need you to go home and be safe or I will not be able to do what I must."

She nodded and backed away to rejoin the Thayer twins, who were now entrusted to Morgan's charge. He'd see them safely home.

Chapter Seventeen

When Lord Morgan had delivered Gina home and come in to give Andrew the news about Charles, the ruckus had woken everyone but Mama, who always took laudanum to sleep—a habit she'd acquired after Cora's death. Moments later, Lord Morgan and Andrew had left together, but not before Andrew loaded a pistol and pushed it in the waistband of his trousers. She had no doubt they were off to rouse Lord Lockwood, the eldest Hunter brother. Oh, how she wished she were a man and could be doing something instead of waiting!

She took advantage of her mother's habit and filched an extra vial from her mother's night table and poured a measure for herself—anything to dull the horror and allow her to sleep. She could think of nothing but the events of the past hour. Mr. Booth dead. Charles Hunter at death's door. What could possibly happen next?

She sat in the overstuffed chair before the fireplace in her room, staring into the banked embers and thinking that the bitter taste of the laudanum was vaguely familiar. With an uncomfortable jolt, she realized that this was what the

Brotherhood had drugged her with. Even now the effects were seeping through her, making her drowsy.

The small mantel clock struck three times, stirring her from her reverie. Nancy had gone to bed long ago, so she sighed deeply and stood to remove her dress. The French-blue gown was simple, since it fastened in the front, but her stays took longer to loosen.

And there, at the end of one lace, was the little key for which she still hadn't found a lock. A key that Mr. Metcalfe had given her. Mr. Metcalfe—another man who was now dead because he had tried to help her. How would she ever gain absolution for being responsible for so much pain and devastation?

She untied the key and lay it on her writing desk. If she did not find the lock before she left for Ireland, she would give the key to Jamie. Perhaps he would find the lock one day.

Her dressing gown lay across her bed and she slipped it on and tied the sash and blew out her candle. The embers in the fireplace cast eerie shadows on the wall behind her. Something in the flicker made her shiver, and she thought she saw a movement in the deeper shadows near the window. Was it the effects of the laudanum?

Ridiculous. She was imagining things. The events of the evening had disturbed her. But there it was again. Ah, her own reflection in the cheval mirror in the corner. She gazed at herself, wondering where the carefree Eugenia O'Rourke of Belfast had gone. Forever changed. Because of Cora. Because of Jamie.

The reflected gleam of her eyes caught her attention and she went closer to the mirror, as if she would find the answer to her questions in her own eyes. But it was not her in the mirror. It was the girl she'd been *that* night. Helpless, she watched as the scene played out in her mirror.

She lay on a cot or pallet of some sort that had been placed on a bare stone floor. She tried to open her eyes, but couldn't. She was not witless, but helpless. Deep, quiet voices floated around her, speaking words she couldn't recall. But there were names she recognized. Hunter. Daschel. Henley.

She forced her eyes open, a monumental task. Shadowy figures in deeply hooded robes moved about her, stripping away her clothing, touching her, anointing her with sickly sweet oil and laughing. Then there came a softer voice. A woman's voice. She leaned close, her face still in shadow, and cooed something in Gina's ear, something that had terrified her then but she couldn't remember now. Others came to touch her but, oddly, she couldn't feel them. Her senses were deadened. It seemed as if these things were happening to someone else—dreadful things that made her close her eyes again and forget.

Gina blinked and the vision in the mirror shifted. Now she was wearing a transparent gown of pleated lawn, fastened low between her breasts and dropping to the tips of her bare toes. Her dark hair, crowned by a diadem, was loose and fell to the middle of her back. One of the robed men produced a carved box and turned it upside down. He took a small packet from the drawer and poured the contents into a cup, which was brought to her and pressed to her lips. A heavy wooden door swung open and she heard a distant chanting. Her head was tilted upward by a robed man and she was forced to drink a bitter brew as distant church bells chimed. Lethargy. Torpor. She could not think, could not move, merely stand in a witless state.

It's time, someone whispered in her ear as men on each side of her took her arms and led her forward. The shadows shifted, and she was lying supine on a stone altar as a dagger descended toward her throat....

Gina gasped, sucking in deep breaths of night air as her hand went to her scar. She was trembling, barely able to stand.

Oh, she'd prayed to remember, and now she had. Memory or dream? Did it matter? She knew those things she'd seen in the mirror were real. Somewhere between her anointing and being dressed in the Egyptian gown, her mind was still blank, but the rest was finally clear.

She held to her bedpost to keep from sinking to her knees. All those horrid memories, and she still didn't have the answer to her question. But Jamie knew. She could only assume the worst, and that he had been trying to spare her pride by remaining silent. But he wouldn't lie to her. Jamie never lied.

She had been ruined, and nothing could change that. Nothing could ever make her clean again, or worthy of Jamie's love. And he knew it, too.

And Henley would have to pay.

Henley. Oh, the box! Henley's little box—the box in her vision! She went to her writing desk and took the carved box from a drawer. She tried to push her key into the lock Mr. Renquist had forced, but it didn't fit. She turned it over and felt along the carvings for something to trigger the little drawer into opening. She found it in the curve of a flower. The slightest pressure tripped a spring to pop the drawer back. There, in a drawer shallow enough to avoid detection, was a folded piece of paper and a small paper packet that held yellowish brown flakes.

She sniffed and recoiled, knowing only too well from the bitter odor what the packet contained: opium. But the paper? She unfolded the sheet and found a list of names. Were these the men Mr. Booth had told her about? The men Mr. Henley was blackmailing? She ran her finger down the list and stopped at—

James Hunter
Charles Hunter
Andrew Hunter

Adam Booth
Stanley Metcalfe
Marcus Wycliffe
Eugenia O'Rourke

And other names she did not know. Could Mr. Henley be blackmailing Jamie and his brothers? Impossible. Why, she was on that list, and it was no secret they'd all been at the chapel that night. They'd rescued her and Bella. No need to pay hush money. But two of the men on that list were dead, another wounded, and God only knew how many more of the names she did not know were dead.

She squared her shoulders, determining to give the list to Jamie as soon as she saw him. He would know what to do with it. But she would keep the opium and the key. She might still have use for them. *Two more days. Two more nights.* She would make the most of them.

Dawn was breaking before Charlie stirred and groaned. Jamie shot out of his chair and leaned over his brother. "Charlie, are you awake?"

"Aye." He sighed, still not opening his eyes. "Am I going to live?"

Jamie jerked the bell pull to alert the staff at Lockwood's London mansion to summon his other brothers. "Of course, you dolt. The doctor said the ball did not do much damage. As long as you do not infect the wound, you'll be weak awhile but otherwise right as rain."

Charlie opened his eyes at last and tried to push himself up until Jamie propped him and pushed pillows behind his back. "Then why does it hurt so deuced much?"

"Because you are father's secret daughter."

Charlie chucked. "Womanish, am I? That's what I like about you, Jamie. Y'don't waste time with sympathy."

Jamie smiled. Coddling Charlie would be the surest way

to alarm him. "Sympathy would be lost on you anyway. And the doctor said you'll be up and about in a day or two."

Lockwood burst into the guest room, Drew and Devlin Farrell fast on his heels. "Charlie?"

"Good God, all my brothers in the same room! It must be worse than I thought."

Drew went to pull the draperies back from the window, exposing a violet-pink dawn above adjacent rooftops. "Sarah will be given the news as soon as she rises, so I expect she will be here soon."

"We'd best get down to business before she starts hovering—fluffing pillows and spooning porridge," Lockwood said. He took a chair near the foot of Charlie's bed. "Tell us what happened."

Charlie frowned and lay back against his pillows. "Damned if I know. Booth was in deep conversation with Miss O'Rourke for a time, then greeted a few people and departed. I thought it was time he and I had a chat, so I followed him out to the street. That is when he was shot."

"Did he say anything before he died?"

"He was shot in the gut—couldn't catch his breath before he expired. There was no time to search him before Jamie and the others arrived. Then…" Charlie shrugged and winced when the action caused him pain.

Drew squeezed Charlie's other shoulder. "An inch or two lower, and it would have pierced your heart, Charlie. You were very lucky."

"Yeah. Lucky."

"You mentioned the Gibbons brothers," Jamie reminded him.

"Didn't know they were such crack shots," Charlie said. "I always thought if they came after me, it would be with a knife. I did not see them—anyone, in fact—but the shot came from the alley. Perhaps I smelled garbage, but I thought it was them."

"Little difference between the two," Lockwood assessed.

"If Morgan hadn't chased after them, they'd likely have picked Jamie off."

"What made them so bold? Most often they are like rats, doing their business in secret."

"Jamie threw down the gauntlet when they wouldn't cooperate and he refused to pay them for nothing," Charlie said.

Devlin rolled his eyes. "A bit rash, eh, Jamie?"

"In retrospect."

"But I think it just as likely that Charlie is acquiring quite a fearsome reputation in the rookeries." Devlin sighed deeply and shook his head. "I warned you it would gain you respect, Charlie, but it also makes you a target."

"So Wycliffe was right about there being a contract out on a Hunter. Just the wrong Hunter."

"Or all of us," Drew concluded. "He'd have reason enough."

"The question is, what shall we do about it?"

Jamie assessed the gathering. Lockwood was looking every inch the family patriarch, Drew appeared rather deadly, Charlie had an angry look about him and Devlin was, as always, unreadable. And Jamie? Well, he was suddenly considering Wycliffe's veiled suggestion that the Gibbons brothers were a danger to society a bit more seriously.

Lockwood sighed deeply and stood. "I shall have to think on this, perhaps discuss it with Marcus." He went to the door and paused. "Oh, and I hear that Mrs. O'Rourke and her daughter are leaving day after tomorrow."

Drew slid a sideways glance at Jamie. "I must say that I will not miss her much," he confessed. "But I will be sad to see Eugenia go."

"And you, Jamie?" Lockwood asked.

Jamie crossed the room and went to stand by the window. "I had hoped Mrs. O'Rourke would change her mind, but I collect that is not to be."

"And Miss Eugenia?"

"Yes, damn it. I will be sorry to say goodbye."

"Have you considered…?"

Jamie gave Charlie a nasty look. Just how much had he told their eldest brother? "I have considered everything, Lockwood. It is hopeless."

"Everything?"

He gave Lockwood a curt nod.

"Then I am very sorry for you, Jamie. Such opportunities rarely come twice in a lifetime. But since she will be going home, I suppose the least we can do is see that justice is served."

Sunday at noon was not a usual time to pay calls, but Gina had hoped the family would be gone to church, and that she might have a private word with Christina. And now, studying the hollows beneath her friend's dark eyes, she was glad she'd come. Christina did not look well.

"Have you been out at all?" Gina asked. "Just a short stroll through your garden might be the very tonic you need."

Christina looked at Gina with an air of hopelessness. "Father told me this morning that Mr. Booth was killed last night."

She nodded. "That is why I've come."

"To tell me about Mr. Booth? But I already know."

"To ask your help again, Christina. I feel as if there is more that you know. Perhaps something you have not thought about, or something you forgot. Something that will help us put an end to all this."

"Us? But what could we do, Gina?"

She took Christina's hand and led her toward the door to

the garden, unwilling to risk being overheard by the servants. "Mr. Henley should be stopped by whatever means necessary. And you, Christina dear, are my safeguard. I shall tell you everything, and you will report to the authorities in case something…untoward should happen to me."

Christina blinked in the bright sunlight and clutched Gina's sleeve. "Do not tell me anything, Gina. Too much knowledge is a dangerous thing."

"Then tell me Mr. Metcalfe's secret."

She shook her head and covered her heart with one hand. "There is really nothing I can tell you."

She was hiding something that could have damaged her fiancé! Gina knew that instinctively, just as she'd always known when her own sisters were hiding something. Did it regard Mr. Henley's paramour? "Can you think of a woman Mr. Henley might have been close to? Someone he kept company with? One of your friends, perhaps, or a widow who could go about unchaperoned?"

Christina's eyes widened and Gina knew she'd come close to her secret. "Stanley and I used to keep company with Mr. Booth and Missy, but that was more so that Stanley could keep an eye on her. He always said she was wild. Sometimes Mr. Henley would accompany us but he would not bring a woman. That is why I was surprised when he brought you to that tableau."

"He was cozening me, Christina. Trying to make me trust him so that I would go with him when the time was right."

Christina sat heavily on a bench in the middle of the garden and turned her face up to the sun. "And you did…"

"But there must have been others. Someone he favored at balls and soirees?"

"Just me and Missy. And once, Mrs. Huffington."

Gina recalled hearing that name before but she could not put it with a face. "I do not believe I have met her."

"She is the ward of Lady Caroline Betman. The orphaned child of a dear friend, I think. Widowed twice though quite young."

Would that fit with what Mr. Booth had told her? But what would Mr. Henley want with a poor relation? He was a money-grubbing extortionist, intent upon amassing a fortune from other men's coffers. Could he have been cozening Mrs. Huffington for the same purpose as he'd cozened Gina? Or was there more? A young woman widowed twice? Could there be something, well, murderous about her? Something that complemented Mr. Henley's nature?

Suddenly Christina blinked, took her hand and squeezed tightly. "Gina, you must go home immediately. I have had the most extraordinary feeling…oh, what if you are the next to be killed?" She stood and hurried back toward the garden door. "We should not be outside."

Gina followed, curious at Christina's sudden change of mood. The moment they were inside and the door was closed, Christina turned to her, earnestness written clearly on her face. "You must listen carefully to me, Gina. About Mr. Henley. He used to watch Missy as if he wanted to seduce her. I always thought that odd—after all, he was Stanley's friend."

"I rather thought Mr. Henley wanted to seduce most every girl he met," Gina said.

Christina led the way straight through the sitting room toward the front door, leading Gina with a hand on her arm. "It occurs to me now that he may have been planning to put Mr. Booth out of the way so he could have Missy even back then. I shall send her a letter at once, but you must also warn her at the first opportunity. Come to me tomorrow. I need to think. It is all so confusing."

Gina nodded as she was fairly thrown out the door and into Nancy's waiting arms. How very astonishing!

"Did you make her angry, miss?" Nancy asked as they entered the foot traffic on the street.

Gina paused to look back at the door. A curtain moved in an upper window, as if someone had been watching her. "I must have."

They walked slowly, since Gina had no desire to return to the house where her mother would be in a frenzy of packing and making arrangements for their departure. She knew she and Nancy would have to pack the trunk that had been delivered to her room that morning, and she was surprised by her own reluctance. A month ago, she'd have given anything to be going home. But today?

Today she only wanted to enjoy the afternoon, which had turned crisp as a precursor to autumn. She wanted to think of seeing James at the family dinner Lord Lockwood was hosting to mark their departure, and the musicale after. She wanted to think of anything, in fact, but her imminent departure.

Nancy tugged at her sleeve. "Oh, miss! There's Tom, the milkman. Might I have a word with him? Who can say if I will be seeing him again?"

The lament was so akin to Gina's emotions that she could only smile and nod. An empty park bench beneath a tree offered her refuge, and she sat where she could watch her maid talk and flirt with the strapping young milkman.

She had just lulled into a pleasant lassitude when a hand on her shoulder and a voice from behind her interrupted her thoughts.

"No. Do not turn around, Miss O'Rourke. I have a knife at your back. I would hate to use it so soon. No scenes, eh?"

Everything inside her screamed with terror. Mr. Henley! She would recognize his voice anywhere now. She took several deep breaths to steady her nerves before she could speak. "What do you want?"

"I hear you may be leaving in a day or two, m'dear. Is that so?"

She nodded.

"Ah. Well, I had been putting our meeting off until a bit later, but now I think I shall have to move it up."

"You would not kill me here. I would scream. Half the park would see you and give chase."

"You underestimate me. I do not intend to kill you *here,* chit, unless you force my hand. If I wanted you dead, you would be dead. I've had more opportunities than you know. No, I only wanted to inform you that you will never be safe from me. I will have my revenge—sooner or later, here or in Belfast. I will come for you. You owe me, and I will damn well collect."

Cold anger drove her fear away. She would not be his victim yet again. She braced herself, catapulted from the bench, and spun around to face him. His look of utter amazement at her boldness was reward enough for the risk she'd taken. "Your days are numbered, Mr. Henley. You cannot elude James Hunter for long. He grows even more weary of your threats than I. Do your worst or slink back into the hole you came from."

His eyes darted right and left as if measuring his chances of killing her and escaping. "*Your* days are numbered, Miss O'Rourke. Yours and everyone who ever helped you."

She watched him run toward the street before she sank back to the bench, her knees turning to water. The moment she caught her breath, she would ask Mr. Renquist for a pocket pistol. Mr. Henley could not come for her if she went for him first.

Chapter Eighteen

Jamie watched Gina, in conversation with Sarah and the Thayer twins, across the music room at Lockwood's manor. She wore a greenish concoction that put him in the mind of spring and everything fresh and new. Her frequent glances in his direction had not gone unnoticed by Drew, who nudged him with a question.

"Are you really going to let her go back to Ireland? Have you asked her to marry you?"

He'd started to. And then she'd told him she'd only made love to him to discover if she'd been virgin or not, and *he'd* felt like a deceived maiden. Even as the hurt resurfaced, he knew he'd been an idiot, let his wounded pride get in the way. Gina would never have slept with him if she hadn't felt something.

"No," he admitted.

"Time is running out. 'Twould be a bit unfair to ask her at the docks, eh?"

"I do not know if she loves me, Drew."

His brother laughed. "Then you're deaf and blind. Charlie

told me weeks ago. I could see it the moment Mrs. O'Rourke announced her plans. In fact, everyone seems to know but you."

Gina chose that moment to look toward him and a faint smile lifted the corners of her mouth. He returned the smile and was rewarded with a soft blush. She loved him? Only two weeks ago, she had told him that he was a reminder of all that had happened to her, and that she was uncomfortable in his presence. When had that changed?

He had taken a step toward her when Drew stopped him. "You haven't said how you feel, Jamie. Do not speak for her if you cannot match her feelings."

"If she loves me half as much as I love her, I'll be content."

Gina appeared nervous when he arrived at her side and gave a small bow. "Miss O'Rourke, might I have a word with you?"

She looked askance at his sister and, at her nod, she accepted his hand. He could have sworn he detected a little tremble there. After all they'd been through, how could she possibly be afraid of him?

"I wished to speak with you, too. There are some things I must give you."

He led her to the terrace and stepped out to the balustrade, his curiosity piqued. "What things?"

"I have uncovered something new. There is a woman associated with Mr. Henley. I do not yet know how, but she is someone who has been helping him. Perhaps hiding him."

"How do you know that?"

"I...I saw a packet of letters. One of them said that the woman was working on a solution to his problem, and that he should be patient. Oh, and that she intended to meet him again at the usual place on Tuesday."

Jamie had seen that very letter just yesterday in Wycliffe's

office. It, along with several others, had been left anonymously on his desk. At this very moment, a number of agents
and runners were trying to track those letters back to their
writer. "*You* found them?"

"There is more."

Jamie sighed, not missing that she hadn't answered his
question. What was she up to?

She plucked a small folded paper from the center of her
décolletage and presented it to him. He accepted the paper,
still disconcertingly warm from her skin, unfolded it and read
the lines. "A list of names?" And a very curious list, indeed.
"Where did you get this, Gina?"

She looked at him straight on and squared her shoulders,
the endearing gesture that warned him not to ask too many
questions. "I believe that is Mr. Henley's handwriting."

Jamie would have to compare the list to other documents
in order to verify her conclusion, but he did not doubt her.
He read the names again. Booth, Metcalfe and half a dozen
others were dead. Frisk had fallen down a flight of stairs,
Destin had been run over by a coach when crossing a street,
Warren had been thrown from his horse onto the cobbles and
cracked his head. Accidents? That many coincidences were
unlikely in view of this list. Charlie had been shot last night
and, but for the grace of God, would also be dead. And then
there were the attempts on his own life.

"A murder list," he concluded.

She shivered. "That is what I feared. Charles…"

"Upstairs being coddled by every maid Lockwood employs.
He intends to break free tomorrow." And then he registered
her name on the list. Eugenia O'Rourke. Henley wanted Gina
dead. He took her arm and turned back to the house. "We
need to get you safely home and under guard."

She shrugged his hand away. "I am not going anywhere,

Jamie. One day is all I have left. Tomorrow will be my last day in London."

"You have no choice. Once I tell Wycliffe—"

"You won't tell Lord Wycliffe. Nor will you tell your brothers. Not unless you and everyone else on the list is locked away, too. Even then, I doubt it would stop Mr. Henley. He found me in the Morris garden, he found me at the theatre and he found me in the park this afternoon. He told me I was not safe, even when I return to Belfast, and that if he wanted me dead already, I would be. He promised he would come for me when he was ready. He will find me anywhere I go. I cannot hide, Jamie. So I may as well fight."

Such cold fury gripped Jamie's heart that he could happily have snapped Henley's neck like a twig. Gina's bravery was admirable and her logic was irrefutable, but both were far too dangerous.

"If it wasn't me? If it were Hortense or Harriett, would you be so unreasonable? Or would you allow them to avenge themselves?"

Damn. She was right. Hadn't he and Wycliffe allowed Bella to flirt with disaster in order to get to the bottom of the Brotherhood? And wasn't Gina every bit as determined as Bella had been? But this was Gina. *His* Gina. How could he refuse her anything she asked? "Do not leave my side, Gina. Is that understood?"

She brightened and touched his cheek. "Thank you, Jamie. You will not regret this."

"I already do."

She turned to the terrace doors, prepared to go in now that their conversation was over, but he hadn't concluded his business yet. He slipped his arm around her and pulled her against his chest. She looked surprised and not a little curious. He lifted her chin with his forefinger and kissed her plush lips with as much tenderness as he felt in his heart. And when it was done, he uttered the words he'd never thought to say to any woman.

"I love you, Gina O'Rourke. Marry me."

Her eyes widened and her mouth opened. "I...I..."

"You cannot be surprised how I feel about you, Gina. It is plain enough that all my brothers and half the ton knows."

"But you never indicated...never said...love. Why, you've never even answered my question."

"What question is that, my love?"

"Am I...was I...virgin?"

That damned question! Why wouldn't she let it go? "Take it on faith, Gina."

"Faith? But why?"

Because he did not have the answer she needed to hear, and he could not lie. There had been no telltale stain on his sheets, but that alone did not answer her question. Many women did not go to their marriage beds intact, and time, circumstance, accidents and nature could account for the lack of evidence. But, more importantly, he feared that if she believed Henley had used her while she was unconscious, she would destroy her life over it. And his.

"It doesn't matter," he said. "Leave it alone, Gina."

She looked at him with such incredulity that he wondered what he'd said wrong. She opened her mouth, then closed it to a tight line, as if talking to him would be a waste of time, then spun around and went back into the music room, leaving him there without an answer to *his* question.

Oh! That infuriating man! Why wouldn't he just say it? He would not have balked at telling her that she'd been virgin. But he hadn't, so why wouldn't he simply tell her she'd been raped—which most certainly had to be the answer. She glanced over her shoulder to see him staring after her, a look of utter astonishment on his face.

And that remarkable proposal! How she wanted to say yes! She'd marry him in an instant if she only knew that she was worthy. How could she ever answer his question unless he answered hers?

Had she not been looking over her shoulder, she would not have bumped into a beautiful girl dressed all in pale yellow—not a good color for her since her pale yellow hair faded against the backdrop. Still, nothing could have dulled her lively green eyes.

"Eugenia O'Rourke, is it not?"

"How…how did you know?"

"Why, you are all the talk of the ton."

People were gossiping about her? "What are they saying?"

"That you are the woman who has brought James Hunter to heel. If that is so, Miss O'Rourke, well done! I gather that is quite an accomplishment."

Jamie had followed her back through the doors and had gone to stand by his brothers, watching her with a brooding look.

The girl followed her gaze and raised her eyebrows. "My! That is a very dark look Mr. Hunter is giving you, Miss O'Rourke. Did you quarrel?"

She laughed. "Do you think that society will still imagine I have brought him to heel?"

"Love and hate are but two sides to the same coin." She dimpled. "I am Mrs. Huffington. Georgiana Huffington. I fear I am a virtual stranger to London and have met almost no one. I only arrived early in June."

Georgiana Huffington? Divine intervention? That was the name Christina had associated with Mr. Henley, and an opportunity not to be missed. "What a coincidence, Mrs. Huffington. We have friends in common."

"Have we? Well, I've been told London is actually a small

town dressed in city clothes. Who, might I ask, do we have in common?"

"Mr. Cyril Henley."

Mrs. Huffington's smile dropped and her face drained of color. "I...I have met the man, but I would not call him a friend."

Gina gave her a reassuring pat on her shoulder. "Have you seen him recently?"

"I saw him at a garden tea not a week ago, but we did not speak. When he saw me, he went in the other direction. I think he was not there long."

Had Mr. Henley fled because of Mrs. Huffington? "If you do not mind me asking, how did you meet?"

"A mutual friend. I met Miss Melissa Metcalfe through Harriett Thayer, and it was Miss Metcalfe who introduced me to her brother, Mr. Booth and Mr. Henley."

They had walked near the fireplace and Gina was relieved to note that they were quite alone. She had detected a note of reluctance in Mrs. Huffington's voice and did not want to risk being overheard. "Am I correct in thinking you are not pleased with the association?"

"Miss O'Rourke, I scarcely know you. I conceive we are having an unusual conversation for two women who are so recently acquainted. I am not accustomed to speaking so frankly to casual acquaintances."

"And you do not wish to speak ill of anyone, I am certain. I hope you will not think me presumptuous, but my family has had some dealings with Mr. Henley, and I would like to solicit your honest opinion."

"You would do better to ask someone more closely acquainted with him. We have only met on two occasions."

"I gather that was enough to form an opinion?"

Mrs. Huffington looked down at her feet. "Yes."

"An unsatisfactory opinion?" she guessed.

"I think, under the circumstances, I will have to trust you. If I can spare you what I suffered, I feel it is my obligation. But what I have to say is for your ears only, Miss O'Rourke, or I shall say nothing at all." Mrs. Huffington looked around, almost as if she expected to find Mr. Henley lurking nearby. Servants were placing chairs about the room in preparation for the performance and not paying the least attention to them.

Gina nodded, her heartbeat racing. If she could trust Mrs. Huffington, she could enlist her aid in locating Mr. Henley.

"I met Miss Metcalfe at a crush in early July," Mrs. Huffington began. "I recall that precisely, because I was fresh out of mourning and we had just come to town. Miss Metcalfe and her brother were part of a large group of merry-makers. They invited me to join them in an excursion to Vauxhall Gardens. Lady Caroline, my aunt, said she could see no impediment after the group was vouched for by Lord Daschel, whom she knew quite well."

Gina scarcely blinked at the mention of that loathsome name. Lord Daschel had been a founder of the Brotherhood, and responsible for seducing Cora into meeting him the night they killed her.

"We took a barge across the Thames, laughing and jesting the whole way. It was then that I met a Mr. Booth and Mr. Henley. I thought I had truly 'arrived,' if you know what I mean—terribly flattered to be a part of such a haute gathering."

A smile came to Gina's lips. She knew the feeling quite well. She, too, had wanted to belong.

Mrs. Huffington removed a lace-edged handkerchief from the little reticule dangling at her wrist and dabbed delicately at the corners of her eyes. "In the beginning, it was great fun. We danced and watched the fireworks, and then Mr. Henley brought us libation, toasting often and encouraging us to drink deeply."

Just as he'd done with Gina when they'd left the theatre and gone to another part of town for the tableaus. She recalled growing quite tipsy rather quickly, and had begged off subsequent glasses of wine. Even so, she'd been quite ill the next day.

"I began to feel fuddled," Mrs. Huffington continued. "Then Mr. Henley took my hand and asked me to walk with him. I thought there could be no harm in that and that perhaps it would clear my head. The walks were well lit and there were people all about. But we were no more than out of sight of the rest when he led me down quite another path. I learned later they call those paths 'dark walks' or 'lover's walks' because they are not lit.

"I did not grow alarmed until Mr. Henley stopped and began to press me for favors." She twisted her handkerchief as she recalled the events of that night. "Perhaps it was because I am a widow that he thought I would be receptive to such a ploy, but I demanded he stop at once. He did not. The more I struggled, the more…inflamed he became. I think…I really think, he enjoyed my terror."

Gina covered the woman's hand with her own. "You needn't continue, Mrs. Huffington. I perceive the drift of your story."

"There is more, but I have not spoken of it since that night. I have not even told Lady Caroline. I was afraid she would not trust my judgment after that."

"My experience was much the same. But we went to a tableau at a mansion somewhere in Kensington." Though she had been much more naive than Mrs. Huffington. She had gone back that second, nearly fatal, night.

Mrs. Huffington shuddered. "It was dreadful. I actually feared I would not escape with my virtue. But when he'd nearly ravished me, he stopped and said he wanted to 'save' me. Do you truly think he was remorseful and wanted to save my virtue?"

She thought it much more likely that he wanted to save Mrs. Huffington to be a victim for the ritual, for all that, as a widow, she could not be a virgin. "Did he call on you afterward? Or invite you to join his group another time?"

"Yes, but I declined to go. I have not spoken to any of them since."

"Did you know that Mr. Booth and Mr. Metcalfe are both dead?"

Her green eyes widened in astonishment. "Gracious! Were they in an accident? How perfectly dreadful. I shall have to call upon Christina tomorrow."

Gina shook her head. "No accident, I fear. I desperately need your help, Mrs. Huffington. We need to find Mr. Henley before anyone else dies."

Mrs. Huffington took two steps backward and narrowed her eyes. "I am sorry, Miss O'Rourke, but I cannot help you."

The guests began to take seats facing the pianoforte and Gina knew she would not have time to cajole Mrs. Huffington's assistance. Plain speaking would have to suffice. "Lives may hang in the balance, Mrs. Huffington."

But the lovely woman merely shook her head and backed away. "I wish you luck, Miss O'Rourke."

After the last note had been played, Jamie's attention was divided between his conversation with his brothers and watching Gina. Despite their earlier agreement, he was certain she was up to something. He had meant to leave her alone until it was time to take her and the Thayer twins home, but now he thought he would have to nip any plot Gina might be nurturing in the bud.

Marcus Wycliffe and Devlin joined their little group and Jamie only half listened to the conversation when one word caught his attention.

"Gibbons? Sorry, what did you say?"

"Artie Gibbons is dead," Wycliffe repeated.

"How?"

"Bullet," Devlin said. "I wonder if he had any last words."

Jamie nearly choked on his wine. Lilly had gone a long way in civilizing Devlin, but he was glad to see that Devlin still maintained his wry humor.

"And Dick?"

"As you might imagine," Wycliffe said.

"I might imagine nearly anything where Dick Gibbons is concerned. Either devastated and grief stricken or furious."

"Devastation would require some actual humanity."

Then it would be hell to pay for anyone Dick suspected of the deed.

"After the botched attempt on Charlie, I suspect Dick will be going after every Hunter and anyone attached to them."

"Only if Artie had something to do with the attempt on Charlie."

Devlin snorted. "If? Do cockroaches scurry from the light? Aye. Whether Artie held the gun or just stood by Dick as he pulled the trigger, the attack on Charlie was engineered by a Gibbons. Dick will make that connection."

Jamie glanced at Gina, who had wandered closer to the group, and he wondered how much she'd heard. Enough to widen her eyes, it seemed.

"I warned them that they did not want to cross a Hunter, but you know how they are…were," Devlin continued. "So blasted sure they could do whatever they pleased without consequence. They got away with everything else they've ever done, so I believe we owe our thanks to whoever pulled that trigger."

They all raised their glasses in a silent toast to one another and Jamie wondered which one of them had actually "pulled that trigger." Lockwood and Wycliffe were more than capable of it, Drew had not come to Charlie's side until this morning, and Devlin might have even considered it his duty. Hell, Jamie would have done it himself if he hadn't been keeping watch by Charlie's bedside.

He drank to Devlin's toast and then reminded them, "Alas, the job is only half done."

"Dick will be harder to kill." Drew nodded. "He'll be looking for it."

They grew thoughtful for a moment and then Wycliffe changed the subject. "I hear there is to be a tableau at Marchant's tonight."

"I know some find them entertaining, but I find them deucedly dull," Devlin said.

Lockwood placed his empty glass on a tray borne by a passing footman. "That would depend upon the subject being reenacted. A Waterloo battle scene might be amusing."

"I believe tonight's subject is great works of art."

Devlin yawned and glanced toward his wife, across the room in conversation with guests. "I think I shall find something infinitely more amusing to entertain me."

Drew laughed. "I will pass, Wycliffe, but perhaps Jamie could join you."

Jamie had his own plans, and they didn't include watching members of the ton dress up in costumes to replicate works of art on a stage. He had an idea of where he might find Henley's mystery woman. "I have to pass. Perhaps another time?"

Wycliffe chortled. "Well, if I cannot lure anyone into sharing my misery, I believe I will drop by my office to see if there is any news, then go home and make an early night of it."

Chapter Nineteen

The night had turned cold by the time Gina arrived home, escorted by Andrew and Bella instead of Jamie, who had made his apologies and then promised to come see her tomorrow afternoon. Or had he merely been trying to avoid her? Regretting his proposal?

She had waited an hour before donning her cloak and sneaking out the garden door to meet Ned. She'd overheard Lord Wycliffe's announcement of a tableau at Marchant's. A few discreet questions had revealed that this was Lord Marchant's palatial home in Mayfair, and therefore not the same location as the erotic tableau where she'd met Christina Race. But, if Mr. Henley favored tableaus, perhaps he would be there. And if he was, she would summon the authorities at once.

Ned was waiting for her, barely perceptible in the shadows of a tree partway down the street. He emerged and came to her side. "Where to t'night, Miss Gina?"

"Do you know where Lord Marchant's house is?"

"Aye, miss. Follow me, eh?"

As they rounded the corner, a dark form stepped in their way. "Oh, I do not think so," he said.

She and Ned both squeaked in fright before they realized it was Jamie standing there, apparently waiting for her.

"Oh!" she gasped. "You frightened us to death!"

He looked them up and down. "A slight exaggeration. But do not think to divert me from the point, Eugenia, which is that you were not to investigate anything unless you were at my side."

"And yet you were going out without me."

Jamie pressed his lips together and pointed at Ned. "Hie back to your crib, boy. Miss O'Rourke will not need you further tonight, or any other night, for that matter."

After a nod from Gina, Ned took off at a lope, but she knew he'd be there tomorrow night, too, if she needed him. The moment Ned was out of sight, she turned and faced Jamie.

"Where are we going, then?"

"You're going home. I suspected you were up to something, so I came by here before going about my business. Home, Gina, where you will be safe and sound."

She shook her head. "Together."

He took her arm and turned her back home. "Where I am going, no decently raised woman would go."

Decently raised? Insufferable. "Tell me."

"I am going to a gaming hell. Thackery's, to be precise. It is not the sort of place decent women go."

"Since you will not answer my question, I do not know if I am decent or not. So shall we go without further delay?"

"Gina—"

"I can guess your arguments. My reputation. My good name. My safety. But those things mean nothing if I am already ruined. And nothing in view of the fact that I am leaving England after tomorrow. Who will remember me a fortnight hence? Who will care where I went or with whom?"

"No."

"Why are you going, Jamie? For gambling? For a woman? Or on my business?"

"Henley is not just your business. He taints everything he touches, and he must be stopped."

"Then do not worry over me. I am already tainted, am I not?" Oh, those words were bitter, but they finally hung in the air between them—his to refute or not.

He looked helpless, and she knew he could not counter her argument. Instead, he pulled the hood of her cloak over her head and draped it to shield her face. "The fewer people who recognize you, Gina, the better."

His coach was waiting around the corner and he called an address to the driver and handed her in, settling himself beside her. "When we get there, Gina, try to say as little as possible. Do not speak to anyone I have not introduced you to, and keep your head down. Perhaps we will get out of this without damage."

"What is our purpose there?"

"I am hoping we can discover who Henley's mystery woman is."

"At a gambling hell?"

"This one is a bit more democratic than the others. Courtesans, the demimonde and better cyprians frequent Thackery's and mingle with the guests. More business than gambling is done above stairs. More to the point, when he was free to go about in society, Thackery's was Henley's favorite establishment. Any woman who kept his company would be familiar with the place."

Cyprians? Did he mean prostitutes? "Is it squalid?"

Jamie laughed. "Very fashionable, actually, and clean. The food and drink are a bit more than passable. Only the customers are squalid."

Gooseflesh rose on Gina's arms. They would find the woman there, she was sure of it now. "And if we find her?"

"If so, I intend to persuade her to tell us where to find him. At the very least, once we learn her identity, we can set a watch on her and she will eventually lead us to him."

Eventually. Gina did not have *eventually*. She only had tomorrow. She looked up at him and slipped her hand into his to give it a little squeeze. "You...you will write to me and let me know when he is captured, will you not?"

He gave her an infinitely sad smile. "Immediately."

She nodded her understanding and was silent for the remainder of the ride, though Jamie did not release her hand and she gathered strength from that. She wanted to feel his determination, his warmth, as long as possible.

When the coach pulled up to an indiscriminate building near St. James Street, he got out, lifted her down and adjusted her hood. "Remember, keep your head down. With luck, we shall get our answer soon and not be here long."

Inside, she allowed a footman to take her cloak, realizing she'd be conspicuous and draw more attention with it on. Jamie smiled at her, evidently approving her choice.

He led her into a large central room, a gambling salon with many tables throughout. There were cards, wheels and dice, and men clustered about to watch the play. Raucous laughter, quiet curses and the even tones of the croupiers punctuated the low tones of a three piece orchestra playing quietly in one corner.

A set of wide stairs led upward to a mezzanine that surrounded the room where men and brightly dressed women strolled, looking down on the players below. A massive chandelier that glittered with a thousand crystals hung from a gilded ceiling. Gina was ashamed to say that she was fascinated with the place. It was unlike anywhere she'd ever been—part palace, part carnival.

Jamie purchased a stack of counters and gave her a few. "If they think you are about to play, they will not bother you or make you go upstairs."

"What is upstairs?"

"A ladies' salon and a few private rooms, for those who have had too much to drink, and others who…are seeking other diversions."

She glanced upward again, looking more closely at the ladies. Some were beautiful and dressed expensively, others were a bit more worn looking, and not quite as well turned out. Cyprians. Women who sold their favors. Women she'd never thought to mingle with, but who were now more like her than not.

She glanced down at her own gown, nearly scandalous by the standards of the ton, but prim in this place. She had the sudden urge to tug her bodice a bit lower just to fit in.

"'Lo there, Hunter. This your new mistress?"

She turned to look at the man who had just addressed Jamie. He was flushed and obviously in his cups. Jamie seemed annoyed, but he forced a smile and tucked Gina a bit tighter against his side. "She is, and I'll thank you to keep your hands off her, Cavendish."

"Just in from the country, I vow. Haven't seen her before. Leave it to you to find the freshest meat, eh?"

She almost laughed when Jamie's jaw tightened.

"What's your name, poppet?"

She opened her mouth but Jamie interceded. "Mary."

"Mary? I vow 'twould be Merry if you came with me, girl. And I vow I'd make merry, as well." The man laughed with hardy enjoyment of his own joke.

Jamie didn't bother with a reply and led her toward the staircase instead. "Stay within sight of me should we get separated, Gina. I am going to talk to some of the regulars to see if Henley has been around at all, then ask who they last saw him with."

How clever. "I shall converse with some of the ladies, too," Gina said.

"Ladies?" He laughed as they began to climb. "I think you had better stay close to me, *poppet*."

And before she could catch her breath, she was in a smaller salon than the one downstairs, with softer lighting and mirrors and murals the length and width of the room. Pastoral scenes or...or...oh! Horned satyrs and naked women cavorted across the countryside and appeared to be copulating in every possible manner! Chubby-cheeked Pan-like creatures spilled wine over couples, and Gina wondered at the symbolism of such a thing until she saw one figure licking the libation off another. Her cheeks burned and she knew she was giving her naïveté away.

Jamie pressed a wineglass into her hand. "Breathe, Gina, and take a drink. It will steady your nerves."

Bringing Gina to Thackery's was a monumental mistake, but he hadn't been able to figure any way around it. He did not fool himself that he could have taken her home and she would have stayed there. Keeping his eye on her would be considerably better than letting her wander about London unprotected. He could only hope that she would go unrecognized, although, as she'd been quick to point out, she would be gone in another day.

At his side, Gina took a long drink of her wine and then smiled up at him. "I believe I am better now. Thank you."

Ah, she'd suppressed that little lilt in her voice he loved so much and that betrayed her origins. Not that it would fool anyone, but any edge she could get would make her feel better. He wanted her confident, but not too confident.

He could not help but note that she was drawing attention

from males and females alike—being sized up by her competition and being measured for pleasure by the buyers. He'd best make it clear immediately that she was spoken for, at least for this evening.

He lifted her chin with his forefinger and bent close, making his intent obvious. "Make this look good, Gina, or you will be fending off eager supplicants the rest of the evening."

She raised on her tiptoes and fit her mouth to his. Not a tender offering but a deep and passionate kiss. No man would ever mistake her intentions, and no woman, either. In fact he, who knew it to be false, was having a difficult time reminding himself that the kiss was for the benefit of the salon, and not for him.

When she slowly withdrew, he whispered, "Well done, poppet."

She chuckled at his jest and straightened his cravat just as an attentive mistress would have done. Lord! How could he leave her side long enough to ask his questions?

"Well met, Hunter. Why don't you introduce me to your new lady love?"

He turned to find Henry Lector grinning ear to ear. "I am not ready to share, Henry."

"Now, is that fair? Have you signed contracts? Is she a one-man woman?"

Gina blinked and he was afraid she'd give herself away, but when she merely tilted her head to one side and said, "One at a time, anyway," he nearly guffawed.

Lector nodded and moved away, not entirely discouraged but willing to wait his turn. But there'd never be a turn. Jamie would see to that.

One thing was clear, Gina was a distraction to his purpose. Any conversation he would have with her by his side was bound to disintegrate to a flirtation if not an outright proposition. With reluctance, he released her hand.

"Will you be all right if I talk to some of these men alone, Gina? It should only take a few minutes."

"I will sit quietly in that corner." She nodded to a far corner where a bench sat in an alcove devised for tête-à-têtes.

"I shan't be long."

He watched Gina until she had taken a seat and began studying the murals with obvious interest. With a niggling feeling that he would regret leaving her alone, he joined a group of Thackery's regulars, positioning himself so that he could keep an eye on her.

Edward Tully was the first to greet him. "Well met, Hunter. We were just talking about Charlie. Is it true?"

He nodded. "Just a scratch. He should be up and around by tomorrow."

"Catch the bloke?" Albert Howland asked.

"One of them."

"How many were there?"

"Two, we suspect. But I did not come to Thackery's to discuss my brother. I've been looking for an old friend."

Tully regarded him with a jaundiced eye. "Who would that be?"

"Cyril Henley."

Eyebrows went up at that. "Friends, eh? I'd never have figured you two would have much in common," Howland said.

"We have some friends in common. People I'd like to locate, if possible."

Tully drank from his glass before he spoke. "Haven't seen him in a couple of months."

"I did. Now, let me see. Where was that?" Howland frowned and stared at the ceiling as if he expected the answer to appear there. "Was it here, or at the Morris masquerade?

Yes, the night Stan Metcalfe was killed. He did not stay long, though. Said he had some place to be."

"Busy man," Tully said noncommittally.

Jamie was reasonably certain Tully knew more than he was saying. "Quite. Has he not been around here with his mistress?"

"Ah, yes! That's it. He was here a few nights ago. After the Morris masquerade. He and Misty. That's what he calls her. Play on words, what?"

"How so?"

"Mystery. Misty. She always wears a domino, don't y'know. We've speculated endlessly about her true identity. We gather she's from the ton, or why the domino?"

"But you haven't recognized her?"

Howland laughed. "We scarcely look above her neck since she wears her gowns so low. But I'd recognize those breasts anywhere."

Tully chortled. "Sweetest little mole just at the top of her left nipple. We've taken bets, but no one has proven yet whether that mole is the result of nature or artifice. My money is on nature."

"And mine is on artifice. There is not much natural about that saucy wench. All I can say for certain is that she is by nature a blonde." Howland drank deeply and winked.

Blonde? Hell, he knew half a dozen blondes who'd known Henley. That was not much help. But Misty? Damn! There was something pricking the back of his mind. The description, vague though it was, sounded familiar.

Subtle questioning of a few more men confirmed Tully and Howland's information. Misty, whoever she was, was a favorite of the men. She asked nothing of them but their attention and was generous with the views she provided to one and all, and generous in more ways to a few; she had been known to go to a room with other men if Henley was not available.

He could not imagine Gina behaving in such a manner. He turned to check on her and groaned. He'd almost rather have found her talking to a man than his former mistress.

"So you are our Jamie's newest obsession, eh?"

Gina turned from her study of the mural and smiled at the beautiful Frenchwoman. She wasn't certain what to say. *Our* Jamie's newest obsession? Did he patronize all the women of Thackery's?

"We could 'ardly miss that kiss, mademoiselle. That is unlike 'im—to show public affection. 'E must think you are very special, eh?"

The thought warmed her. She shrugged. "Perhaps."

"Your name, mademoiselle?"

"Mary. And yours?"

"Suzette. Ah, do not worry over me. I am Charlie's now."

Good heavens! Did the Hunter brothers share their...cyprians? "I am not certain if I am Jamie's or not."

"'E 'as not made up 'is mind? Well, do not fret, little Mary. Even if it is only for tonight, 'e is most generous." Her delicate hand went to her throat and she flicked a diamond and sapphire necklace there. "'E gave me this at our parting."

Uncertain what to say, she ventured, "I am sorry."

Suzette laughed, a musical trilling sound. "No need, Mary. It is the nature of our profession, yes? A man grows bored, a man moves on. I would 'ave missed 'im more if 'is brother was not as good."

"Charlie gives you good gifts, too?"

The girl laughed again. "La! You are most amusing, Mary. But I 'ave come to ask if Jamie 'as mentioned Charlie. I wish to go see 'im, but I think Lockwood would not admit me to 'is 'ouse."

"Oh, of course. Charlie is quite well, I believe. I recall that

Jamie mentioned he would be up and around tomorrow. He is weak, but otherwise well."

"So well informed? Well, I am glad to 'ear it. If Charlie is weak, I shall be 'appy to do all the work." She laughed again. "Quite 'appy, *n'est-ce pas?* Though 'is skill is greater than my own. A skill as great as our Jamie, eh?"

Gina was certain she had missed something. She was about to ask for an explanation when Jamie arrived before them.

"Suzette," he greeted her. "I see you have met Mary."

"She is so precious, Jamie. I am impressed. I would not 'ave thought you would be amused by such…innocence."

Ah, it was an insult! She eyed Suzette and stood, taking Jamie's offered hand. "Oh, but I was not worried over you at all, Suzette. In fact, Jamie has never even mentioned you."

Suzette's eyes narrowed.

Jamie gave just the slightest bow as he turned her away.

"Really," she said under her breath. "You might have warned me I'd be running into your cyprians."

He laughed. "Suzette is my former mistress. I do not frequent cyprians."

"And you've passed her on to your brother. Is it a family thing?"

This time he guffawed. "'Tis only polite. Suzette has… skills."

"Odd. She said the same of you."

They had reached the top of the stairs and taken no more than two steps downward when Jamie halted at the sound of greetings from below. "Bloody hell!"

He spun her around and topped the stairs, then turned her down a corridor past the salon.

"What—"

"It's Gilbert Sayles and his friends. Lady Annica's cousin? You danced with him at your first ball. He was smitten, Gina. He will recognize you."

He threw a door open at the end of the corridor and she hurried in, dreading the thought that she might shame Lady Annica by her presence here.

Even the solid click of the door closing and locking could not pull her away from the vision in front of her. A single candle burned by a lavish bed, but the light of the single flame was reflected in what seemed to be a thousand mirrors. The walls were lined with them, and even the ceiling over the bed bore one. The draperies and bed hangings were either purple or deep violet—she could not tell which in the flickering shadows. But one thing was certain. This was a room made for illicit assignations.

"Sorry," Jamie said. "We will have to wait him out."

A carafe and glasses waited on one bedside table. Jamie poured himself a little and tasted it. "Brandy," he said.

She nodded. "Just a bit."

As she watched him pour measures into two glasses and bring one to her, she noted how interesting it was to see him from both sides. The mirrors were truly amazing. Had she ever noticed the tight curve of his buttocks before? The lean strength of his legs? The broad set of his shoulders? Had she been blind?

She took the glass from him and lifted it in a silent toast. "Will you have to pay for the room now that we've availed ourselves of the amenities?"

He grinned. "Should I have let you run headlong into Gilbert?"

She shook her head, thinking of her own tarnished condition amid cyprians and mistresses. "I think I am where I am supposed to be." She was certainly where she *wanted* to be. Here. With Jamie. For whatever time they had left together.

His expression turned serious. "Gina…"

Tonight. That was all she had. Tonight. And then there

would be no more Jamie. No more tenderness and soft sighs. No more honesty.

But there was still tonight.

Chapter Twenty

The raw emotion in Gina's eyes took his breath away. She wanted him. Could he take her tonight and let her go tomorrow? Could he leave now, never to make love to her again? No, he couldn't. A paradox. A riddle with no answer. He could only stand there, waiting. Wanting. Praying.

She took a step toward him and he started breathing again. When she entered his arms and he closed them about her, he felt whole. As if he held all that mattered in the world. And when she lifted her lips to his, he took them as they'd been offered—completely, sincerely, with a raw truth that humbled him.

He fumbled with her clothing as they kissed, undoing her gown quickly, but slowed by the corset laces. He did not take the time to unfasten them entirely, just loosen them enough to push the offending corset and chemise down over her hips, leaving her in only her white stockings and slippers. He carried her to the bed and threw the coverlet back, wanting to see her against the crisp linens, but she dragged him with her, her fingers working the knots of his cravat. He tossed her slippers over his shoulder but decided to leave the silk stockings as an erotic reminder of the sensuous nature of their encounter. His jacket, his waistcoat, his shirt, boots, breeches and drawers were quickly shed, and he lay on the bed beside her.

Her hair had come undone, tangling around her shoulders like a dark mantle. Her cheeks were flushed with the heat of her passion, and he loved her as much for that as anything. That she wanted him so desperately in this way was immensely satisfying. That she would give herself over to his handling was a sacred trust.

Tonight he would love her as she deserved.

He kissed her deeply, sighing when she invited him in with her tongue and her soft little moans. Oh, God, the sounds she made when he did something new—found a tender spot or deepened a caress—inflamed him, and he used them as a guide to her pleasure. He took his time, cherishing every moment.

When she could scarcely breathe, he left her mouth to kiss his way down to her breasts and cherish them both by turns. Her ripe, berrylike nipples were sweet on his tongue, teasing him, promising him delights to come, and he took them greedily.

He could read her heightened state of arousal in her rapid breathing and the restless way she arched to him. She would need release soon or he would lose her to the darkness of the other side of passion—pure lust without the refinement of love. His own need was mounting with alarming intensity, but he could not slake it at her expense. He pushed it back with all the determination he had, knowing the reward would be everything he wanted.

The woman-scent of her refused denial and he trailed his tongue lower, lower, still lower, until he found that other berry that pulsed against his tongue and told him that she was his for as long as he could hold her on the razor edge of release—not completely there, but on the brink. He knew how much pressure she would need, and the precise moment to apply it, but kept her keening for that release, denying it to intensify it when he granted it. She was like wildfire, burning hot and fast. For him. Only for him.

"Please...please...please..." she chanted.

And still he waited, savoring the sweet-salty taste of her, the scent that aroused something bone-deep in him, a primitive need.

She curled upward, her fingernails biting into his shoulders to drag him over her, to force him into her, but he pushed her back. Soon. A moment more. Just one moment more...

And there it was—the gasp and catch in her breathing that told him she was seconds from swooning. He flicked his tongue and pressed firmly as she arched, her head thrown back as the first shock wave crested. He rose above her and thrust deeply, entering her at the precise moment her climax began, and she screamed with the pure ecstasy of it. She was new to this depth of eroticism, but she had mastered it quickly.

She was snug and tight, her inner muscles rippling and tightening around his shaft in a slow, deep roll that drew a growl of primordial pleasure. But he was not quite done. He carried her along to another climax when her body gripped him as he thrust again and again, deeper and faster until his own release mingled with hers. The world spun out of control, blocking reason and thought. All that existed was pleasure, pure and primal.

Translucent tears trickled from the corners of her eyes as the storm passed and he came back to the moment. And to her. She was glorious, the most arousing thing he'd ever seen, and he loved her as he'd never thought he'd love anyone or anything.

She reached up to touch his face and trace the line of his

jaw as he hovered over her. "Ah, Jamie. I have no words to express…"

There was passion written in her every touch and sigh, speaking what she could not. Still rooted within her, he grew hard again at the vision of her beneath him. When she felt his quickening, she smiled and stretched her arms above her head, opening herself to him and giving him the gift of her trust.

The gift humbled him and he vowed to cherish it. He returned her smile even as he accepted her invitation, moving again, building her arousal with a patience born of self-denial. Oh, she had much to learn about the depth of a man's passion, and he was committed to teaching her.

Gina looked around at the ruins of her room. Open trunks, a wooden crate, boxes and tissue were scattered everywhere. She scarcely knew where to begin, and Nancy was too busy helping Mama to spare a moment for her.

And, oh, she did not want to be leaving so soon. She had too many reasons to stay in London now. And one reason greater than all the rest. James Hunter. Her knees grew weak just thinking of the things he'd done last night. Things she'd never imagined in her wickedest, wildest dreams. Things that left her trembling and sated and exhausted today. And, yes, things she wanted to do again and again. But only with Jamie, and therein lay the problem.

After today, she would not have Jamie in her life. He wanted her, but not enough to answer her question. And with that uncertainty always hanging in the air between them, she knew she could not build a life with him.

But they still had tonight, and she would not squander that. If he would not take her to his flat, she would go back to Thackery's with him and race for the dock in the morning.

"And this is what you get for waiting so long to pack, miss," Nancy told her as she stood at Gina's bedroom door.

She looked at the mound of gowns laying across her bed. "I cannot pack the French-blue gown, Nancy. It is my favorite, and I think I will wear it again tonight. Heaven only knows when I will find a chance to wear it in Belfast."

"And that's another thing, Miss. You ought not to be going out tonight. Mrs. O'Rourke arranged for a coach to be here before dawn to take us to the dock. Why, you'll barely be home and changed by the time we'll have to leave."

There would be sufficient time for her to sleep on the ship, but tonight would be her last chance to see Jamie. Her last chance to tell Hortense and Harriett how much they meant to her, and to thank the ladies of the Wednesday League for their help, and for carrying on once she was gone. Yes, tonight would be her final farewell to what might have been. And to Jamie.

She shook her head. "Ought or not, I am going. There are people I need to see and say goodbye to, and there is no purpose to me pacing in my bedroom."

Nancy shrugged. "I would think you would want to say your goodbyes to your sisters, miss."

"They will be at Lady Sarah's crush tonight. The guest list is quite large, so please do not wait up for me, Nancy. I may be dancing 'til dawn." Oh, what an accomplished liar she was turning out to be.

Nancy harrumphed. "Your mother says she wants you home before midnight."

"Midnight? But I cannot possibly be home so soon."

"The boat leaves at dawn, miss. You'd be boarding in your ball gown."

Her stomach knotted as she pictured herself standing on a deck waving goodbye to her sisters and Jamie. Pictured leaving everything and everyone she loved behind.

"Then...then a ball gown it shall have to be," she said.

"I am sorry, miss, but you know your mother will be having apoplexy if you are not home by midnight. Because of what happened to Miss Cora, I would not put it past her to alert the night watch if you are not." Nancy closed the door behind her with a note of finality.

Midnight! Too soon! Why did Mama have to choose today to care when she came in? There would be no time to tryst with Jamie. No time to say a proper farewell or to hoard memories for the lonely days ahead.

She stubbed her toe on the little carved box peeking out from under her bed and stared. How had she forgotten? Henley. She knelt and opened the lid. There, just as she'd left them, the key, the packet of opium and the pocket pistol she'd borrowed from Mr. Renquist lay secreted.

Here, at least, was something she *could* do. Her last chance to find Mr. Henley.

Gina, dressed in the seductive French-blue gown, stood in conversation with her friends, smiling and laughing as if nothing else mattered. As if *he* did not matter. They hadn't been able to find a moment alone since he'd called for her earlier this evening and found Hortense and Harriet waiting with her. Had she engineered that?

Perhaps she'd been right not to trust him alone with her. Even standing across a room, his body responded to the memory of her beneath him, twisting with passion, tangled in the sheets, gripping him and holding him inside her, calling his name. He could not conceive that this night would be the end of it all. He needed her like he needed air to breathe. She was more potent than whiskey and coursed through his veins like thick, raw honey.

"Good God, Hunter!" Marcus Wycliffe said. "That hot

look could melt glaciers. Have a care if you do not want the entire ton to know what you are thinking."

"Blast the ton," he muttered.

"Is it true? She's leaving in the morning?"

"Less than twelve hours." He glanced at the tall case clock in one corner as it struck ten. "By my reckoning, eight."

"And you've not spoken for her?"

"Oh, I've spoken. She will not have me."

Wycliffe made a sound that was suspiciously like a laugh. "What of your formidable powers of persuasion?"

"She wants an answer...a truth...I cannot give her."

"Ah, yes. And the truth is everything to you, is it not?"

Everything? More than Gina? More than love? Or were Gina and love the only truth that mattered? "It has always been my bulwark," he admitted.

"I hope it will comfort you when she is gone," Wycliffe said.

He was growing tired of hearing that. Did they think he did not dread it—his brothers and Wycliffe? "Is that what you came to talk about, Wycliffe? Or was there something else?"

"Ah, yes. Dick Gibbons."

"Have you brought him in?"

"He's gone to ground. No one has seen him since Artie was killed. No funeral arrangements, nothing. I cannot decide if he simply does not care or if his brother's body and a decent burial means nothing to him. Only animals walk away from their dead, but I doubt Dick is any better than that."

"So now what?"

"I want you on the case. If anyone can find him, you can."

"Ask Devlin. He's got eyes everywhere."

"Jamie, since you're so fond of the truth, do you know who got to Artie?"

He grinned. Wycliffe suspected Devlin. "What makes you think I know?"

"A bit too coincidental, don't you think, that Charlie was shot and not twenty-four hours later, a Gibbons turns up dead."

"It could have been any of us," Jamie admitted. "But you chose Devlin because he has the ruthlessness for a cold kill. If I knew, I wouldn't lie about it, but I wouldn't tell you, either. Whoever killed Artie Gibbons did London a favor."

Wycliffe crossed his arms across his chest. Jamie knew the man was pragmatic enough to realize that what Jamie said was right. But he would also be concerned about any of his operatives who might have overreached the law by taking matters into their own hands.

"It wasn't you, Jamie. You stayed by Charlie's bedside all night. Where were Lockwood and Drew?"

"I must assume they were having brandy in Lockwood's library, assuming that I was at Charlie's bedside."

Wycliffe gave him a long look and then nodded. The matter was closed and he changed the subject. "Give me the name of Mrs. O'Rourke's ship and I'll find a reason to hold it in harbor. Will a week be enough to change Miss Eugenia's mind?"

"Thank you, Marcus, but no. I've already used my best argument. If I couldn't sway her with that, I can't imagine what else I could do." Jamie sighed and slapped him on the back.

Perhaps one last try? He approached her group and greeted the ladies, then requested a dance. Gina placed her hand in his as he led her toward the dance floor. "You are well, I trust?" he asked.

The color in her face heightened. "Tolerable."

He laughed. "Only tolerable? If I recall, you were doing quite well last night."

She smiled shyly. "Actually, I have a small ache…"

Of course she did. He'd been an idiot not to realize she would. Considering the extent of their activity, a small ache was likely an understatement. "I'm sorry. Unaccustomed muscles. 'Twill pass, and quickly, I think. Is it of consequence enough that you would prefer not to dance?"

"A stroll in your sister's gardens might suit me better."

Suit him better, as well. He would prefer to have her to himself. He led her out the terrace doors and she shivered in the night air. He began to shrug out of his jacket but she waved it away, so he slipped his arm around her instead and she nestled against his side. "Will you meet me later, Gina?"

Her pause was so long that he knew it would be a refusal. "Mother expects me home by midnight. We leave at dawn."

He stopped by a fading rosebush. "Can I not persuade you to stay?"

"The cost would be too great."

That question. That damned question that had ruined more than Gina's pride. She would have to give it up, or he would have to destroy her with an inconvenient truth. And neither of them could compromise without denying who they were. He turned her in his arms and leaned down to place a kiss on her lips, still swollen from last night.

"Faith," he whispered against those dewy petals. "Can you not find a little faith?"

"No more than you can lie."

Why did she have to be so blasted stubborn? Would she really throw everything good away for the sake of a single forgotten moment? Was her pride—or whatever it was that drove her—more important than her future? Than him?

He tamped down hard on his rising anger and tried to reason with her. "And if you should find yourself back in Belfast with a growing belly?"

By her look of surprise, he gathered she had not thought of such an eventuality. "I... Surely not."

As for him, he had no intention of fathering a bastard. "You would not be the first woman to be surprised by such an event, Gina. A hasty marriage two or three months from now would have society counting the arrival of our first-born on their fingers. Is that what you want?"

"No, but…I did not mean for any of this to happen. What we did—" She stopped to sigh and start again. "My mother has already lost one daughter forever, and two to marriage. All she wants is to go home. I cannot delay her further."

"If your mind is made up, Eugenia, I will not beg. But, should I find out in the future that you have given birth and not given me the chance to make it right, there will be hell to pay." He took her elbow and led her back to the ballroom. He had to control his anger before he said something he would regret, but with her name on Henley's list, he could not leave her where she was vulnerable. Once inside, he gave her a formal bow and left her.

Chapter Twenty-One

Gina wavered between grief and anger. How could she leave Jamie? How could she stay if he would not answer her? His stubborn refusal to say the words that would end her agony of uncertainty infuriated her because, without that answer, she was surely leaving on that ship in the morning. And now she could only watch him join his brothers across the room and feel the emptiness of her life.

And his threat! *Should I find out in the future that you have given birth and not given me the chance to make it right, there will be hell to pay.* Hell to pay? Absurd. But then she realized her hand had gone to cover her belly without her realizing it. Oh, she could not think about that now.

The weight of the pistol in the pockets beneath her gown and the key tied to her corset strings reminded her what she had to do. Tonight was her last chance to find justice for Cora. And for herself.

"You are looking quite thunderous, Miss O'Rourke."

She turned to find Georgiana Huffington standing beside

her and forced a smile. "Really? I was only thinking of all I have yet to do before I can leave tomorrow."

"I wish we had met sooner, Miss O'Rourke. I think we might have been friends. As it is, we shall have to be content with friends in common. I called upon Christina Race today. I wished to condole with her over the loss of her fiancé. Mourning is something I have had a fair amount of experience with."

"Did you find her well?"

"Melancholy, but fit enough. She gave me a message for you." The woman handed her a folded paper.

Her curiosity was piqued. "Will you excuse me a moment, Mrs. Huffington?" She did not wait for a reply before she unfolded the page and scanned the lines, barely pausing to note that it had not been sealed.

My dear Eugenia,

After considerable introspection, I have come to believe that Stanley would not have wanted me to keep his secret in view of what has transpired over the last several days. For better or worse, you should know, though what you will make of it, I cannot say.

The night of his death, Stanley confessed to me that he had participated in Mr. Henley's rituals. His guilt over that troubled him more than he could express. He wanted to make amends, but did not know how without bringing his family shame. Perhaps the following will help you find the answers you seek and make whatever amends are possible.

Stanley was terribly concerned regarding his sister, Missy. Despite her flirtation with Mr. Booth, Stanley believed she had formed an "unhealthy" friendship with Mr. Henley. It was, in fact, Stanley's belief that she and Mr. Henley had become lovers, and that Mr. Henley was wielding undue influence over her. If she is, indeed, close to Mr. Henley, perhaps she will be able to answer your questions.

I am, as always, your staunch friend,
Miss Christina Race

Gina's head spun. Missy Metcalfe? She did not particularly like the girl, but could Missy have fallen for Mr. Henley's superficial charm? Been so deeply under his spell that she had lost all restraint and good judgment?

Mrs. Huffington placed her hand on Gina's arm. "Are you well, Miss O'Rourke? You've gone quite pale."

"Yes. Yes, I am fine. I must thank you for bringing this to me so promptly. I may yet be able to use it."

The woman blushed. "I confess I read it. My curious nature is my greatest failing. I do not know what any of it means, but I fear it could mean danger for you."

Gina shrugged. There was only one way to find that out. She gathered reassurance from the weight of the pistol in her pocket. "I must speak to Miss Metcalfe at once. Do you know where she lives?"

Mrs. Huffington's green eyes widened. "Is that wise, Miss O'Rourke? Surely, in view of Christina's letter—"

"I really have no choice, Mrs. Huffington. She may be the only one who can help me find the answer to a question."

The woman seemed to consider this for a moment, and then made a decision. "I saw Missy here earlier. Shockingly, I have seen her at other fetes since her brother's death. I do not know what she is after, but she makes me very nervous, indeed."

"Here? Where?"

"In the gardens. As if she were waiting for someone."

Gina glanced at the terrace doors. Did her answer lie on

the other side? She had taken several steps in that direction when Mrs. Huffington halted her with a hand on her arm.

"Oh, please, Miss O'Rourke, I do not think this is wise."

Most likely not, but how long could it take to wheedle an answer from Missy Metcalfe? "If I have not come back inside within half an hour, please inform Mr. James Hunter of what I've done."

Mrs. Huffington watched her leave, a worried look on her face. As Gina turned to close the terrace doors behind her, the girl was already turning to Jamie. Pray she did not tell him soon enough to frighten Miss Metcalfe off before she'd gotten the information she needed.

Quite alone on the terrace, she went the few steps down into the garden, shivering in the cold and wondering if Missy might have watched her and James kiss earlier. She strolled conspicuously down the center path to a fountain, then sat on the edge, contemplating the various paths that converged there.

The rustle of skirts alerted her and she looked around to the path behind her and schooled her face to unconcern. Yes. It was Missy, cloaked in mourning black. "Good evening, Miss Metcalfe."

"As I live and breathe, Miss O'Rourke. What are you doing alone in the garden?"

"Thinking of you, actually. I was just given a letter from Miss Race, explaining that you might be able to help me."

The light from a nearby lantern fell on Missy's face as she sat beside Gina. She was undeniably beautiful, but there was something secretive in her smile. "I shall be pleased to help you in any way you require, Miss O'Rourke."

"Excellent. Then can you tell me where I might be able to find Mr. Henley?"

"La! How should I know that?"

"Miss Race said you knew him quite well."

"Did she? Then I am amazed she has not asked me. Why, just this afternoon when we had tea, she told me she had a message for you and asked if I would deliver it."

Gina could not hide her surprise at this. Two messages from Christina? "Do you have it with you?"

"She would not trust it to be written, but bade me deliver it in person. That is the reason I am here. I pray I am not too late."

"Too late for what?"

"Why, to warn you against Mrs. Huffington."

How very curious! "Does she mean me some harm?"

Missy stood and took Gina's hand, drawing her to her feet. "Christina did not know for certain, but she felt you should not trust her. She said that Mrs. Huffington is...well, *involved* with Mr. Henley, and that you have been looking for him. She seemed to be concerned that you might believe lies the woman might tell. Has she talked to you, Miss O'Rourke? Told you anything that you might find difficult to believe?"

Mrs. Huffington? Involved with Mr. Henley? Could it be possible? She proceeded cautiously. "We exchanged pleasantries. No more."

Missy sighed. "Thank heavens she has not filled your head with falsehoods."

"What could she possibly say? And why would she want to mislead me?"

"Who knows, Miss O'Rourke. 'Tis rumored she had something to do with her husbands' demises. And the woman is an incorrigible liar. Perhaps she is trying to protect Mr. Henley. But what Christina told you is true—I may know how to find Mr. Henley."

Gina's heart beat so rapidly that she feared it might beat out of her chest. She squeezed Missy's hand. "Now? Could you tell me where he is now?"

"Perhaps we could find him if we leave immediately."

"I shall just fetch my cloak and—"

"No time. We must hurry if we are to catch him. 'Tis now or never, Miss O'Rourke."

"But where is he?"

"There are several places he might be."

Was Missy the liar? Or Georgiana Huffington? Or could Christina, herself, have misled her in both directions?

"Are you coming, Miss O'Rourke?"

'Tis now or never, Miss O'Rourke....

"How long ago?"

"I... Half an hour. She said to wait half an hour before telling you."

Jamie cursed and raked his fingers through his hair. He wanted to shake Mrs. Huffington, but she couldn't have known the danger Gina was in. "Did she say where they might have gone?"

"No. I brought a letter to her from Miss Race. She read it, and when I mentioned Missy Metcalfe was in the garden, she went there immediately. I was to tell you only if she hadn't come back within half an hour. Before I came to you, I looked outside, Mr. Hunter, and neither of them were in the garden."

"Thank you, Mrs. Huffington. If you will excuse me." He bowed and went to the foyer, signaling Wycliffe along the way. The footman brought their coats and Jamie waited until they had entered the street before he spoke.

"Miss O'Rourke has gone missing."

Wycliffe's eyebrows shot up to his hairline. "You jest."

Jamie did not deign to answer what was surely a rhetorical question. "The question is where she has got to."

"Ideas?"

"A few. First, we shall call on Miss Race."

"Christina Race? What has she to do with all this?"

"Likely nothing beyond her connection to Stanley Metcalfe. But Mrs. Huffington said she'd given Gina a note from Miss Race, and Gina had gone off to the garden almost immediately. Something is afoot, Marcus. She was angry with me, but I don't think she'd have gone with Missy unless she thought she had matters well in hand. I'm hoping Miss Race will know where they might have gone."

"Give me time to summon the watch."

"To hell with the watch. Get Devlin and my brothers. Catch up with me at Miss Race's."

She'd known before they arrived where they were going. There it was, rising out of the fog. The Ballinger estate, the spire of its eerie chapel rising like a stake from the heart of the grounds. The very place she'd been going to come tonight with her little key after everyone had retired.

Would she find, at last, the door it opened? Missy guided her through the iron gate and to a path that curved around the house and led to the chapel.

The pistol in the pocket that lay against Gina's thigh comforted her. "Do you think he's here?"

"If he is not here now, he will come soon. He… Christina said this is his favorite place."

She shivered with more than the cold. Christina, indeed! Henley loved this place because it was the scene of all his debaucheries. The scene of her disgrace. Her hand went to her throat as she paused at the chapel door.

"Come, Gina. It will be warmer inside," Missy cajoled.

She stepped into a small vestibule, waiting for a memory or a feeling of familiarity, but nothing came. She must have been unconscious or heavily drugged when she'd been brought here.

Missy lit a candle, opened another door and nodded for

Gina to precede her into the vestry. Black cowls hung on pegs and were scattered on the floor, and an overturned bench gave testament to the chaos of that long-ago night.

A bone-deep chill seeped through her. Anxious to dispel the aura of evil, she passed through the vestry to the nave. A barren altar lay ahead of her, and in front of that, a red rug thrown back from an open trapdoor.

Her stomach clenched. Though she had no memory of it, she knew she had been carried down those wooden steps into the inky darkness below. She slipped her hand into the slit in her seam to accommodate the pocket and gripped the handle of the pistol, taking comfort from the fact that, this time, she was prepared to defend herself.

Missy passed her and opened a door behind the altar—the sacristy, where vestments and sacred vessels were kept. She retrieved a pewter chalice and a bottle of sacramental wine. "I am parched, Gina. Mr. Henley is obviously not here yet. Shall we have a sip of communion wine?" She giggled as she poured the wine into the chalice.

Gina looked down into the chamber beneath the trap door. "Are you certain he is not here? He could be down there."

"Nonsense. Had he heard us, he would have come up. We shall have time for a drink before we go below to wait for him."

"How will he know to look for us there?"

"He… I have heard he lives down there." She busied herself placing the chalice on the altar and pouring a generous measure of wine into it.

The list Mr. Renquist had found! *Candles, tinderbox, blanket, wine.* They'd suspected Mr. Henley was setting up new quarters, and so he had. Ah, but Missy had known it, too. And now Gina knew what she had to do.

* * *

Miss Race entered her sitting room, a look of astonishment on her pretty face and her parents behind her. "Mr. Hunter, Lord Wycliffe. What… How can I help you?"

Jamie wondered how much her parents knew about the events that had led them there. He had no wish to cause trouble for her, but he needed information quickly. No time to cozen or cajole. "Miss O'Rourke is missing, Miss Race. Do you have any idea where she might be?"

Her dark eyes widened and her hand went to her heart. "No! Oh, I pray he has not got her."

"Who, Miss Race?" Wycliffe asked.

"Mr. Henley, of course. She was looking for him, but I have prayed that she would not find him. It can mean nothing but trouble for her if she does. Stanley said…"

Jamie remembered the list of names in Henley's writing and finished for her. "He said Miss O'Rourke was in grave danger, did he not?"

Miss Race nodded. "Stanley said Mr. Henley considered her 'unfinished business.'"

"Do you have any idea where he might have gone? Where she might have followed him?"

"I fear not. She called upon me yesterday, and I thought she was going back to Ireland. When Georgiana called today, she did not mention her. Well, but I asked Georgie to give Miss O'Rourke a message for me."

Jamie tamed his sense of urgency. "What did it say?"

Miss Race blushed and glanced over her shoulder at her mother and father, then squared her shoulders in a way so like Gina that his heart twisted. "I told her that Stanley and I believed that Missy had become Mr. Henley's secret lover, and that perhaps Missy would have the answers Gina so desperately needed."

So desperately that she'd risk her life. He'd been a bloody

fool to think he could spare her that pain. If only he'd had the sense to answer her question, perhaps she'd be safe in his arms this very minute. But then he realized that answer alone would never have been enough. She'd wanted justice for her sister, as well.

He sighed deeply. "Is that all, Miss Race?"

"Yes."

"Thank you," Wycliffe said as they turned to go. "Sorry for the interruption of your evening."

Miss Race followed them to the door, and placed her hand on Jamie's sleeve. She lowered her voice to a whisper. "Missy came to call today, too. She asked ever so many questions about Gina—where she was going to be tonight, when she was leaving for Ireland, that sort of thing. I did not think much about it then, but…I wonder if she had something to do with Gina's disappearance."

Hell yes. "If she did, Miss Race, do you have any idea where she might have taken Gina?"

"No. But I keep thinking of what Stanley said about unfinished business. What do you suppose Mr. Henley wants with her?"

Unfinished business? And then it all fell into place. Where else would Henley conduct his lethal business? He leaned down and gave Miss Race a quick kiss on the cheek. "Thank you, Miss Race."

Missy swirled the wine in the chalice. "I think it is a bit stale," she said as she offered the untasted cup.

Gina closed her fingers around the folded packet in her pocket as she lifted the cup to her lips with her other hand. She pretended to drink and then jumped, as if something had startled her. "What was that?"

Missy frowned. "What?"

"I thought I heard something. In the vestry."

A tiny uplift at the corners of Missy's mouth betrayed her. "I shall see if anyone is here. Meanwhile, drink up, Gina."

How foolish did Missy think she was? The minute she started for the vestry, Gina poured the contents of the chalice down the trapdoor and quickly dumped the packet of coarse powder into it. When Missy turned back, she lifted the chalice again and tipped it up as if finishing the last drop, then managed a look of chagrin.

"Oh, sorry. I drank it all. My thirst was greater than I thought, and you were right—the wine has turned. Quite fusty and bitter, but still drinkable." She went to the altar and poured more wine into the chalice before handing it to Missy.

Missy hesitated as she looked down into the cup. "There is likely more wine below."

"It is not that bad. Surely you will not make me drink alone."

Missy shrugged and took a deep drink, making a face when she was done. "Ugh. Quite nasty. That should teach Henley to leave bottles lying about."

Gina breathed easier. She wondered how long it would take for the drug to have an effect.

"Shall we go down?" Missy asked, taking the candlestick and joining her by the trapdoor.

Praying she wouldn't slip on the spilt wine, Gina began to descend the uneven stone steps. She could smell the spilt wine, but couldn't see it. Then other odors assailed her—dust, damp and faint traces of pungent incense—teasing the back of her mind, awakening the dim impression of foreign sensations.

At the bottom of the stairs, she found herself in a narrow antechamber with a small closed door to her right. The first uneasy stirrings of actual memories began to wrap their tendrils around her. Ahead lay an arched opening, and she had a vague memory of a crypt beyond.

Behind her, Missy stumbled, caught herself by leaning against the stone wall and giggled. "Clumsy me. The wine must have gone straight to my head."

Gina hoped something had, though she guessed it would be the contents of that packet. "Here, let me help you," she said, taking the candlestick from Missy before she could drop it and plunge the antechamber into darkness.

"You? Help me?" Another giggle.

"Sit, Missy, before you fall."

"What're you say…say…saying?"

"If my experience bears out, Missy, you are about to have a nice long nap."

Missy's blue eyes widened with disbelief. "You…you… tricked me."

"Yes, I did. Now sit down before you fall and crack your head."

Missy sat with a soft thump. "He'll kill you…for this."

Or for any number of things, she supposed. For exposing him. For escaping him. For hunting him down. It didn't matter why, because it didn't change the facts. And he wasn't going to kill her. Quite the opposite.

Missy's heavy sigh told her the girl had surrendered to the drug. She wondered how long she had before Mr. Henley would appear. She would have to work fast.

She tried the latch to the side door. Locked. Of course it was. She reached inside her décolletage and plucked her corset string, pulling upward until the key appeared. She fit it to the lock and turned. The door swung open with a faint creak.

She could not seem to make herself take that first step over the threshold, so she held the candle high to illuminate the room. It was the room in her dreams—though small, the dark stone walls seemed to swallow the light. A cot stood in the center of the room and there was an empty sconce that would have held a torch. A cup lay overturned on the floor, and crumpled in one corner was the pink gown Gina had worn to meet Mr. Henley that night.

It was true, then. All of those vague impressions, those demivisions were true. She'd been drugged and stripped here, and dressed in that filmy thing that had been removed at the altar.

And more. The hands touching her, anointing her with some sort of oil. She remembered Mr. Henley's face, leering down at her, leaning over her and saying something that still eluded her. And…and Missy, shrouded in one of the dark cowls, her eyes glittering with excitement.

And, still, the answer to her question eluded her.

Any remaining scruples she'd had about drugging Missy disappeared in the midst of those memories. She closed the door but did not lock it. There was nothing there to frighten her anymore. She paused to check on Missy's breathing before squaring her shoulders and passing under the arched opening to the crypt.

The evil in that chamber struck her like an open hand. Gooseflesh rose on her arms and raised the fine hairs on the back of her neck. She touched her candle to an unlit torch in a sconce by the entry and the room danced to life in the flickering light. Each stark detail had been etched on her mind, just waiting for the right stimulus to bring it back in its full horror.

A row of vaults bearing past generations of Ballingers was set into the stone walls, and she wondered what they might have thought of the way their final resting place had been desecrated. A brazier was tipped over and long-dead coals lay scattered on the floor. Everywhere, the scent of cloying incense had permeated the stones and now bled out measured doses into the air.

Gina gagged, the odor pulling her deeper into her memories. She spun around, finding the stone altar, a pagan symbol rising behind it. She thought of Cora, splayed on that altar, her blood staining the stone beneath her. Was it still there? Cora's blood? Her blood?

Fascination drew her to that slab, and she found dark stains upon it. Bile rose in her throat and she grew dizzy. The scar on her neck throbbed as if the dagger had only now pierced her. Her hands flat on the altar, she braced herself until the waves of nausea passed and a deadly calm overtook her.

She regained her balance as she heard a sound behind her. She turned to find Cyril Henley, dressed in the black cloak he'd worn each time she'd seen him, not ten feet away. He'd come down one of the tunnels that fed into the crypt. She backed against the altar, wanting something solid at her back.

"Mr. Henley," she acknowledged in a voice so calm she smiled.

Chapter Twenty-Two

"Miss O'Rourke. How convenient to find you here."

"Convenient? Did Missy not tell you she would lure me to you?"

He grinned. "So you know about Missy, eh? Where is she?"

"The antechamber."

A brief look of concern passed over his face. "What did you do to her?"

"I gave her the contents of the packet in the little wooden box you left behind."

He circled her to the right, keeping distance between them as he edged toward the arched door and the antechamber to take a peek into the darkness where Missy lay. "All of it?"

She shrugged, matching his manner of unconcern. "I believe she drank it all."

"You stupid cow! You could have killed her."

"I really wouldn't know. I just assumed it was the same dose you gave me in July. How much was in *that* packet?"

"She'll be insensible until this time tomorrow."

"Ah, well, then. A pity she will miss all the excitement." She slipped her hand into her pocket and felt the butt of the pistol.

"Do you think you'll escape this time, Miss O'Rourke?"

"I'm fairly certain of it." She removed her hand from her pocket and pointed the pistol at Mr. Henley's heart.

He laughed. "You don't have the nerve for it. If you did, I'd be dead now."

How odd that she felt so calm—as if everything for the past two and a half months had led her to this place and time. "You would be dead if I didn't want something from you."

"I have nothing of yours, chit."

"You have answers. I have questions."

He laughed, a manic sound that made her certain he was quite mad. "I thought you knew everything."

"I want to know if you are the one who killed Cora."

His grin spread. "Ah. Cora O'Rourke. Sweet thing, she was. Looked a bit like you."

She would not be distracted. "Did you?"

"Hmm. There were several of us who held the knife. 'Twas Daschel who carved her up, but yes, I might have been the one to deliver the coup de grâce."

Her finger twitched. Oh, how she wanted to pull that trigger. But not yet. Not quite yet. "You are a pig, Mr. Henley. Not human at all."

He shrugged. "I've worked at it, little Gina. I may call you that?"

"No." She braced her arm with her other hand as the pistol began to waver. "What of Mr. Metcalfe? Mr. Booth? Charles Hunter and the others?"

"Metcalfe was a personal delight—tried to talk his way out of it. Someone else took care of Mr. Booth for me. That idiot Artie Gibbons botched the job on Hunter and his brother. Still, there's no escape for them. I've posted bounties on them all. Sooner or later, one of the Whitechapel scum will succeed."

"Were I to guess, Mr. Henley, I'd say the threat will cease to exist when you do. Without the reward, there will be no incentive."

"Canny little bitch, aren't you? But that is supposing I cease to exist instead of you."

"One more question, Mr. Henley, and I may let you live if you answer honestly. Did you rape me in the antechamber before the ritual?"

He blinked, then a salacious smile spread over his hateful face. "You don't remember, Gina? How very amusing."

"I frankly do not care what amuses you. Just answer me, Mr. Henley."

"I am crushed you could forget our time together. Well, I wouldn't call it rape, exactly. You did not put up much of a fight. You just lay there and let it happen. I rode you hard, you know."

Her jaw clenched and her hand began to tremble again when she lowered her aim to Mr. Henley's crotch.

"Aye, when the others left, I had my way with you. What did it matter if you were virgin on the altar or not? I was to have first breach anyway."

But his jovial, almost taunting manner had changed ever so subtly to carry an undercurrent of anger. And he would not be angry if he were telling the truth. Dear God! He was lying! He hadn't defiled her! *That* was the unfinished business he had with her and the reason he had not simply killed her when he'd had the chance! He still wanted to rape her. She laughed at him.

His smile drew back to a sneer. "You weren't laughing then, Gina. You bled like a stuck pig."

She was almost weak with relief. "Poor Mr. Henley. Second

best to Daschel, and a complete failure on your own. Why, you do not even lie well."

They glanced toward the arch at the clatter of boots on the stone stairway. Jamie? Or Henley's friends? He glanced at her and back at the door and she knew he was measuring his chances of escape. Her hand wavered as she tightened her finger on the trigger. "Do not move, Mr. Henley."

"Gina!"

Jamie's voice carried from the antechamber. They must have found Missy and feared the worst for her.

"Whore!" Mr. Henley cursed and lunged at her.

He caught her off guard, landing across her middle, driving her to the ground and rolling to put her on top to use her as a shield, the pistol locked between them. If she pulled the trigger now, she was as likely to shoot herself as Mr. Henley, who was now trying to wrest the pistol from her hand.

"Release her," she heard Jamie demand in a cold voice somewhere near the entry to the crypt.

"Easy, Henley," another voice soothed—Lord Lockwood, she thought.

"Back away," Henley said, his voice muffled beneath her.

"You won't get away this time, Henley," Andrew told him. "Give up."

Should she pull the trigger? There was an even chance of the ball hitting Mr. Henley. She took a deep breath, gripped the pistol still crushed between them with her whole strength and rolled to expose Mr. Henley's back. She could not pull the trigger for fear of killing herself, but neither could she allow him to use the pistol against Jamie or the others.

He jerked his hand in an effort to wrest the pistol from her, then twisted as she rolled sideways. Her wrist gave way from the stress, leaving Mr. Henley with possession of the pistol.

He laughed and swung the barrel up to her heart, forgetting everyone else in his hatred of her.

Time slowed as she watched his finger curl around the trigger. She squeezed her eyes shut, not wanting to see his triumph. A single shot reverberated in the crypt and, miraculously, she did not feel a thing. She heard the sound of a pistol dropping to the floor and suddenly she was being dragged upward.

"Gina?"

She opened her eyes. Jamie was holding her, studying her, his gaze traveling the length of her. "Are you hurt?"

Weak with relief, she sagged against him. "I am fine, Jamie. He did not hurt me."

She could feel the tension leave his body as he held her tighter. "Thank God. Thank God…."

He turned with her in his arms and she saw Lockwood and Andrew bending over Henley's still body. It was over. Finally over. She was shivering violently and realized she must be suffering shock. And all she could think was that, "You can put me down now, Jamie. I have to be home by midnight."

He only laughed and held her closer.

Epilogue

September 25, 1821

The summons to Andrew's library before dawn did not come as a surprise. Charlie had brought her home last night, leaving the others to clean up the mess she'd made. And, after Mama's vapors, she had written a letter of gratitude to the Wednesday League. She never could have gotten through the last weeks without their support and understanding. They had understood and helped her reclaim her pride and her life. Without them, she would still be cringing in corners. Then she'd managed to get a few fitful hours of sleep and had just begun dressing for the voyage. Now she was prepared for almost anything as she passed the stacks of crates and trunks in the foyer and knocked on the library door.

At a soft call, she entered.

It did not appear as if any of the brothers had been to bed. Charlie, his arm still in a sling, and Andrew, looked relaxed while Jamie and Lockwood appeared as if they'd just returned from some errand or other. There was an empty chair in front of Andrew's desk and he motioned her toward it.

She perched on the edge of the seat and took a deep bracing breath. She could not tell from their faces if the news was good or bad. She risked a glance at Jamie and was reassured by a little smile lingering on his lips.

Andrew poured her a cup of tea from the silver pot on his desk. "Breakfast should be ready soon, Eugenia, but we wanted to talk to you before the others come down."

She nodded and accepted the teacup and saucer.

"Cyril Henley, as you know, is dead. There will be a short obituary in the *Times* tomorrow. Nothing will be said of his activities or the nature of his demise."

She smiled, pleased that there would be no gossip. She could not bear the thought of her family being caught in controversy and speculation again.

Andrew cleared his throat and continued. "We took Miss Metcalfe home and explained her condition to her parents. To say they were shocked and mortified is an understatement. They are making immediate arrangements to remove to a small village in Tuscany to complete their mourning. Mr. Metcalfe will return after a few months, but Miss Metcalfe will remain. Lord Wycliffe made it clear that her only hope of escaping prosecution is to remain abroad.

"As for your name on Henley's murder list, Devlin has put out the word that Henley is dead and there will be no reward for any further attempts on anyone's life—yours most especially, Eugenia."

She glanced quickly at Charlie and Jamie.

Andrew caught her look. "There are a number of cutthroats who are now out of work, and one in particular we are still in search of, but I feel it safe to say that *you* are no longer in danger."

She took a sip of her tea and realized that everyone was

looking at her. "I, ah, thank you all. I am dreadfully sorry for any trouble or inconvenience I have caused—"

"Inconvenience?" Jamie repeated with a little quirk to his mouth. "You have hunted Henley to ground when the Home Office could not. To the contrary, we owe you a debt of gratitude."

She smiled. "If only I could handle Mama half so well."

"Your mother is handled," Jamie told her. "It seems your ship has been delayed. Whatever decision she makes, you will have sufficient time to make yours."

"Mine? Is there some decision I have to make?" They seemed to have taken care of everything.

Andrew stood and nudged Charlie while Lockwood opened the library door. "Jamie has asked for a private word with you. Do you mind?"

Heat washed through her. Mind? She shook her head as Jamie came toward her and took her hand to lift her to her feet. The library door closed softly, and they were alone.

He pulled her into his arms and tilted her chin up to him. "Eugenia O'Rourke, I love you to utter distraction. Will you marry me?"

Yes, her heart cried, but she could not help teasing him one last time. "And?"

"The question." He nodded and took a deep breath. "Yes, my love. You were virgin."

She laughed. "Oh, Jamie. I adore you. I cannot tell you what it means to me that you love me enough to try to lie."

He looked indignant. "Confound it, woman! It is the truth," he protested.

"Even when you attempt a lie, you tell the truth. Because it is true, Jamie. Mr. Henley gave it away before you arrived last night."

He lowered his lips to her, dropping small kisses on her cheeks, her lips, her throat as he spoke. "That never mattered to me. In every important way, you were. I am the first man you've lain with, the first man you've given yourself to, the first man you've loved. And if luck is with me, I will be the only man you ever need."

"Yes," she answered his question and confirmed his wish. He was the only man she would ever need. She'd wanted a simple answer. Uncomplicated and true. He'd given her the only one that mattered. The truest one of all.

* * * * *

The Rake's Final Conquest

Dorothy Elbury

Chapter One

'I'm so dreadfully cold, Miss Flint! Have we very much further to go?'

'Not far now, Lydia, my dear,' replied Sophie, in as cheerful a tone as she could muster, given that she too was feeling chilled to the bone. Putting aside her own discomfort, she reached across her charge and tucked the travelling rug more snugly around the girl, before peering through the misted glass of the carriage window at the snow-blanketed scene beyond. 'We do seem to be running a little late, but I imagine that this unexpected fall of snow must have *required* our coachman to lessen his normal speed somewhat.'

'Been crawling along like a slug for the past half an hour or so,' grunted the stout, ruddy-faced man opposite. 'Should never have left the Reading stage at all, in my opinion. I warned him that the weather was going to worsen before the day was much older, but would he pay any heed to the worldly wisdom of an old sailor? Not a bit of it—and now see where we are!'

'Hold hard, sir!' exclaimed the elderly gentleman seated at Sophie's right, the clerical collar at his neck clearly indicating his profession. 'One has to remember that these stagecoach drivers are under contract to adhere pretty strictly to the advertised timetables! The poor fellow is seemingly doing his best in what must be the most trying of weather conditions. Surely we should all be applauding his efforts, rather than seeking to find fault with him!'

A low moan emanating from the far corner then directed all eyes towards the couple who occupied the carriage's two remaining seats. As a self-conscious flush covered his cheeks, the young man pulled the woman more closely to him, before saying, 'I am sure that it cannot have escaped your notice that my wife is in a somewhat—er—delicate condition! We had expected to arrive at our destination in Maidenhead with more than enough time to spare but now I feel bound to advise you that it is becoming vital that we reach shelter with all possible speed!'

Since none of the carriage's other occupants could have failed to observe the young woman's advanced state of pregnancy upon boarding the stage at Bath, it was hardly surprising that her husband's words were greeted with a rather ominous silence.

'Fear not, dear lady,' said the reverend gentleman bracingly, leaning forward to give the young woman a reassuring pat on her knee. 'You may be sure that our doughty driver will do whatever is necessary to bring us all safely to the Maidenhead stage well before—'

With a juddering creak the coach slithered slowly to a halt, leaving the rest of the clergyman's intended words of comfort unspoken. The unmistakable sound of the guard clambering down from his perch caused all six passengers to eye one another in varying degrees of alarm. Seconds later, the wrenching open of the nearside door brought about a concerted gasp of dismayed protest as a brisk flurry of snow whirled into the carriage, covering its occupants in a fine layer of ice cold crystals.

'Sorry about that, sirs and madams,' puffed the guard, as he pulled himself up and dragged the door shut behind him. 'Come to inform you that we have hit a bit of a snag. Seems that this snowstorm's a good deal worse than we expected!'

Ignoring the florid ex-captain's grunted, 'Told you so!' he went on, 'Looks to be buildin' up into a fair old blizzard, it do! Driver can't see a blessed thing and the horses is getting fair spooked!'

'You're surely not suggesting that you intend for us just to sit here and weather the thing out?' demanded the young father-to-be. 'My wife is already in a really bad way and I fear that we may well be needful of the services of a midwife before very much longer!'

Cutting through the perturbed silence that followed these disquieting words, the sudden forward lurch of the carriage brought a gleam of satisfaction to the guard's wizened features.

'Peckers up, folks!' he crowed, as he reached again for the door handle. 'Looks like Old Jim's decided to try retracing our steps! Said he'd caught sight of a roadside inn of some sort a while back, so he must be aiming to take shelter there. Just until this infernal wind dies down, at any rate, if we can find the place!'

A second blast of icy weather billowed into the carriage as, once again, the door was thrown open and the guard stepped out to face the harsh elements beyond. Although it was not yet five o'clock in the afternoon, the combination of badly misted windows and thickly swirling snow made it well nigh impossible for any of the passengers to make out exactly what was happening outside the vehicle. Eventually, however, it became apparent that, despite the fact that the turnpike was already inches deep in snow, the driver and his mate had managed to persuade their trepid team of horses into executing a complete turnabout and, now that they no longer found themselves trying to battle against the oncoming blizzard, the edgy foursome seemed to have calmed down at least enough to allow themselves to be led through the snowy wasteland back in the direction from which they had just come.

Throughout the entire manoeuvre the seventeen-year-old Lydia Crayford, her eyes wide with apprehension, had been clutching at Sophie's arm.

'Oh, Miss Flint!' she wailed, as the carriage began to inch its way forward once more. 'Now we will be even later than ever! I cannot begin to imagine what Mama will say when we fail to arrive at the Swan at eight o'clock, as instructed!'

Having borne the brunt of her employer's vituperation on more than one occasion during her six month tenure as governess to the Crayfords' two younger offspring, Sophie had no need to exercise her imagination over the matter. She had little doubt that any blame for returning Lydia late to the bosom of her family would be placed squarely at her door, despite the fact that the assignment upon which she had been dispatched could hardly, in the normal way, have been considered as forming part of her accustomed duties.

Having received urgent notification of a suspected outbreak of chickenpox at the highly regarded Bath seminary at which her stepdaughter boarded, Mrs Crayford, disinclined to allow the event to interfere with her own busy social calendar, had done her utmost to try to persuade her stepson Arthur to take on the task of posting down to Bath to fetch his sister back to the safety of her own home. When that young dandy had flatly refused to be seen 'carting about the countryside with a blessed schoolgirl in tow' Mrs Crayford had simply delegated the undertaking to her own children's governess.

Furnishing Sophie with the cost of one return and one single ticket, plus a shilling or two for any necessary refreshments, she had sent her off to the staging post in Lad Lane, with instructions to board the evening coach to Bath, collect Lydia without delay and bring her back home on the early morning stage.

'That way there will be no need for you to put up overnight,' she had informed Sophie grandly, as she had handed her the five guineas that were intended to cover the full cost of the trip. 'You will have ample time to catch up on any lost sleep on the way. Roberts will be at the Swan at eight o'clock tomorrow evening to meet you. Kindly return here with all speed, for I shall require the barouche to take me on to the Messinghams' rout at nine o'clock.'

Now, wearily reflecting on her mistress's parsimony, Sophie loosened the drawstring of her reticule and, with considerable perturbation, calculated the extent of the small change therein. There was barely enough left for a decent meal between the two of them, let alone an overnight stay! It was to be hoped that Lydia had brought some money with her, otherwise they were going to find themselves deeply embarrassed, always assuming that they eventually succeeded in reaching the shelter the driver sought!

Suddenly conscious that the conveyance had veered sharply to the right, and was now running down a steep incline before eventually coming to a halt, she leaned across her charge and pressed her nose against the windowpane. Through the swirl of the thickly falling snowflakes she could just make out a pair of squat buildings, huddled together in a small hollow just off the side of the post road. Her heart sank, for it was clear that the 'inn' to which the guard had referred was little more than a hedge tavern or local alehouse, and most definitely not the kind of place that would be likely to meet with Mrs Crayford's approval, should it prove necessary to inform her of their unscheduled stop.

Scarcely more than a minute or two had elapsed, however, before the unwelcome sound of raised voices met the ears of the waiting passengers, causing a good many troubled glances to be shared between them. Captain Gibbons frowned and shook his head.

''Tis naught but a den of thieves!' he scoffed, as he peered through the glass. 'Won't be catching me going in there, that's for sure! Strip you of every penny-piece you own and throw you to the wolves as soon as look at you, that sort would!'

'Except that it would seem that we really have very little choice in the matter,' returned Sophie tartly, as she rose from her seat. 'Either we choose to take our chances inside or we stay out here and freeze to death! Come along, Lydia!'

And, holding out her hand, she proceeded to pull the decidedly unenthusiastic Lydia to her feet. Opening the door to the elements, the pair stepped down from the carriage, only to find themselves up to their ankles in several inches of freshly fallen snow. After her initial gasp of shock, Sophie, gritting her teeth, turned back to face the others and advised the young father-to-be that he had better be prepared to carry his wife, since she doubted that the young woman would be able to manage the somewhat treacherous terrain without some sort of assistance.

Determinedly ploughing her way through the rapidly drifting snow towards the building's lighted doorway, Sophie, keeping Lydia's hand firmly in her own, did her best to reassure her shivering companion that she would soon be warm and dry again. Upon reaching the shabby dwelling-place, however, it became clear that the driver was having difficulty in persuading the landlady to provide his passengers with the necessary shelter.

'Oh, miss!' breathed the elderly woman as, with a sigh of relief, she caught sight of the two young women approaching. 'Please tell your driver here that I'd be only too glad to help you all if I could but, as I keep tellin' him, neither the potman nor the young skivvy who usually helps me have shown up—hardly surprisin', I dare say, what with this sudden fall of snow! But even so, miss, I just don't have the facilities for puttin' folks such as you up!'

'You have no rooms at all?'

'Well, it's true that we do have three small bedrooms, miss, but none of them fit for the likes of you and your companions. Plus there's no fires lit, and none of the beds are made up, and without any help I'm just not in a position to assist you, much as I would like to oblige.'

'Three rooms will do very nicely,' said Sophie, eying the woman steadily. 'The young lady who is in the process of alighting from the coach at this very minute is due to give birth at some time in the very near future—unless you wish me to direct her towards your stable in the time honoured fashion?'

'Lord bless us, no, miss!' exclaimed the woman, clapping a hand to her mouth in dismay. 'I'll just go and look out some sheets and blankets—we don't get that many paying guests around these parts—it's only the lack of help that's bothering me, not being as young and fettlesome as I once was!'

A sudden smile lit up Sophie's face. 'Well, then, let me assure you that I'm perfectly fettlesome and only too willing to lend you a hand,' she said decidedly. 'If we could just get Mrs Lucan into bed first, we can take our time sorting out the rest of the party.' Then, with a nod at her young companion, she added, 'Come along, Lydia, I dare say that we will be able to find something useful for you to do, too!'

'But I have the most fearful headache and I do not even know how to make beds!' complained the youngster, as she trundled sullenly after the governess. 'I cannot think what Mama will say when she hears about this!'

Since she preferred not to dwell too heavily on what her mistress might or might not have to say about the matter, Sophie chose not to reply, and applied herself, instead, to helping the inn's landlady extract a number of sheets and pillowcases from a large linen press on the first floor landing.

Quilts and blankets for the bed allocated to the young couple expecting the baby were found in a shabby ottoman at the foot of the room's half-tester and, while Sophie proceeded to instruct her none-too-willing charge in the niceties of bed-making, both the landlord and his wife, Webster by name, set themselves to lighting all the bedroom fires.

Consequently, when the somewhat out of breath Jack Lucan shuffled through the doorway, bearing his whimpering wife in his arms, the first of the three small bedrooms was already beginning to lose its original chill and, since Mrs Webster had also had the forethought to fetch up a couple of hot bricks from the kitchen range, the young woman was slightly overcome to discover that the bed itself was as warm and as cosy as it was possible to be, given the unusual circumstances.

Discovering that both of the two remaining rooms were even smaller than that which had been assigned to the Lucans, Sophie elected to commandeer the smallest of them for Lydia's use, it being furnished with only a single bed and a marble-topped commode, leaving just enough room at the foot of the bed for the straw pallet that the highly apologetic landlord had managed to locate from somewhere or other. Reassuring Mr Webster that such a makeshift bed would serve her perfectly well for the enforced overnight stay, Sophie then brought a relieved smile to the man's face by adding that she had frequently been obliged to bed down in far less salubrious conditions during her recent travels with her soldier father.

Although neither Captain Gibbons nor the Reverend Palfrey were particularly happy at finding themselves obliged to share the bed in the last of the three rooms, they were both far too relieved to be out of the cold to complain, albeit that the ex-sailor was frequently to be heard muttering somewhat uncomplimentary remarks about the drawbacks of travelling with such a cut-purse coaching company, along with his intention to deliver the owner a pretty sharp set-down the minute they arrived at their destination.

Leaving Mr Lucan to attend to his wife's immediate needs, Sophie, having accompanied their hostess into the inn's kitchen, then enquired as to the extent of provisions available. Luckily, it soon transpired that Mrs Webster was a great believer in the keeping of a well stocked larder, so it seemed that there was very little likelihood of her unexpected guests going hungry—were it not for one unfortunate setback.

'I don't know as how I could rig up a meal for such a large number,' exclaimed their hostess, wringing her hands together in considerable apprehension. 'I've never been obliged to cook for more than two or three at a time—Mr Webster were goin' to kill a chicken for our tonight's dinner, but I don't see as how the one bird can be made to feed the ten of us!'

'It most surely can, if it is made into a hearty stew!' returned Sophie swiftly, as she rolled back her cuffs. 'And, having seen your splendid store of winter vegetables, that should not prove too difficult a task for the pair of us.'

So saying, she sat herself down at the large pine table in the middle of the kitchen and proceeded to attack the heap of mixed vegetables that the landlady was already beginning to pile on to its well scrubbed surface.

'You're a bit of a strange one, miss, if you don't mind me sayin' so,' remarked Mrs Webster, as she took a seat opposite and picked up a potato to peel. 'I'd have said that you must have been in service at one time, if it weren't for the way you speak—sort of genteel-like, if you'll excuse me sayin'.'

'Well, I suppose you could say that I was in service once—in a manner of speaking.' Sophie laughed as she neatly quartered an onion and tossed it into the large stew pot that the landlady had placed on the table between the two of them. 'For the past twenty years or so my mother and I have been following my soldier father wherever his army campaigns chose to take him. We were obliged to spend a good deal of our time arranging sleeping quarters and making the most of whatever provender we were able to get hold of, so I suppose that this kind of thing does seem to come as some sort of second nature to me.'

'A hard life for a young lady, that,' observed the elderly woman. 'Had you no brothers or sisters?'

'Oh, yes!' confirmed Sophie, with a smile. 'I have a fourteen-year-old brother, Roger, but he's away at school now. Mama was determined that his education should not be allowed to suffer as a result of...' Her voice tailed away and her eyes began to mist up, causing her to clench her teeth as she made a determined effort to regain control of her emotions. Even after all these months, just the thought of her father's death the previous year still had the ability to knock her sideways.

'Lost your pa in the war, did you, miss?' Mrs Webster's voice was full of sympathy.

At Sophie's brief nod, the landlady let out a deep sigh. 'Our Jamie was taken, too,' she said quietly. 'Just over four years ago, it were—some place in Spain called Badhow or Bardhoff—never could quite get my tongue around the name.'

'Badajoz,' responded Sophie, much calmer now. 'Yes, I know it well. Such a dreadful battle it was, but our soldiers fought so courageously—you must be very proud of your son.'

'Well, yes. Dare say I am,' returned the other flatly. 'But I'd still far rather he'd stayed at home with us!'

The resultant silence that followed this critical observation might well have continued for quite some time had not the return of the landlord, bearing aloft his freshly slaughtered chicken, served to interrupt the mutual melancholia.

'Biggest one I could get hold of!' he bragged as, sit-

ting himself down next to his wife, he proceeded to
pluck out the bird's feathers.

Some three hours later, fully replete on double help-
ings of the hearty chicken and dumpling stew, chased
down with a glass or two of Mrs Webster's highly intoxicating homebrewed ginger wine, the exhausted travellers
declared themselves ready for their beds.

Having offered to take a tray up to the Lucan couple,
Sophie had found the pair fast asleep, entwined in one
another's arms and, since she did not have the heart to
awaken them, she had crept quietly away, judging that a
peaceful night's sleep was likely to be of far more benefit to the expectant mother than a plateful of stew.

A rather more immediate concern, from her own
point of view, had been her young companion's constant sneezing and shivering fits throughout the evening, both of which seemed to indicate the beginnings
of something ominous. She could only hope and pray
that Lydia had not already succumbed to the dreaded
infection from which she had been despatched to remove
the youngster!

Luckily, Mrs Webster was able to supply Sophie
with a couple of headache powders, but it was not until
she had administered one of these to Lydia, tucked a
wrapped hot brick at her feet and settled her down for
the night, that she was able to turn her mind to her own
needs. Having set out from London with the intention of
being back in Lennox Gardens before nightfall, she had
brought nothing with her apart from the clothes she was
wearing! Had she thought of it before her young charge
had drifted off to sleep, she might well have considered
asking Lydia for the loan of one of her nightdresses,
since they were of an almost similar size. As it was,

having hung her plain but serviceable grey kerseymere gown over the fireguard, in the hopes that the fire's heat might remove the worst of its creases, she was obliged to resign herself to sleeping in her flimsy muslin shift.

Although the straw-filled palliasse was not the most comfortable of mattresses, it was impossible not to smile as she had, as she'd told the landlord, known far worse sleeping quarters, and she quickly reminded herself that, had their doughty driver not found them this little jewel of a lodging, they might yet be sitting in the carriage, probably freezing to death in a snowdrift somewhere!

Snuggling under the heavy quilt with which Mrs Webster had insisted upon providing her, she felt her eyelids droop and sleep was all but ready to claim her when a sudden thought flashed through her mind.

Her reticule! Unable to recall exactly where or when she had last set eyes on the little purse that held the sum total of her wealth, she pulled herself up out of her warm cocoon and, with the help of the flickering firelight, began to peruse the various surfaces of the tiny room. In one of the pockets of her pelisse, perhaps? But, no, she remembered having checked both pockets before handing her damp coat over to Mrs Webster to hang up on the ceiling dryer in the kitchen! As panic threatened to overcome her, she forced herself to take a deep breath and concentrate. And then, as sanity prevailed, it all came back to her. She had placed her reticule down on the parlour windowsill before coming upstairs to help Mrs Webster with the bed-making. She found it hard to believe that any of the other passengers would have helped themselves to it, but then, one could never tell these days! So, judging that it would be better to be safe than sorry, she crept over to Lydia's portmanteau, extracted a large paisley shawl from within and, after thrusting her feet into her half-boots, made her way over to the doorway and peered out into the dimly lit passage beyond.

Chapter Two

Just as she had supposed, the house was completely silent, with every one of its exhausted occupants presumably wrapped in the arms of Morpheus! Tiptoeing swiftly down the single flight of stairs, with only the light from one wall sconce to guide her, she made at once for the parlour. Finding the door shut, she turned the knob gently, unwilling to risk waking either of her hosts who, as she had recently ascertained, slept in the room directly opposite to this one. As she stepped inside, her boot immediately encountered a creaking floorboard, causing her to freeze in her tracks, but then, by the light of the still glowing logs in the fireplace, she spotted her reticule, lying just as she had left it upon the windowsill. Her courage returned and, making a quick dash across the room, she reached out her hand to snatch up the precious object.

'Well, well, well! And what have we here? A cosy little armful come to keep me company, eh? How very accommodating!'

At the unexpected sound of the drawling male voice, Sophie spun round in dismay—only to find herself almost face-to-face with its advancing owner who, as she was soon to discover, seemed bent on relieving her of her shawl. Clutching the totally inadequate covering more tightly about her person, she attempted to back away towards the door.

'Not so fast, my pretty one!' came the stranger's purring undertone, as his hand shot out to catch hold of the shawl's trailing end. Then, with one swift jerk, he yanked it from her shoulders, to leave her cowering before him clad only in her flimsy shift.

'You clearly came with the sole purpose of entertaining me in my hour of need, my sweet, so let's waste no more time on this feeble pretence at maidenly modesty, I implore you!'

And then, before the utterly transfixed Sophie even had time to speculate upon what his intentions might be, the man had stepped forward, pulled her into his arms and, after tipping her head back, set about capturing her lips with his own!

Her initial sense of stunned outrage was almost overwhelmed as an inexplicable trickle of excitement ran up and down her spine, and for countless seconds she found herself seized by the wildest of temptations to simply allow these confusing emotions to run away with her. It was not until one of the stranger's hands slid down her back to cup the softly rounded cheeks of her buttocks that her misplaced wits suddenly leapt into action and, with a swift wrench, she succeeded in tearing herself away from what was becoming an increasingly enthusiastic onslaught on her person.

Breathless with disbelief, she tried to haul herself

out of his reach, but he was too quick for her, his hand shooting out and capturing her wrist.

'Let me go!' she panted. 'Please, let me go, sir. I beg of you!'

A puzzled frown puckered the man's brow, and as the sound of Sophie's voice gradually penetrated his perception a sudden stillness came over him. *No serving wench this, as the girl's cultured tones instantly informed him!* With a strangled oath he dropped his hold and, stepping hurriedly away from her, held up his hands in a gesture of surrender.

'My mistake, ma'am,' he grated, as he lurched back to sink into the fireside chair that he had so eagerly vacated at Sophie's unexpected entrance. 'I fear that I seem to have partaken of—'

But Sophie, seizing her chance, was in no mind to wait to hear whatever explanation her attacker was about to drum up to excuse his extraordinary behaviour. Snatching up the discarded shawl, she dashed towards the door and, dragging it open, fled along the passageway and up the stairs as if all the devils in hell were at her heels!

Raising his head just in time to catch sight of her shapely calves and trim ankles disappearing from his view, Marcus Wolfe, Viscount Helstone, let out a self-deprecating groan. Well aware that it had been sheer madness on his part to have set out from Bradfield on such a night, he could not help but feel that he had been well served for his inanity. Whilst it was true that another hour spent in his father's company might well have driven him into doing or saying something that he was sure to have later regretted, he was not so foxed that he was unable to recognise the possible bumblebath into which he had landed himself, with his attempted seduction of a female who, rather than having been a serving girl eager to earn herself a few shillings in return for services rendered, as he had originally supposed, had turned out to be one of the inn's benighted coach party passengers!

Not that he was especially worried about any consequences that might arise as a result of that rather unproductive foray—past experience had taught him that the passing over of a thick wad of notes was usually more than enough to silence the complaints of even the most devoted of husbands and fathers! He shrugged. In any case, life was too short to allow such petty irrelevances to overset him! Not for nothing had his closest associates designated the Viscount with the soubriquet Hellcat!

Tossing back the final dregs of the bottle of rather inferior brandy with which the landlord had provided him—presumably as some sort of sop for failing to accommodate him with sleeping quarters more appropriate to his position—Marcus sprawled back in his chair with a low growl of discontent. Far from being too short, his life, as far as he was concerned, was well on the way to being too damned long and a sight too dreary for words! Small wonder that his father had termed him a worthless wastrel, much preferring the company of Giles, the younger of the two Wolfe scions. Giles the brave—Giles the hero—good old never-put-a-foot-wrong Giles!

Good grief! What in God's name had got into him that he had actually sunk to reviling his beloved brother, a man whom he loved and respected with every fibre of his being!

As he stared down into the fire's dying embers, Marcus's shoulders slumped in a fit of self-revulsion. It seemed as if the endless round of drinking, gambling and whoring of which his life consisted was finally beginning to affect his reason. It was beyond question that Giles, who for the past six years and more had fought his way across two continents, surviving countless bloody battles to emerge virtually unscathed as a highly decorated war hero, deserved every bit of praise and admiration that could be heaped upon his twenty-seven-year-old shoulders.

It was not that Marcus begrudged his brother even a single one of that young man's well deserved accreditations. His abiding feeling was simply one of envy, laced with a generous helping of resentment—a deep and bitter resentment at having been born the elder of their father's two sons, thus precluding him from opting for the much desired military career that his younger brother had been allowed to pursue. Whilst it was true that a good many members of the nobility had been seen to encourage their eldest sons to join in the campaign to rid the civilised world of Napoleon's tyranny, it had been as a direct result of the loss of so many of those promising young lives that Marcus's father, the Earl of Bradfield, fearing the possibility of losing both his heirs, had flatly refused to countenance his elder son purchasing the commission on which the Viscount had set his heart.

The badly thwarted Marcus, having pointed out that there was more than one way that a fellow might choose to sacrifice his life, had then proceeded to demonstrate several of them, thoroughly outraging his father by occupying his hours with every possible degeneracy known to man.

In direct contravention of the Earl's wishes, Marcus appeared to have gone out of his way to dice with death and had, in the past eight or so years, been obliged to turn up to defend his name in dawn encounters on more than one occasion. Although he had, as yet, never actually killed a man—his aim being so impeccable that a harmless nick in an opponent's upper arm or shoulder had proved more than enough to decide the day.

Whilst he could, if he so chose, drink most of his friends and colleagues under the proverbial table, he had for the most part learned to hold his liquor, preferring to keep a sober head both for his card-playing and for other, more pleasurable activities. For, although he kept two mistresses in comfort in different parts of Town, he did not feel that such arrangements necessarily prohibited him from taking advantage of the many other casual liaisons that offered themselves up to him—a goodly proportion of the females in the upper echelons of the society in which the Viscount moved had proved to be remarkably lax in regard to the marital vows they had taken, hence those somewhat frequent dawn encounters! And, had his skill at cards not been so amazingly superior to that of his opponents, Marcus might well have lost the fortune he had inherited from his maternal grandmother, thereby obliging him to depend upon hand-outs from his father—a situation to be avoided at all costs, as far as Helstone was concerned.

As it was, he could not help but be aware that he was in grave danger of becoming not only an out-and-out rakeshame but also the 'worthless wastrel' his father had termed him earlier that evening—an epithet that did not sit too readily on Helstone's shoulders and one that had caused him to quit the family mansion in a towering fury.

Having finally managed to stumble, half-dead with cold, into this tiny wayside tavern on the Reading post road, only to discover that all its rooms were already occupied, he had been obliged to try and make himself comfortable on one of the most uncomfortable of fireside chairs that he had ever encountered, but with his boots off, a roaring fire at his feet and a half bottle of brandy at his disposal, he had been quite prepared to make the best of it, reasoning that by morning the snow would more than likely have disappeared and he would be back on his way to his Grosvenor Square mansion well before noon.

Although he had been slightly taken aback at the unexpected appearance of the rather comely young woman who had seen fit to invade his privacy, he had merely taken her arrival as yet another token of the landlord's regret at not having been able to furnish him with a suitable bed for the night, as was his due! And, although the girl had turned out not to be the accommodating chambermaid of his fancy, she had certainly been a highly curvaceous little creature, in addition to having been blessed with quite the most kissable lips that he had had the pleasure of tasting in some time.

Throwing on a couple more logs, he stoked up the fire and, thrusting a cushion behind his head, stretched out his legs and placed his feet on the leather-topped log box, having reached the happy conclusion that, provided he got away at first light, he could avoid any inherent complications of coming face-to-face with his late-night visitor—not to mention any irate husband or father that lady might have in tow!

In the event, however, it seemed that the Viscount's good intentions were to be brought to nought. On pulling back the curtain at around six of the clock the following morning, in order to check the state of the weather outside, he was dismayed to find that, rather than having improved overnight, as he had supposed it must, the situation appeared to have worsened to an even more worrying degree.

Despite the fact that the fierce wind of the previous day looked to have finally blown itself out, the continuously falling snow had enveloped the entire landscape in a soft white blanket as far as the eye could see. Whilst this highly picturesque scene was, without doubt, one of awe-inspiring splendor, and more than enough to cause Marcus to draw in his breath in appreciative wonder at Nature's handiwork, it was not long before it came to him that the hasty departure on which he had set his mind was now totally out of the question. It was becoming increasingly obvious that the depth of the snow that filled the little hollow wherein the tavern nestled would make the reaching of the post road well nigh impossible—given that the drifts outside his window were already somewhere in the region of three feet deep! It would take three or four men half a day at least to dig out a passageway up that steep incline to get to the highway, and even then one could not be entirely sure that the post road would even be traversable—there had certainly been no indication of any passing traffic for the past hour or so, as far as he had been aware!

Stifling a yawn, the Viscount ran his fingers over the bristles on his chin and wondered how long it would be before anyone would think to fetch him some hot water in order that he might wash and shave. He had heard various sounds of movement emanating from the passage outside his room, and the welcome smell of freshly brewed coffee had been wafting its way into the little parlour for some time now.

He stood, undecided, for a further moment or two but then, as the smell of the coffee grew ever more enticing, causing his empty stomach to growl in anticipation, he plonked himself back down on the fireside chair and began the almost Herculean task of pulling on his boots—something of a masterly feat, in his case, considering the lack of both valet and boot-horn!

It was while he was attempting to smooth the creases of his crumpled cravat into some sort of acceptable order that, on turning his head, he happened to catch sight of a small brown leather object that had somehow become lodged behind one of the legs of the side table that stood against the rear wall of the parlour. Curious, he reached down to pick it up. No sooner had he recognised the object for what it was—a lady's reticule—than his lips began to curve in amused recall of the previous night's thwarted encounter.

So, this was what the young woman had been after when she had come creeping into his room! It must hold something of immense value to have caused her to leave her bed and wander, half-clad, into a gentleman's sleeping quarters! Not that she was likely to have known that it was anyone's sleeping quarters at the time, he was quick to remind himself, as he unwound the thongs of the shabby purse and tipped its meagre contents into the palm of his hand.

A puzzled frown creased his brow as he stared down at the sum total that he held—a single half-crown, three sixpenny pieces and a few odd coppers! Less than five shillings, all told—hardly worth anyone going to so much bother to retrieve, he thought dispassionately, as he returned the coins to the reticule and retied its leather thongs before thrusting it into his jacket pocket.

Finding the passageway deserted, he made for the door at its far end. Having been ushered through that same door the previous evening, he had no doubts about it leading him to the kitchen and to that much needed cup of coffee!

Pushing open the door, he quickly surveyed the scene in front of him. A lace-capped serving wench, clad in a plain grey kerseymere gown, overtopped by a clean white apron, was bent over the range with her back to him, heavily preoccupied in stirring the contents of one of the pots thereon.

'Coffee, if you please, and quick about it!' he ordered authoritatively, as he sauntered across the room and took a seat at the large pine table that dominated the tavern's kitchen. 'And then ham, eggs and mushrooms to follow, I think!'

Straightening up in shock, Sophie swung round to face him, her heart stuttering almost to a stop as she got her first real look at her midnight assailant. Pausing momentarily to take in his remarkably handsome if slightly dishevelled appearance, she found it necessary to take in quite a deep breath of air before she felt able to summon up the necessary self-assurance to respond to his communication. Having spent the better part of the night trying to rationalise the quite bizarre happenings in the parlour—particularly in reference to her own out-of-character behaviour—she had reached the conclusion that, since it had seemed to her that the man must have been in a very advanced state of intoxication to behave in the way he had done, there was every chance he might well have woken with no memory of what had occurred between them.

Not that anything of great moment had actually taken place, as she hastily reminded herself! Merely a fumbled kiss, followed by his slurred attempt at an apology— hardly a matter to get wound up over and, if she were honest, an experience nowhere near as unpleasant as those she had suffered at the hands of Arthur Crayford, whose constant attempts to waylay her whenever his stepmother was not in the offing were beginning to cause her considerable disquiet!

'Wake up, girl! I said coffee, if you please!'

She started. It seemed that the man had not recognised her! Which was hardly surprising, really, considering all the effort she had made to bundle her unruly chestnut curls into some sort of chignon, prior to covering her entire head with one of the highly unattractive lace caps she had taken to wearing in her attempts to hold young Crayford at bay.

'There is no more coffee, I'm afraid,' she replied, in as gracious a tone as she could manage in the circumstances. 'Mr Webster has had the last of it—he slipped on the ice while going to collect logs and has been obliged to take to his bed with a badly sprained back. As a result of which, the range fire is now almost out, but should you care to go and fetch some logs yourself, I daresay I might be prevailed upon to provide you with a fresh jug of coffee!'

Thoroughly taken aback, Marcus rose from his seat and in two quick strides he was standing in front of her, an angry expression upon his face.

'I believe you are forgetting yourself, miss!'

'As indeed are you, sir!' Sophie fired back at him, her former apprehension instantly swept aside in her growing indignation at what she felt was an unnecessarily imperious manner on the man's part.

Marcus stared down at her, his eyes narrowing. 'What the devil do you mean by that remark?' he demanded, somewhat belligerently. 'Is it or is it not your duty to wait upon the guests in this establishment?'

'I hardly think so,' she countered, in the most dulcet of tones. 'Since I myself am also one of the guests.'

A puzzled frown shifted across his brow as he continued to peruse her face until all at once realisation began to surface. 'Good God! You're her, dammit, aren't you?'

'She,' corrected Sophie automatically. 'I am she, not "her"—if you are referring to the female who inadvertently invaded your sleeping quarters last evening, that is!'

Marcus's eyebrow quirked in exasperation.

'Never mind the blessed semantics,' he grunted. 'Perhaps you will have the goodness to explain to me what you mean by going around giving folks the impression that you are a serving maid?'

'I believe that was your mistake, sir, not mine!' she answered cheerfully, as she turned back to the porridge pot to give it another quick stir. 'I am merely doing my best to help an old couple who, quite without warning, have found themselves landed with a house full of uninvited guests. Apart from our doughty driver and his guard, who have spent the past two hours clearing a path to the stables and woodshed, it would seem that I am the only one of our party who is capable of being of any practical help to them.'

'Ah! At last I begin to understand,' returned Marcus with an expressive nod. 'I must suppose that this is also the reason you are togged up in that apron and wearing that hideous monstrosity on your head.'

'I beg your pardon!' flashed back Sophie indignantly. 'I'll have you know that my cap is perfectly respectable and generally considered to be quite in keeping with my position.'

'Whatever position that might be I cannot begin to

imagine,' he riposted quickly, having already ascertained that her fingers were unadorned with rings of any sort. 'You are quite clearly not a widow, and unless I am much mistaken a fair few years from being counted an old maid!'

'Really, sir!' retorted Sophie, beginning to feel distinctly nettled at the man's indefensible lack of civility. 'I fail to see that who I am or what my situation is can be any possible concern of yours!'

Whilst it was true that in normal circumstances such pointed questioning of a young woman might be considered rather improper, Marcus suddenly found himself relishing the thought that, given their present situation, no such conventional restrictions need apply.

'Oh, come now!' he cajoled, favouring her with a lopsided grin, the like of which was usually more than enough to leave even the most straitlaced of females quivering in her shoes. 'Since it would seem that we are likely to be cooped up together for who knows how long, it occurs to me that the polite interchange of names might not be considered amiss.'

Then, executing a perfect leg, he added, 'Marcus Wolfe, at your service, ma'am.'

Whilst his roguish smile was certainly enough to bump up her heart rate more than just a notch or two, Sophie's unconventional upbringing had taught her to recognise such guile for what it was worth, and, dipping him what was intended to be a mockingly servile curtsey, she replied, 'Miss Sophie Flint, governess—if it so pleases your honour, sir!'

He laughed, showing a set of even white teeth. 'It pleases me greatly, thank you, Miss Flint and, if you will allow it, I should like to take this opportunity to apologise for that rather unfortunate misunderstanding last evening—I suspect that your impromptu visit was actually intended to retrieve this piece of property. I assume that it *is* yours?'

And, having thrust his hand into his pocket as he spoke, he extracted Sophie's reticule and held it out towards her.

At the sight of her shabby brown leather purse, the blush that had been forming on Sophie's face at the man's mention of the highly discomfiting events of the previous evening quickly disappeared. All at once her summer blue eyes lit up in delight and she favoured the Viscount with a smile of such joyful sweetness that he was momentarily lost for words.

'Oh, thank you, Mr Wolfe!' she exclaimed, as she reached forward to accept the purse. 'I was beginning to fear that I might have seen the last of it!'

Not having seen fit to introduce himself by his correct title, Marcus was unable to bring himself to rectify Sophie's unwitting error. In fact, having experienced a somewhat disconcerting sensation in the pit of his stomach the moment their hands touched, he was very soon of the opinion that, for the short time that they were to be forced into one another's company, to be known as Mr Wolfe might serve him rather well—especially since the yawning, night-capped landlord had been too busy apologising for the lack of a suitable bed to get around to enquiring his name upon his arrival the previous evening.

Forcing his eyes away from her elated expression, he shot a quick look at the dying fire.

'I suppose if I am ever to get that cup of coffee I am so desperately in need of, I had better go and see about these blessed logs,' he groaned, at the same time simulating a world-weary sigh. 'Exactly where is this woodshed of which you spoke?'

Unable to hide her amusement at his feigned expression of virtuous suffering, Sophie raised her hand and indicated the back door. 'Directly opposite,' she replied. 'As I said before, part of the yard has already been cleared of snow and—oh, yes, I'm afraid I forgot to mention—should you happen to require milk in your coffee, you will find Daisy waiting in the adjoining cowshed!'

'Daisy?'

Marcus stopped and turned, a mystified frown on his face.

'The Websters' cow—she is yet to be milked.'

But then, seeing the Viscount's look of utter astonishment, she added hurriedly, 'That was intended merely as a jest, Mr Wolfe. One could scarcely suppose it likely that you also number milking amongst your undoubted talents!'

He gave a low chuckle and a mischievous glint lit up his eyes. 'Such talents as I do happen to possess might surprise even your good self, Miss Flint,' he murmured softly. 'In fact, if you would just do me the service of removing that ghastly monstrosity from your head, who knows what hazardous activities I could be persuaded into!'

The challenging look he cast at her was more than enough to cause Sophie's cheeks to flame in mortification, it having instantly brought to mind her almost wanton behaviour of the previous evening.

'Logs!' she choked, as she gave him a swift push towards the door. 'And quickly—before the fire goes out!'

Kissing the tips of his fingers, he sent her a quick

salute as he exited from the room with the words, 'Your wish is my command, dear lady!'

As she stared at the now closed door, a perplexed frown creased Sophie's brow and she tried her utmost to make some sense out of the somewhat odd sensations that the very vexing Mr Wolfe seemed to have engendered within her. Unable to reach a satisfactory conclusion to her ruminations, however, she gave a brisk shake of her head and forced herself to return her attention to the porridge pot from where, after giving it one final stir, she spooned out a small bowlful to take up to her still ailing charge, along with the very last drop of milk in the jug.

That Marcus Wolfe was the most accomplished rake she had ever come across was without question, and, given his rather autocratic manner and the obvious quality of his perfectly tailored jacket and fine leather riding boots, it would seem that he more than likely belonged to that high-flown set of men about town whom lesser beings such as Arthur Crayford craved vainly to emulate. Clearly the sort of dangerously attractive man that all well brought up young females were taught by their mothers to be on their guard against, and, bearing in mind the rather disconcerting effect that his very presence already seemed to be having on her, Sophie was quick to realise that she would need to keep all her wits about her if she meant to keep her heart safe from Wolfe's compellingly magnetic charisma.

Having spent most of her growing years in the company of men from all walks of life, she could not recall a single one of them having had quite the same effect on her pulse as did this man, who was little more than a stranger to her. Whilst she had never been averse to a light flirtation with the occasional junior officer under her father's command, her heart had always remained entirely her own, and now that she was forced to make her own way in the world she had reached the conclusion that it must continue to remain that way.

With her mother reduced to taking in paying guests in a rented house in Dulwich village, in order that Roger, Sophie's fourteen-year-old brother, might continue his public school education at the nearby college, an advantageous marriage might have been thought to be the ideal solution to the Flint family's financial difficulties. Unfortunately, given that Sophie's current situation as a governess to two young children was something of a drawback insofar as regular contact with unmarried members of the opposite sex was concerned, she had grown accustomed to the idea that the chances of receiving a suitable offer for her hand were distinctly remote. Indeed, it was entirely due to having found herself the unwitting recipient of rather too many highly *unsuitable* offers during her six month tenure with the Crayfords that she had privately determined to consign all gentlemen below the age of sixty-five or so to Hades—or to some other persecution of an equally unpleasant nature!

Her inexplicable reaction to Wolfe's stolen kiss had set her at odds with her normally down-to-earth self, and she could only pray that she had it in her to drum up sufficient tenacity to withstand his flirtatious banter—not to mention the incredibly melting effect he seemed to have on her every time his lips curved in that particular smile of his! In fact she was disconcerted to discover, as she made her way up the stairs towards Lydia's room, it seemed that even the memory of it was enough to make her heart skip more than the odd beat.

Chapter Three

Once she stepped inside the bedroom door, however, one glance at her young charge was more than enough to banish all such heady thoughts from her mind. *Oh, dear Lord*, she thought in dismay, as she stared down at the girl's flushed and perspiring face, *the poor child really looks quite poorly! Now what am I to do?*

'Could you just try and sit up for a moment, Lydia?' she coaxed, and she sat down on the bed where, slipping one arm beneath the girl's shoulders, she eased her gently into a sitting position, before carefully plumping up the pillows behind her back to help support her.

'Oh, Miss Flint!' wailed Lydia, clutching at the governess's hand. 'My head aches so and I feel truly dreadful! Please do not tell me that I have developed the chickenpox, after all—Mama will be so cross with me if I should end up with a host of unsightly scars on my face!'

'Hush, my dear, you must not think such things,' soothed Sophie. 'You have caught a very bad cold, that is all, and if you wish to get better quickly you must try to eat some of this lovely porridge that I have brought you.'

'But I hate porridge!' cried the youngster, eying Sophie's offering with considerable distaste. 'I would much rather have a glass of cold milk!'

Finding herself at something of a stand at the girl's plea, Sophie dipped the spoon into the bowl and lifted it towards her lips.

'As soon as you have eaten all of this,' she encouraged, mentally crossing her fingers as she did so, 'then you shall have as much milk as you want, I promise you, my dear!'

Even if I have to go and milk the blessed animal myself! she averred silently.

Fortunately, since it took every scrap of Lydia's energy to take in and swallow every mouthful of the detested oatmeal, all she wanted to do when she had finished the dreaded ordeal was to slump back against the pillows and drift off to sleep again.

Placing her hand upon the child's fevered brow, Sophie could not help but feel that Mrs Crayford had landed her with an almighty problem. What if Lydia was really sick? Supposing that she *had* caught the chicken-pox? Without a doctor, and only Mrs Webster's headache powders to hand, it seemed that there was very little that she could do to alleviate the youngster's suffering. But then, castigating herself for such negative thinking, she started to ask herself what her own mother, the calmest and most practical of women, would have done in such circumstances—her tender ministrations to the sick and injured having become almost legendary during the family's years in the Peninsular.

Lemon barley water, of course! Mrs Webster is sure

*to have those ingredients, at least! And then I must
bathe Lydia's arms and legs with warm water to bring
down her temperature.*

But after shooting a quick glance at the dying fire,
she could not help but wonder how successful Mr Wolfe
had been in his bid to secure logs—only to experience a slight flutter of dismay when it suddenly came
to her that the future health and safety of the entire
household might well depend on the reliability of that
undeniably handsome but decidedly suspect character
downstairs!

Raised voices from the next room soon had her on her
feet, making for the door. Surely Captain Gibbons and
the Reverend were not at each other's throats again, so
early in the day? She had hoped that, after yesterday's
disturbing goings-on, the ill-matched pair would have
been only too happy to remain in their bed until at least
mid-morning. Apparently not, if the noises emanating
from their room were anything to go by!

Glancing across at the bed, she could see that Lydia
was now asleep, although her restless tossing and turning
did not bode well for a swift recovery. Quickly making
up her mind, she tossed the last of the logs on to the
fire's still glowing embers, left the room, and rapped
sharply on the door of the neighbouring bedchamber.

The wrangling from within ceased instantly, followed
by a moment's silence before the door was flung open
by the Reverend Palfrey, to reveal both of the room's
nightshirt-clad occupants clutching at a tangled heap of
bedclothes.

'I hesitate to bring it to your attention, sirs,' she began,
without preamble. 'But there are sick people on either
side of you, and the walls of this cottage are exceedingly

thin! Kindly lower your voices to a minimum, if you would!'

'But he keeps taking more than his fair share of the blankets!' protested Captain Gibbons, tugging frantically at the quilt that the reverend gentleman, despite his lesser stature, was quite determined not to relinquish.

'The situation is quite the reverse, I assure you, ma'am,' gasped the outraged parson. 'I have awoken time after time throughout the night to find myself totally devoid of bedding. I was merely endeavouring to rectify the matter when this—this—!'

When the epithet he was searching for failed to materialise, his shoulders slumped, and with a resigned sigh he released his hold on the quilt, allowing his adversary to clutch it to his chest in grinning triumph.

'Really, gentlemen!' Sophie admonished the pair. 'One would have thought that you had sufficient wit between you to have reached some sort of reasonable compromise. It seems to me that you have more than enough bedding to accommodate the pair of you. Why not simply divide it in half and each of you roll yourselves up into a separate little cocoon? It's a method that has always served its purpose perfectly well in military circles, I've found, and since it appears that we are to suffer one another's company for a good deal longer than was originally supposed, you might well consider putting it into practice without further delay!'

For a long moment neither of the two men moved nor uttered a word, but then, giving a slow, appreciative nod, the Captain let go of the quilt.

'T'lass is quite right,' he said, with a hoarse chuckle. 'Makes no sense two grown men argifyin' over a set of bedclothes—you take hold of this, sir, and I'll make do with what's left. What say we bed down for another couple of hours before we brave the chill below?'

'Whilst I am perfectly agreeable to that suggestion, my dear fellow,' returned Palfrey, with an acquiescent bow, 'I must insist that you retain the quilt. I am more than content to avail myself of the remaining blankets.'

'Not at all, sir!' exclaimed Gibbons. 'The quilt is yours—these fine blankets will do me just proud!'

Seeing that another argument between the disparate pair seemed about to ensue, Sophie, throwing up her hands in despair at their ludicrous behaviour, turned on her heel and hurriedly left the room, having come to the conclusion that any further intervention on her part would be pointless.

Just as she was closing the door behind her, however, she came upon Mrs Webster, who was just on the point of exiting the Lucans' room.

'Any further progress in that direction?' she enquired of the landlady, in a low voice.

'Slow goin', I'm afraid,' whispered Mrs Webster, with a pensive shake of her head. 'My guess is that the poor lass will be some little while yet—not that I've any great experience in these matters, only havin' had the one myself, you understand.'

'Then we must just hope and pray that this appalling weather improves sufficiently for us to summon the local midwife to help us out,' declared Sophie bracingly, as she followed her elderly hostess down the stairs. 'How is Mr Webster faring, after that nasty fall?'

'Well enough in the circumstances, thank you, miss,' replied Mrs Webster, pushing open the kitchen door. 'Although how on earth we are going to manage without his help, I can't begin to—great heavens above!'

The landlady having stopped dead in her tracks at the doorway, Sophie found herself obliged to peer over the woman's shoulder in order to discover the cause of her astonishment—only to find herself equally taken aback at the extraordinary scene that met her eyes.

There at the kitchen table stood Marcus Wolfe, his shirtsleeves rolled up to his elbows and minus his neck-cloth, unconcernedly ladling milk out of a wooden pail into a large blue-and-white-striped pottery jug. A quick look across at the cheery flames leaping up between the bars of the range's firebox soon ascertained that he had fulfilled his pledge to replenish the supply of logs. Hesitating for only the barest moment, Sophie, her eyes agleam with amusement, raised her hand and, whipping off the lace cap, stuffed the offending article into her apron pocket before following Mrs Webster into the room.

At the sound of their entry, Helstone looked up and smiled, his lips curving to an even greater extent as he registered the lack of covering on Sophie's now slightly tousled chestnut tresses.

'Mrs Webster, I presume?' he said, laying aside the ladle and sketching the landlady a brief bow. 'Marcus Wolfe, at your service. No doubt your husband has already informed you that he was obliged to offer me shelter last evening. I trust that he has not suffered serious hurt from his unfortunate fall?'

'Just twisted his back slightly, sir,' returned the woman, staring at the milk pail in some confusion. 'You've been out and milked our Daisy, sir? How very good of you to put yourself to so much bother!'

Helstone raised a disaffected shoulder and indicated the jug of freshly made coffee simmering gently on the top of the kitchen range. 'Had to be done, if we were to have milk in our coffee.'

It having been a good many years since he had been anywhere near a cow, let alone milked one, Marcus's initial attempts at the activity had met with little success. Daisy had greeted his nervous fumblings with considerable mistrust, jostling him off the stool and kicking away the pail in her impatience to rid herself of his decidedly amateur ministrations. It had taken sheer bloody-mindedness—along with the virtual ruination of a perfectly good pair of leather riding breeches—to finally persuade the recalcitrant animal to succumb to his advances, but once he had managed to get back into the swing of things the old memories had come quickly flooding back.

Milking cows, collecting eggs, haymaking, picking apples and chopping logs—there had been very few activities in which the Viscount had not involved himself during his boyhood on the family estate. Sadly, his ongoing feud with his father had brought about an instant demise of any undertaking that smacked even vaguely of husbandry, in whatever shape or form it might have appeared. Indeed, for the past six years or so he had resolutely refused to involve himself in all matters that had to do with the running of the family estate—to his own detriment, more often than not, as his recent unexpectedly pleasurable activities were now starting to bring home to him.

It had been while he was splitting the logs into a more convenient size that it had begun to occur to him that he actually enjoyed involving himself in this sort of manual labour. Even as the snow had continued to fall in gusting billows all around him, its icy wetness gradually penetrating the fine wool of his expensive riding jacket, he had not been able to help but feel that there was something infinitely wholesome about expending one's energy for the benefit of others—a feeling of healthy satisfaction that even several hours spent in Gentleman Jackson's salon or at the fencing parlour failed to emulate. Sophie's unspoken message that the entire well-being of a handful of total strangers might well devolve upon his being able to keep the house supplied with firewood had brought about the first real sense of purpose that he had experienced for many years. Indeed, just the thought of finding himself the recipient of another of her devastatingly captivating smiles was more than enough incentive to have him attacking even the largest of logs with considerable relish.

And as to the milking! It was beyond thought that he was ever going to allow a mere animal to get the better of him! Aside from which, he was quite determined not to set a foot back inside that blessed kitchen without bearing a reasonable quantity of milk—he'd have that confounded cap off the saucy little madam's head if it was the last thing he did!

His dark eyes gleaming with satisfaction, he now considered Sophie's greatly improved appearance. Freed from the constriction of the cap, several strands of her hair—the colour of which he could only liken to that of ripe chestnuts—fell about her neck in a teasing tangle, instilling in him a sudden urge to rip out the confining pins of the remains of her bundled chignon just to see if the total effect was truly as glorious as his alcohol-fuelled fantasy of the previous night had imagined it to be.

Drawing in a deep breath, in order to steady his rapidly increasing pulse rate, he turned his attention back to the landlady, who had been marvelling at the huge pile of logs stacked beside the chimneypiece.

'There's a good bit more just inside the door of the taproom, ma'am,' he said, jerking his head in the direction of the saloon bar. 'I took the liberty of piling it there, since I doubt that any of your regular clients will be likely to pay us a visit during the next couple of days or so.'

'Still no sign of a let-up, then?' queried Sophie, as she collected three bowls from the dresser and doled out a healthy serving of porridge into each of them.

'Sadly not,' he replied, taking a seat at the table. 'That driver of yours seems to be of the opinion that we're stuck here for the duration. Having very sensibly taken the precaution of pulling the carriage into the barn as soon as they arrived, he and the guard have made themselves up a couple of very comfortable looking beds on the squabs. Organised themselves quite a cosy little set-up out there, they have—even got a brazier burning in the middle of the barn.'

'It sounds as though they must have been soldiers at one time.' Sophie laughed. 'Many's the time my little brother and I were obliged to bed down in such a manner.' Then, stealing an impish look at him, she went on, 'I dare say you must quite envy the pair of them, given your own rather Spartan accommodation.'

Mrs Webster gave a quick nod. 'Yes, we must see if we can't do something about that, young man,' she declared. 'There are a couple of cushioned settles in the tap room—not ideal, certainly, but a sight better than what you had to put up with last night, I feel sure!'

'Oh, I've known worse, I assure you!' he said, flashing a mischievous smile at the now somewhat rosy-cheeked Sophie. 'Nevertheless, I daresay another cushion or two would be most welcome—I'll bring them into the parlour after I've eaten, if I may—although I rather fear that my being obliged to commandeer the room for my own personal use will disadvantage your other guests to some extent.'

'Can't be helped,' retorted Mrs Webster, getting to her feet and moving towards the pantry. 'Needs must, as they say—now, what do the pair of you say to a nice dish of bacon and scrambled eggs?'

'I say yes, please, and thank you very much,' replied Marcus with a quick nod of his head, as he spooned the last of his porridge into his mouth. 'Best porridge I've tasted in years,' he then averred, fixing Sophie with another of his slightly lopsided grins and causing her to experience all sorts of problems with her breathing processes. 'Although I feel bound to confess that I haven't touched the stuff since I was in leading-reins!'

'It's amazing what one will eat if one is hungry!' she returned somewhat distractedly, gripping her hands tightly together under the table in an effort to still the frightening rapidity of her heartbeat. 'My brother and I were often obliged to eat all manner of strange concoctions during our years with the military—but it certainly taught us to appreciate good food when it was offered to us.'

'I appreciated every mouthful, I promise you,' he assured her quickly, his sharp eyes not having missed the rather forlorn look that had suddenly crept across her face as she spoke of her past. 'However, I cannot help but wonder about these strange concoctions of which you spoke. Pray enlighten me.'

Pushing back her chair, she stood up, affecting an airy little laugh. 'Best not to describe such delicacies in detail, I assure you, and certainly not while you are about to eat Mrs Webster's delicious breakfast!' she said, determinedly busying herself with the collecting up of the empty bowls before carrying them over to the kitchen sink.

His eyes following her progress across the room, Marcus's lips curved in appreciative recall of the softly rounded curves that dwelt beneath the ill-fitting grey gown she wore, the memory of which brought about the all too familiar clenching of his gut followed by the usual pulsating throb of his loins. Gritting his teeth, he forced himself to concentrate his attention on the very appetising-looking meal that Mrs Webster had placed before him, ruefully reflecting that any sort of casual dalliance with the comely governess in these present conditions looked to be very much against the odds. Not only had it transpired that Miss Flint was sharing her room with her young charge, but—even given that his chances of persuading her to venture there a second time were probably a hundred to one against—his own accommodation hardly lent itself to the sort of activity he had in mind.

Heaving back a sigh of regret, he did his best to dismiss the several enticing images that were beginning to crowd his brain and, reaching for his knife and fork, endeavoured to apply his concentration to the heaped platter of eggs and bacon in front of him, being very careful to avoid looking directly at the object of his lustful thoughts when she returned to the table and took her place opposite him.

'At least the pump hasn't frozen,' she remarked cheerfully, as she reached across the table and helped herself to one of Mrs Webster's hastily cooked griddle scones. 'I was afraid that we might have to resort to melting buckets of snow for our water!'

'Lor' bless you, no, Miss!' chortled the landlady. 'That's one thing we won't have to worry about, thanks to the fellow who built this place originally. Comes up from the well right next to the back wall, the water does. We have to wrap the outside pipe with a bit of sheepskin every winter to be on the safe side, of course, but apart from that we've never had a hap'orth of trouble.'

'I dare say you've been obliged to do that as well,' remarked the Viscount, chancing a quick look at Sophie.

She looked puzzled. 'Wrap pipes with sheepskin, you mean?'

He shook his head and a reluctant grin crept across his face. 'No, I was referring to your reference to the melting of buckets full of snow—I assumed that you must have been involved in such an activity during your days with the military.'

'Once or twice.' She nodded, her face clearing. 'It can get very cold in the mountain areas of Spain and Portugal.' She paused, as a little furrow creased her brow. 'I take it that you chose not to volunteer your own services?'

There was a moment's silence, then, 'I had my reasons,' returned Marcus curtly, as he pushed back his chair and rose from the table, his meal scarcely half finished. 'If you will excuse me? I really ought to go and check my horse over.'

'Touched a sore nerve there, it seems,' murmured Mrs Webster, after he had exited the room. 'Yon driver told me he'd fed and watered all the horses first thing, before him and his mate cleared the yard. Our Mr Wolfe looks to be sufferin' from a bit of a guilty conscience, if you want my opinion.'

'Probably just not cut out for that sort of life, Mrs

Webster,' said Sophie. 'Judging from the quality of his boots and the cut of his jacket, I should imagine that Mr Wolfe spends most of his time lounging in the high-class drawing rooms of the rich and famous—although I feel bound to admit that his undoubted expertise with the axe did come as somewhat of a surprise to me.'

'And may the heavens be thanked for it,' returned the landlady, with a slight shake of her head. 'Where we would have been without the lad, the Lord only knows. Your old driver and his mate have been workin' nineteen to the dozen keepin' the yard clear of snow, as well as seein' to the horses, but I doubt if either of them could chop up a log to save his life. Even my Walter would be hard put to it these days—our potboy usually deals with the likes of that sort of thing!'

'Well, we definitely shan't go cold, at any rate,' said Sophie, rising to her feet and beginning to gather up the dirty dishes. 'And, thanks to your excellent housekeeping, it seems unlikely that any of us will starve. Shall we take a peek into your larder and see what we can conjure up for dinner between us?'

'I've a nice leg of ham hanging there,' began Mrs Webster, as she made her way across the room towards the storeroom. 'I had thought of keepin' it for…'

The rest of her sentence was cut off as the sound of running footsteps on the stairs heralded the arrival of a white-faced Mr Lucan, who burst into the kitchen, calling out for immediate assistance.

'My wife!' he gasped, as he clutched at the doorjamb to steady himself. 'She thinks the babe is on its way! Somebody help her, I beg of you! *Please!*'

Whipping off her soiled apron, Sophie started for the door, only to find herself being pulled back by Mrs Webster.

'Not you, my dear,' cautioned the landlady. 'This sort of thing is not at all suitable for a young unmarried lady such as yourself. I'm not exactly up to the mark myself, but I shall do what I can. You stay here and see to the dinner.'

'Nonsense!' averred Sophie cheerfully. 'I've helped deliver dozens of babies—midwives were few and far between on the Peninsula, I assure you!'

Turning to Lucan, she bade him to calm down and then instructed him to make himself useful by filling all the pots he could find with water and putting them on to boil.

'Why ever 'ave you set 'im to doing that?' whispered the mystified Mrs Webster, as the two of them hastened up the stairs in the direction of the plaintive wails issuing from within the Lucans' bedroom. 'I disremember anyone doin' any such thing when my Jamie was born.'

'Just gives the poor fellow something to occupy his mind,' replied Sophie, with a slight chuckle. 'Expectant fathers are known to become somewhat beside themselves at such times—we always found it better to keep them well out of the way until the worst of the business was over and done with. Speaking of which—do you have some old sheets we could use?'

Chapter Four

Having spent the best part of the past hour exchanging ribald jokes and anecdotes with Driver Lapworthy and his guard, Marcus was in a far better frame of mind when he eventually returned to the kitchen, only to find himself confronted by the sight of a white-faced Jack Lucan, anxiously pacing the floor of the room, quite oblivious to the argument going on between the Reverend Palfrey and Captain Gibbons who, having finally ousted themselves from their bed, had come down to the kitchen in the expectation of finding a meal waiting for them. Finding no one available to serve their needs, they had raided the larder and were now noisily debating the merits of frying eggs as opposed to scrambling them.

'Do you actually have any idea how to scramble eggs?' demanded Gibbons scathingly, as he attempted to extricate the skillet from the parson's hands. 'At least I've fried a good few in my time!'

'And nasty greasy things they were too, I'll be bound,' retorted Palfrey, determinedly clinging to the pan. 'A lightly scrambled egg is far better for a delicate stomach.'

'Well, my stomach ain't in the least bit delicate,' roared the Captain, having finally managed to wrench the utensil out of the weaker man's grasp. 'It's just grumbling from lack of sustenance!'

'Please, please, gentlemen,' interposed the distraught Lucan. 'Have a little consideration for my poor wife in her hour of need.'

Casting sullen looks at one another, the two elderly squabblers ceased their wrangling and did their utmost to appear suitably chastened at his appeal.

Stepping forward, Marcus reached across and relieved Gibbons of his recently acquired trophy.

'Since there appear to be at least half a dozen cooking pots readily available,' he commented sagely, 'it would seem sensible for each of you to have his eggs in whichever way suits him best. If you would care to sit yourselves down at the table, gentlemen, I am sure I can attend to both your requirements.' Then, turning to Lucan, he added, 'You too, my good sir, if you please— from your agitated demeanour I must assume that your wife is at this moment doing her best to provide you with an heir. I hasten to point out that you will do the young lady no favours by collapsing at her bedside for want of an egg or two.'

Although he cast a somewhat piteous look in his direction, the young father-to-be obeyed the Viscount without comment, reluctantly sitting himself down at the table while Marcus proceeded to break three eggs into the already sizzling frying pan, before turning his attention to the whipping up of several more prior to tipping them into a butter-laced pot.

What an extraordinary day this is turning into! he

mused, as he stirred the eggs in one pan and flipped the others over in the skillet. *Chopping logs, milking cows and now—by all that's marvellous—acting as kitchen maid to as big a set of nincompoops as I've ever come across! Damned lucky I spent so much time down in the kitchens at Bradfield when I was a lad. What next, I wonder? Just so long as they don't expect me to deliver the blessed baby!*

At this thought he frowned, having suddenly realised that the continued absence of both Sophie and Mrs Webster seemed to indicate that the two of them were engaged in that very task. *Hardly a suitable occupation for an unmarried girl, surely?* Although, from what he had already gathered from her earlier remarks, it would seem that there were few things at which that particular young lady would demur from attempting, if the need arose.

His lips twisted as Sophie's query as to his involvement in the country's recent hostilities returned to haunt him, and, as always, a hot surge of resentment ran through him as he recalled his father's absolute obduracy over the matter throughout the past six years. Although why it should now concern him what conclusion a virtual stranger might have reached over his apparent lack of participation, he was hard put to fathom. Yet for some unknown reason it did.

The faint smell of singeing alerted him back to the task in hand. Hastily he slid the pan of frying eggs away from the hotplate before any real damage was done, and skilfully tipped the contents on to Captain Gibbons's plate, then returning to the range to collect the pot of scrambled eggs, which he placed on the table and exhorted the other two men to 'dig in' while his offering was still at its best.

Sadly enough, Mr Lucan had barely dipped his fork into the minute portion of the creamy mixture to which he had helped himself before the passage door sprang open and a laughing-eyed Sophie was informing the assembled company of the safe arrival of one Master John Henry Lucan.

'I believe your wife would like to see you now, sir,' she said, shooting the new father a mischievous smile. 'She is rather tired, of course, but has asked if you could manage to spare her a few moments of your time…?'

Dropping his fork, Lucan was on his feet in a flash, had dashed through the doorway and was halfway up the stairs before any of his table companions could even draw breath to offer him their congratulations.

Heaving a deep sigh, the now slightly tearful Sophie turned to look at the coffee-pot, simmering at the back of the range. 'I believe I have earned a cup of that, if one of you gentlemen would be good enough to pour it for me,' she murmured, as she lowered herself into Mrs Webster's fireside chair and, leaning her head back against the cushions, closed her eyes.

Marcus had sprung to attention before either of the other two men had even registered her words, and in no time at all he was at her side, offering the requested refreshment.

Having reluctantly managed to pry her eyelids apart, Sophie was startled to find herself immediately confronted with Marcus's dark brown gaze, only inches from her face. For a moment it seemed that her heart had stopped beating and her entire body seemed to be flooding with the oddest sensations, the like of which she had never before experienced. An inexplicable feeling of panic ran through her, causing her to shoot bolt upright, and it was only Marcus's quick reaction to her sudden movement that prevented her from being deluged with the scalding contents of the cup he held in his hand.

'Whoa, steady, there!' he cautioned, as he laid the cup down on the hearth. 'A breath of fresh air is what you really need, you know,' he said, frowning in concern as he took in the faint shadows beneath her eyes. 'I believe it stopped snowing some time ago. If you would care to step outside for a few moments, I should be more than happy to keep you company.'

Sophie rose to her feet, desperately trying to control the violent wave of trembling that still beset her.

'I—I'll just get my pelisse—it should be dry by now—Mrs Webster kindly hung it on the drying frame for me...'

She had the distinct feeling that she was talking gibberish but could not seem to get a grip on herself. Before she could even attempt to extricate her pelisse from the overhead frame, Marcus had reached up and unhooked it and was, even now, coaxing her into sliding her arms through the sleeves. Ignoring her muted protests, he proceeded, in the most matter-of-fact way, to pull the coat-fronts together and fasten the buttons, before standing back and regarding her with a quizzical frown.

'Not exactly the warmest coat I've ever come across,' he observed, with a crooked smile. 'You had better have my scarf.'

Tucking her arm into his elbow, he led her across to the back door where, after collecting his thick red woollen scarf from the hook on the wall, he wrapped it firmly over her head and around her neck before opening the door and leading her out into the stableyard.

'Oh, goodness me!' she gasped, stepping back as the cold air hit her. 'I'm not sure I wouldn't rather have stayed by the fire!'

'A little bit of exercise will soon get the blood flowing,' he teased and, bending down, he picked up a small handful of snow, compressed it into a ball and gently tossed it towards her, taking great care to avoid actually hitting her.

'Why, you…!'

Filling her hands with snow, she balled it and flung it at him, missing him by several feet. Stooping to gather up more ammunition, she found herself obliged to dodge the hail of missiles that Marcus had seemed able to conjure up before she had managed to collect even the one—although she quickly came to the conclusion that his aim was no better than hers since very few of his snowballs ever made real contact with her person. Nevertheless, dashing from one side of the stableyard to the other soon had her feeling warmed from the tip of her nose right down to her toes, and it was not long before she was obliged to seek refuge against the cowshed wall where she held up her hands and laughingly begged him for mercy.

'Only if you pay the time-honoured forfeit.'

He walked towards her, his lips curved and eyes gleaming with unsuppressed amusement. Standing directly in front of her, he reached out his hands and began busying himself with a purposeful rearrangement of her head covering, which had gone somewhat adrift during their boisterous frolic.

'F-forfeit?'

Sophie cast a wary glance upward and then wished she had not done so, for the look in his eyes as he stared down at her was more than enough to have her heart doing that very same stop/start dance that had brought her out here in the first place. She was almost certain that he was about to kiss her and she was not at all sure if that was such a good idea. She had been kissed before, it was true—swift, daring pecks on the cheek by bashful sub-lieutenants, for the most part, as her upbringing, though irregular, had been somewhat meticulous in certain respects. But, given what she had experienced the previous night, coupled with the strangely disturbing feelings that he seemed to engender within her simply by catching her eye, she could not help feeling that allowing herself to be kissed by Marcus Wolfe would prove to be a very big mistake.

Carefully easing one hand behind Sophie's neck, the Viscount, hardly daring to breathe lest he broke the spell that he had succeeded in conjuring up, bent his head to claim his much-desired forfeit.

Quick as a flash, Sophie ducked beneath his arm and spun out of reach, only to find herself suddenly sliding sideways across the snow-covered ground in the most inelegant fashion. With a startled oath Marcus grabbed at her falling figure, whereupon he too found himself sliding on the ice. Concerted cries of dismay emanated from the pair as, wildly clutching at each other and powerless to prevent their descent, they fell headlong into a nearby snowdrift.

'Deuce take it, woman!' gasped Marcus, when he had recovered sufficiently to take a breath. 'What in God's name was that all about?'

With the full weight of his body on top of her, Sophie was finding it impossible to concentrate her mind on the whys and wherefores of her precipitate action, but, as the melting snow began to make its presence felt through the thin fabric of her pelisse, the need to extricate herself became paramount. 'Kindly remove yourself!' she grated through clenched teeth. 'The snow is soaking through my coat.'

'Hardly surprising,' he snapped, as he clambered to his feet and reached down to haul her out of the drift. The whole experience had left him feeling decidedly irritated. Hardly had he had time to react to Sophie's unexpected rejection of his advances before he had found himself pitched ignominiously into a heap of snow where, to his everlasting shame and annoyance, he been unable to control his all too swift reaction to the soft imprint of her curves as they pressed against his body. The powerful sensations that had swept through him had left him in a state of stunned bewilderment which had, somehow or other, exacerbated his feelings of umbrage towards the wet and shivering creature standing in front of him. 'You really need to furnish yourself with a much more suitable outfit, my dear, if you will insist on long-distance travel at this time of year,' he ground out tersely.

Now thoroughly chilled to the bone, Sophie was in no mood for such high-handed observations from someone who clearly had no notion of how it might feel to be inadequately clad and all but penniless.

'Some of us have little choice in the matter of what we are obliged to wear,' she flashed back, doing her level best to stop her teeth from chattering. 'We don't all have fat purses and wardrobes full of furs!'

He stilled, staring down at her, a mental picture of her sprawled across his bed draped in white furs suddenly filling his imagination. 'You could have all of that and more if you really wanted it,' he said huskily, his fingertips reaching across to caress her damp cheek. 'I have the neatest little cottage in Chelsea—'

'How dare you, sir?'

An ice-cold hand hard across the side of his face brought the trembling Viscount swiftly to his senses.

Good God, he thought, aghast, *was I really about to offer a* carte blanche *to an impoverished governess? I must be losing my mind!*

Shaking with a curious combination of heart-wrenching desolation coupled with out-and-out fury, Sophie angrily divested herself of the Viscount's scarf and, after flinging the offending article at him, started back towards the inn, taking very careful steps across the now visibly melting snow. She had almost gained the back door when the faint but unmistakable jingle of horses' traces reached her ears. She stopped, straining hard to identify the sound. Yes, there it was again! There was traffic moving on the road above. Her eyes shining, she whirled round to face the still rigidly motionless Viscount.

'There!' she cried. 'Do you hear it? The road must be passable again. We must all set to and dig out a pas-sageway for the coach. We could be away first thing tomorrow if we put our backs into it!'

'Dig out a passageway?' returned the Viscount, with a disdainful curl of his lip. 'Who? You, me and those two old has-beens in the stable, I suppose? It would take us until a week next Friday to clear that amount of snow!'

She stared at him in disbelief, then shook her head. 'You can take it from me that neither Lapworthy nor Hastings will be so faint-hearted when they hear that the road is open,' she said, before adding disparagingly, 'It's little wonder that you chose not to join the military. I doubt that you would have even survived the Channel crossing!'

Clenching his fists, Marcus took a single step for-ward, then stopped.

'Had you been a man, you would have paid dearly

for that insult,' he ground out. 'Let me assure you that you'll get your passageway, Miss Flint—even if I have to carve it out with my bare hands. Might I suggest that you take yourself off and devote your efforts to attending to the needs of those who clearly appreciate your company more than I do?'

With that, he turned on his heel and stalked towards the door of the stable, from which were already emerging the elderly coach driver and his guard, each of them carrying an assortment of tools.

'Did you hear it?' called the guard, as he rolled up his sleeves and started to shovel at the softening snow. 'That be the four o'clock mail out of Bath, sure as my name's Gus Hastings. Trifle tardy, to be sure, but they allus keeps the mails runnin', no matter what! Bit o' fierce diggin' and we'll be out of here before the cat can spit!' Then, turning to the Viscount, he added, 'How's about it, sir? You'll be up for it, I'm sure.'

'Lead on, Macduff,' murmured Marcus resignedly, as he divested himself of both his greatcoat and jacket, at once revealing the hefty muscles in his arms and thighs, courtesy of his many hours spent in Jackson's parlour, sparring against the great man himself. 'At a guess, I'd say it's about fifty or sixty yards to the turnpike.'

With a brief nod, the driver screwed up his eyes and stared across the snow-covered terrain in front of them. 'Uphill, too,' he said tersely, as he gathered together his chosen implements. 'We'll be slippin' an' sliding all the way—puts me in mind o' that winter when we was holed up in Lisbon, Gus. Do you recall?'

'Hard to forget!' came his companion's cheerful reply. 'Still, at least we don't 'ave to cross a flooded Douro on this occasion!'

Laughing together, the pair set to, but it soon occurred

to Sophie, who had been unable to drag herself away from the scene, that the advanced ages of the driver and his guard would eventually tell against them, for in spite of their obvious courage and determination it was clearly all they could do to stay abreast of Marcus, who was shovelling away as though his very life depended on it. Which, in the terms of bolstering up his dented pride and filling him with a much-needed sense of achievement, perhaps it did.

'I'll show the cold-hearted shrew,' he muttered to himself, as he tossed yet another hefty shovelful of snow to one side. *'I'll have her out of here by morning, if it's the last thing I do!'*

The sight of the damp shirt clinging to his rippling muscles was more than enough for Sophie to begin to regret her earlier outburst, for it was becoming increasingly clear that Marcus Wolfe was hardly the chicken-hearted poltroon that she had all but accused him of being. After watching him for some minutes she turned away and, with hot tears pricking at the back of her eyes, re-entered the inn to do as he had suggested and concentrate her attentions on the needs of the three invalids—at least they seemed to appreciate her efforts, she thought as, with a plaintive sniff, she wiped away the unbidden tears.

The snow-clearing operation continued well into the evening, when the lack of light brought such proceedings to a halt. Even Lucan had insisted upon taking his turn, and had done sterling work for almost an hour, despite the fact that neither he nor his wife were likely to be in any position to complete their own journey for some days. Even the doughty Captain managed a couple of feet or so, before a violent bout of coughing sent him back into the welcoming warmth of the inn's kitchen.

Throughout the entire range of shift-changing, however, Marcus pressed on, oblivious to the various recommendations that he should stop and take a well-earned rest. Sheer dogged determination drove him on—to give up now would be to admit defeat, and there was no way he was going to allow Sophie to witness failure at this stage of the game!

In the end, however, despite the fact that the ever-cheerful Gus Hastings had brought out a lantern to help the Viscount carve his way through the waist-deep drifts that had formed throughout the previous night and earlier part of the day, the growing darkness finally overcame even his obdurate resolution.

'Best jack it in now, mate,' advised the guard. 'A good night's sleep and we can 'ave at it again come first light—less than twenty yards to go now, by my reckonin'.'

Utterly spent, and with every muscle in his body crying out for reprieve, Marcus at last agreed that it was time to quit, and, after virtually dragging himself back to the sanctuary of the kitchen, he collapsed into the chair by the fireside and thankfully accepted Mrs Webster's offer of a hot toddy.

'I'll take myself off to my bed now, if you have no objections,' he croaked wearily, after he had downed half of the spicy mixture. 'If you could manage to dry my shirt by morning, I'd be most grateful.'

'No problem at all, sir,' Mrs Webster assured him, as she draped a large towel over his heaving shoulders. 'I've put extra rugs and cushions on the settle, so you should get a fairly decent sleep tonight. Just pass me out your shirt and I'll have it clean and ready for you when you need it.'

Ignoring the rest of the assembled company, the

Viscount headed for his makeshift bed in the parlour, unbuttoning his soaking wet shirt as he went. Once inside his room, he peeled it off and passed it out to the waiting landlady, bidding her a weary goodnight as he closed the door.

'Young fool was practically killing himself out there,' observed the Captain, with a concerned shake of his head. 'Must be desperate keen to get on his way.'

Desperately keen to get away from me, more likely, was Sophie's forlorn thought, as she finished drying the last of the supper dishes. Having been watching Marcus out of the corner of her eye, in the vain hope of seeing some sign of conciliation from him, it had been made clear to her that he had no intention of giving her any chance to apologise for her recklessly hurtful remarks, the constant memory of which now filled her with a burning sense of self-recrimination. She found herself thinking that even the fact that he appeared to have been about to suggest that living under his protection might be preferable to the penury of her present position could not really be regarded as ample justification for the unbridled discourtesy of her response. Her six-month tenure with the Crayfords had left her with few illusions as to how the so-called *haut monde* conducted their lives. Indeed, she had soon learned that many females in circumstances similar to her own would have been only too glad to jump at such a generous offer especially—as she found herself obliged to admit, albeit with a some- what rueful sigh—from so personable a man as Marcus Wolfe!

But then, she reasoned, as she lifted her chin and squared her shoulders in preparation to bidding her fellow travellers goodnight and quitting the room, her parents had brought her up to place a high regard on her self-respect, and, although it was true that her situation within the Crayford family was far from ideal, she was not yet reduced to selling herself in order to survive!

This spirited resolve was doomed to falter slightly as she made her way past the door to Marcus's sleeping quarters and was unable to prevent herself from conjuring up a picture of his bronzed and muscular torso—shirtless now, of course—only to find herself then wondering if he slept in those thigh-hugging leather breeches or...!

Pulling herself up sharp, she all but fled up the stairs to her own bedchamber, where she was more than pleased to find that her young charge, having been liberally dosed with Mrs Webster's willow-bark powders throughout the day, was now almost back to her normal petulant self. So much so that she was quite adamant in her refusal to allow her governess to borrow one of her many nightgowns, forcing Sophie to spend yet another night in her flimsy shift.

Rolling off his cushioned settle well before any sensible-minded lark would even consider the possibility of rising, Marcus flexed his aching muscles, pulled on his breeches and opened his bedroom door—to find there on the floor, just as promised, his shirt, newly washed and ironed. Even the hardly surprising discovery that none of the other stalwart navigators had yet risen from their beds did not deter the Viscount from rescuing his discarded shovel from where he had tossed it the previous evening and applying himself once more to his gruelling self-appointed task.

Having spent much of the night doing his best to dismiss all thoughts of Sophie from his mind, he had found himself racked with an unfathomable remorse at having treated her in such a cavalier manner. *What in God's name could I have been thinking of?* he had asked himself over and over again. With two perfectly satisfactory mistresses already at his disposal and any number of bored young matrons indicating their willingness to make themselves available to him, his needs in that particular direction were more than adequately served. So what it was about this chestnut-haired, startlingly blue-eyed nobody that had managed to get under his skin he was hard pressed to comprehend. It was true that he had been without a woman for almost a week now, but surely, he thought savagely, as he dug his shovel into the snow, his sexual proclivities were not so all-consuming that he needed to latch on to the first pretty wench that he came across after a mere seven days? If so, heaven help him! He must really be turning into the godforsaken wastrel that his father had dubbed him! At that thought he could not help but let out a deep chuckle. If the old man could but see him now—knee-deep in a snowdrift! Knee-deep? He paused, leant on his shovel and stared at the blanketed terrain around him, suddenly realising that the snow's depth, which had been well over three feet down at the lower part of the dig, was now down to less than two the closer he got to the highway. In just a couple of yards it would be possible to simply scrape it to one side to allow the carriage free access.

And so it was that, shortly after ten o'clock that same morning, the three other men having applied themselves to the task with extra vigour once they realised that their goal was no longer as insurmountable as it had seemed eighteen hours earlier, the passage was pronounced navigable. A hasty breakfast was gulped down as quickly as was humanly possible by those intending to travel, and by eleven o'clock the horses were poled up, the luggage strapped on to the roof and the driver declared the coach ready to depart.

With her four shillings and ninepence still intact—Mrs Webster having waved away all attempts at any sort of payment from her, on the grounds that she had achieved far more in the past two days than the absent local girl usually managed in a week—Sophie climbed into the carriage and took one of the window seats, with the well-wrapped-up Lydia at her side and Gibbons and Palfrey seated opposite. The Lucans, of course, would not be travelling to the Maidenhead post with them, but Sophie had promised to get a message to Mrs Lucan's anxiously waiting mother, in order that that lady might set about organising her family's safe removal from the little inn.

Looking out of the window, she could see that Jack Lucan and Marcus were standing ready to apply their shoulders to the rear of the vehicle, should the precipitous slope prove difficult to negotiate. She tried focussing her gaze on the back of Marcus's head, desperately willing him to turn and look in her direction so that she could at least wave him farewell, but to no avail.

After two failed attempts to chivvy the lead horses up the slope, the coach at last began to move, and with Gus Hastings encouraging the horses at the front, and Marcus and Lucan hefting their backs at the rear, the ancient vehicle gradually began to lumber slowly through the man-made passageway.

Once on the turnpike, however, it was clear that the going had been made easier by the passage of several other vehicles already. Added to which, the sun had finally come out from behind the clouds and the snow was now beginning to melt quite rapidly. By midafternoon, Marcus hazarded, as he stood at the top of the incline trying to get his breath back, most of it would in all likelihood have disappeared completely, leaving him with nothing but a few painful memories that he could well do without. Time to saddle Jupiter and continue his own interrupted journey, he reminded himself dismally. On to London, his original destination, or back to Bradfield to try and make peace with his father? At this point, he had no real idea of what he wanted to do.

Heaving a deep sigh, he turned to watch Gus climbing up on to the box next to Lapworthy. In doing so, he was unable to prevent himself casting a quick glance towards where Sophie was sitting, next to the carriage's already misted-up window. Having made up his mind to avoid all contact with her since their altercation in the yard, he had not even joined in the round of farewells that had taken place when the travellers were ready to depart, electing instead to busy himself with the strapping on of the luggage. But now, as his eyes made contact with hers, his heart stopped, his stomach seemed to turn over and a sudden disquieting panic threatened to overwhelm him.

Barely stopping to think, he stepped forward, wrenched open the door of the carriage and, dipping his hand into his jacket pocket, extracted one of his calling cards. Thrusting it into the startled Sophie's hand, he exhorted her to contact him should she ever require his help, then, slamming the door shut before she could deny him, he stepped away from the vehicle just as the driver gave the lead horse the office to move on.

A heartening surge of relief seemed to flood through his veins as he stood back and watched as the coach pulled away. Now, at least, she was not lost to him for ever. By giving Sophie his card he had made it possible for him to call on her in the socially accepted manner. After that—well, who knew what Fate might have in store for them? But even as the Viscount sought to console himself with this comforting thought, the cold trickle of impending disaster proceeded to sweep it abruptly away as all at once it came to him that he had not the slightest idea of Sophie's place of residence—nor did he even know the name of the people who employed her! Any thoughts that he might have had about contacting her within the next few days were clearly doomed to failure!

Letting out a loud groan of dismay, he started after the carriage, though he was well aware that, with a team of frisky horses having been cooped up for two days at its head, his chances of catching up with the now swiftly moving vehicle were somewhat less than nil. After a fruitless dash of some fifty yards or so, he dragged to a gasping halt, his shoulders slumped in despair, and, disconsolately retracing his steps, he made his way back to the inn, hoping against hope that Mrs Webster could furnish him with the information he needed—information that had, for some inexplicable reason, suddenly become a most vital necessity!

Chapter Five

'I still fail to understand why finding this blessed female is of such vital importance to you. Have you fallen in love with her, or what?'

'Don't talk rot!'

Strolling with his brother Giles down Oxford Street's wide thoroughfare, Marcus let out a dismissive bark of laughter. Two weeks had passed since his return to the capital and he was still no further forward in his search. The tavern's landlady having informed him that she knew very little about Sophie's personal history, other than the fact that her father had been killed in action at Waterloo and that she had a younger brother who was away at school somewhere, Marcus had been reduced to enlisting his brother's help. The Major, in his capacity of Chief Intelligence Officer at the Home Office, was equipped with the necessary seniority of rank to pull all sorts of strings that were unavailable to the Viscount himself. So far, however, it would seem that even Giles's investigations had drawn a blank.

'Well, as I've already told you, the only Flints that I've been able to get any leads on are a young rifleman from the ninety-forth and a Scottish Colour Sergeant, neither of whom were married with children. There was one other—for what it's worth—but he was a highly decorated Lieutenant-Colonel, name of Pendleton-Flint. Can't see that he would fit your—where in the hell are you off to now?'

Left standing speechless as he watched his brother tear across the road, dodging in and out of the heavy press of traffic and taking his life in his hands, Giles was set to wondering—and not for the first time during the past fourteen days—whether Marcus had suffered some sort of weird brainstorm when he had been benighted by that freak blizzard. That the Viscount had been acting rather oddly since that time would be something of an understatement, to say the least, especially in regard to the puzzling rekindling of his once close relationship with his brother Giles, from whose side Marcus had hardly strayed since his arrival back in town. No all-night drinking and gambling sessions, no mad escapades with those equally notorious associates of his and, somewhat more disturbing, not a single minute spent in the company of either of his rather comely mistresses! Instead, an apparently single-minded dedication applied to the task of uncovering the whereabouts of some mysterious governess—a task to which he had also managed to persuade Major Wolfe to devote not only his expertise but quite a significant portion of the manpower at his disposal, in addition.

With a groan of dismay, Giles heaved in a choking gasp of despair as he witnessed his brother narrowly managing to avoid being crushed under the wheels of a heavily loaded brewer's dray before leaping up on to the pavement opposite, where he skidded to a breathless halt in front of the rather drab-looking wench who was walking amongst the press of people there.

'Mr Wolfe!'

Although her eyes had widened with delight at the unexpected pleasure of seeing Marcus again, Sophie's cheeks immediately flushed scarlet as she realised how she had addressed him. 'I do beg your pardon, my lord,' she substituted hurriedly. 'H-how nice to see you! H-how are you keeping? Well, I trust?'

The mere sight of him had reduced her to talking gibberish again, and she knew it. A fortnight of sleepless nights, tossing about on her hard, lumpy mattress, doing her best to put all thoughts of Marcus Wolfe out of her mind, had done little to improve her appearance. Her hair was, once again, encased in the dreaded lace cap, and both her nondescript bonnet and pelisse were as grey and as shabby as they had ever been. Since her shocked discovery that plain Mr Wolfe was—as indicated by the card that he had thrust into her hand at their parting—none other than Viscount Helstone, heir to the Bradfield earldom, and, according to what she had overheard of the servants' chatter, more generally referred to as 'Hellcat Helstone' in the gossip columns of the popular press—she had alternated between thanking her lucky stars that their acquaintanceship had been cut short so precipitately and ruefully wondering how it might have developed had she been bold enough to accept his outrageous offer.

Mrs Crayford having held her personally responsible for Lydia's severe cold on their belated return to the capital, the quality of her life in the Lennox Gardens residence had continued to deteriorate and, since there had been no snow in or around the centre of London at the time, her employer had refused to concede that the weather could have been so bad as to prevent their return at the pre-arranged time. This had not been helped by her daughter's input that 'There really didn't seem to be that much snow about, as far as I could recall'—an unsurprising evaluation of the situation, given that the girl had spent the whole of the two days in bed, being waited on by her luckless companion.

Added to which, the young Arthur Crayford, his objective having been made only too clear on any number of previous occasions, had recently taken to waylaying Sophie in some deserted part of the house or other and pressing his lubricious attentions on her—a rather taxing situation that was beginning to cause her real concern.

Marcus, gazing down at her pale drawn face, could not help observing that she seemed to have lost weight since their last meeting, and as the possibility that she might be being deprived of food invaded his mind he found himself beset by a hot flood of rage.

'I'm fine,' he said, in reply to her garbled question. 'How about you?'

'Very well, thank you,' came her automatic response, which might have caused the Viscount to laugh out loud, had his attention not been drawn to the dark shadows under her eyes.

By this time Giles had managed to cross the road and was standing to one side, waiting for his brother to introduce him to the waif-like creature in the shabby attire.

At his discreet cough, Marcus flushed, as he belatedly remembered his manners.

'My brother—Major Wolfe,' he said, not taking his eyes from Sophie's stricken face as he waved a careless hand in Giles's direction. 'This lady is my Miss Flint, Giles.'

'Good God!'

Marcus's use of the possessive pronoun, followed so swiftly by his brother's explosive epithet of astonishment, brought yet another rosy flush to Sophie's cheeks, but on this occasion it was a flush of indignation. Raising her chin, she stared pointedly at Giles, favouring him with an example of one of the chilling glances that generally had the effect of putting even the most recalcitrant of her charges firmly in their place.

It worked, rendering the Major duly admonished.

'I beg your pardon, ma'am,' he stuttered as, casting a furious glare at Marcus and registering the unrepentant gleam of amusement in his brother's eyes, he collected himself sufficiently to execute an elegant bow.

Before Sophie was able to respond to the Major's gallant gesture, however, she felt herself being shunted forward as someone barged into her from behind, throwing her completely off balance. Letting out a cry of dismay, she would certainly have fallen to the ground had not Marcus, uttering an angry curse, thrown out his hands to grab at her and pulled her quickly towards him. For an instant the sudden surge of joy that cascaded through her at finding herself wrapped in the Viscount's arms once more wiped all vestige of sense from Sophie's mind, filling her entire being with a wholly primitive need to return the unexpected embrace. Almost of their own volition her hands reached up, and might well have attained their goal had she not suddenly become aware of the fact that her small beaded reticule, which normally dangled by its chain at her wrist, was no longer in its accustomed place.

Groaning in exasperation, she hauled herself away from Marcus, crying, 'Oh, not again! My purse—it has been stolen!'

Pushing the bewildered Viscount to one side, she quickly took stock of the crowds milling all about them. Then, with an angry cry, she pointed to the raggedy barefoot youth she had spotted fleeing towards a nearby side alley. 'There!' she cried. 'See? That little devil has it in his hand!'

'Leave it to me!' responded Giles, and, taking off with all speed, he made after the fingersmith, leaving his brother to comfort the now highly irate Sophie.

'You had better come and sit down,' he urged, catching hold of her hand and directing her towards a nearby tea shop. 'You are shaking all over.'

Once inside, he signalled to a waiter and ordered tea. 'Best thing for shock,' he said, casting a concerned eye over Sophie's white-set features. 'Or so I have been told.'

'I'm not suffering from shock,' she retorted, through clenched teeth. 'What kind of a weak-kneed creature do you think I am? I'm just so utterly furious!'

'I can see that you must be,' sympathised the Viscount. 'I'm just glad that you weren't hurt. These young sneak thieves are getting more audacious by the day.'

Still frowning, Sophie did not reply.

'Did you lose a great deal?' he then asked, recalling the pitifully small cache of coins that she had had with her at the inn.

She gave a slight shrug of her shoulders. 'Do I really look as if I'm worth robbing?' she demanded, hurriedly blinking back the angry tears that threatened. 'Three shillings and sixpence and my last good handkerchief, if you really must know. All the rest went with my other purse yesterday morning.'

'You're not telling me that the same thing happened to you yesterday, too?' exclaimed Marcus, with a shocked expression.

Sophie gave him a weary nod. 'While I was taking my charges for their afternoon walk in the square gardens—I would have gone after the little devil, but of course I was unable to leave the children.'

'What truly damnable luck. You won't allow me to reimburse you, I dare say?'

She stared across at him, exasperation plain on her face. 'Certainly not! I thought I had made my position perfectly clear in that respect at our last meeting.'

'Well, yes, you did rather,' replied Marcus, his lips curving slightly as he lifted his fingers and patted the cheek she had slapped. 'This, however, is a somewhat different matter. I wouldn't care to think of you going without, for the sake of a few shillings on my part.'

Sophie shook her head. 'I shan't go without,' she assured him. 'It was money I had set aside for a book— an atlas I am in need of—I was on my way to the bookshop to enquire after it when we met.'

Leaning closer, he stretched out his hand and laid it on hers. 'Then at least let me purchase the book for you,' he said eagerly. 'Surely you must agree that it would be quite unexceptional for you to accept so mundane a gift from a friend?'

At his touch, Sophie's heart-rate shot up by several notches and, raising her teacup to her lips in order to hide her confusion, it was all she could do to prevent her hand from shaking. 'Thank you, my lord, but that really isn't necessary, I promise you,' she eventually managed and then, having struggled to get her emotions under control, added, 'In any event, I need to have words with the bookseller. I still have not received the book he promised to find for me, yet he has sent me the most ridiculous bill of sale. It's just fortunate that I was carrying it in my coat pocket; otherwise I would have lost that, too.'

A wide grin crept over Marcus's face. 'Well, I've often heard of bills being referred to as irritating, but "ridiculous"? That's certainly a new one on me!'

'Well, this one *is* ridiculous, I assure you,' retorted Sophie and, dipping her fingers into the pocket of her pelisse, she withdrew a folded sheet of paper and spread it out on the table in front of him. 'As you will see for yourself, if you care to examine it.'

At first, as far as the Viscount could see, the document looked like any other bill of sale, until he realised that, although it had 'Miss S. Flint' and—to his secret delight—Sophie's full Lennox Gardens address written clearly on the reverse of the sheet, the bill itself was, in fact, invoiced to a Mr Matthew Nyne.

'A simple misdirection, I'd say.' He smiled, handing it back to her.

'Yes, that's what I thought, at first,' she said, staring down at the missive. 'If it weren't for the fact that the arithmetic is quite bizarre. Look more closely, my lord, if you would.'

Although he was finding Sophie's continual use of his title somewhat jarring, Marcus thought it best to refrain from commenting on the matter. Reaching for the proffered document, he proceeded to give it his full attention.

<u>*Urgent Attn. Matthew Nyne*</u>

	£ : s : d
To Items	9 : 5
.. ..	5 : 4
.. ..	2 : 1
.. ..	2 : 2
To Items	2 : 4
.. ..	3 : 7
.. ..	5 : 4
To Items	5 : 1
.. ..	5 : 11
.. ..	2 : 2
.. ..	2 : 1
.. ..	3 : 8
Balance	£7 : 13 : 5

'Good grief!' he exclaimed eventually. 'Your book-seller clearly needs a few lessons in accountancy! Here! Take a look at this, Giles!'

This last was to his brother who, having failed in his pursuit of the guttersnipe who had made off with Sophie's reticule, had just this moment peered into the tearooms, in search of the missing pair.

'Tea! Good—oh!' he said, eyeing the teapot with satisfaction as he joined them. Then, catching sight of the piece of paper in Marcus's hand, he queried, 'What's to do? Not got behind in settling up your debts, have you, bro?'

After giving the Major's ankle a swift but harmless kick under the table, Marcus grinned and shoved the bill under his brother's nose while Sophie busied herself with the tea things. 'What do you make of that, then?' he asked.

Giles cast a cursory glance over the figures, and his

expression was at first quite indifferent. Then, stiffening, he shot a quick sideways look at Sophie and said quietly, 'May I ask how you came by this document, Miss Flint?'

'It was delivered along with yesterday morning's post,' she replied, somewhat taken aback at his abrupt manner. 'Why do you ask?'

'You were expecting an invoice from this Mr Broomfield?'

'In a manner of speaking, yes, but my bill would only have been for three shillings and sixpence, and as you see…'

'Yes. Quite.' Giles nodded, continuing to stare at Sophie in the most searching manner.

'Steady on, Giles!' protested Marcus, laughing. 'Why the interrogation? Miss Flint is not the one who has got her sums wrong!'

'Yes, I am aware of that,' said the Major abruptly, shooting his brother an exasperated glance before turning once more to Sophie and asking, 'Would it be possible for me to borrow this invoice for a day or so, I wonder? I would like to have one of my men take a copy, if you have no objection.'

'Take a copy!' exclaimed Sophie in astonishment, while Marcus simply looked at his brother in dumbfounded incredulity. 'Whatever for? Surely Mr Broomfield just needs to tell his clerk to sharpen up his ideas?'

'Possibly,' replied Giles briskly, rising to his feet, his tea still untasted. Folding the bill of sale carefully, he raised his eyebrows questioningly at Sophie and, at her mystified nod, tucked it into his jacket pocket, bowed neatly and bade them both farewell, before exiting the tea shop in considerable haste.

'Well, I'll be well and truly damned!' muttered Marcus under his breath, as he glared at his brother's departing figure in mystified disbelief.

Her sharp ears having caught his nonchalant profanity, Sophie was all at once put in mind of the scurrilous tales she had heard the servants whispering about the notorious Viscount, causing her to ask herself what on earth she thought she was doing, sitting in a public tea shop with so infamous a character as Hellcat Helstone. 'Oh, I do hope not,' she murmured softly, as she allowed her eyes to drink in the never to be forgotten contours of his features.

He, not having missed her words, stared across at her, a sardonic smile tugging at his lips.

'It would appear that your earlier opinion of me has undergone little alteration since our last encounter,' he sighed. 'Doubtless you have spent the past two weeks perusing the gossip columns—might I venture to suggest that I'm not actually as black as I have been frequently painted?'

A sudden flush covered her cheeks as she recalled her previous ruthless assessment of his worth.

'I seldom have the opportunity to read gossip columns,' she said, carefully avoiding his eyes. 'I usually prefer to make up my own mind about people.'

She paused, her brows furrowing slightly as she searched for the words. 'I am, however, sometimes a little too swift to reach conclusions,' she added, albeit somewhat reluctantly. 'My father was often obliged to remind me never to judge people on first appearance.'

His pulse quickening, the Viscount leant forward eagerly, finding himself inexplicably keen to learn whether her former opinion of him had changed.

'And so, after due consideration,' he said, hiding his

innermost feelings behind the light bantering tone that he was wont to employ when he was not entirely in command of the situation, 'may I be so bold as to enquire what conclusion you have now reached in regard to my reprehensible character?'

Frowning, Sophie gave a quick shake of her head. 'I have decided that I really don't know you well enough to have formed any worthwhile opinion, my lord,' she replied carefully. 'And, whilst your sterling efforts back at the tavern were certainly more than enough to revise my original view of you, I still do not understand why you felt it necessary to hide your true identity from all of us there—were you afraid that someone might try to take advantage of your lofty position?'

Shifting uncomfortably, the Viscount gave a noncommittal shrug. 'It has been known,' he replied. 'But I have to say that on that particular occasion it all came about rather by accident. I supplied my name—which *is* Marcus Wolfe, as it happens—and merely failed to qualify my title. Besides which...' Here he gave a rueful grin, before continuing. 'Following my behaviour towards you on the previous evening, I judged that it might be more circumspect to remain relatively anonymous for the duration of my stay there—I fear my reputation in that particular direction has the habit of preceding me.'

'Yes, I imagine that it must,' returned Sophie in a somewhat distracted tone of voice, unable to prevent her colour heightening as the well-remembered sensations of that encounter once again flooded through her being. But then, as she observed the almost imperceptible slump of his shoulders, her heart turned over, causing her to add gently, 'That being so, I have to say that, whilst you may not be quite as black as rumour seems to have painted you, you do appear to be verging on a rather dark shade of grey!'

At this, Marcus tipped back his head, letting out a sudden shout of laughter that reverberated across the room, causing several of the other customers to turn and cast disapproving frowns in their direction.

Still grinning, he then rose to his feet and held out his hand to her. 'Thoroughly hoist, then, I would say!' he chuckled. 'Let us hie ourselves off to your bookshop, then—it seems clear that I am desperately in need of a tome on moral rectitude, and you, my dear Miss Flint, seem to be the very person to point me in the proper direction.'

'But I no longer have the bill of sale to take to Mr Broomfield,' protested Sophie, as she got to her feet and began to pull on her gloves. 'What am I to say to him?'

'There is no need for you to mention anything about it—the fellow's not to know that you received the wrong invoice. The other note—the one that this Mr Nyne is now very likely in possession of—was probably to tell you that the book you had asked about had arrived. That being so, it will be perfectly in order for you to call into the shop and enquire after it.'

Yes, she could do that, thought Sophie, her eyes brightening at the notion of extending this chance meeting for a further half hour or so. Having given up all expectation of ever setting eyes on Marcus again—especially once she had been made aware of his true identity—there was no way on earth that she was even going to consider rejecting such an opportunity. Besides which, she reasoned, surely there was little need for her to concern herself with all those unproven rumours of the Viscount's less than perfect reputation since, after today's out-of-the-blue reunion, the chances of the pair of them ever crossing each other's paths again were extremely unlikely. That being so, the mere idea of spending even just a few more precious minutes in his company was far too tempting an offer on which she was prepared to turn her back. Regrettably, however, there was still that one troublesome drawback to consider…

'But if Mr Broomfield should happen to have my atlas in stock,' she felt constrained to point out, 'he will be expecting me to pay for it there and then, and—'

'Let's not cross that particular bridge until we get to it, shall we?' retorted Marcus, cutting her off before she had a chance to remind him of her lack of finances. 'I merely wanted a plausible excuse to take a quick peek at this numbskull clerk of his. My brother seemed extraordinarily interested in that invoice of yours—maybe this bookshop of yours is the hub of some shady goings-on and this Mr Broomfield is some sort of master criminal!'

Taking hold of her elbow, he manoeuvred her across the tea shop's threshold and out into the busy street where, on a sudden impulse, he beckoned over a nearby flower-seller and selected a large bunch of violets from her tray. Dividing the bunch into two halves, he drew Sophie towards him, and before she had any idea of his intent he had tucked one small posy into the top buttonhole of her threadbare pelisse.

Smiling down at her, a mischievous glint in his eye, he held the remaining flowers out towards her, allowing their delicate fragrance to waft into the air.

'I believe I have already earned the right to relieve you of that confounded cap, but if milking a cow is what it takes, I dare say I could prevail upon one of the milkmaids in the park to allow me to manhandle one of her charges!'

'Oh, but I couldn't possibly—' she began, uncomfortably aware of the crowds milling all about her, but then, as the powerful look of entreaty in the Viscount's eyes threatened to stop her breath entirely, a soft flush covered her cheeks and she began shakily to unravel the bow of her shabby grey bonnet, saying, 'I really cannot imagine what it is about the poor thing that annoys you so!'

'Apart from it being quite hideous in its own right,' he retorted softly, as he reached across and whipped the offending article from her head, before stuffing it into his jacket pocket, 'it makes you look about a hundred and five. But, more to the point, it has the damned effrontery to cover up your glorious hair.'

And then, before she was even aware of what he was about, he had tucked the stems of the remaining violets under the top ribbon of her bonnet, settled it back on to her head and was busily engrossed in retying the bow.

'Well, really, my lord!' exclaimed Sophie in stupefied amazement as, stepping back, the smiling Viscount gave a satisfied nod. Even though she was thoroughly astonished at his quite audacious behaviour, she could hardly help but feel secretly delighted at his rather gratifying comments regarding her hair, for, as she well remembered, her father had always considered her bright chestnut locks to be her crowning glory. It had been only as a result of Arthur Crayford's insidious pestering that she had taken to covering up what she had decided must act as some sort of catalyst to his repulsive conduct. Not that her actions appeared to have dissuaded the youth to any great extent, she was obliged to remind herself. But then, as Marcus, an oddly intent expression in his eyes, reached out and fingered a wayward curl that had escaped its confinement, all thoughts of Crayford and his irritating ways were wiped immediately from her mind.

Chapter Six

'So where exactly are we heading?' enquired Marcus, as he skilfully steered her through the heavy throng of Saturday afternoon promenaders. 'I thought I knew all the book emporiums in this part of town but I don't recall ever seeing a Broomfields.'

'His establishment is in an alley off Gilbert Street,' explained Sophie, somewhat guardedly. 'It is not a very grand place, but one of the assistants at Hatchards was good enough to recommend it to me as a possible source of the atlas for which I was searching.'

He looked down at her, his curiosity fired. 'And what's so special about this particular atlas?' he asked.

'It has some rather nice sketches in it, making it more suitable for younger children.'

'And Hatchards don't stock it?' The Viscount sounded surprised. 'They are usually pretty well up to snuff with that sort of thing, if my memory serves me aright.'

'As a matter of fact they did have several copies in stock,' replied Sophie, after some slight hesitation. 'But they were priced at three guineas each, and I—well—as you know—'

His face clearing, Marcus nodded. 'Ah! Now I begin to see! I take it that your Mr Broomfield is more of what we might term a *"used"* bookseller? May I ask how much he is asking for his copy?'

'Just three shillings and sixpence.' She sighed, uncomfortably aware of the fact that she no longer had such wherewithal available. 'He told me that he was sure that he had one somewhere in his stock—it really is most vexing!'

'I still don't understand why you feel it necessary to purchase the book yourself. Surely that sort of thing falls within your employer's domain? I should have thought that any household capable of employing a governess would be equipped with an adequate supply of necessary textbooks.'

'That's probably because you never have to involve yourself with people like the Crayfords,' muttered Sophie under her breath, but then, having reminded herself that this unexpected bonus of an hour or so in the Viscount's company was far too precious to be marred by petty grievances about her daily life, she tipped back her head and awarded him one of her most brilliant smiles—the effect of which was to cause Marcus to veer awkwardly into the path of an extremely stout gentleman who was struggling under the weight of a large assortment of boxes and packets.

'I say! Have a care, young fellow!' yelped the man, clutching at his mound of parcels.

Inwardly cursing, Marcus stooped to retrieve the lone packet that had fallen from the pile, before returning it to its former position with a bow and an apologetic smile. *No second-hand books for this extravagantly dressed figure of fun,* he thought bleakly, having instantly recognised Hatchards' distinctive wrapping paper on the neatly packaged item.

All of a sudden the fact that Sophie should feel obliged to make do with someone else's cast-off reading matter filled him with a red-hot fury the like of which he had never before experienced. That her employers were clutch-fisted upstarts was becoming increasingly clear to him, and to think of her having to live her life in so penurious a manner was becoming almost more than he could bear. He was consumed with an overpowering desire to sweep her up into his arms and carry her off to some secluded retreat where he could lavish upon her every luxury at his disposal—silks, satins, jewels, furs, perfumes—whatsoever she might wish for. He would be only too happy to see her every desire fulfilled—not to mention one or two of his own! Not that there was the least likelihood of being able to persuade the lady in question to even consider such a plan, he was obliged to remind himself as, with a painful jolt, the realisation that they had finally reached their intended destination brought him swiftly back to earth.

Still, he mused, standing back and allowing himself to drink in the reflection of Sophie's lovely features as she peered through the bottle-glass window of the bookseller's cluttered-looking premises, *hope springs eternal, as they say, and in the meantime the odd little gentle nudge in the right direction can't do any harm!* For now that he had finally managed to run his chestnut-haired temptress to ground, the Viscount had no intention of allowing her to slip through his fingers again. *It's high time my sweet Sophie started to learn that I can be quite as intractable as she is,* he thought, carefully hiding a self-satisfied smile as he pushed open the door to allow her to precede him into the shop.

'Good afternoon, sir, and what may I have the pleasure of doing for you?'

The small, bespectacled, bald-headed man who was peering out at them from behind a huge pile of books located on a desk to one side of the shop being the only creature in sight, Marcus could only suppose that this was, indeed, Sophie's Mr Broomfield.

'I believe that you are keeping a copy of an illustrated atlas for Miss Flint here?' he said, motioning Sophie forward.

Casting her a condescending glance, the bookseller gave a deprecating nod before turning to rummage in a nearby box for several moments. Finally extracting a decidedly tattered-looking version of a map book—one that Marcus had little difficulty recognising as having been one of his own childhood favourites many years back—he slapped it down on the desk in front of the Viscount. 'Three shillings and sixpence!' he announced, holding out his hand.

'Is that the best copy you have available?' asked Marcus stiffly.

'It's the cheapest I could find,' returned the shopkeeper with a careless shrug. 'The young lady was quite firm on that point, as I recall.'

Conscious of a slight tug at his elbow, Marcus turned, only to be confronted with an expression of earnest entreaty in Sophie's eyes. Heaving back a sigh, he bent his head in her direction.

'This book is perfectly adequate for my purpose,' she murmured into his ear. 'If you would be so good as to advance me the money, you have my promise that I will very soon find the means to reimburse you.'

At the thought of her being obliged to skimp and scrape to gather together such a pitiful outlay, Marcus felt his anger deepen and, turning back to the waiting Broomfield, he curtly ordered him to have the book wrapped.

'Bargain books don't usually warrant—' began the man, but, catching sight of the steely glint in the Viscount's eye, he gave a quick nod and, picking up the atlas, began to make his way to the rear of the shop.

'You stay here for a moment,' Marcus directed Sophie as he made after the shopkeeper. 'I just want to take a quick peek at that clerk of his.'

Although she was finding it well nigh impossible to comprehend how merely looking at the fellow could possibly determine his ability to add and subtract figures correctly, Sophie gave the Viscount a brief acquiescent smile and sat herself down on Broomfield's rather rickety-looking chair to await further developments.

'No need for you to come along, sir,' protested the shopkeeper as he observed Marcus's intention.

'Just want to see that you do the job properly,' came the Viscount's reply. 'Wouldn't do for Miss Flint's parcel to fall apart while I was carrying it, now, would it?'

Mumbling crossly to himself, Broomfield pushed open the door to the tiny back room that served as an office. Seated before a high desk, his head bent in deep concentration as he carefully inscribed a row of figures on one of the bookshop's bills of sale, was a sharp-nosed gangly youth of possibly sixteen or seventeen summers. *Not exactly the stuff of subterfuge or other under-the-counter deeds of derring-do,* thought Marcus, as he stepped across the room's threshold and studied the clerk. *Easy to understand the accounting errors, though!*

* * *

Emerging from the office some few minutes later, he found Sophie immersed in a book of Shakespeare's sonnets.

'Would you care to have that too?' he asked, smiling down at her.

'Oh, no!' She laughed, jumping up and placing the book carefully back on its pile. 'I already have my own copy—I was just enjoying reading them again, that's all.' Eying the neatly wrapped volume under his arm, she then observed, 'It was very good of you to go to so much trouble on my behalf.'

'No trouble at all,' he assured her, as the now surprisingly compliant Broomfield stepped forward and cheerily ushered them both out of the shop. 'My pleasure entirely.'

'You do seem to have quite a remarkable habit of winning people around,' she said, the shopkeeper's *volte-face* having thoroughly confounded her. 'I suppose it comes with being born with the proverbial silver spoon in your mouth?'

'Shouldn't be surprised,' replied Helstone nonchalantly, as he raised his hand to signal an approaching hackney carriage.

Realising his intention, Sophie immediately let go of his arm and stepped away from him. 'Oh, I'm not at all sure that I can agree to this,' she said pensively. It had temporarily slipped her mind that her very agreeable companion was still none other than the notorious Hell-cat Helstone, and, while sitting in a public tea shop with him and strolling along London's busy thoroughfares whilst surrounded by scores of other shoppers might be considered quite unremarkable, climbing into a hackney carriage with so infamous a character might be regarded in a somewhat different light.

Raising his eyebrows at her uneasy expression, the Viscount let out a soft chuckle. 'My days of seducing females in carriages are long gone, I assure you,' he twinkled, as he unceremoniously bundled her up into the cab. 'Decidedly uncomfortable business it was too, as I recall! I just figured that we might avoid the inevitable battering experience if we resorted to wheels for our return journey?'

In point of fact, being closeted in such a confined space with so charismatic an individual as Marcus was showing himself to be was turning out to be the icing on the cake as far as Sophie's afternoon was concerned. Throughout the whole of the journey from Gilbert Street to Lennox Gardens the Viscount had no difficulty keeping her fully entertained with his charming and witty observations. At least now she would have plenty to fill her dreams in the coming lonely days and nights, she thought, mentally hugging herself with delight as she gazed across the carriage at the Viscount's smiling countenance. Although on the other side of the same coin was the painful realisation that this short afternoon spent in his company could only serve to bring her greater heartache when the inevitable parting finally came. And come it must, she was forced to concede, given the wide disparity of their respective circumstances.

'I do hope that my employers don't see me arriving home in a hackney,' she ventured, with a nervous laugh. 'They will begin to think that they are paying me too high a salary!'

Having spent the whole of the past fifteen minutes or so fighting off a rapidly growing desire to haul her into his arms and feast his lips on hers, this disagreeable reminder of Sophie's disadvantaged situation was too much for Marcus to bear.

All at once he was at her side as, with a despairing groan, he pulled her towards him, murmuring huskily, 'Accept my offer, then, why don't you? How can you think of going back to humiliations of that sort when I could give you everything your heart desires!'

And then, before Sophie had either the wit or sense to prevent him, he had captured her lips with his and her whole world seemed to explode into a million sparkling fragments. Every single fibre of her being suddenly leapt into life as he trailed the tip of his tongue across the contours of her lips before finally forcing entry and deepening the kiss. Her entire body was awash with such indescribable feelings of rapture that the temptation to give in to his request was almost too much for Sophie to resist. The thought of never again having to bite back a stinging retort to one of Mrs Crayford's constant put-downs, never again having to grapple with Arthur Crayford in unexpected corners of the house, having a home of her own—with a fire in every room, should she so desire it, a well-stocked larder and wardrobes full of the most fashionable wear imaginable. Why, mother and Roger would—

At that sudden thought she froze and, wrenching herself away from his grasp, shunted to the far end of the seat, crying, 'How could you? You led me to believe that you would not attempt anything of that nature! Can it be that you truly are as black as you are painted?'

His jaw set, the Viscount flinched visibly at her accusation and, his body still aching with unfulfilled desire, sank back against the squabs, struggling to catch his breath as he tried to come to terms with his inexplicable behaviour.

What the hell is happening to me? he thought, as he stared across the carriage at Sophie's dumbfounded, wide-eyed expression. *Have I lost my wits entirely? Am I really reduced to behaving like an unfledged stripling on his first outing?*

'Please accept my apologies,' he managed eventually, desperately trying to summon up his customary air of insouciance. 'I really had not intended that to happen—some sort of fleeting aberration appears to have overruled my better judgement.' Summoning up a smile, he held out his hand. 'Come,' he said. 'It won't happen again, I promise you. Please don't let us part as enemies.'

Having had all her newly formed dreams so violently fractured, it was as much as Sophie could do to shake her head and wriggle herself more securely into her corner, and, since she was conscious of the carriage slowing down, she kept her eyes firmly fixed on the door handle, ready to make as speedy an exit as possible the minute the vehicle stopped.

But then, to Marcus's bewilderment, just as she leant forward to wrench open the carriage door, upon raising her eyes to peer out of the window she slumped back into her corner, her fingers to her lips, and uttered a moan of dismay.

Leaning across and staring through the glass in order to ascertain what it was that could have caused her such unease, the Viscount could see nothing amiss. The hackney driver had pulled his vehicle up outside number twelve, as instructed, and apart from the rather flashily dressed young man who was in the process of mounting the steps to the front door of the house there was no one else about.

Somewhat perplexed, he sat down again and studied

her, a frown forming on his brow as he registered her apprehension.

'What is it, my dear?' he said, leaning forward. 'It is perfectly safe to alight, I promise you. I saw no signs of curtains twitching or anything of that nature.'

Suddenly straightening herself, Sophie seemed to flare into life. 'My cap!' she ordered him. 'You have it in your pocket. Please give it back to me!'

Still mystified, the Viscount shrugged, drew out the requested article and handed it to her, watching in growing confusion as she hastily dragged off her bonnet before proceeding to stuff the abundant coils of her hair back into their former confinement. Glancing down at her bonnet, prior to replacing it, she caught sight of the tiny bunch of violets that Marcus had tucked into the ribbon just an hour or so earlier. She hesitated, a soft sigh escaping her lips, but then without further ado plucked them from their place, did likewise with those in the buttonhole of her pelisse. She stuffed the now badly crushed blossoms into her pocket and, leaning forward again, reached for the door handle.

But Marcus, his face clearing now that he had at last begun to fathom out what was troubling her, was ahead of her. *Now, this I can do something about,* he thought in satisfaction as, thrusting open the door, he leapt nimbly out on to the pavement and held out his hand, giving Sophie no opportunity to do other than accept his proffered assistance.

Having heard the carriage, the young Crayford had turned to see who might be visiting his home at such an unusual hour for calling. His expression, when he witnessed his younger siblings' governess being handed out of a vehicle and escorted up the steps by one of the Town's most notorious rakes, was something to behold.

'L-Lord Helstone?' he stammered in disbelief, half paralysed with nerves as, tugging at his cravat, he made the Viscount an exaggerated leg.

'Ah, Mr Crayford, I believe,' drawled Marcus, eyeing the youngster gravely. 'I have been wanting to have a word with you, if you could spare me a few moments of your time?'

That such an out-and-out Corinthian was even prepared to stop and pass the time of day with him, let alone engage him in any sort of conversation, was almost too much for Crayford to comprehend.

'You wish to have words with me?' he squeaked, the hue of his cheeks glowing even more brightly than the strawberry-pink brocade of his waistcoat.

'If you would be so good as to open the door for Miss Flint?'

Without sparing Sophie even the briefest of glances, Crayford at once sprang to attention, applying the knocker with such vigour that its strident clanging reverberated halfway down the street.

Whilst it was perfectly clear to both Sophie and the Viscount that the elderly manservant who opened the door was decidedly unimpressed with his young master's peremptory use of the knocker, Crayford was too far up in the boughs to notice the man's barely disguised expression of contempt.

'Ah, Hawkins, there you are,' babbled the youngster, almost pushing an unresisting Sophie through the entrance, before turning to Marcus and asking eagerly, 'Would you care to come into the library, my lord? My father has a halfway decent sherry I can offer you.'

'Thank you, but no,' replied Marcus, pausing only to

flash an encouraging smile at the somewhat distracted Sophie, as the manservant offered him a courteous bow before finally closing the door. 'What I have to say to you won't take long.'

Then, reaching out, he grasped hold of Crayford's neckcloth and pulled the startled youngster towards him, his tone unmistakably menacing as he murmured, 'If I should hear that you have dared to lay a finger on so much as a single hair of Miss Flint's head ever again, I will make it my business to have both you and your father barred from every club in Town. Do I make myself clear?'

Satisfied that the youngster's petrified gurgle was intended to signal some sort of assent, the Viscount nodded and released his hold.

'Very well—now, here is my card,' he continued, almost conversationally, and he took out his card case and extracted the pasteboard rectangle that held his noble details. 'You may inform your mother that I have called, and will be doing so again at some time in the very near future.'

From what he had been able to gather from Sophie's occasional references to her employer, the Viscount was reasonably certain that the parsimonious Mrs Crayford would turn out to be a social climber of the very worst sort. He had little doubt that within hours news of his visit would be circulating like wildfire amongst her cronies. Dissolute reprobate though he was considered to be, as the wealthy heir apparent to a long-established earldom he could hardly help being aware that there were few members of the *Ton* who would not give their eye teeth to have him grace their functions with his presence.

Society hostesses were known to go to extraordinary

lengths in their endeavours to secure his attendance at their balls and soirees, and not merely for the fact of his undoubtedly compelling charm, for he was, after all, an extremely eligible bachelor. This being so, he judged that it was fairly safe to assume that not a single member of the Crayford family would be likely to take issue with Sophie if they received the impression that their humble governess was someone he held in high regard.

His lips twisting in distaste as he recalled the damage that he had already done to that otherwise gratifyingly blossoming friendship, he passed his card to the still quivering stripling on the doorstep, inclined his head briefly, and sauntered casually down the steps before climbing into the still waiting hackney carriage.

Chapter Seven

Having managed to reach her attic bedroom without further intervention, Sophie, wanting nothing more than to throw herself onto her bed and sob her eyes out, thrust open the door and stepped inside—only to be met by the heartstopping sight of every single one of her precious possessions strewn in haphazard fashion across the bare floorboards, with the now empty drawers of her chest tossed into a careless heap in the room's far corner.

Collapsing onto the bed and staring at the jumbled mess with disbelieving eyes, she began to suppose that she must be living in some sort of ghastly nightmare. As though having been relieved of both of her purses, her one comb, two handkerchiefs and the bulk of her hard-earned savings in the space of twenty-four hours were not enough to endure, this must surely be regarded as the crowning touch to one of the most disagreeable days she had had the misfortune of experiencing for quite some time.

Even what had started out to be a joyful reunion with

Marcus Wolfe—or Viscount Helstone of Bradfield, as it had transpired—had ended in disastrous disappointment, when the libertine that he clearly was had finally chosen to revert to his true colours.

Angrily brushing away the gathering tears, Sophie dropped to her knees to make a start on returning her possessions to some sort of order. *I should have listened more carefully to what the servants were saying about him,* she chastised herself. *It's all very well making grandiose statements about paying no attention to gossip and arriving at one's own conclusions about people, but, really, with all that information at my fingertips, I must have been mad to allow myself be played on his line like the veriest gudgeon!*

Yet those rapturous sensations that had all but overcome her resolve the moment his lips had touched hers had been akin to a sort of madness, she was forced to admit to herself. Another few moments and who knew where such careless passion might have led? Thank heavens that timely vision of her mother had prevented her from forgetting herself entirely.

At the thought of her mother, a sudden frisson of alarm ran through Sophie, and, her hands shaking with panic, she began a feverish search through the heaps of articles that the disrespectful Henry—it *had* to be that beastly little devil, Sophie was almost certain, for no one else but the eight-year-old mischief-maker would think to harass her in such a petty manner—had tossed so carelessly about the room.

When at last her eyes lit upon the sleeveless flannel spencer that her mother had insisted on tucking into her travelling-box 'in case the weather turns cold', Sophie grabbed at the garment and ran her fingers hurriedly along its lower hem where, with a sob of relief, she discovered that the two crowns she had slid into the jacket's hem for safe-keeping were still there. She tossed up a prayer of thanksgiving for her mother's sensible teachings during the family's years with the military that, should the possibility of sudden evacuation ever occur—which it had frequently done—such a hidden source of money might serve to save their lives. Ever since those days, it had been Sophie's habit to tuck all of her loose change into the hem of the never-likely-to-be-worn flannel jacket. As it happened, the ten shillings that she had put aside from her quarterly salary of three pounds was intended to bolster up the meagre pension awarded to her mother by the War Office, in recognition of the late Lieutenant-Colonel's services to his country. On glancing up from her position on the floor, however, Sophie chanced to see the splendidly wrapped package that lay on her bed, and she realised, to her sorrow, that she would be obliged to ask her mother to make do with only five shillings on this occasion, since paying Helstone back his three shillings and sixpence had now become more a point of honour than a matter of principle.

Getting to her feet, she sat down on the bed and began to unravel the string that surrounded the parcel, ruefully recalling the vibrant joy she had felt at simply being in the Viscount's company. Was it possible that one could love someone and yet dislike them in almost equal measure at one and the same time? she wondered, as she unwrapped the package, only to find as the wrapping paper fell from her fingers that the book that now lay on her knees was not the tattered version that Mr Broomfield had offered to her in his bookshop but an almost pristine edition of the same work!

She stared down at the book, a mixture of wild fury

and disbelief coursing through her veins. It seemed that the duplicitous Helstone had hoodwinked her yet again, in the certain knowledge that she did not have the resources to fulfil so great a debt! For one awestruck moment she was not certain whether she wanted to laugh hysterically or scream her anger to the four walls.

In the event, a sharp tap at her door prevented her from venting her aggravation in either fashion, and as one of the maids poked her head around the door with the message that the mistress required her presence downstairs on the instant, Sophie could only suppose that the day's misfortunes had not yet reached their pinnacle. Evidently, it would seem, Arthur Crayford had informed his mother of her arrival in a hackney carriage in the company of one of the Town's most notorious rakes. Instant dismissal was clearly on the cards yet again, she thought, as she made her way down to the drawing room to confront her employer, dismally conscious of the fact that this threat dropped from Mrs Crayford's lips with monotonous regularity, wherever and whenever things failed to go exactly as she had planned them.

To her surprise, however, Mrs Crayford stood up and moved forward to greet her on her entry into the room, saying, 'My dear Miss Flint! How nice to see you looking so well. You enjoyed your afternoon off, I trust?'

Considerably taken aback at her employer's over-effusive welcome, Sophie glanced suspiciously at the young Mr Crayford who, skulking nervously behind his parent, seemed reluctant to meet her gaze.

'Do sit down, my dear. I have just rung for tea.'

Motioning her to the chair nearest to her own, Mrs Crayford reseated herself and regarded Sophie with what the startled governess surmised was meant to be a look of affection.

'Arthur tells me that you came home in the company of Viscount Helstone,' she then gushed, before leaning across and tapping Sophie playfully on the knee with her fan. 'You really should have mentioned that you were acquainted with the gentleman, you naughty girl! What must he think of us for having failed to invite him to the various soirees and musical evenings that we have given during these past few weeks? Clearly we must see to it that such a grievous omission is rectified without delay—is that not so, dear child?'

Still finding herself to be in a state of shocked disbelief, Sophie was unable to summon up a suitable reply. Not that one was necessary, it appeared, since Mrs Crayford then proceeded to outline some of her ill-thought-out schemes for entertaining the Viscount during the coming months, barely stopping to take a breath as she set off on a wild flight of fancy that included such things as ice sculptures, chocolate fountains and the like.

Sliding her glance across to where Arthur Crayford was sitting, nervously fingering his cravat and staring back at her in an apprehensive manner, Sophie was struck with the oddest impression that he was expecting her to leap up and attack him at any minute.

Suddenly the reason for all this ingratiating obsequiousness became horrifyingly apparent. Having marked her agitation when she had caught sight of the young man on the doorstep, Helstone had obviously drawn his own conclusions as to her uneasiness and, as soon as the front door had closed, must have set about intimidating Crayford in some way or another—which would explain the youngster's conspicuously edgy demeanour. And, whilst Sophie was decidedly annoyed at finding herself presented with yet another example of the Viscount's high-handed interference in her life, she could not help but experience a warm ripple of pleasure at the thought of him having gone to such trouble on her behalf.

Mrs Crayford's wildly extravagant plans, on the other hand, were another matter entirely, and Sophie knew that she had to find some way of putting a stop to them before they got out of hand. The mere thought of Helstone being invited to come and go as he pleased—as seemed to be her employer's heartfelt ambition—was enough to send her senses skittering in all directions. Even worse, it now appeared, when she had surfaced sufficiently to take in yet more of Mrs Crayford's revised plans for the Season, that she herself was to be included in all this jollification!

'But I do not have a suitable wardrobe to wear on such occasions,' she interjected in dismay, the minute Mrs Crayford at last paused to draw breath.

'Not to worry, my dear,' declared her employer, waving a dismissive hand. 'Lydia has more gowns than she can possibly wear—she shall loan you some of hers. You are of a size, I believe. The child can scarcely object, after all,' she went on, her eyes glowing in anticipation. 'With so noble a patron, the possibilities for her are endless!'

Biting at the inside of her lip in an effort not to burst out laughing at the thought of so infamous a rake as Helstone being persuaded to sponsor the Crayford's seventeen-year-old daughter into Society, Sophie was obliged to concentrate her attention on the slightly faded patterning of the room's Aubusson rug.

'So, that's settled then,' declared her employer, in a satisfied tone, as she rose to her feet. 'I shall write to his lordship at once and invite him to take dinner with us on Tuesday next—that will give Mrs Hawkins ample time to have all the glass and silverware polished to perfection.'

'Oh, no! I fear that won't do at all,' cried Sophie, clutching at straws. 'I believe his lordship mentioned that he would be out of town all next week—possibly longer,' she added, in desperation.

'Hmm.' Pausing in her tracks, Mrs Crayford swung round to frown at her son. 'Did you not tell me that the Viscount said that it was his intention to call upon us shortly?'

'Very near future, was what he said,' gabbled the youngster, standing up and clutching at the back of his chair for support. 'Took that to mean in the next day or so—but I couldn't swear—'

'Never mind,' interrupted his mother, turning back to face Sophie. 'You will just have to ascertain his lordship's movements for the coming weeks, so that I can plan my functions accordingly. I shouldn't care to find myself going to a host of trouble for nothing—we have to be sure of the dates that he will be available. You must write him a note straight away and I will have Fisher take it across.'

'Oh, but I couldn't possibly,' began Sophie, her eyes widening in dismay. How was she supposed to explain that the Viscount was merely a passing acquaintance when he had, it would seem, chosen to give Crayford the impression that he and she were close friends of a long standing. Telling the truth would merely serve to blacken her own character to such an extent that she really would be in danger of losing her position, and then where would she be? Realising that, unless some miracle should occur to prevent the inevitable revelation, there was nothing for it but to appear to go along with Mrs

Crayford's plans, she gave her employer a resigned nod of acquiescence and, at that lady's continued insistence, took her place at the escritoire, desperately wondering how best she might pen such a note.

Having divested himself of his jacket, waistcoat and boots, Marcus had taken up residence in one of the two leather fireside chairs that straddled the fireplace in the library of his Grosvenor Square mansion. His brother Giles, in similar garb, lounged wearily back in the other.

'Bit of luck you running into that Flint female this afternoon,' observed the Major, as he took a hefty swig of the brandy that his brother had just poured him. 'Finally managed to get one of my chaps to decipher these damned coded messages that have been causing us such difficulty these past couple of weeks.'

'Some devilment afoot somewhere, then?' enquired Marcus lazily, his brain more intent on conjuring up sweet visions of kissing Sophie than paying a great deal of attention to his brother's words.

'Another plot to assassinate old Hookey, by the looks of it,' returned Giles complacently. 'Must be at the least the sixth this year, by my reckoning.'

'Does it bother his grace—this new-found antagonism towards him after all that adulation of last year?'

'He says not.' The Major laughed, leaning forward to top up his glass from the brandy decanter positioned on the table between the two of them. 'Noticed that he's made a start on having railings erected round Apsley House, though—had a couple of rocks heaved through one of his windows the other day, apparently.'

'Teach him to stop mouthing off about the country's need for greater mechanisation. The last thing we want now is more riots, what with the number of unemployed men piling into the capital.'

'Good God, Marcus!' exclaimed his brother in aston-ishment. 'Don't tell me you're developing a social con-science at long last—the old man will never believe it when I tell him!'

'Then don't,' returned Marcus shortly, before taking another pensive swig of his drink. 'How is the old devil, by the way? Still cursing the day I was born, I imagine?'

'Not to my knowledge. As a matter of fact, he's not been too good this last week or so—ever since you rode off into that blizzard he's been surprisingly quiet on the subject of your descent into dissolution. You really ought to go down and make your peace with him, you know.'

Marcus nodded. 'Yes, I shall—as soon as—'

Stopping abruptly, he coloured and swiftly changed the subject. 'This code business, then—how did Miss Flint's bill of sale help solve the puzzle?'

'Pretty clever, really,' said Giles, leaning forward. 'We'd already intercepted a similar invoice to a Mr Luke Fower, and hadn't been able to make a great deal of sense out of it, but as soon as we got hold of the one addressed to Mr Matthew Nyne it all began to fall into place.'

'I'm not sure I follow your line of reasoning.'

'Quite simple. One of my newer chaps—part-time lay preacher, as it happens—finally twigged the connection. Luke Fower and Matthew Nyne! Get it?'

At his brother's continued expression of puzzlement, the Major, after a brief pause, proceeded to explain. 'Luke Four and Matthew Nine—books and chapters of the New Testament, old chum! Once our chaps had hit on that, of course, the rest was pretty plain sailing—just a matter of working on the whys and wherefores. The first number indicated a verse, the second a letter in that verse, so Miss Flint's invoice, when correctly deciphered, actually reads "BOW SWAN FINAL"—presumably signifying a final meeting of some sort at the Swan Inn at Bow. The invoice's erroneous total, cleverly spotted by that sharp-eyed little governess of yours, spells out the time and date of the meeting—hence seven pounds, thirteen shillings and fivepence translates as seven o'clock on the thirteenth of May—just two weeks away, as it happens.'

He sat back, looking extremely pleased with himself. 'I've got two men keeping an eye on the bookshop, in order to see exactly how Broomfield and his clerk might be involved, and with this new information at our fingertips we should have no difficulty in catching the beggars red-handed, so to speak. All thanks to your Miss Flint and that invoice of hers!'

'Which would explain why someone was so keen to get hold of the thing, then,' murmured Marcus, almost to himself. 'She told me that was the second of two purses she'd had stolen in as many days—I'd thought it was mere coincidence, but now—good Lord!'

Starting up, he reached forward and grasped his brother's arm.

'You realise what this means, of course?' he demanded and, at the Major's bewildered shake of the head, exclaimed, 'The fact that there is no such person as Matthew Nyne surely suggests that, had not Broomfield's clerk carelessly mixed up the addressees, the invoice that was delivered to Miss Flint must have been intended for one of the other occupants at the Crayford residence!'

His eyes sparkling with triumph, he sat back. 'It just

remains for you to find who got hers and you'll have your man!'

'That's not necessarily as simple as you might suppose,' remarked his brother dryly. 'Do you have any suggestions?'

Marcus shook his head. 'Ordinarily, my money would be on the odious Crayford junior, but from what I've seen of him I take leave to doubt that he's got the nous to involve himself in any sort of political activism—all puff and no blow, if you get my meaning!'

'I wouldn't be too sure of that, if I were you,' returned Giles, with a pensive frown. 'In my experience it's often the most unlikely seeming character who turns out to be the villain of the piece!'

'Oh, I can't imagine the little toad—good grief!' The Viscount shot his brother a startled look. 'Are you saying that wretched performance of his could just be a clever blind?'

At the Major's nod, Marcus's face paled visibly. 'Merciful heavens!' he groaned. 'Here am I, getting slowly foxed, when that poor sweet creature might be in who knows what sort of danger from that foul swine!'

Leaping to his feet, he swayed violently before being obliged to sit down again, landing back in his seat with a heavy thump. 'Dammit!' he exclaimed angrily. 'She was quite right! Fat lot of use I'd be in an emergency!'

Frowning in concern, his brother reached over and removed the almost empty glass from his grasp. 'This young woman is really getting to you, isn't she, bro? I can't recall ever having seen you working yourself into such a state over a female since that time when you were about sixteen and swore that you were going to elope with one of the dairymaids. The customary treatment soon put paid to your over-excessive enthusiasm, if I remember rightly. I take it that you haven't managed to work your usual magic spell on this one?'

'Go to hell!' rasped Marcus, and he snatched up his glass from the table and refilled it, tossing back half of its contents before sinking into a morass of brooding silence.

Shaking his head in bafflement at his brother's decidedly out-of-character behaviour, Giles got to his feet and began to prise himself back into his snug-fitting military jacket, hazarding a guess that there was likely to be little further sensible conversation from his brother on this occasion. That being so, he decided, with another quick look at his uncommunicative sibling, he might just as well go back to his own apartment and carry on with his investigations into that other rather interesting matter that he had been working on.

On exiting from the library, however, he narrowly missed colliding with one of Marcus's footmen, who had been just on the point of tapping on the door to announce a lately delivered missive for his master.

'Just arrived, sir,' he said, nodding his head to indicate the presence of a second liveried person standing in the hall. 'Been told to wait for an answer.'

'He'll be lucky!' muttered the Major, as he picked up the letter from the tray and began to retrace his steps. Tapping Marcus briskly on the shoulder, he bade him open his eyes. 'Urgent message, old chap,' he announced, while giving his brother another vigorous prod. 'Looks like a female hand—might be from that new lady-love of yours!'

As Giles's laughing words began to penetrate his befogged brain, the Viscount heaved himself upright, grabbed at the missive and, his fingers trembling with impatience, ripped it open—only to find the words swimming blearily across the page.

My lord. You must excuse my presumption in writing to you like this, but your earlier actions have left me with an unfortunate predicament. My employer is now labouring under the misconception that we are closely acquainted and has insisted that I obtain your agreement to attend some of her forthcoming functions. I apologise for this intrusion, but wonder if it would be possible for you to write to her and explain that you have other commitments which will prevent you from accepting any of her invitations? I would be most grateful for your co-operation in this matter.
Yours &c.
S.F.

Swiping his hand across his eyes, Marcus had to concentrate hard to keep the neat script in focus. Even so, it took him three attempts before the meaning of the words finally sank in. 'Not mine, unfortunately,' he growled, as he let the paper slip from his fingers before slumping back into his seat. 'And not nearly as grateful as I would like her to be!'

Grabbing at the missive before it floated into the fire, Giles cast a quick glance over the words, but was unable to make sense of their content. 'Seems the lady needs your help,' he said, somewhat awkwardly, since he had no idea what sort of brouhaha his brother had got himself into this time. 'Messenger's waiting for a reply.'

Muttering scabrous imprecations, Marcus stumbled to his feet again, staggered over to the nearby bureau, snatched up a piece of crested writing-paper and, after stabbing a quill into the inkstand a couple of times, shakily scrawled '*3 p.m. tomorrow. M.H.*' across the sheet. Folding the paper with careful precision, he picked up a stick of sealing wax and stared down at it in some confusion.

'Might be better if you left that to me, old boy,' came his brother's gentle voice from behind him.

With a weary nod, the Viscount passed the sealing wax to Giles and, blinking rapidly, watched as the Major lit a candle, melted the wax and sealed the letter.

'Pass me your ring!' commanded Giles, holding out his hand.

Easing the crested band from his finger, Marcus slid it across the desk towards his brother who, wordlessly retrieving the item, proceeded to press its raised design into the blob of wax, leaving on its hardening surface the clear imprint of an upright lance along with the ancient family motto—*nunquam cesseris*—never give in!

Pulling the missive towards him, Marcus stared dumbly down at the inscription for some moments, before his lips twisted in a wry grimace. Then, straightening his shoulders, he lifted his chin and rose cautiously to his feet.

'I can do this,' he muttered, his teeth clenched tightly together as he eased himself around to face the library door. '*I can* do this.'

Then, to Giles's amazement, he proceeded to cross the room with barely the faintest hint of having over-indulged himself. Swinging open the door, the Viscount then poked out his head, beckoned to the still waiting messenger and pressed his reply into the man's hand, along with the requisite shilling.

It was only after the visiting footman had bowed and

taken his leave that the flash of an incomplete memory leapt into Marcus's still somewhat befuddled brain. He was sure that it was connected to something he had seen in the bookshop, but he was damned if he could call it to mind.

Returning to the fireplace, he pulled at the bellrope to summon his butler. 'Sorry about that pathetic display, Giles,' he said with an awkward grin. 'A large jug of black coffee seems to be in order. It's high time I started making a few much-needed changes to my life, I believe.'

Chapter Eight

Even though her living conditions seemed about to take a turn for the better following Mrs Crayford's wrongful assumption of her relationship with Helstone, Sophie was not at all sure that she cared for such a change, since it appeared that from now on she was expected to join the family at dinner, instead of taking the meal with the two younger Crayford children in the nursery parlour, as had previously been required of her.

Nor did it add to her sense of wellbeing to have Lydia march into her room the following morning and deposit a huge pile of miscellaneous articles of clothing onto her bed, with the words, 'You may have these—I no longer have any use for them!' before letting out a barely disguised snort of laughter, clapping her fingers to her lips and running from the room.

Even the discovery that several of the garments appeared never to have been worn before was of no great consolation to Sophie, since it was clear that every single item had been designed for someone a good few years younger than her own three and twenty, in both fashion and colour scheme. But even as she stared down in dismay at the pale pastel-shaded gowns, every one of them complete with more than its fair share of frills, flounces and furbelows, she was well aware that, other than appearing at the table in one of the three serviceable grey gowns that comprised her limited wardrobe, she had little choice but to comply with her employer's instruction that she wear one of Lydia's repugnant cast-offs that evening.

Neither had Helstone's message that he intended to present himself at three o'clock that afternoon brought her any solace. The fact that he had chosen to ignore her request had already cost her a sleepless night, as her exhausted brain endeavoured to fathom out his reasons for hounding her in this manner. By his impetuous actions he had made it very clear that he was attracted to her but, given that he was a man who could have the pick of the most beautiful women in Society—and probably already had, if the truth be known—his apparent determination to add a provincial nobody to his list of conquests had left Sophie feeling confused and ill-equipped to deal with any further onslaughts from him. For, as she was gradually being forced to admit to herself, the plain fact of the matter was that she was already more than halfway in love with the charismatic devil—a situation which only served to make his continued importuning of her all the more difficult to resist, when all she really wanted to do was to shout, *Yes! Yes! Yes! Hold me in your arms and kiss me to distraction!*

Not that she could ever imagine herself acting in such a wild and abandoned manner, she concluded with a disapproving grimace, as she stared at what she could see of her reflection in the pock-marked mirror that stood on her chest of drawers and ruefully contemplated the likely effect of the least offensive of Lydia's gowns when held up against her own rather more curvaceous figure. *Perhaps I am just more strait-laced than I had otherwise supposed?* was her next thought. *Although, whilst it is true that my upbringing might have been somewhat out of the ordinary, Mama was always quite strict in certain matters, and I am perfectly sure that she would never approve of me even considering such a shameful course of action!*

Heaving a sigh, she tossed the over-embellished pink-spotted muslin back on to the bed and selected another from the pile—pale green this time, and almost identical in design to the former, apart from a deep flounce of figured lace at its hem. *Hmm…* she then thought. *If I unpick all those ridiculous bows and folderols, this might well serve the purpose for this evening. Not that anyone will give a fig as to how I look—apart from the odious Arthur, of course—although, thanks to Helstone's timely intervention, the little creep does seem to have drawn in his horns somewhat. Oh, dear! I really must learn to count my blessings, as Mama is often wont to say!*

Unfortunately, unpicking the numerous bows and other unnecessary ornamentation on the gown took Sophie rather longer than she had expected, and as she reached for a clothes hanger upon which to hang the completed garment her eyes happened to fall on the little clock that stood on her bedside table. Good grief! It was a quarter to three already and she had barely left herself with enough time to wash her hands and brush her hair!

She was just in the process of stabbing the last hairpin into her hastily constructed chignon when a tap at her bedroom door heralded the appearance of the maidservant, bearing the message that the mistress wished to inform Miss Flint that Lord Helstone had arrived, and would she be so good as to join the family in the drawing room?

Brushing her fingers down the front of her grey cambric gown, in a vain attempt to smooth out the creases that had formed during her needlecraft activities, Sophie followed the girl down the stairs to the ground floor where, pausing outside the drawing room, she took a deep breath, stiffened her spine and pushed open the door.

'Ah, come in, my dear Miss Flint,' cried Mrs Crayford at her entry. 'As you can see, your cousin has kept his promise to call on us!'

Cousin! Great heavens! What other barefaced lies had the wicked devil been constructing during her absence?

It was all Sophie could do to stop herself from exclaiming out loud. Inwardly fuming that Helstone had had the audacity to claim a non-existent kinship with her, she dipped him the briefest of curtseys and refused to raise her eyes to meet his, knowing full well that they would be regarding her with their usual mischievous glint.

'It was good of you to come, my lord,' she managed, through partly clenched teeth.

Marcus bit back the grin that threatened. Sophie's indignant reaction to his spurious assertion was proving to be much as he had expected, but, having finally decided his course of action, he was quite prepared to make some sacrifices in order to achieve his intended goal. The past ten or more minutes spent engaged in pointless conversation with the inept and decidedly doddery Crayford senior, along with his unbelievably bourgeois and graceless wife, having been the first of such sacrifices, the Viscount was only just beginning to realise exactly how much of a challenge he had set himself. But then, as he was quick to remind himself, *to the victor the spoils*—or so the saying would have it.

Not that there was any real chance of him failing in his chosen pursuit, he thought complacently. There never was. Once he had set his sights on a particular target, it merely remained to find ways of persuading the object of his interest to succumb to his advances. This method had always served him perfectly well in the past, and the Viscount could see no reason why it should fail him on this occasion, having already reached the conclusion that the mounting ardour he felt for Sophie was simply some sort of adverse reaction to her continued refusal to accept his offer. The trouble was, as he was now obliged to admit as he sat back in his seat and covertly studied her set expression, he was just not used to being turned down—rather the reverse, in the majority of cases!

'His lordship has expressed the desire to take you for a drive in his curricle this afternoon,' gushed Mrs Crayford, coyly batting her eyelashes at the Viscount. 'In the ordinary way, of course, such a suggestion would be out of the question, but now that he has explained your relationship I see no reason to refuse his request—although I do think that you might prefer to go and change into one of your prettier gowns before you depart?'

This last was to Sophie, to whom her employer shot a fierce look of disapprobation—doubtless for her having chosen to appear before the noble guest dressed in her customary colourless fashion.

'I cannot think that his lordship would care to keep his horses standing any longer than absolutely necessary,' returned Sophie mutinously. Torn between wanting to reject Helstone's offer out of hand and a pressing need to take him to task for falsifying their relationship, she had opted for the latter. Nevertheless, she had no intention of primping herself in Lydia's outmoded cast-offs just to oblige Mrs Crayford's *déclassé* ideas of propriety. 'I will just go and collect my bonnet—if you will excuse me?'

Dipping another quick curtsey to no one in particular, she left the room before her employer could summon up an adequate reply.

'So impetuous—I sometimes find it quite difficult to keep up with the girl!' exclaimed Mrs Crayford gaily, in a failed attempt at merriment, as she feverishly applied her fan to her reddening cheeks. 'Do sit down again, my lord—another glass of sherry, perhaps?'

'Thank you, but no,' replied Marcus, bending to retrieve his hat and gloves from the arm of his chair. 'Miss—er—my cousin is quite correct in her assumption that my horses have been left standing quite long enough. I will take my leave of you now, if you will excuse me? Thank you both for your indulgence.'

'Oh, our pleasure entirely, my lord!'

Doing his utmost to construct a bow at the same time as reaching for the bell-pull in order to summon the butler to escort his esteemed visitor from the premises, the doddery Crayford senior lost his footing and all but tumbled into the fireplace. His ungainly recovery brought forth a barely suppressed snigger from his son, whose apprehension over the Viscount had rendered him virtually speechless throughout the entire visit. A questioning glance from Helstone, however, soon put him firmly back in his place. A bright flush crept across his cheeks as, mortified once more, he hunched up his shoulders and did his best to appear invisible, mentally swearing eternal damnation to Helstone and all his kind.

Blissfully oblivious of the vicious maledictions being cast against his person, Marcus strode out into the hallway just as Sophie stepped off the bottom stair. Hurrying across to meet her, he felt his heart execute the same extraordinary somersault that it had done at every other one of their meetings. Catching his breath as he offered her his hand, he could only put the inexplicable sensation down to his recent over-indulgence of liquor which, he was forced to admit, seemed to have increased out of all proportion of late—a matter that clearly needed addressing.

Tucking her gloved hand into the crook of his elbow, he led her out of the house and into the late April sunshine, glancing down at the fine woollen shawl on her shoulders.

'Are you sure that scrap of stuff is going to be warm enough?' he asked in concern as he handed her up into his curricle, before taking the reins from his tiger and climbing into his own seat. 'The breeze will tend to feel quite brisk once we're on the move.'

'I trust that you are not about to give forth with one of your usual panegyrics regarding the supremacy of the fur stole over the humble woollen shawl,' said Sophie wearily, and she attempted to edge herself further along the seat, away from Helstone's impossibly charismatic masculinity. 'After spouting that inexcusable falsehood, I wonder that you have the audacity to face me at all!'

'Needs must.' He laughed, nodding to the tiger to let go the horses' heads. 'How else was I supposed to get you out of the house? That old cat of an employer of yours is a sight too inquisitive for my liking. I was obliged to invent all manner of relatives to satisfy her curiosity. I'm still not entirely sure that she trusts me to return you in one piece!'

'Then your reputation has clearly preceded you,' retorted Sophie tartly, clutching at the side rail of the highly sprung vehicle as it swung sharply around a bend in the road, while secretly in awe of the way the Viscount's strong, shapely hands manipulated the reins to control his team. Hands that had held her so firmly against his chest—

'Do you have to drive so fast?' she gasped, desperately trying to banish that oft recurring image from her mind. 'You will have me tipped over the side if you're not careful! Where are we going, anyway? This isn't the way to the park.'

'Too busy, and too many prying eyes for my liking.'

A frisson of unease shot through her. 'I trust you aren't thinking of attempting to repeat yesterday's sordid activity?' she challenged him.

His eyes gleaming with laughter, Marcus shook his head. 'Don't worry. Your virtue is quite safe this time, I promise you. Besides which,' he added, jerking his head over his shoulder, 'Kimble is here to see that you come to no harm—isn't that so, Kim?'

'Whatever you say, guv,' returned the tiger, with a nonchalant shrug.

'Very confidence-inspiring, I'm sure!' muttered Sophie. 'I dare say you pay him extra for helping you abduct helpless maidens!'

'Not my style,' retorted the Viscount, shooting her a sideways glance. 'Besides which, I've never thought of you as particularly helpless—you had little trouble fighting me off, as I recall.'

'Probably because your conscience got the better of you!' she flashed back at him.

'Conscience!'

Letting out a scornful hoot, Marcus tightened his hands on the reins, signalling to his team to slow down to a trot. 'I can't imagine what has given you the impression that I have any sort of a conscience.'

'Everyone has a conscience if they dig deeply enough,' she replied smugly.

When he did not answer, she glanced across at him. Though his eyes were fixed on the road ahead, he had a frown on his face, and as she watched a small tic appeared at the side of his lower lip. She opened her mouth to ask him if something was wrong, but then, thinking the better of it, remained silent.

Eventually he spoke, with a slight grate to his voice. 'Did you really mean it when you described my kissing you as "sordid"?'

'I—I—!'

Her cheeks aflame, Sophie was temporarily lost for words.

'I had the distinct feeling that, for a moment or two at least, you were actually enjoying the whole experience quite as much as I was,' he continued, still concentrating his gaze to the front. Then, with a jerk, he pulled his team to a standstill and swung round to face her, his eyes boring into hers. 'In fact, I defy you to tell me that you didn't enjoy it!'

'I—I—that is—it was wrong of you to pounce on me like that!' she floundered, finding it totally impossible to withstand the blatant heat of his compelling gaze.

'That's not what I asked!' he rasped, ripping off his

glove before reaching out and cupping her cheek so as to prevent her turning her head away. 'Look me in the eye and tell me that you didn't enjoy it as much as I did!'

Endless minutes ticked slowly by, as the Viscount's unremitting gaze seemed to strip away every one of her defences and lay open her very soul, until at last, as a little sob escaped her lips, Sophie was forced to tear her eyes away from his with the broken whisper, 'I—I cannot—you know full well that I cannot!'

A hot flood of elation pulsed through him. *I knew it! I knew it!* Marcus told himself exultantly, clenching his fists and almost punching at the air in his utter delight at having forced the admission from her, but then, as his gleeful eyes turned once more to confront her, a bewildered frown furrowed his brow. Sophie's face was turned away from him, but there on her right cheek the slow trickle of a single tear was clearly visible. All of a sudden his heart seemed to stumble to a standstill, and what he had previously regarded as a resounding victory swiftly deteriorated into the most crippling of defeats.

Motioning to Kimble to get down and hold the horses' heads, the Viscount reached across and took hold of Sophie's hands, only to feel his heart lurch once more. Even through the thin fabric of her cheap cotton gloves the trembling of her fingers was marked.

'Don't,' he murmured hoarsely, as he gripped her hands tightly in his. 'Please don't—I'm so very sorry—I didn't mean to browbeat you so—I really cannot think what came over me to behave in such a way. I can't apologise enough—please tell me that you forgive me?'

Sniffing back her tears, Sophie tried her best to extricate herself from his hold. 'If you would be so good as to let go of my hands, I really would like to wipe my nose,' she mumbled crossly.

Although Helstone's ruthless badgering had undermined her confidence considerably, she was determined not to let him see the extent of her humiliation. She felt thoroughly wretched and was quite certain that the Viscount, despite his extensive apologies, must think her behaviour ridiculous. When all was said and done, it was hardly the end of the world to have been obliged to admit to having enjoyed his embrace—especially since she had thought of little else since it happened. Although, what had caused his lordship to get so fired up about the whole matter was a complete mystery to her. *He probably keeps a little black book of all his conquests, marking off the names whenever he achieves a success,* she concluded, giving another despondent sniff at the thought of having allowed herself to be just another ticked-off name on some well-practised womaniser's list.

Relief flooding his face at Sophie's return to normal, Marcus let go of her hands and, reaching into his jacket pocket, drew out his handkerchief and set about mopping up the damage her tears had done to her face. His gentle, ineffectual dabbings achieved so little success, however, that Sophie was obliged to relieve him of his handkerchief and complete the job to her own satisfaction.

'Am I forgiven?' he asked anxiously, when she finally sat motionless, her eyes fixed on the balled-up handkerchief in her gloved hands. 'Do we proceed or would you prefer that I took you back home?'

Home! The mere idea of the Crayfords' residence being described as 'home' was almost enough to reduce Sophie to tears once more. She and her family had never really had a home of their own—plenty of rented or even commandeered dwellings as they had travelled the continent, but nothing of any long standing. Even the little house in Dulwich that her mother had managed to acquire could hardly be classed as a home, since it was really too small to accommodate all three of them, especially now that two of the rooms had been rented out in order to help Mrs Flint make ends meet. It would seem that a place that Sophie could truly call "home" was forever to remain the "castle in the air" daydream it had always been, rendering the thought of a quick return to her attic bedroom in Lennox Gardens even less appealing than usual.

'We might just as well go on,' she said, stifling a sigh. 'Now that we've come this far—you presumably set out with a particular objective in mind?'

I did indeed, thought Marcus somewhat ruefully, as he now began to wonder whether he might not have been just a little too precipitate in his planning for this afternoon's excursion. Despite having woken up with the very devil of a headache, he had set about carrying out his previous evening's intention of wearing down Sophie's resistance with a series of delightful treats, having convinced himself that all that was required was a few tastes of the high life to make her rethink her stubborn refusal to put herself under his protection. He had spent much of the morning organising the delivery of champagne, hot-house strawberries and an unlimited number of baskets of all sorts of other luxury comestibles to his intended destination, and he had been hoping to overwhelm her with such bountiful largesse.

That the delightful cottage and grounds would speak for themselves he had little doubt, he himself having been thoroughly charmed with the tiny estate when he had first come across it some months ago. He owned several other properties, of course, including the two that presently housed his current mistresses, but neither of them had received a visit from him for almost a full month now—as certain parts of his body were only too aware—due to his having allowed himself to become thoroughly preoccupied with a chestnut-haired vision who had inadvertently crept into his bedchamber in the middle of a snowstorm!

Now, however, thanks to a careless lack of judgement on his part, it was beginning to look as though his original plan might have to be postponed. Not that that need prevent the two of them spending an idle hour or so at the cottage, he thought, brightening. Indeed, it would be a great shame to allow all that food to go to waste, and after all Mrs Bellamy had been warned to expect him, and had, in all probability, gone to a great deal of trouble on his behalf…

'Just a little way beyond the next village,' he said, having finally made up his mind, and, whistling for Kimble to return to his perch, he took up the reins and once more pointed his team in the direction of Laurel Cottage.

Having been too engrossed to pay much attention to the landscape during the earlier part of their journey, Sophie found herself wondering exactly where they were. She vaguely recalled travelling along the Knightsbridge Road and turning into Sloane Street, but now that they were out in the country, with her limited knowledge of London's environs, it was difficult for her to guess where they might be—somewhere in the region of Chelsea Village, she assumed.

Chelsea! Sitting bolt upright, she swivelled herself round and fixed Helstone with a piercing glare.

'We wouldn't be heading for your "neat little cottage in Chelsea" by any chance, would we, my lord?' she asked, her voice dripping with sarcasm. 'Do you never give up?'

'In the blood, I'm afraid,' he replied, with a slightly self-conscious half-laugh. 'You need have no fear for your virtue on this occasion, however. The house comes fully equipped with as highly respectable a staff as you are ever likely to come across—the formidable Mrs Bellamy would doubtless have at me with a frying pan if I so much as lifted a finger in your direction!'

'I cannot suppose that that has ever prevented you from turning up with a succession of opera dancers and other such lightskirts,' she returned frostily.

'Not so,' he drawled, before skilfully swinging his equipage through an arched gateway and up an attractively curved driveway flanked by laurel bushes. 'I have never felt the need to associate with females of that sort and, much as it may surprise you to learn, you are the only lady of my acquaintance who has ever been invited to cross the threshold of this particular establishment. There!' As the carriage drew up outside the front door steps, he swept out his arm to encompass the surrounding vista. 'Tell me what you think.'

No sooner had her eyes lit upon the graceful lines of the simple but charming two-storeyed building, surrounded by a profusion of neatly stocked flowerbeds and set in a wide expanse of carefully tended lawn, than Sophie's throat started to contract painfully, making it impossible for her to take a full breath. For there in front of her, in all its splendid glory, stood her dream home, almost exactly as she had always pictured it.

Utterly lost for words, she could only sit and gaze about her in silent awe, causing Marcus to experience a sharp stab of disappointment when the expected words of approval failed to materialise, since he had already convinced himself that the peaceful beauty of the place would appeal to Sophie in much the same way that it had attracted him.

'I take it that you're not overly impressed, then,' he said abruptly as, tossing the reins to the already descended Kimble, he leapt lightly from the driving seat and walked around the carriage to help Sophie alight. Doggedly resisting the impulse to fasten both his hands about her waist and haul her down into a crushing embrace, he gritted his teeth and held out only the one hand, in the total expectation of Sophie's making use of its assistance to help her down from her seat. But no! It seemed that she was still so heavily engrossed in the view that she remained completely oblivious to both his words and his actions. A baffled frown appeared on his brow as he registered the thoroughly stunned and awed expression on her face.

Good Lord! he thought, as he let his arm fall limply to his side. *She is as entranced with the place as I had hoped she would be. Round one to me, it seems. It would appear that the lady is well and truly hooked!*

Filled with a deep sense of satisfaction, but well aware that the battle was not yet won, the Viscount, clearing his throat briskly, reached out his hand again and tapped Sophie gently on the arm.

'I hate to interrupt your reverie, my dear, but I fear that the horses are starting to get restive!'

At the unexpectedness of his touch, Sophie found herself jerked back to the far-from-dreamlike reality of her present situation. *How typical of the devil to have stumbled across the very place that might cause me to change my mind,* she thought crossly, as she placed her hand into Helstone's and allowed him to help her down from the carriage. *Nevertheless,* she vowed, *he will soon find that I still have no intention of becoming his paramour, no matter how impossibly perfect his beastly cottage might be!*

Not that the idea was without a certain appeal, she was obliged to concede, casting up a quick sideways glance at the Viscount's handsome visage as he escorted her up the front steps and through the cottage's already opened door. *Would it really be so very wrong to agree to his proposition in order to acquire the tenancy of this splendid house?* she conjectured wistfully, as she stepped inside the elegantly appointed hallway. But even as she felt the heat of so enticing a notion coursing through her veins, she forced herself to thrust it instantly away. To exchange a future lifetime of pain and regret for a few months of vicarious pleasure could in no way be considered any sort of a bargain, she castigated herself impatiently. For, despite having had a rather limited acquaintance with the subject, she was not so foolish that she did not understand that the sort of liaison in which Helstone had suggested she might care to involve herself was well known to have a somewhat limited tenure. It was not difficult to fathom out what might become of women in such situations once they were cast aside—the very thought of which was enough to make her own dreary existence seem almost palatable by comparison!

'Good afternoon, my lord. I trust that you had a pleasant journey?'

Returning her thoughts to the reality of her present situation, Sophie became aware that the Viscount was being addressed by a tall, stately looking female of indeterminate years, clad in a black bombazine gown with a neat frill of white lace at its neck. *Mrs Bellamy, the housekeeper*, she supposed, doing her utmost to adopt an air of detached nonchalance in the face of the house-keeper's expected attitude of disparagement. *Not that I should expect anything less from the poor creature,* she reminded herself. *Unaccompanied young ladies of good standing do not accept invitations to the secret love-nests of well-known libertines. The good woman has probably already formed her own opinion of my doubtful worth—especially since my mode of dress is likely to be somewhat dowdy when compared to that of his lordship's usual doxies!*

Lifting her chin, she stared defiantly at the house-keeper, daring the woman to show her disapproval.

'Pleasant enough, thank you, Mrs Bellamy—although a trifle more breezy than I had anticipated. Perhaps you would be so good as to direct Miss Flint to a chamber where she might wash her hands and tidy her hair?'

'But of course, sir—do come this way, ma'am.'

To Sophie's surprise, the housekeeper's tone was in no way starchy or censorious. In fact, as she led her up the broad staircase to the upper floor, Mrs Bellamy's face creased in a friendly smile. She showed her into a prettily decorated bedchamber and invited her to make use of its facilities.

'I shall have hot water sent up directly,' she said, directing Sophie's attention to the washstand beside a fully equipped dressing table. 'You will find combs and brushes there—they are all brand new, of course, so please do not be afraid to avail yourself of them. I was beginning to doubt that they would ever be used! His lordship has owned the property for well over six months now, and you are the very first visitor ever to have set foot inside it!' Pausing, she shot Sophie a somewhat shrewd glance, before going on to say, 'I do so hope that you approve of all the decorations and improvements that have been made.'

That the housekeeper should consider her opinion to be of any value came as something of a surprise to Sophie, given that she was just a casual visitor and hardly likely to come here again. But then it occurred to her that the woman was merely looking for some sort of acknowledgment for all the hard work that she and her staff had put in.

'I really cannot imagine that anyone would be able to find fault with a single thing, Mrs Bellamy,' she assured her earnestly. 'Everything looks so clean and bright— it's quite the loveliest cottage that I have ever seen, and the gardens, well, who could possibly ask for a more delightful view?'

Crossing over to the open window, she poked her head out, only to find her senses almost overwhelmed by the fragrant scent of the densely blossomed honeysuckle bush, whose branches had spread their tendrils right across the cottage wall just below the room's windowsill. And then, as her eyes travelled slowly across the neatly laid out gardens before her, they fell upon an arching rose arbour at the far end of the side garden, beyond which another glorious aspect threatened to take her breath away. There, with its gently sloping banks edged with aspen and willow trees—complete with all the obligatory bulrushes, water lilies, swans and assorted ducks of her childhood imaginings—lay a small but picturesque lake, its limpid waters sparkling invitingly in the afternoon sunshine. The entire prospect was so devastatingly awe-inspiring that she was rendered almost speechless.

'Perfect,' she breathed softly. 'Truly perfect.'

'I am so glad you approve, ma'am.' The housekeeper

beamed as she turned to leave the room. 'I have always thought it a most pleasant view, myself. And now, if you will excuse me, I must go and see about that hot water I promised you.'

Chapter Nine

Tentatively retracing her steps down the stairs some ten minutes later, Sophie was well on the way to convincing herself that Viscount Helstone must be something of a mind-reading magician for, having brought her to this delightful cottage, presumably with the sole intention of persuading her to accept his offer, he seemed to have managed to conjure up almost every one of the wild and wonderful fantasies that she had held dear for most of her childhood years and beyond. *How Mama would love all this,* she thought dreamily, as she ran her fingers over the smooth, lovingly polished surface of the mahogany banister rail. *And what an incredible place for Roger to come home to in the holidays! All those trees, just waiting to be climbed, and the lake—how he would revel in fishing there—possibly he could even have a boat of his own! We could have picnics by the lakeside, and in the winter, when the water froze...*

'A penny for them, Miss Flint!'

The sound of Helstone's deep voice at her elbow

wrenched her from her daydream. With a gasp of dismay, she spun round, her cheeks aflame. *What could she have been thinking, to let her imagination run away with her in such a foolish manner? To accept Helstone's offer would mean totally cutting herself off from her family, just as her father had done from his all those years ago. There would be no way on earth that she would ever see her mama strolling across these lawns twirling her parasol, and her brother would most likely never be allowed to speak to her again, let alone climb the apple trees in Laurel Cottage's orchard!*

'Hardly a sufficient offer, perhaps?' continued the Viscount, easing himself away from the doorframe against which he had been leaning while watching Sophie's preoccupied descent of the stairs. 'I have the feeling that your thoughts were worth a good deal more than that—but I shan't press you, so your secrets are perfectly safe, I promise you.'

Which is probably just as well, thought Sophie, steadfastly refusing to look at him. *If he had the slightest inkling of where my thoughts were leading me, I cannot begin to imagine what his reaction would be!*

'Come,' he said, holding out his hand. 'Mrs Bellamy tells me that she has laid tea in the pavilion—it seems a pity not to take advantage of the sun while it is still shining.'

A pavilion too? Sophie could hardly believe it. Was the man supernatural?

'I didn't see a pavilion when I was looking out of the window,' she said, as she tucked her hand into the crook of his arm and allowed him to lead her out of a side door onto a path that led through the abundantly stocked flower gardens down towards the lake.

'No, you wouldn't,' he explained. 'It is hidden away

on the other side of the rose arbour—I found that the trellising helps to ward off the wind.'

'You designed all this yourself?' Sophie could not conceal her astonishment.

'Not all,' he replied, a soft smile tugging at his lips as he registered her incredulous expression. 'Just a few minor improvements here and there. Do you approve?'

'I'm utterly overwhelmed—it would be difficult to imagine anything more perfect. It is so kind of you to allow me to see it all.'

Kind! Marcus blanched. Kindness had been the last thing on his mind when he had drummed up this idea. Total seduction of Sophie's senses had been his original intention, followed by...

Grimacing, as the only too familiar ache in his groin assailed him once again, he bit back a groan. *Take it easy,* he rebuked himself. *Slowly does it—it wouldn't do to frighten the lady away entirely!* Apart from which, he found himself admitting there was something oddly refreshing about Sophie's refusal to bend herself to his will—a distinct change from his many past conquests, who had been only too eager to bestow whatever favours he required in exchange for some paltry bauble or other. Sophie, on the other hand, had even made a point of turning down his offer to pay for that damned atlas of hers, insisting that she would somehow find the money and reimburse him! Having managed to scotch that plan by getting Broomfield to exchange the tattered copy for a much newer version, Marcus was surprised that Sophie had not yet tackled him over that particular subterfuge. *Probably saving it up to attack me with it when I least expect it,* he concluded ruefully, as he attempted to ply her with the various sumptuous dishes that Mrs Bellamy had laid out for them.

'But there is far too much food here for just the two of us!' she protested, laughingly waving away his offerings. 'I couldn't possibly eat that amount of veal pie—you must cut that slice in half, at the very least!'

'But you've taken scarcely enough to feed a kitten,' he complained. 'Do try some of this chicken. It is utterly delicious, I swear. We can't have Cook thinking that we don't appreciate her culinary arts—good cooks are very hard to come by.'

'Well, just a little, perhaps,' conceded Sophie, holding out her plate in order that he could serve her a slice of the succulent meat. 'But I really need to save a little space for those delicious-looking strawberries—I can't remember the last time I had any and I do enjoy them so.'

In fact, her enjoyment of the whole afternoon was such that she had all but ceased to be chary of him. After all the deprivation that she had suffered during the past few months, she was finding the Viscount's dedicated attention to her every need so very heart-warming. Not only that, but the sheer beauty of her surroundings was threatening to dazzle her entirely, making her uncomfortably aware of the fact that, should Helstone happen to choose this particular moment to launch another one of his amorous assaults on her, she very much doubted that she would be able to find either the strength or the willpower to resist his advances.

Fortunately for her peace of mind, the Viscount's thoughts appeared to be elsewhere.

'You've led a most unusual life, haven't you?' he asked, reaching forward to pass her a generous helping of the ripe red fruits. Then, repositioning himself comfortably against the stone bench's fat cushions, so that he could indulge himself in witnessing Sophie's sheer delight in what was, to her, yet another unexpected luxury, he murmured, 'Care to tell me about it?'

'Our life was no different from any other family who chose to follow their loved ones to war,' replied Sophie, somewhat evasively. 'My mother travelled with my father when his unit was sent to Ireland back in ninety-two, and we always accompanied him thereafter—that is,' she amended, 'Mama and I did. Roger, my brother, was sent away to school when he was eight. When Papa was killed, of course...' Her voice trailed away and her eyes were suddenly filled with desolation. Biting back the tears that threatened, she attempted a mocking laugh. 'The rest you know—lack of finance required me to seek some sort of position, but, since I had nothing to show in the way of references, I was obliged to settle for the Crayfords' offer.'

Although he was tempted to remind her that his own proposition far outweighed the Crayfords' in terms of generosity, Marcus held his tongue, having just recalled the chance remark made by his brother the previous day.

'Your father,' he said, leaning forward. 'He must have been an officer to have been allowed to have his family travel with him. What rank was he, may I ask?'

'He was a Lieutenant-Colonel,' responded Sophie instantly, her chin held high. 'He died attempting to move his unit to higher ground and was awarded for his bravery—not that such an accolade is a great deal of help to us now,' she added bitterly. 'But I am still immensely proud of him, nevertheless.'

'And rightly so,' returned the Viscount, much moved. 'He was clearly a credit to his country.' He paused, slightly unsure of how to phrase his next question. 'My brother once spoke to me of a Lieutenant-Colonel Pendleton-Flint,' he then said. 'He wouldn't have been your father, by any chance?'

'Yes, he was,' she replied dully. 'And if you are wondering why I do not use my full name just ask yourself how many people would wish to employ a companion or governess with a double-barrelled name. The employment agency advised me to discard the Pendleton, on the grounds that it might give prospective employers the idea that I had ideas above my station!'

'But that's nonsense!' protested Marcus angrily. 'Surely everyone is entitled to use their given name, no matter what their walk of life?'

'It would appear not, my lord,' rebutted Sophie, as she rose from her seat. 'Needless to say, I would appreciate your discretion in this matter—I already have enough with which to contend after your claiming to be a cousin of mine, without having to explain my reasons for not using my full name.'

She paused and then, fixing him with an angry glare, went on, 'Which reminds me—I believe I am in your debt for an even greater amount than the three shillings and sixpence we originally agreed upon. Perhaps you would let me know the exact figure and I will do my best to see that you—'

'Heaven preserve me from idiotish females!' exploded Marcus, jumping to his feet and cutting her short. 'You know perfectly well that you haven't a hope in hell of being able to pay me back this side of Judgement Day, so will you kindly desist from mentioning the subject again?'

Sophie's face whitened. 'Was the book so very expensive then?' she persisted, quite resolute in her determination to refund the Viscount the full amount of her indebtedness, regardless of how long it might take.

'What does it matter what the damned thing cost?' he cried, clapping his hand to his brow. 'I shan't accept a single penny from you and that's final! No!' he ordered, as she opened her mouth to protest. 'I won't hear another word on the subject! If you imagine that I'm going to stand here arguing over a paltry ten shillings, you are— oh, damn it to hell!'

As the sound of Sophie's barely suppressed chuckle filled the air, a rueful smile spread across Helstone's face. 'Rolled up, lock, stock and barrel!' he groaned, as he threw himself back onto his seat.

'Don't fret, my lord,' cooed Sophie gleefully, reaching forward and patting him on the hand. 'I was bound to have found out eventually—I had it in mind to ask Mr Broomfield had you refused to tell me!'

Marcus stared at her, shaking his head in self-disgust. Then, as the seed of an idea planted itself in his brain, 'How much do these Crayfords actually pay you, then, Miss Moneybags?' he asked carelessly.

'Twelve pounds a year, all found,' replied Sophie, caught off guard by his casual tone.

'Good God!' The Viscount was visibly shocked. 'The miserable skinflints—even my sister's governess gets twenty pounds a year and her husband is the most tight-fisted clutch-purse known to man! How, in God's name, do you manage on such a pittance?'

'There are plenty of people who survive on a good deal less,' she retorted dryly. 'I have more than enough for my own needs and I even manage to put a little aside every quarter to send to my mother.'

'And you would rather live like that than…?' he

asked, eying her wonderingly. 'Hardly the most flattering thing I've ever been told!'

Sophie shrugged. 'It's just a question of self-respect, my lord. That and—' She stopped, her cheeks flaming.

'And what?' he prompted, impatient to know her true reasons for continually turning him down.

Blinking rapidly, she turned away, so that the Viscount could not see her face.

'I've always supposed that I would—give myself to someone that I loved and who loved me in return,' she said, in a low voice. 'And, even though marriage is denied me, I see no reason to relinquish my principles.'

Marcus stilled, his eyes focussed on her back. Then, 'In what way is marriage denied you?' he demanded hoarsely. 'You are quite lovely.'

Turning to face him, she gestured impatiently. 'I am a dowerless, impoverished governess, and the only gentlemen who cross my path are those whose inclinations are as far removed from thoughts of marriage as are your own, sir!'

He stiffened as hot colour mounted his cheeks, struck silent by her damning words and heavily conscious of the fact that the charge was impossible to deny. In fact, no one knew better than he that his recent behaviour in regard to this chestnut-haired siren had been well outside his normal code of conduct, and the disquieting awareness of which, it had to be said, had caused the Viscount a good many sleepless nights of late. From the very first moment he had set eyes on her, he had felt himself drawn to her in a way that was both compelling and yet at the same time quite mystifying. Sophie's departure from the tavern had left him feeling so bereft that he had, unaccountably, badgered his brother into helping him search for her, and now that he had found her again he knew that his life meant nothing unless she agreed to be part of it. Now, however, since she had made it quite clear that the final objective was to be denied him, regardless of anything he might say or do, any attempt on his part to continue with his carefully thought-out plans to persuade her to succumb to his desires now seemed totally pointless.

Apart from an offer of marriage, of course, he allowed, with an inward grimace, supremely confident in the knowledge that should he, as heir to the Bradfield earldom, ever care to cast his hat into that particular ring, he would have the pick of the Season's debutantes scrambling to take up his offer. *Should I be mad enough to venture into that hornets' nest!* thought Marcus scathingly. *No, thank you! I'm more than happy to leave the question of succession to Giles—let him put his head into the parson's mousetrap, if he must. Marriage is most definitely not on the cards, as far as I'm concerned!*

At his continued silence, Sophie returned to the table and, holding back a disconsolate sigh, picked up her discarded napkin and proceeded to fill it with random scraps of food.

'With your permission, I shall go and feed the ducks,' she said, casting a questioning glance at the Viscount's scowling visage.

'As you wish,' returned Marcus, with a careless shrug. He was beginning to regret his decision to bring Sophie to Laurel Cottage. From now on this peaceful bolt-hole would be forever tainted with tantalising images of her walking down the stairs, strolling through the gardens admiring his designs, daintily sipping champagne in the pavilion—his very favourite spot of all—and now…

Against his better judgement, he let his eyes drift over to where Sophie now stood at the water's edge. Having leaned forward to toss a handful of crumbs towards the flock of ducks now heading swiftly in her direction, she had let out a loud peal of laughter and was clapping her hands in delight as the comical antics of the noisy jostling birds captured the whole of her attention.

At the sight of her laughing face Marcus felt his stomach give a violent lurch, and it was all he could do to stop from hurling himself across the grass and dragging her into his arms. His entire body ached to feel the soft roundness of her curves pressed against him and to taste the incredible sweetness of her lips again. *God, but it's going to be difficult to give her up!* He groaned inwardly, steeling himself to descend the pavilion steps and walk towards the water's edge with a modicum of dignified composure.

'Watch out for the swans,' he advised, as he approached. 'They are apt to go for the hand, if one isn't careful.'

'Oh, what a pity!' she said, turning her attention to the far side of the lake, from which she could see two majestic-looking swans making a graceful approach. 'I didn't think that they would come while there were so many ducks squabbling for my offerings and now it has all gone!'

Rising to her feet, she shook the final few crumbs into the water, setting off another clamour, as the flapping, squawking waterfowl jostled one another witlessly in their frenzied attempts to get at the offerings.

'There's plenty more back there,' offered Marcus with a light laugh, jerking his head towards the plates full of untouched delicacies still sitting on the table in the pavilion. 'Enough to satisfy even the most voracious of their appetites, I should think.'

'Thank you, but I fear that I really ought to be thinking of leaving now,' returned Sophie, casting a last regretful look at the swans, now drifting in aimless circles in search of long-gone provender. 'Mrs Crayford distinctly said "afternoon drive", as I recall, and it must be getting close to five o'clock by now, I should think.'

'A quarter to,' supplied the Viscount, after pulling out his watch and flipping open its lid to check the hour. 'I'll have the carriage brought round.'

Probably for the best, he told himself sternly as Sophie gave a swift nod and turned to make her way back to the house. *I'll just have to accept the fact that she means what she says and let her go to get on with her own life.*

'I trust that you've had no further attacks on your person since our last meeting?' he then added, as if by afterthought.

'No, of course not,' she replied, with a vehement shake of her head. 'I should have mentioned it had I done so. Apart from having to clear up my room after all the mess that my dear pupil caused, my life has gone on much as usual.'

'Your pupil ransacked your room?' Marcus bit back his anger. 'When did this happen?'

'I discovered it upon my return yesterday afternoon,' she said in reply. 'I must confess that I found it a trifle dispiriting at the time.'

Hardly surprising, reflected the Viscount, with a wry grimace. *Coming on top of my boorish behaviour as it did! The perfect ending to a perfect day!*

'Does the boy make a habit of that sort of thing?' he asked.

'Not as such.' She sighed. 'He did set a host of frogs free in my room shortly after I arrived, and is inclined to be somewhat insolent at times, but he has never before gone to such a spiteful extreme.'

'You administered a suitable punishment, I imagine?'

'No, I refuse to give him the gratification of thinking that it bothered me. I have learned that, in Henry's case, at least, children are apt not to repeat things that fail to have the effect they had hoped for. He won't do it again.'

'You're quite certain that the lad was the culprit, I suppose?'

Faced with this latest piece of information, Marcus was seriously beginning to doubt that Sophie's errant pupil had been to blame for the ransacking of her room. Since the unwitting governess had already been the unfortunate victim of two-bag snatches in a matter of hours, it was hardly a long shot for him to infer that the retrieval of the misdirected cipher had been the real purpose for each of these robberies. If so, and rather more to the point as far as Marcus was concerned, it was not difficult to deduce that the ransacking of her room could be laid squarely at the feet of whoever had been responsible for the bag snatching. A cold trickle of unease ran through him as it then became clear that what he had vaguely suspected all along was no longer open to any doubt. *One or other member of the Crayford household was behind all three attacks!* And, much as the Viscount would have taken great pleasure in being the one to apprehend the craven individual and teach him a much needed lesson in civility, he had sufficient sense to appreciate that such things were best left in the more competent hands of Giles and his team of experts. He could only thank God that Sophie no longer had the damned invoice in her possession!

A slight furrow appeared on Sophie's brow as she pondered his question.

'Reasonably so,' she replied cautiously. 'I admit that I did, at first, suspect Arthur Crayford, but, having seen him leave the house just before I myself left, I was obliged to discount him. Apart from which,' she added, her tone more scathing, 'I cannot imagine him going to so much trouble for so little return—his methods are far more confrontational.'

Not any more, they aren't, reflected Marcus with a certain amount of satisfaction. But then, bearing in mind his brother's remarks regarding the sometimes dual personalities of hardened criminals, he realised that it might be unwise to dismiss the coxcomb entirely.

'You always keep your bedroom door locked, I imagine?' he then asked, as they were about to re-enter the house. 'An open door is often regarded as an open invitation, in certain quarters.'

Giving him a reassuring smile, Sophie replied, 'I hadn't always done so—except at night, of course. But I shall be sure to do so from now on.'

'Very wise,' agreed the Viscount somewhat inattentively, since his mind had instantly latched on to Sophie's veiled reference to the nightly locking of her door. *That evil toad Crayford at his tricks again*, he supposed, harnessing his fury at the thought of Sophie having been obliged to endure such iniquitous harassment. Hopefully, yesterday's warning should have put a stop to the noxious little swine's activities, but, if not, Marcus was in no doubt that he would soon find a way of dissuading the young wretch in some other, possibly less gentlemanly fashion.

Not that Sophie's future well-being was really any concern of his, he was at pains to remind himself. Now that she had made her intentions clear, it merely remained for him to see her safely home, put in a cursory appearance at the Crayford soiree and simply put the whole sorry business out of his mind as though none of it had ever happened.

If only life were that simple…

Chapter Ten

An open curricle, as Mrs Bellamy had been swift to point out upon their departure, was not, perhaps, an ideal mode of transport for what was to be a somewhat chillier journey back to Town, but to Sophie's undisguised delight Helstone had already thought to cater for such an eventuality. Having equipped himself with one of the soft woollen rugs that were draped over the backs of the sofas in the cottage's parlour, he had tucked it behind his driving seat, in the event of an emergency.

At the first sign of Sophie's shivering, he swung his equipage over to the side of the road and, pulling out the rug, draped it neatly about her shoulders saying, with a somewhat wry smile, 'Since you insist upon denying me the pleasure of lavishing you with furs, at least allow me the privilege of ensuring your comfort for the duration of this trip.'

Snuggling blissfully into the cosy warmth, Sophie gave a contented sigh. 'You are very kind, my lord, and I really must thank you for a most enjoyable afternoon.'

Pausing, she then cast him an uneasy glance before continuing. 'I'm truly sorry that we failed to see eye to eye over—um—a certain matter, but I feel sure that, once you have had a chance to review the situation, you will agree that it is really for the best that we do not continue to see each other.'

Whilst it cost her a great deal to make this pronouncement, Sophie was convinced that it was the right and proper thing to do. She already had an inkling that the Viscount had accepted the fact that she was never going to agree to become his mistress, and, that being so, there could be no further need for him to remain in touch with her. She would go her way and he, no doubt, would continue to go his. He would never know the true extent of her feelings for him and she would have to learn to live with the knowledge of what she might have had, had she been a little more courageous or even a little less prideful, perhaps!

'That might prove a little difficult,' replied Marcus, in response to her ultimatum. 'I have already accepted an invitation to attend this function that the Crayfords are holding on Tuesday evening. I feel that it would be rather discourteous of me to default at this stage.' Not that he really gave a tinker's cuss as to what the Crayfords might think or feel about his failure to attend their pathetic little soiree, but, even though his carefully laid plans had failed to tempt Sophie away from her chosen path of virtue, the Viscount still had every intention of finding some way of persuading her employers to treat their governess with a little more respect than hitherto.

Unable to think up an adequate reason as to why Helstone should not fulfil his commitment, Sophie remained silent, although her thoughts were chaotic. The Viscount's having agreed to put in an appearance

at the Crayfords' rout would mean that she too would
be obliged to attend the hastily arranged function, occa-
sioning even more time in his company—a situation that
she was desperately keen to avoid, well aware that every
minute spent in such close proximity with him took her
yet another step closer to her eventual undoing.

As the carriage swung sharply around a bend in the
road, she could feel the warmth of Helstone's disturb-
ingly muscular thigh pressing hard against hers, causing
a hot spiral of longing to course throughout her entire
body. Desperately trying to edge herself away from his
enticing nearness, Sophie racked her brains for some
topic of conversation that might help take her mind off
the all too alluring images that her thoughts were presently conjuring up.

'You don't happen to know what your brother did
with my bill of sale, I suppose?' she asked.

'He used it to help him solve some puzzle or other,'
replied Marcus off-handedly, achingly aware of her presence next to him. Sophie's vain attempts to put more
space between them had not passed him by, but had
merely served to underline what he could only suppose
was her growing antipathy towards him. Despite this
rather dispiriting conclusion, however, he still had every
intention of carrying out the task he had set himself. By
the time he had finished with the Crayfords, he vowed,
they would be blessing the day that Sophie had chosen
to cross their threshold. With a surfeit of friends and
acquaintances who owed him enough favours to serve
his purpose, he intended to call in those favours by way
of obliging several highborn members of the *Ton* to
show their faces at some of the ghastly-sounding functions that the socially inept Mrs Crayford had spoken
of in their earlier conversation. That should ensure that

her indomitable governess slept safe in her bed at nights, if nothing else, he thought to himself in satisfaction.

'Puzzle?' ventured Sophie, breaking into his reverie.

'Apparently, the thing was in code,' he replied, hastily returning his attention to the subject in hand. 'Seems there's some sort of a plot afoot to do away with the Duke of Wellington, and your invoice unravelled the mystery as to the gang's next meeting place.'

'But that's appalling!' she cried, turning towards him, her fists clenched and her clear blue eyes alight with anger. 'His Grace is a national hero! Why, only a few months ago the crowds were pelting his carriage with flowers as he drove down Pall Mall. My father thought him the greatest general our country has ever known. Why would anyone wish to harm him now, after all he has done?'

Unwilling to share his brother's concerns regarding the growing unrest in the country, Marcus thought it best to change the subject.

'Probably just a few crack pots trying to stir up trouble,' he said, doing his best to adopt his normal blasé manner. 'I should put it out of my mind, if I were you. I'm sure that my brother has it all in hand, thanks to that invoice of yours.'

Sophie was silent for a moment or two, apparently digesting this advice, but then, turning to face him once more, she said, 'But surely your brother cannot suspect that decrepit old bookseller of being involved in such a plot?'

'Probably not,' conceded the Viscount, who was now devoting the majority of his attention to negotiating the sharp turn out of Sloane Street into Lennox Gardens. Having brought his carriage neatly to a halt outside the

Crayford residence, he then looked across at her to add, somewhat mischievously, 'But I'm bound to say that clerk of his looked decidedly shifty when I went into the back office to have your atlas wrapped.'

'*Your* atlas, you mean!' she retaliated at once, just as he had known that she would. '*My* atlas is still in the shop!'

'As you please,' he replied, giving her another of his lop-sided grins, before leaping down from his seat and skirting around the vehicle in order to be ready to offer her his assistance.

But instead of holding out his hand, as she had expected, the Viscount reached forward and, placing both hands firmly at her waist, swung her out of her seat to deposit her neatly on to the pavement.

Thoroughly taken aback by his unanticipated manoeuvre, Sophie stood in breathless bewilderment as she waited for Helstone to release his hold on her. When he did not immediately do so, however, her eyes flew up to his face, questioningly.

Helstone's expression, she discovered, was quite incomprehensible; his eyes, as they looked searchingly into hers, seemed to bore deep down into her very soul, setting up such a violent trembling within her that, had his hands not still been at her waist, she would have sworn that her knees were ready to give way beneath her. Her mind in complete disarray, she had almost convinced herself that the Viscount was about to kiss her... out here in the street...in full view of anyone who might be watching...when, with a sudden start, he blinked and, hurriedly releasing his hold, stepped away from her, a perplexed frown on his forehead.

Then, just as if the incident had never taken place, he drew in a deep breath, offered the thoroughly shaken

Sophie his arm and escorted her up the short flight of steps that led to the Crayfords' front door.

Any thoughts that she might have had regarding his strange behaviour were wiped completely from her mind by the fact that, even before the Viscount had reached out his hand to raise the knocker, the front door was opened by none other than Mrs Crayford herself, albeit that the highly indignant features of Hawkins the butler could be seen at his mistress's elbow.

'Ah, there you are, your lordship,' gushed Mrs Crayford, as she hurriedly reversed to allow the pair to enter the hallway. 'We were beginning to fear that you had met with some dreadful accident. How very naughty of Miss Flint to have kept you out for so long—you must be quite exhausted. You will come in and take a little refreshment, I trust?'

'It is exceedingly kind of you to offer,' returned Marcus, affecting an extravagant bow in order to hide his expression of utter disgust. 'However, Miss Flint and I have already dined and, as to our being late, I was unaware that any particular time of arrival had been specified. I was under the impression that my cousin's Sunday afternoons were hers to do with as she pleases.'

'Why, yes, of course,' replied the now highly flustered matron, braving the steely glint in the Viscount's eye to add, with a slight hint of defiance, 'After the children have attended the morning church service, Miss Flint's time is her own.'

'As I surmised,' observed the Viscount smoothly. 'My sister, the Duchess of Marchmont, practises a very similar arrangement with her children's governess.'

Marcus's casual reference to one of Society's most admired hostesses at once claimed Mrs Crayford's entire attention, as had been his intention. That he had then gone on to liken her domestic arrangements to those of the illustrious Duchess was almost enough to deprive the coarse vulgarian of her power of speech.

'One tries to be fair,' she eventually managed, vigorously fanning her reddening cheeks with her handkerchief, while Sophie did her best to control the expression of sheer disbelief that threatened.

In point of fact, not a single Sunday afternoon had passed since Sophie's arrival without Mrs Crayford having plied her with some secretarial chore or other. At the very start of her employment Sophie had been far too grateful to have been accepted for the position to even consider putting up any sort of resistance to this continual encroachment into what was meant to be her free time, as a result of which her employer now seemed to take it for granted that her children's governess would be prepared to make herself available to her as and whenever her services were called upon. Especially since Sophie's non-complaining lack of resistance obviated the need for Mrs Crayford to employ a secretary, thereby allowing her employer to put the generous quarterage that she received from her husband to cover the household expenses to what she considered far better use—namely, her own self-adornment.

Having done his best to raise Sophie's stock a little higher, Marcus made ready to leave. Executing another elegant bow in Mrs Crayford's direction, he turned to bid farewell to Sophie, but just as he did so his eyes chanced to fall on the footman who was waiting to open the door. Recognising him at once as the fellow who had delivered Sophie's message to him the previous evening, the Viscount was again beset by the feeling that he had come across the man before, in some other capacity.

'What's that chap's name?' he murmured under his breath, as he lifted Sophie's hand to brush his lips across the tips of her fingers. 'I keep getting the feeling that I know him from somewhere.'

Although she was quite startled at being questioned in such a covert manner, Sophie strove to maintain an impassive mien. Dipping his lordship a quick curtsey, she mouthed the word 'Fisher' at him, before straightening up and offering him her grateful thanks for 'a most delightful afternoon'.

'My pleasure entirely, dear coz,' he said, as he stepped away from her. 'We must endeavour to repeat the experience in the very near future.'

Ignoring her reproachful frown, he tossed another brief nod at her employer before turning smartly on his heel and striding towards the front door, still racking his brains as to why the footman's features should seem so familiar to him.

Before he was halfway out of the door, however, Mrs Crayford, suddenly galvanised into action, dashed across the hallway and grasped at his arm.

'You haven't forgotten our little soiree on Tuesday evening, have you, my lord?' she gasped anxiously.

Steeling himself not to rip her clutching fingers from his coat-sleeve, the Viscount forced a smile to his lips, saying, 'I shall be here, ma'am—you have my word.'

Then, without further ado, he ran lightly down the steps, hoisted himself up into his driving seat and, after signalling Kimble to let go the horses' heads, flicked the reins and headed towards his Grosvenor Square establishment.

Having come to the conclusion that there was little point in bemoaning the afternoon's lack of success in the seduction stakes, he set his mind to concentrating

on the recurring puzzle that the footman's appearance
had set him.

A pasty-looking, sharp-featured individual…eyes set
too close together…distinctively pointed nose…

His unanticipated jerk of the reins had Kimble almost
out of his seat as the two grey thoroughbreds skidded
to an abrupt halt.

'Have a heart, guv!' protested the tiger, ruefully mas-
saging his bruised knee. 'Nearly had me under that there
coal wagon.'

'Teach you not to fall asleep on the job,' retorted
Marcus. 'Hop down and help me head 'em back up
towards Bond Street.'

'Thought we was going home,' muttered the aggrieved
Kimble, reluctantly doing as he had been bidden. 'Took
me eyes off the road for the barest mo, only to find
meself hanging on to me perch for dear life—a bit of
notice wouldn't have gone amiss!'

'Sorry about that,' returned the Viscount, shooting
his groom an unrepentant grin as the man wheeled the
greys around until the entire equipage faced in the opposite direction. 'I give you leave to drown your sorrows in
the King's Arms—I find I need to have an urgent word
with the Major.'

Having been unable to fathom Helstone's untoward
interest in the Crayfords' footman, Sophie found herself
casting the manservant a surreptitious glance—only
to find Fisher regarding her in an equally disquieting
manner. Hurriedly dropping her eyes, she made for the
stairs, but was immediately forestalled by Mrs Crayford's sharp insistence that she should join the family
in the drawing room.

'For I'm sure we are all agog to hear how the pair

of you spent your afternoon. And fancy his lordship choosing to take you out to dine—you simply must come along and tell us all about it.'

Groaning inwardly, since she was not at all disposed to sharing a single minute of her enchanting afternoon with her invidiously prying employer, Sophie made up her mind to ignore the implicit command.

'Thank you, but since I still have tomorrow's lessons to prepare I really ought to get on,' she said, lifting her foot in readiness to mount the stairs.

Unfortunately, Mrs Crayford refused to be denied.

'Oh, but that can wait a few more minutes, I am sure,' she said, waving a dismissive hand. 'Mr Crayford and myself are really most eager to hear about your trip.'

Very much doubting that Mrs Crayford's elderly, timorous spouse was in the least bit interested in the comings and goings of his children's governess, Sophie curbed the facetious retort that hovered on the tip of her tongue and then, conscious that her employer had left her with very little option but to comply with her demands, felt obliged to concede.

'As you wish,' she replied dispiritedly. 'But, I daresay you will excuse me for a moment or two while I take my things to my room and tidy my hair.'

'Well, if you really must,' pouted Mrs Crayford, eying with disfavour the prim grey gown Sophie had insisted upon wearing, despite her mistress's very clear objections to the contrary. 'And, while you're at it, you might care to change into one of those very pretty gowns that Lydia was so kind as to pass on to you—I really cannot understand why you felt it necessary to accompany his lordship in your workaday clothes when you have so many other lovely dresses to choose from!'

Her lips clamped firmly together, in order to prevent

the inadvertent emission of some choice but highly unladylike profanity regarding the loveliness or otherwise of the aforementioned offerings, Sophie sensibly demurred from making any reply and, her whole body seething with tightly suppressed fury, proceeded to climb the three flights of stairs that led up to her attic bedroom. On reaching the second floor, however, she was startled to find herself waylaid by none other than the footman, Fisher, who emerged from the entrance to the servants' stairway just as she was about to pass.

'A word, Miss Flint, if you please,' he hissed, his sharp eyes darting anxiously hither and thither in order to satisfy himself that his clandestine apprehension of the governess had remained unobserved.

Unfortunately, Sophie's recent unsatisfactory encounter with Mrs Crayford had left her in no mood to deal with what she considered to be an overly theatrical performance on the part of the footman. 'I'm sorry, Fisher,' she said, as she skirted past him and continued on her way. 'I'm afraid I don't have time to stop and chat with you just at the moment. The Crayfords are waiting for me.'

'But I have something...' he began, digging his hand into his pocket and withdrawing a tightly folded piece of paper. 'There was a mistake in the direction...'

Suddenly alert, Sophie came to a halt and, spinning on her heel, she stared down at the servant in wide-eyed incredulity.

'You have my invoice?' she cried, starting back down the stairs and holding out her hand.

But instead of handing her the missive, as she had expected, Fisher thrust his hand behind him. 'You'll get it back as soon as you return the one that was intended for me,' he grunted.

'But I don't—' began Sophie, but then, having suddenly realised that the orchestrator of all the ills that had befallen her over the past two days was standing here in front of her, did a swift rethink and went on, considering her words with a good deal more care. 'Unfortunately, I don't have it on me at the moment—I will bring it down to the servants' hall later. Now, I really must get on before I incur Mrs Crayford's wrath.'

With that, she turned on her heel once more and ran up the remaining stairs to the upper floor, reasonably confident that, since both the purse-snatching and the ransacking of her room could now clearly be laid at Fisher's door, the manservant might well think twice before attempting to follow her up onto the attic floor.

Not so. He stared up at her for only the briefest moment, before an uncouth grin spread slowly across his face and he started to climb the stairs after her— only to be suddenly halted in his tracks as the sound of a nearby door opening echoed down the passageway.

'Ah, Fisher—just the man.'

Never in her whole life could Sophie have imagined that she would actually be glad to see the loathsome son of the house hove into view. Fisher, muttering a crude imprecation, hastily regained his former position on the landing and quickly bent down, in order to give the approaching Crayford junior the impression that he had merely paused to tie up his bootlace.

''Fraid I've just kicked over my chamber pot—made a bit of a mess—get someone to see to it, there's a good chap,' called Crayford over his shoulder, as he unconcernedly continued on his way along the corridor and down the stairs.

Taking this opportunity to make good her escape, Sophie scuttled quickly to her chamber where, after dashing inside, she hurriedly locked the door. Not that this fairly basic precaution would necessarily keep her free from harm, she realised, since not only did Mrs Dixon, the housekeeper, possess a full set of keys to every room in the house, but there was also the spare set which hung inside the butler's pantry, in the event of a fire or other emergency. Meaning that just about anyone in the household was free to invade her privacy whenever they might choose to do so.

Gasping for breath and collapsing on her bed, she could not help wondering whether the plodding continuance of her formerly uneventful existence had not been a sight more preferable to the ongoing turmoil of the past couple of days. Not that this unexpected hiatus was likely to last for very much longer, she reminded herself brusquely. Not beyond Tuesday evening, at any rate. Having finally made her attitude clear to him, there was nothing else for her to do but wait and see whether Helstone would have the sense to cease his ridiculous pursuit of her and walk away, leaving her to her own devices. But even as she contemplated the prospect of so bleak a future the haunting image of his very perceptive glances swam into her thoughts and a sudden shiver rippled through her. It would be so very easy to allow herself to succumb to his persuasive entreaties and simply agree to his demands, she thought, as she closed her eyes and endeavoured to recapture the unbelievable thrill of that first breathtaking moment when the Viscount's firm, warm lips had finally made contact with her own. It had been as though every one of her recent dreams had come to fruition, only to find themselves suddenly dashed into a million irreparable fragments and cast to the four winds.

With a soft sigh, she rose to her feet and began to

undo the buttons of her gown. The die, it seemed, was well and truly cast, for had not she herself been the one to cast it? She had made her decision and all that remained was for his lordship to abide by his agreement to respect her wishes. Provided that she held fast to her resolve for the next forty-eight hours or so, she could see no reason why her life should not slide back to its former mundane tenure.

In the meantime, there was still the problem of Fisher to be addressed, but, since the footman was also entrusted with the house messages, it was difficult to see how she was going to manage to get word to the Viscount to inform him of her recent discovery. Even if she were able to persuade young Monks the Boots to take a note, she doubted that she could do so without drawing Fisher's attention to the fact. The problem, it seemed, looked to be insurmountable.

Chapter Eleven

Marcus stared at his brother in disbelief.

'Are you telling me that you have been aware of this Fisher chap's involvement all along?' he demanded, slamming down his glass and rising to his feet in a fury.

'Steady on, old son,' entreated Giles, as he hurriedly thrust out his hand to prevent the still full glass from tipping its contents over the edge of the table. 'The information was passed to me scarcely an hour or so ago. Once we'd got hold of Miss Flint's invoice I deemed it necessary to check out everyone in the Crayford household—I'd already put two men to watching the bookshop, as I told you. Anyway, as soon as it was learned that the footman and the clerk shared the same surname, it was not difficult to put two and two together.'

'And yet you've still not done a thing about it!' Marcus was incensed. 'Soph—Miss Flint's life might well be in danger and you're prepared to sit back and allow that fiend to run loose in the house!'

'Well, I didn't know about the lady's room having been ransacked until you informed me of that fact less than five minutes ago,' returned his brother, in his own defence. 'That sort of information does tend to put a different complexion on the matter.'

'But, if you are sure that these two are your men, why haven't you already had them both taken in charge?'

'Because we don't want to scare off the entire gang, that's why. It would be difficult to arrest the clerk without word getting out, thereby sending the whole bunch of them to earth. Additionally, we have reason to believe that the recipients of the coded message are group leaders—possibly running cells of four or five contacts each—which would explain Fisher's anxiety to get hold of his list of instructions.'

'Which Miss Flint no longer has in her possession!' pointed out Marcus, in some irritation. 'What if he decides to confront her head on? No one in that establishment is going to rush to her defence. I can assure you of that! The son is lily-livered; the woman is a self-centred sycophant and the husband appears to have the wits of a four-year-old!'

'Crayford senior is somewhat advanced in years, that's true.' The Major nodded. 'The blonde pea-goose is his second wife, I'm reliably informed.'

'Yet another fine example of married bliss, I dare say,' grunted Marcus, getting to his feet and glaring down at his brother. 'More than enough to put a fellow off for life! But enough of this chit-chat. Do you mean to sort out this Fisher chap or do I have to deal with the devious swine myself?'

'I think you had best leave the apprehension of felons to the experts, old son,' returned Giles briskly, as he leaned across and reached for the bell-rope. 'It is true that I had hoped to have returned the lady's invoice before matters reached such a crucial stage in the proceedings, but it now appears that I could have been just a little more incisive in my planning—ah, come in, Peters. It would seem that we might have some sort of crisis on our hands.'

Thus it was that, barely five minutes into Mrs Crayford's fervent cross-examination of Sophie, a wide-eyed Hawkins thrust open the drawing room door and stumbled inside, bearing the shocking news that two constables had invaded his kitchen and were now in the process of arresting the footman! At which point the mistress of the house promptly dissolved into one of her habitual vapourish fits and the elderly master of the house seemed unable to do anything other than shake his head at the thoroughly discomposed butler while murmuring, 'Well, 'pon my soul—two constables—in the kitchen—well, 'pon my soul, whatever is the world coming to?'

Since both Arthur and Lydia appeared to be similarly mesmerised by Hawkins's astonishing declaration, Sophie, mentally counting her blessings, realised that some sort of decisive action was required.

'Pray do not distress yourself, Hawkins,' she advised the still clearly shocked butler. 'No fault can be laid at your door, of that I'm sure. Nevertheless, do you not think that it might be wise to return to the kitchen in order to ascertain exactly what is happening? Added to which, I do feel that Mrs Crayford's maid ought to be informed of her mistress's apparent need of her *sal volatile* bottle.'

Then, getting to her feet, she approached Crayford senior and laid her hand on his arm. 'I imagine that you will wish to speak to the constables, sir,' she said gently.

'What—me? Oh, no, I couldn't possibly—Eleanor's the one—she'll sort it all out.'

His bottom lip trembling, he shook his head, refusing to meet her eyes.

'But Mrs Crayford is not well, sir. Hawkins has gone to fetch her maid.'

Receiving no response to her observation, Sophie gave a frustrated sigh and turned her attention towards the other two members of the family, who were now regarding her movements in a fascinated silence.

'Do try to rally your father, Arthur,' she urged him. 'Surely you can see that the poor man is in a considerable state of shock—the constables will be upon us shortly and might well want to ask questions.'

'Why should they want to question us?' returned the youth belligerently. 'We haven't done anything wrong!'

'Do you suppose he has murdered someone?' breathed Lydia, clutching at her brother's arm, her eyes wide with excitement. 'Slit their throat with a carving knife or stabbed them in the back, perhaps?'

'Who? Pa?' exclaimed Crayford junior, impatiently shrugging himself away from her. 'Don't be so stupid! You read far too many of those paltry Minerva mysteries!'

'I was referring to Fisher, you great clunkhead!' retorted the girl crossly. 'And I shall tell Mama what you just said to me.'

'Mama has perfectly good hearing of her own, thank you very much,' came Mrs Crayford's weakly rejoinder, as she thrust herself up into a sitting position. Having discovered that her performance had failed to achieve the effect that it usually commanded, she was not about to allow her governess to take centre stage. 'Help me to my feet, Miss Flint. I need to see what's going on in my kitchen.'

'I have sent for Capstan, ma'am,' said Sophie, hurrying forward. 'Perhaps you ought to wait and take a little *sal volatile* before you involve yourself in anything too energetic?'

'Nonsense!' Mrs Crayford was already on her feet. 'It's clear that the man must have been helping himself to our property—I need to take an immediate inventory of all our valuables in order to see what might have gone missing. Come along, Miss Flint, you can take down the list.'

Raising her eyes to the ceiling, Sophie gave a disbelieving shrug and prepared to follow her employer, only too aware that the exercise in which they were now about to involve themselves was going to prove a total waste of time. 'Might it not be better to go down to the kitchen first and hear what the constables have to say?' she ventured, as soon as they had reached the hallway. 'Perhaps Fisher's misdemeanour has nothing to do with his employment here?'

'Just as long as the dreaded constabulary hasn't advertised its presence to the entire neighbourhood,' moaned her mistress. 'What if that wicked creature has been raiding houses up and down the street? I shall never be able to hold up my head in public again!'

She did, however, agree to visit the kitchen prior to starting on her inventory and by the time they reached the basement Sophie was beginning to feel almost sorry for the footman, whose crimes, in Mrs Crayford's imagination, ranged from petty thievery all the way up to organised crime on the grandest of scales.

* * *

'Sedition?' repeated her employer, staring at one of the constables in some confusion, after he had acquainted her with the charges against Fisher. 'I'm not sure I...'

'Sort of treason, ma'am,' put in the constable helpfully. 'Incitement to riot and all that sort of thing.'

'Not stealing, then?'

Keeping her eyes carefully averted from the spectacle of her only footman standing heavily manacled at the back door, Mrs Crayford sank slowly into the chair that Sophie had had the good sense to position at her rear. 'Thank God it's nothing serious, then,' she murmured, as she clung on to the table-edge. 'But how on earth we are expected to manage without a footman to serve at table defies even my imagination. Why couldn't the selfish creature have put off his stupid sediting until later in the week, I ask you? I can hardly bear to contemplate what his lordship will think of such shoddy service when he next visits us.'

'Oh, I'm sure Hawkins will be able to arrange a suitable replacement by tomorrow evening,' Sophie was quick to assure her, as she cast up a questioning look at the butler who, having recovered from the humiliation of having two burly men of law bursting into his kitchen and apprehending his footman, had managed to revert to his former dignified persona.

'As you say, miss,' he replied gravely. 'I was about to make a similar suggestion myself—I shall deal with the matter first thing in the morning.'

'Well, make sure that you don't get another seditor this time,' snapped Mrs Crayford crossly, as she rose to her feet and prepared to depart. 'You may take yourselves off now,' she added, waving a dismissive hand to the still waiting constables. 'And do try not to cause too much of a commotion outside when you leave. This is a very respectable neighbourhood, you know.'

'But we still have several questions that we need answers to,' insisted one of the men, edging his way forward. 'Where this fellow came from, how long he's worked for you and all that sort of thing.'

'Well, you can hardly expect me to know those sorts of details about people in my employ,' returned Mrs Crayford edgily. 'Hawkins deals with all that kind of thing. He'll tell you anything you need to know. And now, if you will excuse me, I have other far more important matters to attend to.'

The Crayford soiree looked well on the way to becoming quite a resounding success, thought Sophie in considerable surprise, as she took in the bustling scene that surrounded her. The level of noise had already reached ear-piercing proportions and there was scarcely an inch of space to spare in any direction, making the air in both this and the adjoining room decidedly oppressive. The whole event, it would seem, had every sign of turning out to be the sort of crush for which her employer had been craving much of her married life.

Having been the one to whom the task of writing out the fifty or so invitations had fallen, she had supposed that perhaps half of the illustrious personages invited might design to attend such a lowly gathering. The sheer volume of numbers turning up on the front doorstep, however, had come as something of a shock even to Mrs Crayford, who had been obliged to keep pinching herself in order to convince herself that the whole thing was not some sort of wild, improbable dream.

'I really cannot recall having invited either the

Hetheringtons or the Liskeards,' she whispered to Sophie in awe, as still more guests from the upper echelons of Society continued to pour into the lower hallway. 'I can only think that they must be associates of his lordship's—I did tell him that he was welcome to bring along some of his friends if he wished.'

'Well, he certainly seems to have taken you at your word,' returned Sophie, biting back her irritation. All this, presumably, was another of Helstone's far-flung ideas of attempting to give the Crayfords the impression that she came from much more worthy stock than they had originally supposed. But, whilst it was certainly true that the family's attitude towards her had changed for the better since the Viscount's claim to be a distant cousin of hers, it was not hard to envisage the level of antagonism that would be directed towards her when his assertations were found to be untrue and his visits came to a halt—as they most surely would, once this evening's affair was over.

Craning her neck to seek out Helstone's distinctive dark head of hair, she scoured the room but could see no sign of him. Her heart sank at the thought that, after her unsatisfactory performance of Sunday afternoon, he might well have decided not to attend the soiree, after all.

'Looking for anyone in particular?' came the Viscount's deep drawl, from somewhere in the direction of her left ear.

Spinning around, the tell-tale flush still on her face, Sophie gasped, 'But how on earth did you manage to fight your way through that crush of people without me catching sight of you?'

'I had my driver drop me off as we passed the mews and I came in through the back garden,' he said, motioning her gently towards the nearby terrace doors. 'Nice to know that you were keeping a weather eye out for me.'

Taking in a much needed breath of fresh air as she stepped out on to the deserted terrace with him, Sophie gave a careless shrug.

'I merely wanted to ask you whether the extraordinary number of uninvited guests who have turned up this evening is any of your doing.'

'Well, I have to admit that I did call in a few favours,' he replied, with a somewhat sheepish grin that immediately had Sophie's heart executing violent somersaults. 'But I must confess that I didn't expect them all to be repaid on the one night. I trust that her greatness is suitably impressed?'

'Completely overwhelmed, I should imagine,' responded Sophie, letting out a little chuckle. 'Although I am given to understand that such an unforeseen increase in numbers has made considerable inroads into Mr Crayford's stock of champagne, as well as having put paid to Mrs Crayford's idea of setting up a dance area at the far end of the drawing room, as was her original intention.'

'Now, that *is* a pity,' sighed Marcus, who was finding it almost impossible to tear his eyes away from the tantalising sight of the soft swell of Sophie's bosom peeping teasingly above the low-cut neckline of her hastily redesigned evening gown. 'I'm bound to admit that the idea of holding you in my arms again has enormous appeal—even if it's only to whirl you around the room in time with the music.'

Her mind unable to erase the piquant image his words had conjured up, Sophie stepped away from him, doing her best to manufacture a frown of disapproval. 'You really must desist from making that sort of remark—I was under the impression that we had finally reached an agreement over that matter.'

Marcus offered her what was intended to be a penitent grin. 'You can't blame me if my baser instincts threaten to get the better of me whenever I am close to you.'

Her pulse ratcheting up another notch, Sophie took a steadying breath.

'If you refuse to behave yourself, sir, I shall just have to go back inside.'

'No, please don't.' Marcus caught at her hand. 'I shall try to be good, I promise.'

'You really shouldn't make promises that you have no intention of keeping,' she retorted shakily. 'You have already broken your word to me on two previous occasions. I had always been under the impression that a gentleman's word was supposed to be his bond.'

His eyes darkening in exasperation, Marcus stared down at her, frowning. 'I think you'll find that that much used adage generally applies to financial agreements made in gambling dens and other such unsavoury establishments.'

'And only between persons who number themselves gentlemen, presumably?'

'Goes without saying, I should have thought.'

Her eyes widening in indignation, Sophie drew in a sharp breath.

'Are you saying, then, that a promise given to a lady doesn't require to be treated with the same respect as one you might give to a fellow gambler?'

'Why, yes, of course it does,' he snapped, then, hesitating, began to run his fingers through his hair in a somewhat distracted manner. 'Well, not in the same way, perhaps—the two cases are somewhat different. The first is a matter of honour—no, that's not what I mean. They are both matters of honour, of course but—damn, it, woman! How can you expect me to think straight when you look at me in such a way?'

Then, powerless to prevent himself, he let out a deep groan and, reaching forward, pulled her into his arms, slanting his lips across hers. Caught off guard, Sophie melted into his embrace, moulding her curves into the hard contours of his supreme maleness. Her arms twined tightly around his neck, while every nerve in her body responded to the urgent demands of his lips.

Lost in the wonder of the moment, she felt her senses swim, and nothing else in the world seemed to matter but the wondrously exciting feel of Helstone's arms surrounding her and the hot, insistent pressure of his lips on hers.

'Come away with me, Sophie.' He gasped, pulling away from her just long enough to drag in a lungful of air. 'Come away now. I don't think I can stand another night without you.'

Like a dash of icy water down her spine, the sudden shock of his words shattered Sophie's trancelike state, leaving her stunned and shaken. Uttering a faint moan of distress, she tore herself away from the still heavily panting Viscount and clutched at the stone bulwarks of the terrace in an effort to support her quivering limbs.

'No more, please,' she whimpered. 'Must I beg you to leave me alone?'

'Sophie—sweetheart!'

Marcus, still struggling to master his unsated ardour, took an uncertain step towards her and held out his hand. 'You cannot think that I mean to hurt you, surely?' he asked in astonishment. 'You must know that I would sooner cut off my right hand than—'

Trembling with a mixture of rage and some other unidentifiable emotion that she refused to acknowledge, Sophie clapped both hands against her ears, determined not to listen to Helstone's hollow blandishments.

Incensed, the Viscount whipped out his hand and grabbed at her wrist, wresting her fingers away from her head and pulling her towards him. 'Now you're being foolish,' he growled into her ear. 'Next you'll be telling me that you don't enjoy kissing me, when I know damn well that you do—you couldn't respond in that way if you didn't feel as I do.'

Wrenching herself out of his grip, Sophie stepped back and pointed an accusing finger at him.

'You have shown yourself to be the very worst kind of cad, sir. I have rejected your offer on more than one occasion, yet still you persist in pursuing me. How many more times must I tell you that I do not desire your attentions? Please remove yourself and take your worthless promises with you. You are without morals—no better than that odious little reptile Crayford—and I swear I would rather starve on the streets than submit to your improper suggestions.'

His face paling visibly, Marcus stepped away from her, his dark eyes glittering with some unnamed emotion and his mouth curving in a mocking smile.

'That wish may be granted sooner than you think, if I know anything of your employer's tactics,' he ground out abruptly, before turning on his heel and thrusting his way through the terrace doors that led into the crowded reception room. Then, ignoring the concerted cries of protest from the closely packed mêlée, his lips compressed in fury, he proceeded to elbow his way through their ranks before taking the stairs down to the hallway three at a time where, ignoring the waiting butler, he flung open the front door himself and stormed angrily out of the house.

Eventually locating his own carriage some hundred or so yards down the waiting line, he ejected both driver and groom with a curt dismissal and, after hauling himself up onto the box, spat out, 'Get yourselves a hackney home—I'll take them myself.'

Hobbes, the Viscount's driver of many years standing, having opened his mouth to protest at such cavalier treatment, took one look at his master's pursed lips and rigid expression and immediately thought better of it.

'He's in a rare old pelter,' he muttered to the groom, as Helstone inched the team out of the line until the landau was clear and then, cracking his whip at the leader, set off down the road at breakneck speed. 'Can't recall ever seeing him that mad before.'

Chapter Twelve

Letting out a sob of despair, Sophie sank back against the stone balustrade, her heart pounding and hot tears welling up into her eyes. How could she have allowed her temper to get the better of her in such a cruel, malicious manner? she asked herself wretchedly. Just because Helstone had failed to control his ardour, it was surely no reason for her to have reacted quite so imprudently?

Angrily dashing the tears from her cheeks with the back of her hand, she gave a trembling sigh, well aware that the real reason behind her hurtful attack on the Viscount's character had stemmed from the fact that he had spoken nothing but the truth—a truth that she had been fighting against ever since he had first walked into her life. A truth that brought about feelings of embarrassment, shame and anguish—hence her hysterical outburst. For, although the Viscount had been the one to bear the brunt of her resentment, she knew quite well that it was she herself with whom she was most angry—for having been so foolish as to allow herself to fall so desperately in love with a man whose dreams and aims were about as far removed from her own as it was possible to be. Yet, now that she had cast him out of her life for ever, she could not help being achingly aware that, when the tears had ceased and the heartache had finally faded away—if indeed it ever did—those sweet dreams would be all she would have left to see her through the dark and dismal days ahead.

'A most edifying scene, I'm sure—although I have to say that I don't care to hear myself being referred to in such a derogatory manner!'

Letting out a sharp gasp of dismay, Sophie whirled round and saw Arthur Crayford, his fleshy lips curved in a malicious smile, climbing the terrace steps towards her.

'You were eavesdropping!' she cried scornfully, turning away from the advancing youth and making for the doors into the reception room. 'How very contemptible!'

'Not as contemptible as your kissing cousin, it would seem,' he sneered, as he quickly stepped around in front of her, barring her way. 'I believe you owe me an apology. Something rather similar to that which you treated his lordship would serve nicely—at least to begin with!'

'Get away from me, you loathsome little beast!' she hissed, backing away from him. 'How many times must I tell you to keep your hands to yourself?'

'As many as you like, my sweet,' he retorted, as he shot out a hand and, grabbing at her wrist, jerked her viciously towards him. 'The more insults you hurl in my direction, the greater the number of penalties you will pay—so I can't really lose, can I? How about that kiss, for starters?'

A ripple of ice cold dread ran through Sophie's veins as she tried frantically to free herself from Crayford's clutching hands. Having dismissed calling out for assistance as a pointless exercise, given the high volume of noise emanating from the nearby reception room, she quickly realised that her only hope lay in trying to manoeuvre her attacker in the direction of the doors and praying that one or other of the guests might witness her predicament through the panes of glass and come to her aid.

Unfortunately, Crayford was already intent on forcing her into one of the darker recesses, well away from the pools of light that shone from the windows of the reception rooms out on to the terrace beyond. Her heart racing with apprehension, Sophie knew that her only option now was to feign weakness. Letting out a weak little moan, she bent her knees and allowed herself to slump forward, which sudden reversal of tactics had Crayford desperately trying to maintain his hold on her.

'Stand up, you stupid bitch!' he grunted, staggering backwards as he strove to pull her to her feet at the same time as trying to correct his own balance.

Quick as a flash, Sophie seized the opportunity and, ducking under his arm, twisted herself away from him and made a desperate leap for the terrace doors. At that exact same instant, the doors flew open to reveal a livid-faced Mrs Crayford, who charged on to the terrace as though all the devils in hell were in pursuit.

'The guests are leaving in droves!' she babbled almost incoherently, drops of her spittle flying in all directions as she prodded the startled Sophie with her furled-up fan. 'Hawkins tells me that Helstone almost had the front door off its hinges in his fury to quit the premises, and now it seems that the rest of his friends and acquaintances cannot get away quickly enough. They are all going—every single one of them! I shall never live down the disgrace as long as I live! This has to be all your fault, girl! What can you have said to your cousin to put his lordship in such a dreadful taking?'

'She ain't his cousin, Ma,' interrupted her stepson, stepping out of the shadows. 'She just happens to be one of his current ladybirds.'

'Ladybirds?' Mrs Crayford recoiled in distaste, staring at him. 'Kindly explain yourself, Arthur.'

'I was down in the garden, enjoying a quiet blow, when I just happened to overhear their conversation,' he replied carelessly, his eyes gleaming with spite as he cast Sophie a malicious grin. 'Seems our little governess here is no more his lordship's cousin than I am. One of his latest demi-reps, more like, judging by what the pair of them were up to when I chanced upon them!'

Letting out a little snigger at his stepmother's gasp of horror, he gave a quick nod before adding, 'Anyway, seems that little bit of business led to them arguing the toss over something that ended with our Miss Goody Two-Shoes calling his lordship all the names under the sun and him storming off in a rare old dudgeon.'

'But that's simply not—' began Sophie, determined to stop the flow of Crayford's wicked inventions.

'You're not going to stand there and deny that you called his lordship an immoral cad, I trust?' he interrupted her, a challenging flash in his eyes.

'Well, I—' Sophie said hotly, but then, as the full gist of her angry outburst returned to her, her cheeks flooded and she stopped. 'It's not at all how it seems,' she finished lamely.

'Is Lord Helstone your cousin, or is he not?'

demanded Mrs Crayford, now quite beside herself with rage. 'Speak up, girl!'

Biting her lip, Sophie shook her head. She had known all along that this foolish assertion of Helstone's would lead to trouble eventually. 'He is not,' she replied dully. 'He is merely one of the travellers who were caught in that snowstorm last month.'

'And that was when the pair of you started this *affaire* of yours, I presume?' Icy contempt dripped from her employer's lips.

'We are not engaged in an *affaire*!' protested Sophie. 'His lordship is just a-a—' Racking her brain to find a suitable epithet to describe her relationship with Helstone, she concluded weakly. 'He's merely a casual acquaintance.'

'Well, you must hope that this "casual acquaintance-ship" you speak of extends to his helping you find other employment,' snapped Mrs Crayford. 'Between the pair of you, you have succeeded in turning me into a veritable laughing stock, and I refuse to have you in my house another moment. You will go straight to your room, pack up your belongings and take yourself out of my sight without further ado!'

'But it's after eleven,' returned Sophie in bewildered stupefaction. 'Where am I to go at this time of night?'

'That is hardly my problem, Miss Flint,' said her employer, with an indifferent shrug. 'Having put paid to all my carefully thought-out plans with your outrageous lies and subterfuge—not to mention ruining Lydia's entire future—I cannot imagine why you should think I would wish to concern myself over your welfare!'

'Well, I trust that you intend to pay me my outstanding wages,' retorted Sophie, somewhat defiantly. 'I believe I am owed something in the region of five and a half weeks.'

Raising one supercilious eyebrow, Mrs Crayford raked a contemptuous glance over the passed-on gown that Sophie had so diligently altered. 'And I believe that the value of the gown you are wearing will more than cover that amount—needless to say you will return everything else that my stepdaughter kindly volunteered on your behalf.'

Before Sophie could voice her thoughts regarding Lydia's kindness or otherwise, Crayford junior stepped forward, anxious to have his say.

Having remained more or less silent during the whole of the foregoing proceedings, it had slowly dawned on the youth that if Sophie were to be turned out immediately all chance of bedding her would be lost to him. Whereas if he could just persuade his stepmother to allow the governess to remain until the morning there was every possibility that he might be able to creep into her bedchamber and fulfil what had been a long-held ambition of his. *And wouldn't that be one in the eye for the high and mighty Helstone?* He grinned to himself. *Given that the Viscount seemed to be experiencing a certain amount of difficulty persuading the little lady to part with the goods!*

'Might be better if Miss Flint left first thing in the morning, Ma,' he interjected hastily. 'Wouldn't look too good with the neighbours, her leaving with all her baggage at this time of night—especially after all the guests quitting the place in such a tearing hurry. Plus there was that other unpleasant business with the constabulary on Sunday,' he reminded her, in an effort to add extra fillip to his suggestion.

Pursing her lips, Mrs Crayford considered her

stepson's words. 'You may well be right,' she said, giving a reluctant nod. 'Very well, Miss Flint. You may stay until first light—but I refuse to have you in my house a moment longer!'

Sophie's lip curled in disgust as she registered Crayford's expression of smug complacency, for it hadn't required a great deal of intelligence to work out what the devious coxcomb really had in mind. While she was relieved that his intervention might, in the one sense, be regarded as something of a temporary salvation, insofar as keeping her off the streets for the next few hours, it was also clear that it was going to involve her in a long and sleepless night, while she kept a tight and vigilant watch on the doorknob to her room.

Shortly before five o'clock the following morning, Sophie dragged her heavy hamper down the steps of the Crayfords' residence and stood staring down at her pitiful little pile of belongings: one basket, two bulging valises and a couple of paper-wrapped packages—the sum total of her worth, she thought grimly.

But as to how she was going to get her possessions to the coaching station in Piccadilly she still had not the vaguest idea, even though this particular problem had been uppermost in her mind for most of the past few hours.

Just as she had anticipated, young Crayford's attempts at invading her privacy had started almost as soon as the last servant had crept off to bed, but, having taken the precaution of pushing her chest of drawers up against the locked door, Sophie had been able to sit back and enjoy listening to the thwarted youth's vicious imprecations as he twisted the doorknob first this way and then that, in his continual efforts to gain entry to her room. Those attempts had persisted at varying intervals through much of the night, culminating in what had been his final endeavour, and one that had caused Sophie several moments of real panic, since by this time her tormentor, almost out of his mind with a combination of rage and frustrated libido, had managed to get hold of one of the spare keys to her door. It had been due only to a last-minute brainwave on Sophie's part that this final effort was doomed to meet with a similar fate to his previous sorties.

Realising that it would not be long before his key managed to displace her own, she had hit on the idea of jamming a pencil into the aperture, which had had the desired effect of preventing him from pushing her key out and inserting his own. After spending some ten minutes or more involved in various fruitless attempts to dislodge the obstruction, Crayford had finally given up all hope of achieving his ambition and, cursing Sophie to high heaven, hefted one last violent kick at her door before taking himself off to the library, where he'd set about doing his damnedest to drown his disappointment by way of his father's best cognac.

By that time it had already been past four o'clock, and, heartsick and weary as she was, Sophie had known that sleep was out of the question. She was to be out of the house before the maidservants rose to clean the grates and light the fires, and that was less than an hour away.

After stuffing the last of her possessions into the wickerwork hamper that had been her travelling companion on so many other journeys in her life, she had sat back on her knees and given her mind over to the problem of how to get her belongings down to the front doorstep. In the normal way, a footman would have carried her boxes down the back stairs into the servants' hall and thence out through the basement. However, as she was well aware, the main staircase was the most direct route, and her heavy basket would be far easier to manoeuvre on the carpeting than it would on the rough stone steps that the servants were required to use. With the memory of Mrs Crayford's cruel refusal to pay her what she was owed still ringing in her ears, Sophie, setting her chin defiantly, had made up her mind to flout convention and elected to go for the route that suited her purpose best.

In point of fact, she had been obliged to make her chosen journey three times before her task was complete. Luckily, the resonant ticking of the long-case clock in the hallway, coupled with the sounds of Crayford's strident snoring issuing from behind the closed door of the adjacent library, had all but obscured the soft, steady thump-thump of her basket as she had finally dragged it down the three flights of stairs and into the hallway. Pausing momentarily to catch her breath, she had cast a quick look around to satisfy herself that no prying eyes were there to witness her departure and then, pulling back the bolts on the front door, had let herself out into the cool half-light of the new day.

Now that she was here, however, out on the pavement surrounded by her bags and boxes, she was at a loss to know what to do next. She needed to remove herself from the vicinity of the Crayford house with all possible speed, that much was certain, but how? That was the question.

She stared up and down the street, hoping for some inspiration to strike her, but the only movement she could perceive was that of the lamp-lighter, who was making his laborious way up the street extinguishing all the lamps.

A sudden tug on her skirt-hem caused her a moment or two's anxiety until, peering down through the basement railings below her, she found herself looking into the begrimed and anxious face of Monks, the boot boy.

'What are you—?' she began, but stopped the moment she saw him press his fingers against his lips, in an effort to get her to still her tongue.

'Mr 'awkins sent me to get you an 'ack, miss,' the boy whispered hoarsely, while climbing up the steps and out into the street. 'There's usually a few of 'em in the rank on the corner of Sloane Street—shan't be a tick.'

'But I can't afford a cab,' she cried softly, reaching out her hand to grab the boy before he took off. 'I have barely enough money for my coach fare to Dulwich.'

'Not to worry, miss,' replied Monks with a wide grin, as he delved into one of his pockets and produced a shilling piece. 'Mr 'awkins thought o' that, too. This'll get you as far as the Piccadilly stage, 'e said.'

Hot tears flooded Sophie's eyes as she watched the boot boy's skinny figure tearing down the pavement towards Pont Street. In her role as a governess she had been neither fish nor fowl, insofar as her position in the hierarchy of the household had been concerned, and although she had always treated her fellow employees with the utmost respect, she had continued to feel something of an interloper whenever she had had cause to venture into the servants' hall, as a consequence of which, she had elected to take her meals in the nursery wing, along with her two young pupils. So to discover that the butler had held her in such esteem that he was willing to go to these lengths on her behalf was almost unbelievable, and quite the most uplifting thing that had happened to her for some little while.

Within minutes a hackney carriage rounded the corner of Lennox Gardens and, with the boot boy's assistance, Sophie had little difficulty in stowing her belongings into the cab's luggage basket. When the time came for her to take her seat, however, her heart was so full that it was as much as she could do to stop herself from flinging her arms around the beaming youngster and kissing his grimy cheek.

'Oh, 'ang on a minute!' said the boy, grasping hold of the handle and pulling open the door again. 'Nearly forgot—Cook sent you this.' And, thrusting his hand into another of his pockets, he withdrew a neatly wrapped package. 'Thought you might get peckish on the journey,' he added. 'Seein' as 'ow you ain't 'ad any breakfast.' And then, after bestowing another of his cheery grins on her, he turned tail and scampered back down the basement steps, soon to disappear from her sight.

Brushing away her tears, Sophie leaned back against the squabs and closed her eyes, thinking how very sad it was to have learned of the kind-heartedness of her fellow employees at this late stage of their association. She prayed that their actions would remain undiscovered, for she was left with no illusions as to the way in which the vindictive Mrs Crayford's mind worked.

The fare, on her arrival at the Piccadilly coaching station, was exactly one shilling, just as the butler had predicted, and having found himself strangely moved to witness his passenger's distress on departing from her abode, the elderly jarvey even hauled himself down from his box and helped Sophie carry her baggage into the station's left luggage department, accepting her grateful thanks but brushing away her offer of the single groat that she had found in her pocket.

'You keep it, miss,' he said gruffly. 'Buy yourself a nice 'ot drink to steady them nerves.'

After thanking the driver once again, Sophie turned her attention towards the booking office. Having tied her four half-crowns carefully into a handkerchief, for she had no intention of being deprived of her wealth on this occasion, she had kept the handkerchief tucked safely inside her glove. The six mile journey from the staging post in Dulwich had cost three shillings when she had set out to take up her employment at the Crayfords' some months earlier, and she could only pray that the fares had not increased in that time. The baggage clerk had already informed her, on handing her a ticket, that it would cost her sixpence to retrieve her possessions, and she did so want to be able to hand over to her mother as much of what was left of her sadly depleted store as she possibly could.

She had just booked her seat on the midday coach—at an increased cost of three shillings and ninepence, to her dismay—when she felt a gentle tap on her shoulder and, swinging round, found herself staring up into the apologetic face of the hackney driver.

'Nearly left one of your parcels behind, miss,' he said ruefully. 'Found it right at the bottom of the basket when I was about to load up another fare. I oughter've checked more careful, like. Very sorry, miss.'

Eying the package as he passed it over to her, Sophie felt her heart give a little jerk, for it was none other than the atlas that Helstone had procured on her behalf and which she had rewrapped with the intention of returning it to him.

'No harm done,' she assured the jarvey, and thanked

him again for his diligence, conscious that many another driver would simply have kept the package and sold its contents for personal gain. 'It was very good of you to go to the trouble of returning it.'

'No trouble, miss—I hadn't left the yard.'

And, tipping his hat at her, he backed away and disappeared into the thronging mêlée.

Sophie stared down at the parcel in dismay. Short of paying for another left luggage ticket, which she could ill afford, she was going to have to carry the hefty package around with her until the midday coach departed—some six hours hence! She had originally intended to while away the intervening hours by walking in Green Park, and possibly visiting one or other of Piccadilly's circulating libraries, where it was possible to sit and read newspapers and periodicals without fear of interruption. But having to carry so large a parcel about with her was going to hamper her freedom quite considerably. She frowned. The dratted book had caused her nothing but problems from the outset! She had a good mind to—

She clapped her fingers against her lips, her eyes lighting up with excitement. But of course! The answer was staring her in the face. She would take the atlas back to Broomfield's shop and persuade the bookseller to buy it back from her! Helstone had admitted paying ten shillings for it, so Broomfield would surely be prepared to part with seven or eight! The walk to Maddox Alley would help to kill time, and she could eat the breakfast that Cook had so kindly prepared for her in Berkeley Square gardens. The sun had come up, heralding what looked set to turn into a fine warm day. With a determined smile, she straightened her shoulders and, tucking the parcel firmly under her arm, set out in the direction of Broomfield's store.

* * *

'I'd soon be out of business if I was to buy back every book I sold, young lady,' argued the bookseller, as he thrust the atlas back at her.

'But I'm not asking you to pay back the full amount,' protested Sophie, in desperation. 'Even half would do, and you would still make a handsome profit when you next sell it.'

'The way things are going, I could be out of business in a week,' returned the man morosely. 'What with constables trashing their way though all my goods yesterday, and then marching young Fisher off in irons, leaving me with a great pile of unfinished invoices to sort out, I doubt I'll ever find the time to sell another book.'

'Your clerk has been arrested?' cried Sophie, clutching wildly at a possible solution to her problems. 'I can see that that must make things very difficult for you. You are clearly in need of some help.'

'Not easy to get hold of anyone suitable round here,' sighed Broomfield, seeming almost glad to have found someone to whom he could express his grievances. 'Only took the lad on on account of being acquainted with his widowed mother, and now I'm told that both he and his brother have been mixed up in some plot to do away with some high-flown peer of the realm—wouldn't tell me which one, of course, and what it's all got to do with my bookshop, I can't begin to imagine.'

'I can see that it must be very difficult for you,' said Sophie, giving him a sympathetic nod. 'As it happens,' she then added, being careful to exhibit just the right amount of diffidence, 'I am well versed in the intricacies of double-entry book-keeping—as a qualified school-mistress...' Crossing her fingers behind her back, she drew in a deep breath and went on, 'I dare say I could probably stay and help you out for an hour or two, if that would be of any use to you?'

'You mean that you would be willing to sort out those bills for me?' asked Broomfield in amazement, jerking his head towards the huge pile of paperwork that could be seen on the desk in the rear office. 'I've been at it myself half the night, but my eyesight's not what it used to be, and what with customers interrupting—' He stopped, somewhat embarrassed, then endeavoured to hide his confusion by pulling off his spectacles and rubbing them briskly with the hem of his none too clean apron.

'I can stay until half-past eleven,' stated Sophie firmly, as she started to remove her pelisse. 'I must be at the coaching station by twelve, in order to catch the stage, and—' Pausing, she drew in a deep breath. 'You must pay me for my time, of course—I shall require ten shillings.'

'Ten shillings?' returned the bookseller at once. 'That's a great deal of money just to write out a few paltry invoices.'

Sophie raised an eyebrow. 'You would prefer to attend to them yourself?' she enquired sweetly. 'And by my estimation there are close in the region of fifty or sixty—scarcely a few.' Reaching out a hand for her discarded pelisse, she eyed him sternly. 'Ten shillings, Mr Broomfield, and in addition you may keep the atlas. Otherwise…'

'All the invoices?' he asked, his bleared eyes darting back to the pile. 'Every single one.'

'Every one—providing that I can make a start on them right away.'

'Ten shillings it is, then,' he said, backing out of the room. 'I'll leave you to get on with it, shall I?'

'Let me know when it's half-past eleven,' she called out to him, as he quietly closed the door.

Sixty-three invoices later, Sophie at last laid down her pen and, climbing down from the high stool on which she had been perched for the past four hours, pressed her hands into the small of her back to relieve the dull ache and stretched her shoulders. It had been touch and go, for there had been a good many inconsistencies in Mr Broomfield's figures and she had actually run out of ink at one point, necessitating a hurried call to the bookseller to replenish her pot. Since he had been serving a customer at the time, she had been obliged to waste several precious minutes until he could attend to her request. Now the job was done, however, and she was ten shillings to the good, making all her scrupulously checked figuring well worth her while.

'It's just on a quarter past the hour,' Broomfield pointed out, when she re-entered the shop. 'You'll find your ten shillings next to the cash box.' He eyed her enquiringly. 'You wouldn't care to take on the position full-time, I suppose?'

Sophie stared at him, considering. Might his offer be more preferable to going back home to be a burden on her mother's slim resources? she wondered. But then, realising that to accept the position would mean having to take lodgings somewhere in the nearby vicinity, she gave a reluctant shake of her head. The chances of running into Helstone in this area were far too great and a prospect to be avoided at all costs.

The previous evening's ugly confrontation, coupled with its disastrous consequences, had taught Sophie a valuable, if heartrendingly painful lesson, making it vital that she put as much distance as was possible between herself and the Viscount. She could hardly help but be aware of the fact that it was due entirely to his continual interference in her life that the whole compass of her existence had turned completely upside down. Having dissembled his way into the Crayfords' favour, with his disarming self-assurance and thoroughly irresistible smile, Helstone had then carelessly, but quite determinedly, set out to seduce her—very nearly achieving his aim with that unforgettable kiss; a kiss that had unlocked a wild and passionate facet to her nature, the like of which she had not realised lurked deep within her being. Her shock and dismay at being confronted with her own apparent inability to resist the Viscount's highly intoxicating charms had been the real reason for her sudden rage, followed by a primeval urge to unleash her fury on the root cause of her distress.

But then, as she bade the disappointed bookseller farewell and set out for her journey back to the Piccadilly change to board the stage to Dulwich, it was with doleful realisation that it came to her that, despite everything that had happened, that same unanswerable question still continued to niggle at her thoughts. What might have been the outcome had she agreed to Helstone's proposition?

Mentally admonishing herself for her wayward thoughts, she did her best to dismiss the Viscount from her mind altogether and endeavoured to concentrate her efforts on trying to conjure up some sort of acceptable explanation for her mother, since the whole unvarnished truth behind her sudden dismissal from the Crayfords was not a matter that Sophie was keen to share with her estimable parent.

In the event, Mrs Pendleton-Flint was so dismayed at learning of Sophie's constant battle to keep the son of the house at bay during her short tenure with the Crayfords that she could only express her gladness that her daughter had managed to escape the residence with her virtue still intact. Sophie, however, was honest enough to admit to herself that it was not the oleaginous Arthur Crayford who had posed the greatest threat in that particular regard, but the rakish Marcus Wolfe, with his teasing smile and that breathtakingly challenging glint in his eye, the poignant memory of which was to prove the cause of many a damp pillowcase during the long and sleepless nights that followed.

Chapter Thirteen

The reins hanging limply in his hands, Marcus peered abstractedly into the cloudy night-time gloom that surrounded the carriage. From the distressed sound of his horses' breathing, it would seem that he had run the poor beasts into the ground—an action for which he felt bitterly ashamed—in addition to which, he had not the faintest idea of where he had finally pitched up.

Having set off out of Lennox Gardens with no clear idea of where he was heading, the red mist of anger that filled his head had obscured everything but the need to remove himself from the hurtful echo of Sophie's bitter accusations. The toll-gates at Hyde Park corner and Kensington Gore figured vaguely in his memory, as did passing the gates of Chiswick House, but beyond these easily recognisable landmarks his mind was a total blank. That he had travelled some goodly distance at speed was only too apparent from the foam-flecked hides of the two wheelers who were now pawing at the ground in restive agitation.

Cursing himself for an insensitive fool, Marcus grabbed the handful of cloths that Hobbes kept tucked behind the driver's seat and, lowering himself carefully down from his perch, inched his way through the gloom to examine the leaders. Murmuring soothing words of comfort as he worked, he wiped away the excess of sweat from the animals' drenched coats, covering their shuddering backs as best he could with an assortment of rugs and other articles that he found in the box.

Raking his fingers through his hair, he peered around him. From the narrowness of the lane that they were on it was clear that he must have turned off the turnpike at some point, but where, and—more to the point, perhaps—why?

Casting his mind back, he did have an indistinct recollection of slackening the reins and letting the leaders have their heads, but where in God's name had the beasts taken him? With only the dim and gradually diminishing light thrown out by the carriage's twin oil lamps to light his path, Marcus inched his way slowly up the lane in the hopes of coming across a gate or other such feature of the landscape that might point him in the direction of a dwelling-place of some description.

Just at that moment the scudding clouds chasing across the night sky parted momentarily, to allow the full moon to shine down on the scene in all her glory, causing Marcus to blink several times before he could believe the evidence of his eyes. But, even as he threw back his head to let out a whoop of sheer disbelief the moon disappeared to obscure his view once more. Not that the Viscount needed any such light to guide him through the gates of Bradfield, which, as had been clearly revealed in that single instance, lay scarcely twenty yards distant from the very spot on which he was now standing! The clever beasts had brought him back to his ancestral home!

Shaking his head in wonder at the extraordinary ingenuity of these four-legged marvels, he took hold of the leader's harness and set out to guide the exhausted animals up the lane towards the wrought iron gates that opened on to the Bradfield estate. A single pull of the bell brought the elderly lodge keeper, his nightshirt flapping beneath a hastily donned drab woollen overcoat, tottering out of the front door of the lodge.

'Very sorry, your lordship,' gasped the man, as he drew back the bolts and began to pull open the gates. 'Wasn't warned to expect you.'

'Sorry to get you up, Cutler,' returned Marcus, adding his weight to the older man's efforts. 'Didn't know I'd be here myself until a short while ago.' *And that's something of an understatement, if ever there was one,* he thought to himself, with an inward grimace. 'You get yourself back to your bed—I can shoot the bolts myself as soon as I've got the carriage through.'

'If you're sure, sir?'

At the Viscount's insistent nod, the lodge keeper, clutching his coat about his bony frame, hobbled back to his door, where he stood for some moments watching in total confusion as the heir to the earldom led in the clearly shattered four-horse team along with their carriage but minus both driver and groom.

Unleashing the horses from their traces single-handedly proved to be a rather more exhausting procedure than Marcus might have imagined, but, being reluctant to rouse any of the grooms or stable lads from their hard earned slumbers, he doggedly persevered with his self-imposed undertaking until all four animals were unharnessed, rubbed down, watered and safely in their stalls. Only then did he turn his attention to the problem of getting himself into Bradfield Hall without waking up the entire household—as hammering on the great oak front door or tugging at the bell-pull would most surely do.

The Hall, as he knew, would be well and truly secured against intruders—thanks to the diligence of Warren, his father's major-domo, who took a personal pride in seeing that every one of the Hall's many entry points was safely locked and bolted before he retired for the night. Since it was now close to three o'clock in the morning, Marcus doubted that anyone in the house would still be awake.

Looks as though it's going to have to be the well-tried route of previous misadventures, he thought gloomily, as he made his way round to the rear of the building, past the succession houses and into the neatly kept kitchen gardens. *Thank God the clouds have blown away. At least I'll have enough light to see by should I happen to fall and break my neck!*

Eying the ancient walnut tree that stood in the centre of the garden with a certain amount of trepidation, for it was a good many years since he had been obliged to use this method of entry into his bedchamber, he was heartened to observe that the single upper branch that reached as far as his windowsill still looked strong enough to support his weight. Whether he was still sufficiently agile to accomplish the tricky manoeuvre remained yet to be seen. His bedroom window, he was relieved to note, had been left in just the way he always demanded, revealing a welcoming gap of two to three inches in its top sash.

Unbuttoning his jacket, he flexed his shoulders and, after taking a deep breath and casting up a prayer to the heavens above, swung himself up onto one of the walnut's lower branches and started to climb.

Some ten or so minutes later, his hands and face having both been badly scratched in the process of achieving his goal, he found himself balanced somewhat precariously with his left knee on the windowsill of his bedroom and his right foot perched on the none too steady branch of the tree, whose ominous creaking sounds were beginning to cause him serious concern.

Reluctantly letting go of his secure hold on the branch above his head, he grappled feverishly with the window's lower sash, eventually managing to hoist it upwards sufficiently to allow him to haul the upper part of his body across the opening where, breathless from his exertions, he remained motionless for some moments, both legs still dangling limply over the outside sill.

A sudden noise from within the room had him lifting his head in alarm, whereupon, gathering up the remains of his strength, he started to heave himself over the windowsill—only to find himself being grasped by the seat of his breeches and dragged with considerable force into the room, to be dropped, face-first and none too gently, onto his bedroom carpet.

'Righto, my lad,' came Giles's unruffled voice close to his ear. 'That's quite enough of— *Good God! Marcus?*'

'Get your knee out of my back, there's a good chap,' begged the Viscount, gingerly rolling himself over and up into a sitting position as soon as his startled brother had gathered enough wits to comply with his request. 'Obviously not quite as fit as I thought I was,' he added wryly.

'A good deal more dicked in the nob though, it would seem,' retorted Giles, as he reached out a hand to help

Marcus to his feet. 'I took you for a burglar, you blithering idiot! What the devil do you think you're at, sneaking into the house in this underhand manner? What's wrong with the front door, may I ask?'

'As it happens, I was doing my best to avoid waking the entire household,' returned his brother irritably, peeling off his soiled and ripped jacket and shirt and tossing them to one side. 'So, unless you want the whole lot of them down on our heads like the proverbial ton of bricks, I suggest you try and keep your voice to a minimum.'

'Yes, but why *are* you here?' asked Giles, lowering his voice but still staring at Marcus in confusion. 'Last I heard, you were off to do the pretty at the Crayfords'. The fragrant Miss Pendleton-Flint give you your marching orders, did she?'

'You could say that, I suppose,' muttered the Viscount abstractedly, as he threw himself down onto his bed to lie glowering at the silken underside of his tester. 'Seems I lost my temper, somewhat, and made a fool of myself into the bargain!' Swinging his legs over the side of the bed, he sat up with a rueful half-laugh. 'Can't think what's got into me of late—I don't usually behave in such a crass manner—must be getting old!'

'Or just in love, perhaps?' murmured his brother, not quite *sotto voce*. 'It does tend to hit you like that, I'm told.'

'What the hell are you talking about?' returned Marcus impatiently. 'Miss Pendleton-Flint and I simply agreed to disagree and that's all there is to it.'

'Then why are you getting so riled up about it?' asked Giles, eyeing his brother steadily. 'There are plenty of other fish in the sea—as I've heard you remark often enough in the past.'

And with good cause, thought Marcus, with a wry twist of his lips. *But none of them like Sophie.* He closed his eyes in a vain attempt to conjure up the image of her face. Sadly, all he achieved was a resounding echo of the hurtful recriminations that she had thrown at him. 'I was simply trying to make the poor girl's life a little more bearable,' he grunted, clenching his fists. 'It makes me really angry to think of the way that godforsaken bunch of social misfits treat her.'

'Such righteous altruism does you real credit, bro,' observed his brother, with a dry laugh. 'And there was I, thinking that your interest in the female was purely carnal!'

A faint flush covered the Viscount's cheeks as Giles's dart hit the mark. Frowning slightly, he gave a dismissive shrug. 'I won't deny that I find myself very attracted to her—she is so utterly different from any other female I've ever come across. She is so bright and intelligent, and incredibly resourceful, yet she is constantly put upon by her employers—she even spends her own hard-earned cash on books for the schoolroom, would you believe? And yet those misbegotten savages treat her as less than nothing—it makes my blood boil just to think of it.'

Getting to his feet, he began to pace the room. 'I just wanted to get her out of that blasted house. She deserves so much better. If you could have seen her at that tavern, Giles,' he went on, his eyes softening at the memory. 'There didn't seem to be any problem that she wasn't prepared to tackle—I swear that I've never come across anyone quite like her in the whole of my life. In fact, I wouldn't mind betting that more than one of her fellow travellers could well have perished in that snowstorm had it not been for Sophie Flint's down-to-earth capability and sheer dogged determination—she even had me milking a blessed cow—did I tell you that?'

'I believe you may have mentioned it once or twice,' said his brother, turning away to hide the grin that was forming. 'Nonetheless, bro, you know the rules as well as I do—defenceless virgins are out of bounds to men of our class, and as for offering virtuous spinsters such as your little governess a *carte blanche*, I find myself questioning your sanity—apart from which, I should have thought that those two little beauties you already have in your keeping were more than enough for any reasonable man to contend with!'

Giles's pointed reference to Livvy Rayner and Cynthia Bedlington brought Marcus's pacing to a sudden halt. 'Not that it's any of your damned business,' he returned curtly, 'but it just so happens that arrangements are already in hand to discontinue both of those associations.'

Giles let out a long low whistle. 'You're paying 'em off—just like that?' he asked incredulously. 'A touch on the heartless side after all these years, don't you think?'

'Hearts have no place in business arrangements of that sort,' retorted the Viscount, striding over to the mirror to inspect the damage to his face. Grimacing at the livid scratch across his left cheek, he picked up a towel and proceeded to dab at his blood-streaked visage. 'Surely the whole point about setting up a mistress is that one is able to do away with all the emotional claptrap and enjoy a purely physical relationship without any unnecessary ties. Both Livvy and Cynthia were well aware that the association would end some day. And, in case you are wondering, I have made sure that neither one of them will be the loser. I have arranged to have the deeds of their houses made over to them both, along with suitably generous dowries commensurate with their past efforts on my behalf.' A slightly cynical smile crept across his lips. 'I take leave to doubt that it will take either lady long to find herself a new protector.'

Turning to face his brother, he offered him a slightly rueful grin. 'In fact, one could say that both of the little minxes have been shoring up their futures at my expense for quite some time now—if the recent accounts from Rundell and Bridge are anything to go by!'

Although Giles was somewhat taken aback at Marcus's relatively casual parting with his two paramours, both of whom, insofar as his brother was aware, had been under Helstone's protection for well over three years, it took the Major no time at all to realise that this sudden decision of the Viscount's was yet another indication of his growing preoccupation with the Crayfords' impoverished governess.

'So, having disposed of both Miss Rayner and Miss Bedlington to your satisfaction,' he said, eyeing his brother in some disapproval, 'I take it that you were assuming that Miss Pendleton-Flint would be falling over herself to step into the vacancy—which, I must assume from your rather crushed demeanour earlier, is the opposite of what actually occurred when you put the suggestion to her?'

As Sophie's bitter accusations assailed his memory once again, Marcus flinched. Shaking his head in weary rebuttal of his brother's uncannily accurate construal of that unpleasant scene, he said, 'I'd just as soon not discuss the matter any longer, if it's all the same to you, Giles. Suffice to say that I was deeply concerned about the lady's situation and merely harboured a desire to see her in a more fitting environment. However, since Miss

Pendleton-Flint has elected not to accept my offer of help, the subject, as far as I am concerned, is now well and truly closed.'

'Sounds rather more than just a business arrangement you were offering the unfortunate lass, if I'm any judge,' Giles retaliated, as he headed for the door. 'However, enough of your problems. I fear my bed is calling me.' Pulling open the door, he hesitated slightly, then, turning back to face his brother once more, he added, a sly grin forming on his face, 'Although, after what I've gathered from your singular obsession with her, it occurs to me that you might just as well go the whole hog and marry the girl, if you want my opinion!'

'Which I don't!' retorted Marcus, as Giles stepped hurriedly out into the corridor and closed the door behind him. *I can just picture Father's face if I walked in and announced my intention of legshackling myself to a down-and-out nobody who has been forced into earning her living as a governess,* he thought scathingly, as he wrenched off his damaged pantaloons and dived under the coverlet of his large four-poster.

Not that there was anything at all dishonourable about having to earn one's living as a governess, he then amended, somewhat shamefaced that such an idea should have even crossed his mind. *In fact,* he reflected, as the image of Sophie's sweet smile drifted into his mind, *if one were to consider it objectively, dedicating oneself to the education of young children might well be considered to be rather an honourable profession. And as for being a nobody—why, hadn't her father been a highly decorated lieutenant-colonel in one of His Majesty's top hussar regiments? One could hardly class such a fellow as a nobody. And, whilst Sophie's upbringing may have been a touch irregular by conventional standards, it was abundantly clear that her parents had made no concessions, insofar as strict discipline and correct standards of behaviour were concerned—as he, to his eternal damnation, was well able to testify!*

As the memory of those discomfiting episodes surfaced once more, Marcus let out a loud groan and, rolling over onto his stomach, buried his head in his pillow in an effort to blot out the deeply disturbing images that continued to assail his thoughts. But it was no good. The harder he tried to rid his head of all thoughts of Sophie, the more his wayward brain insisted upon seducing his mind's eye with yet another tantalising depiction of her presence: Sophie in that hideous lace cap—Sophie washing dishes—Sophie throwing snowballs—feeding ducks—swans… God! Was there nothing in the world that didn't remind him of the woman?

And then, like a clarion call, his brother's closing shot resurfaced in his mind. He shot upright, his heart pounding in rapid disorder. Dragging in a deep breath, he flung back his bedclothes, heaved his legs over the side of the bed and, for several long moments just sat there, totally impervious to the chill night air as it wafted over his naked flesh, scarcely able to comprehend the impossible thought that had succeeded in worming its way into his brain.

'Damned if I don't do just that!'

No sooner had he spoken the words out loud than everything seemed to fall neatly into place. It was really quite simple, now that he had really given the matter some thought. He had to marry some time, after all; for months now his father been pressing him to attend to his duties and responsibilities as heir to the estate and, rather than settle for one of a number of mealy-mouthed, whey-faced debutantes, fresh from the schoolroom, whose names were sure to figure on his parents' list of suitable bride fodder, he would shackle himself to Sophie Pendleton-Flint!

The more Marcus thought about it, the more appealing the whole idea seemed. As far as he was concerned there was nothing about Sophie that might prohibit her from becoming his Viscountess. She was not only lovely to look at; she was graceful, intelligent and endowed with a rare common sense to which decidedly few females of his acquaintance could lay claim. But, above all else, she was the most fascinating creature that he had come across in all his days.

And so utterly desirable, of course. It was difficult to recall his ever having wanted any woman as badly as he wanted Sophie; his whole body ached with desire just at the thought of making her his wife. He had handed both of his regular mistresses their *congées* without a single pang of regret, since neither Cynthia's pert blonde curvaceousness nor the doe-eyed Livvy's sultry Latin magnetism had the power to captivate him any longer; only the warm glow of a pair of summer blue eyes and the promise of untamed flowing chestnut tresses now had that ability.

Sliding under the covers again, he lay back and closed his eyes, ready for sleep at last, satisfied that the only hurdle that stood in the way of his future plans was his father's possible opposition. Once he'd dealt with that problem, he mused idly, as he felt himself drifting off to sleep, it merely remained to acquaint Sophie with his revised proposal…

As it turned out, both the Earl and the Countess were so relieved to see their elder son safely returned to the fold after such an extended absence that it was some little while before he was able to turn their attention to the subject that had been exercising his mind since the moment he had surfaced from the highly erotic dreamworld of his slumbers.

'As a matter of fact,' he said, in answer to his mother's anxious query as to how long he intended to remain at Bradfield on this occasion, 'I do have something of an announcement to make—I trust it will meet with your approval.' Pausing, he dragged in a deep breath, conscious of the questioning stares of his listeners. 'I am pleased to inform you all that I have decided to take a wife.'

The astounded silence that followed this declaration was broken only by Giles's spluttering cough as the piece of ham he had been chewing became lodged in the back of his throat, threatening to choke him.

Getting to his feet and striding around the breakfast table to administer a hefty thump to his brother's back, thereby relieving his discomfort, Marcus took the opportunity to shoot the scarlet-faced Major a warning look, indicating that *he* would be the one to decide about which aspects of Sophie's history his parents might need to be apprised.

Resuming his seat, he turned to face his still stunned father and said, 'In case you might be wondering, sir, the lady's name is Miss Sophie Pendleton-Flint. It is my intention to bring her to meet you both sometime in the very near future. I would be glad to have your assurances that you will be prepared to receive my— fiancée—and welcome her into the family.'

A suspicious glint in his eye, the Earl regarded his son silently for some moments before saying, 'Somewhat out of character for you, isn't it, this sudden need to observe the proprieties?'

Swallowing the retaliatory retort that had instantly sprung to his lips at his father's contentious barb, Marcus curled his fingers tightly round the stem of his glass. 'Comes to all of us in the end, I dare say,' he said, striving to maintain his temper. 'I should have thought you would be glad to hear that I am finally prepared to meet your demands and relieve you of some of the burdens you carry.'

'Enough, you two. I beg of you!' interposed the Countess, reaching out to grasp hold of her son's clenched fingers. 'This is no time to re-enact past grievances! We must look to the future and I, for one, cannot wait to meet your chosen wife, Marcus. Miss—um—Pendleton-Flint, did you say? It is not a name I recognise—is the family new in Town?'

'The lady is not one of the current crop of debutantes, if that's what you're asking,' returned Marcus hurriedly, as he rose to his feet in preparation of quitting the room before either of his parents could embark upon a surfeit of awkward questions that he was not, in all conscience, fully confident that he was equipped to answer. 'Suffice to say that she is twenty-three years of age and her father was, until his death at Waterloo, a greatly admired and highly revered lieutenant-colonel in one of His Majesty's elite hussar regiments. And now, if you will please excuse me, I have a most pressing matter to attend to—I hope to be able to furnish you with further information regarding my forthcoming nuptials within the next day or so.'

Hardly had he left the room, however, before Bradfield, turning to his younger son, demanded, 'Out with it, Giles! It's quite clear that you know a good deal more about this matter than you are prepared to admit. Has that fool of a brother of yours got some young hussy in the family way and thinks to present us with his by-blow, or what?'

'Really, Edward!' protested Lady Susanna, tossing down her napkin and getting to her feet. 'You have spent the past month bemoaning the fact that Marcus refuses to come home and take up his duties, yet no sooner does he show his face than you are ready to malign him all over again. Little wonder he prefers to remain in Town with his friends. And now, when he has brought us this most thrilling piece of news—which, if I may be so bold as to remind you, is something we have been waiting to hear for some two years or more now—all you can do is reduce it to gutter level. You should be ashamed of yourself, referring to your son's betrothed in such a tawdry manner!'

'Calm yourself, my dear,' exclaimed Bradfield, as he reached for his walking stick and levered himself up out of his chair. 'I have no desire to distress you in any way, as you well know. But I surely do not need to point out that the boy seems to derive a great deal of pleasure from causing me as much aggravation as possible, and I fear that this latest ploy might well turn out to be yet another one of his—'

'I think not, sir,' put in Giles hastily, having registered his father's rapidly heightening colour and taut neck muscles—both warning signs that pointed to a swift rise in the Earl's blood pressure, a situation to be avoided at all costs, given the gentleman's weakened heart condition. Whilst Marcus's announcement had come as something of a bombshell to him, he had observed his brother's cautionary glance and had resolved to keep his counsel. Now, however, torn between a real concern for his father's health and a sense of loyalty towards his older brother, he felt that it was impossible to remain totally silent.

'I have met Miss Pendleton-Flint, sir,' he said. 'And I can assure you both that the young lady is, beyond question, entirely respectable.'

'And Marcus really means to marry the girl?'

Hesitating only briefly, the Major nodded. 'It would appear so,' he confirmed.

'Then this is truly wonderful news,' exclaimed his mother, clapping her hands in delight and turning once again to her husband. 'We must hold a ball to celebrate this great event, my dear!'

'Best wait until Marcus gives you the all-clear on that, Mother,' put in Giles hurriedly. 'You know how he is apt to dig his heels in if he thinks he's being coerced.'

'Only too well,' retorted the Earl moodily. 'A more obstinate example of manhood I have yet to come across.'

He stood for some minutes, idly tapping his finger against his lips, then, turning, exclaimed, 'I have it now! Pendleton-Flint! I had a feeling that the name rang a distant bell but I couldn't quite place it.'

Giles, who had spent some time trying to track down Sophie's father's past history without success, hastened to his father's side and, after helping him into a nearby chair, asked eagerly, 'You were acquainted with the family, sir?'

'Not as such,' replied Bradfield, his brows knitting together in concentration as he endeavoured to dredge up a vague recollection from almost half a century earlier. 'However, if my memory serves me aright, there was a chap at university—couple of years my senior, he was—name of Joseph Flint. Anyway, the *on dit* at the time was that this Flint fellow had been contracted in marriage to the daughter of his father's best friend—one Sir Jacob Pendleton by name. It appears that some sort of pact had been agreed between the two families when the youngsters were still in leading strings—something to do with the complicated entails of both estates, I believe. I wasn't really that interested at the time. I do, however, have a pretty clear recollection of the fact that young Flint was expected to add the Pendleton name to his own upon the actual marriage.' He frowned. 'The Pendleton girl's name escapes me, I'm afraid, although I do seem to remember being told that the poor lass died in childbed barely a year after the marriage had taken place.'

'And the child—did the poor mite survive?' the Countess was keen to know.

'Must have done,' Giles felt constrained to point out. 'A son too, one presumes—otherwise the conjoined name could not have carried on this far.' Then, turning back to his father, he asked, 'Any idea from which part of the country these Flints and Pendletons hailed, sir?'

Lips pursed, the Earl again racked his brain. 'Somewhere in the North Riding, I believe—Harrogate Spa, possibly—I vaguely recollect some tomfoolery regarding a proposed visit to the baths there. Flint seemed pretty well acquainted with the town, if I remember correctly.'

'And this Pendleton fellow was a baronet, you say?'

'Could have been merely a knight—can't be certain, either way—although I definitely recall Flint referring to the fellow as *Sir* Jacob. You could try looking him up in an old Debretts, if you have a mind to, Giles. I believe we still have a copy of the 1802 original somewhere in the library.'

At her husband's words, the Countess beamed. 'It would appear that Marcus's betrothed might not be without a certain standing, then,' she said, heaving a sigh of satisfaction. 'Although why he feels the need to be so very cagey about the young lady, I really cannot imagine. One would think he had something to hide!'

Chapter Fourteen

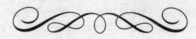

'*What are you saying, man?*'

'I have been advised to inform your lordship that Miss Flint is no longer resident at this address,' repeated Hawkins somewhat warily, the image of Helstone's violent and precipitate exit of the previous evening still vividly imprinted in his memory.

Marcus stared down at the manservant in stunned disbelief. *No longer resident? Impossible! Less than twelve hours had elapsed since he had quit the Crayford premises the evening before.* He frowned. Clearly the butler had been instructed to deny him access—a decision which, insofar as the mistress of the house was concerned, might be considered a rather daring and somewhat foolish move on her part. Although hardly surprising, perhaps, in the light of his abysmal display of temper on his last visit.

'I see,' he said, as he struggled to maintain a grip on his rage. 'Then perhaps you would be good enough to ask your mistress if she could spare me a few moments of her time?'

'I'm afraid Mrs Crayford is not at home, sir,' the butler intoned, his expression wooden. 'Perhaps your lordship would care to leave a card?'

Not at home to me, you mean, thought Marcus sourly as, with a brisk shake of his head, he turned to leave. Having had it made clear to him that he was *persona non grata* insofar as the Crayford household was concerned, the exasperated Viscount was obliged to accept that any further advances from himself were certain to be similarly rebuffed. And, as if that humiliation were not more than enough with which to cope, he was obliged to face up to the fact that Giles—the only person he might have called upon to act as his emissary—had just chosen to embark on some sort of wild goose chase up into the wilds of North Yorkshire, thereby requiring Marcus to shelve all his hastily garnered plans of matrimony until such time as his brother should choose to return.

Not that there's any real point in Giles trying to ferret out any of Sophie's long-lost relatives, he told himself, as he steered his curricle around the mass of vehicles battling to enter Hyde Park for the morning promenade. *I just hope he doesn't spend too long at it, that's all, since he's the only one who can be relied upon to gain admittance into the Crayfords' house and persuade Sophie to agree to meet up with me.*

His dark eyes gleamed with satisfaction as he conjured up her look of delight when he finally announced his altered intentions towards her—a vision that caused him to spend the remainder of the drive back to his Grosvenor Square mansion in blithe contemplation of the various ways in which Sophie might choose to reward him for providing her with so magnanimous a compromise to her earlier opposition.

* * *

Having noted her daughter's uncharacteristically withdrawn demeanour, Mrs Pendleton-Flint could only suppose that Sophie's time with the Crayfords had been rather more of an ordeal than her daughter had been prepared to divulge and she endeavoured to do what little she could to try to take the girl's mind off the experience. By sending Sophie down to the village shops daily on some pretext or other, and keeping her actively involved in as many domestic activities as was possible in such a small household, she sought to encourage her daughter to concentrate her thoughts more firmly on the here and now, rather than dwelling on the past.

Three days had now elapsed since Sophie's enforced flight from the Crayford residence and, although she did her utmost to disguise her unhappiness, the memory of the bitter words she had flung at Helstone on the evening of the ill-fated soiree still continued to haunt her, threatening to reduce her to tears at the most inconvenient times and bombarding her senses with the same unanswerable questions. *How might it have been had she accepted Marcus's proposition? For how long might such a fragile relationship have stood the test of time? Was it possible that he might, eventually, have come to love her in the way she loved him? On the other hand, and, most testing of all, could she really face a future knowing that she would never set eyes on him again?*

As if on cue, the tears would start to well up again and she would be obliged to make some hurried excuse to take herself out into the small back garden, where she would try to busy herself with the tying back of lavender, or some other mundane occupation, in an effort to prevent her mother from witnessing her anguish. And so the interminable days, coupled with the never-ending nights, drifted drearily by.

Returning to the house on the third afternoon of her enforced visit, bearing the small packet of baking powder of which her mother had insisted she was in dire need, Sophie was surprised to see a rather sumptuous-looking travelling chariot drawn up in the street outside the front doorstep. For one foolish moment her heart soared with joy as the thought that Marcus had sought out her whereabouts, having found himself unable to stay away from her, leapt into her mind. One careful look at the painted crest on the carriage's door panel, however, soon disabused her of this idea, for she had seen enough examples of the Helstone family crest on the tableware at Laurel Cottage to have committed the device of an upright lance to enduring memory.

With a disappointed sigh, she made her way into the living room, where she perceived her mother in conversation with a sweet-faced, rather plump lady of middle years, her elegant silk travelling outfit proclaiming a certain affluence. At her entrance the stranger rose immediately to her feet and hurried towards her, hands outstretched and the widest of smiles on her face.

'Oh, my dear Miss Pendleton-Flint! How pleased I am to have finally found you! Elizabeth has spoken of you with such affection—you cannot know how glad I am to be able to thank you at last!'

'Elizabeth? I'm afraid I don't…' began Sophie, only to find herself enveloped in the visitor's arms, her face pressed into the lady's very ample bosom.

'To think that without your aid my poor little Lizzie might well have died,' exclaimed the now quite tearful stranger when she finally set Sophie at arm's length, only to continue to gaze at her in the most disconcertingly soulful manner. 'And that dear little baby—oh, it really doesn't bear thinking about!'

At last Sophie began to understand. It was now obvious that the surprise visitor was none other than the recently delivered Mrs Lucan's mother—the lady to whom the Lucans had been on their way to visit when the snow blizzard had waylaid their coach on that fateful afternoon now some weeks distant.

'Do please sit down and finish your tea, Mrs—?'

Guiding the still weeping matron back to her seat, Sophie shot a questioning glance at her mother.

'Mrs Egremont,' interposed Mrs Pendleton-Flint hastily. 'It seems that the family has been searching for you ever since Mrs Lucan told her mother what a help you had been to her in her hour of need.' Since Sophie had favoured her mother with only the briefest of outlines in respect to that particular occurrence, the unexpected visitor's disclosure had come as something of a revelation to Mrs Pendleton-Flint.

'And it was not until the dear child happened to remember that you had mentioned the name of your brother's school in Dulwich that we were able to make any sort of headway,' sniffed Mrs Egremont woefully, as she dabbed at her tear-drenched cheeks with a lace-edged handkerchief. 'His lordship—Jack's father, as you are no doubt aware—even went to the trouble of engaging two Bow Street runners to seek you out, but to no avail. Although, it is true that they were told to search for a Miss Flint, of course. In the event it was not until your brother's headmaster informed me that Roger's full name was, in fact, *Pendleton*-Flint that we were finally able to ascertain your whereabouts.'

'But I still don't understand why you felt it necessary to go to such lengths to track me down,' exclaimed

Sophie, considerably puzzled. 'What I did was no more than anyone would have done under similar circumstances.' She paused as a sudden awful thought occurred to her, before adding, in a somewhat hesitant voice, 'I trust that your daughter has made a full recovery from the unfortunate experience?'

'Oh, yes, indeed, my dear,' purred Mrs Egremont, leaning forward to clasp Sophie's hand in hers. 'Both she and the babe are thoroughly blooming, thanks to your sterling efforts.'

'Perhaps it would help if I were to acquaint Sophie with a few more of the details…?' ventured Mrs Pendleton-Flint, having registered the still totally bewildered expression on her daughter's face.

'Oh, yes, please do,' replied their visitor, heaving a deep sigh of relief. 'I'm afraid I do seem to become somewhat beside myself whenever I am forced to dwell on what might well have been the outcome of that dreadful occasion, had it not been for the timely intervention of your brave girl.'

And so quite calmly, and in as straightforward a manner as was possible, given the somewhat emotional convolutions of Mrs Egremont's original outpourings, Mrs Pendleton-Flint set about furnishing her daughter with the bones of the Lucan couple's history, from which it soon became apparent that Sophie's chance involvement during that snowbound episode had achieved more than simply helping to bring about the safe delivery of the pair's firstborn child. It had, it seemed—rather more importantly from certain points of view, as it transpired—secured the ongoing line of the Lucan family, along with the not inconsiderable earldom of Whitcombe and all its attached estates.

Having been denied Mr and Mrs Egremont's

permission to marry their seventeen-year-old daughter, the current earl's younger son, the Honourable John Lucan—Jack to his friends—had, it seemed, persuaded his childhood sweetheart into a secret elopement, whereupon, following their overnight dash to the Scottish border to exchange their vows, he had taken her across the Irish Sea and set up residence in a rural retreat in Waterford, from where the pair had cut themselves off from both of their families.

Some eighteen months later, however, finding herself about to give birth to her first child, the young Elizabeth had insisted upon returning to England in order that she might avail herself of her mother's support during her coming confinement. Safely back within the family folds, following their unfortunate incarceration at the inn, however, the pair had been confronted with the tragic news that, shortly following their elopement and self-appointed exile, Jack's elder brother Charles—heir presumptive to the Whitcombe title—had met his death in a riding accident. The ancient title had thereby passed to Jack and, of course, his wife—Mrs Egremont's daughter Elizabeth—who, it seemed, now rejoiced in the lofty title of Her Ladyship the Viscountess Bingham.

'So it would seem that Master John Henry Lucan has inherited a rather more significant role in his family's history than one might have imagined at the time,' exclaimed Sophie, shaking her head in wonder at the amazing tale.

'Both families' histories,' averred Mrs Egremont firmly. 'Lizzie, being Mr Egremont's and my only child, stands to inherit all of her father's lands, which just happen to march in tandem with the Whitcombe estate, making her little boy heir to what will, in all probability, end up as being amongst the largest estates in the entire county!'

Reaching out her hand, she again gripped hold of Sophie's and as the tears began to tumble once more from her eyes went on, 'Had you not been there in that tavern, my poor, sweet Lizzie might well have perished along with her son, meaning that every last inch of Mr Egremont's property would have gone to some unknown cousin of his in the Antipodes. So you will now, perhaps, begin to appreciate the depth of our gratitude to you!'

Pausing momentarily to wipe her eyes, she then turned to Mrs Pendleton-Flint, adding, 'We—both of the families, that is—would very much like to do something to express our truly heartfelt appreciation to your daughter. Can you think of anything that might serve to show our gratitude?'

'Oh, no, really,' put in Sophie with a horrified gasp. 'That is quite unnecessary, I assure you!'

'Absolutely imperative, as far as our families are concerned, my dear child,' returned Mrs Egremont, a look of determination in her eyes. 'His lordship has instructed me to brook no refusal—apart from which, my Lizzie would never forgive me if I were to allow you to go unrewarded for your efforts on her little son's behalf. Surely there must be some way in which we can all show how grateful we all are?'

Sophie was in something of a quandary. From a purely acquisitive point of view she could not help thinking that a nice fat purse full of gold sovereigns would come in very handy, given her family's present financial situation, but, mindful of her mother's teachings, she was also perfectly well aware that any suggestion of a monetary reward would be considered decidedly vulgar.

Her thoughts a complete blank, she sat absent-mindedly chewing at her bottom lip until, in a sudden flash, it came to her.

'Well, then, what I really would like, more than any-thing,' she said, her eyes shining with anticipation, 'is the chance to reacquaint myself with young John Henry and his mother.'

'Oh, my dear!'

As the ready tears sprang once again into Mrs Egremont's eyes, Sophie was safe in the knowledge that nothing she might have chosen could have had the effect of pleasing their visitor more than this simple request, and, after casting a quick glance at her mother's face, she knew that she had done the right thing.

'What a splendid idea!'

Their visitor was quite beside herself with excitement.

'You shall travel home with me this very afternoon—with your mama's permission, of course?'

A questioning look in Mrs Pendleton-Flint's direction assured the now highly exuberant matron that this suggestion met with Sophie's mother's instant approval and, despite Sophie's tentative reservations regarding the woeful inadequacy of her wardrobe, her protests were immediately thrust aside and pooh-poohed as being of less than no importance.

And so it was that, scarcely half an hour later, having carefully repacked her basket with the most suitable of her belongings, Sophie found herself comfortably ensconced upon the pale blue velvet squabs of the Earl of Whitcombe's luxuriously appointed travelling chariot, about to begin the journey to the Egremont residence at Littlewick Green.

* * *

Three days having passed since he had commissioned a man to keep watch on the Crayford property, in the hopes of waylaying Sophie as soon as she emerged, her total non-appearance was more than enough to cause Marcus considerable disquiet. For it was now beginning to look as if the butler had spoken the truth when he had informed the Viscount that the governess was no longer in residence.

Whatever that might mean, thought Marcus, almost out of his mind with despair as, pacing backwards and forwards across his study floor, he raked his fingers distractedly through his hair. *But if Sophie wasn't at the Crayfords', then where the devil was she? It was beyond thought that, having finally managed to track her down following her departure from the inn, he could have been so arrogantly reckless as to allow her to slip through his fingers once again and, this time—God forbid—possibly out of his life for ever!*

Such a prospect was more than he could bear even to contemplate. As total misery washed over him, he sank wearily into a nearby armchair, dropping his head into his hands and letting out an anguished moan. *He just couldn't lose her! He loved her, damn it—he loved her!*

As the full implication of his unuttered words finally hit him, Marcus started back, his eyes widening in disbelief. *Where in God's name had that thought sprung from?* he asked himself incredulously, but then, the more he pondered the matter, the more it began to dawn upon him that his almost total preoccupation with Sophie was considerably more complicated than the simple fact of just wanting to get her into his bed—which he did, of course. That went without saying. In fact, if he were to be honest with himself, the sheer idea of making passionate love to her had ballooned into an all-encompassing desire more powerful than any he had ever experienced throughout the multi-faceted history of all his past *affaires*. But, alongside all of that, it seemed that, without his having been aware of it he had also acquired a deep, almost primitive urge to cherish and protect her and keep her safe from harm. All part and parcel of what one might reasonably expect from a man in love, he thought with a wry grimace, achingly aware that his constant cajoling of Sophie to become his mistress could hardly be regarded in a similar vein. *Small wonder that she had called him a cad.* It would be nothing short of a miracle if he ever managed to persuade her to forgive such reprehensible conduct, let alone agree to become his wife!

Filled with a sudden self-loathing, the Viscount began to take stock of the all too numerous misdemeanours of his recent history, and it gradually began to dawn on him that, at twenty-nine years of age, it was high time he put aside his juvenile resentment towards his father and started conducting himself in the manner that might be expected of one who had at least been born a gentleman—well past time, in fact, to wave an unregretted farewell to all the drunken carousing, gambling, casual assignations and other such excessive behaviour of the past six years and make a start on trying to repair the breach that had opened up between himself and the Earl.

All of a sudden it began to dawn on him that all he really needed to bring true meaning to his life was Sophie—with her at his side, who knew to what heights he might climb, what goals he might achieve? He pulled in a ragged breath, painfully conscious of the fact that, before this highly appealing vision of an unparalleled future with Sophie at his side was likely to come to fruition, he had first to find her. Having wasted precious time sitting around kicking his heels, waiting for Giles to return from his errand in the north, in the hopes that his more diplomatically inclined brother might gain entry into the Crayford establishment in order to ascertain their governess's whereabouts, Marcus was no longer of a mind to wait another second. Swearing that he would beard the lion's den himself, and have the information out of the Crayfords' supercilious manservant even if he died in the attempt, he rose to his feet and started for the door.

He had taken scarcely two steps across the room, however, before there came a tentative tap on the door—which then opened to reveal his butler, bearing a sealed letter on a silver tray.

'An urgent communication from Major Wolfe, your lordship,' intoned the man. 'One of his fellows has just brought it round.'

Thank God! Giles must have finally returned from his abortive mission in the wilds of Yorkshire! Now things can really get moving! was Marcus's initial thought, as he stretched out his hand to relieve Danson of his missive. Breaking open the note's seal, he hurriedly scanned the short and decidedly cryptic message therein.

Grillons. With all poss. speed. Giles.

Having long ago given up trying to fathom the convoluted workings of his brother's mind, Marcus let out a sigh. Crucial though his own mission was, the simple brevity of Giles's message seemed to indicate a more pressing urgency, causing the Viscount to feel that he had little choice but to comply with the Major's summons.

'Have my curricle brought round immediately, Danson,' he ordered as, reaching to one side, he quickly retrieved his hat and gloves from the chair on which he had impatiently tossed them upon his earlier return from a fruitless consultation with his agent in Lennox Gardens.

Upon stepping into the foyer of the Albemarle Street hotel, the Viscount was greeted by Giles who, holding up his hand to silence his brother's questions, proceeded to hustle the thoroughly mystified Marcus up the stairs and through the door of one of the hotel's premier suites where, seated on an armchair by the fireside, the Viscount perceived an elderly female, elegantly clad in a most expensive looking and extremely well-cut gown of lavender coloured silk.

At her visitors' entry the lady rose gracefully to her feet and, holding out her hands, walked forward to greet the two men.

Executing a respectful bow in the lady's direction, Giles said, 'May I present my brother, Viscount Helstone, ma'am?' And to Marcus, 'Allow me to introduce you to Miss Catherine Pendleton—Sophie's great-aunt.'

Chapter Fifteen

From her vantage point at the head of the elegant curving staircase that led down into the Whitcombes' sumptuously appointed ballroom, Sophie anxiously scanned the faces of the guests thronging below, doing her best to persuade herself that there was no real likelihood of Lord Helstone being among their number. Nevertheless, having only just learned this very afternoon that her hosts, the Earl and Countess of Whitcombe, numbered his lordship's parents among their many acquaintances, along with the further information that his family seat was situated barely ten miles distant from Whitcombe Abbey, she could not help but be aware of the fact that the chances of running into the Viscount at so prestigious a function were not entirely beyond the realms of possibility.

Given that scarcely a single day had gone by since her departure from the Crayfords' without the vivid image of Helstone's angry features forcing itself into the forefront of her mind, causing her to have to relive once again the heated exchange of their final parting, it was difficult for her to suppose that he would be prepared even to exchange polite greetings with her—far more likely that he would simply cut her dead, she thought despondently. But then, with a wan smile and brief shake of her head, she was obliged to dismiss such a foolish notion as being totally unworthy of consideration, well aware that, despite his unfortunate shortcomings in certain matters, Helstone would never stoop to such unworthy behaviour. Added to which, she reminded herself, now that her circumstances had undergone such a drastic change there was always the possibility that he might even begin to regard her in an entirely different light...

'Come along now, my dear—that posse of handsome *beaux* you've acquired look to be growing impatient.'

Shaken out of her pensive reverie, Sophie turned to observe Frederick Egremont approaching. Her lips curved in welcome as he joined her, for she had made a firm friend of Elizabeth's genial father during the short time she had been with the family—so much so that it had been Mr Egremont to whom she had gone for advice after receiving the extraordinary missive from her mother telling her of the visit from her late father's aunt—a Miss Catherine Pendleton, apparently—who had come bearing the news that Sophie's brother, having inherited their great-grandfather's title, along with a not inconsiderable fortune, was now in a position to designate himself *Sir* Roger, landed baronet!

Sophie, on the verge of packing her bags and returning to her mother's side, had been dissuaded from doing so by Mr Egremont who, having perused the letter rather more thoroughly than she in her breathless excitement had done, had directed her attention to the hastily scribbled post script on its rear, which exhorted Sophie to remain where she was for the present, since both her mother and brother were about to set out for Harrogate, with their recently acquired relative, in order that they might be on hand to deal with the various legalities that had arisen as a result of Roger's unexpected elevation.

Although she was, naturally, thoroughly delighted to hear of her brother's good fortune, Sophie could not help feeling just a little piqued that Mrs Pendleton-Flint had elected to make such a momentous journey without her daughter's support. Even the discovery of the very generous banker's draft attached to the letter had failed to lift her spirits entirely, until both Elizabeth and Mrs Egremont had taken her gently to one side to point out to her that—since she had been unreasonably stubborn in her refusal to accept even one of the many gifts that both families had done their very best to press upon her—the timely arrival of such largesse would go a long way towards affording her the independence to deal with her own oft bemoaned lack of suitable finery.

Sophie, who had been growing increasingly conscious of the shabby state of the three simple muslin gowns that she had brought with her, but had been firmly polite in her refusal to take advantage of Elizabeth's very generous offers to supplement her meagre wardrobe, had very soon been brought to see the wisdom of her new friends' advice. As a result, she had very soon found herself—following a hastily arranged visit from the local modiste, along with the inevitable measuring and pinning sessions—the thoroughly overwhelmed owner of a whole new set of such gowns and accessories that, in her previous existence, would have been totally beyond anything she could ever have imagined.

No sooner had it been confirmed that Elizabeth was

well enough to receive visitors than, exactly as Mrs Egremont had predicted, the invitations had started to roll in with increasing regularity, culminating in a hectic whirl of non-stop activity, in which Sophie had found herself very much a part. Morning visits, afternoon picnics, routs, soirees and musical evenings, not to mention two full dress balls, had filled almost every hour of the two weeks that had passed since her arrival at Egremont Hall—all of which ought to have left her with no time to dwell upon the rift between Helstone and herself. And yet with each day that passed, and despite all outward appearances to the contrary, the ache in her heart had deepened and the painful memory of their final meeting had grown more and more turbulent. But she had skipped through the measures of the various dances with apparent cheerful abandon, favouring each of her newly acquired admirers with the same bright-eyed smile, and neither they nor her hosts had ever been led to suspect the true depth of her inner despair.

The welcoming smile that she now bestowed upon Elizabeth's father as she greeted him, however, was entirely genuine as, tucking her hand into his arm, she allowed him to escort her down the stairs into the Whitcombes' crowded ballroom.

'One or two of them are inclined to be a little overpowering,' she confided, referring to his earlier remark concerning the growing number of dashing young blades who constantly vied for her attention. 'Lord Bentley keeps sending me the most ridiculous poems—likening the colour of my eyes to a blue jug that stands on his mother's washstand!'

Letting out a loud guffaw of laughter, Egremont patted her hand. 'You should be grateful that the young buffoon didn't choose to use the slopbucket as an analogy!'

'Oh, I am, believe me,' she said, chuckling softly as the two of them made their way across the room to join the group presently paying court to the radiant new Viscountess Bingham. 'Especially as he also mentioned that my hair colour put him in mind of a well-polished hessian boot!'

Marcus, who in the normal way would never have even contemplated putting in an appearance at an event such as the Whitcombes' annual ball, had found himself—owing to a sudden indisposition on his father's part, coupled with the fact that his brother Giles was heavily engaged in tracking down yet another group of subversives in the capital—called upon to escort his mother to the affair.

Ever since that fateful day when Giles had ushered him into Catherine Pendleton's suite at Grillons' hotel the Viscount had been battling with a depression so entrenched that he frequently found it difficult to drag himself out of bed in the mornings. From the moment that the elderly lady had started on her tale the realisation that his cause was lost had hammered itself into his brain. His dismay at learning that his brother had actually managed to make contact with one of Sophie's relatives had been such that his mind had barely managed to register all but the barest details of the explanatory tale that Miss Pendleton had so painstakingly unfolded.

It had transpired that Sophie's father, Jonathan Pendleton-Flint—the baby son of the ill-fated Joseph Flint of Marcus's father's memory—having been raised in the bosom of his dead mother's family had, at the age of twenty-two, formed what his somewhat autocratic grandfather, Sir Jacob, had termed 'an undesirable association' with the local schoolmaster's pretty daughter,

Amelia Dwyer. Having recently inherited the not inconsiderable fortune left to him by his late father, Jonathan had chosen to defy the old man's instructions to curtail the friendship and had instead gone off to marry the young woman, who was, in time, to become mother to both Sophie and Roger. The young Pendleton-Flint, in pursuit of a long-held ambition, had purchased himself a commission in a dragoon regiment that had then been garrisoned in the nearby town of York, thereby beginning a distinguished career which, by virtue of his continuously outstanding courage in the face of the enemy, had seen him awarded various battlefield honours and ultimately achieving the rank of Lieutenant-Colonel—at which point his highly successful military career had reached its untimely end during the last decisive battle of the long drawn-out war against the Emperor Napoleon.

Despite her father having disowned his grandson, and forbidden his daughter Catherine to communicate with him, it seemed that Miss Pendleton, who had been Jonathan's primary carer throughout his childhood, had by dint of various underhand subterfuges managed to keep in touch with her nephew during the early part of his career. But as the years had progressed, with the Pendleton-Flints constantly on the move across the continents, contact between Jonathan and his aunt had gradually petered out, and it had been several years since Catherine had heard anything from her nephew.

Unfortunately, Sir Jacob had not received the report of his grandson's demise until he himself had also been on his deathbed. In fact, it was the opinion of his elderly daughter that it had been the unexpected shock of this harrowing news that had finally pushed the old man over the edge.

Having been made aware that her nephew had fathered a family, Catherine had then made every effort to trace the whereabouts of the remaining Pendleton-Flints, but it had not been until Major Wolfe had finally tracked her down that her quest was to succeed at last. Contacting Sophie's mother had then proved to be surprisingly simple, once Catherine had provided the two men with the name of Roger's school in Dulwich since—as might have been expected, had they but been aware of it—it turned out to be the selfsame one at which his father had been educated.

Forced to consider the fact that whatever reason he might once have had for finding Sophie could now be of no consequence to anyone but himself, and unable to confront the prospect of any tentative overture on his part being dismissed out of hand, Marcus had elected not to accompany the Major and Miss Pendleton on their visit to Dulwich. Subsequently, upon being advised that the Pendleton-Flints had left for the North Ridings, along with their newly acquired relative, Marcus had naturally assumed that Sophie must be travelling with her family. Having finally been forced to face up to the fact that she had gone out of his life for ever, he had shut himself up in his library and proceeded to drink himself into a life-threatening stupor in a vain attempt to expunge all thoughts of her from his mind.

The consequent hangover he had suffered as a result of this massive over-indulgence had caused him to review, yet again, the pointless emptiness of his chosen lifestyle, and no sooner had he judged himself fit enough to travel than he had called for his curricle, his thoughts agog with newly formed aspirations of making peace with his father, relieving him of the greater part of his burdensome duties and generally fulfilling all the Earl's earlier expectations of the heir to his vast estate.

These ambitions, as Marcus was soon to find out, were more easily imagined than achieved, since Bradfield was inclined to view his recalcitrant son's unexpected reformation with a good deal of suspicion—particularly after the Viscount had been forced to admit that the promised engagement of which he had spoken had hit something of a snag and would not now take place.

Nevertheless, and in spite of these unfortunate drawbacks to his somewhat high-flown intentions, the Viscount had managed to buckle down and stick to his guns, and for the past week or so the better part of his days had been filled with the perusal of account books and stock sheets, visits to tenants to discuss property repairs, renovations and so on, along with the overseeing of various planting and breeding programmes with which the estate was involved. All of which, he had been somewhat surprised to discover, had turned out to be rather more satisfying ways of spending one's days than he had formerly supposed.

Not so the nights, however, which had continued to present him with an entirely different problem, and one that persisted in proving utterly unsolvable, no matter how hard he endeavoured to resolve it. Whilst he had no reason to suppose that locating Sophie would involve him in any great difficulty, he was still left with the highly unpalatable fact that he had, on more than one occasion, attempted to persuade the former governess into becoming his mistress. How could he now seek her out and profess his undying love and devotion after having shown her so little respect in the past? Now that Sophie was protected by the wealth and security of her brother's fortune and title, any unexpected keenness on his part to renew their former acquaintanceship must only be regarded with her deepest mistrust, and would surely damn him for ever in her eyes—always supposing that Sophie even chose to receive him, which, after that last violent interchange between the two of them, Marcus was inclined to believe there was every reason to doubt.

And so, night after night, the never-ending search for some sort of answer to this vexing dilemma continued to govern the Viscount's thoughts, playing havoc with his sleep patterns until, as the first shrill cock-crow pierced the dawn of each new day, he would force himself reluctantly from his bed, do his best to banish his growing wretchedness to the back of his mind, and make every effort to occupy the whole of his attention with whatever mundane task his father had chosen to test him.

'…and you must come and say hello to John's wife— you may recall having met her at the Egremonts', when she was just a girl.'

With a sudden blink, Marcus jerked himself back to reality. *Pay attention, man!* he chided himself impatiently, hurriedly stifling the yawn that threatened, and hoping against hope that his mother was of a mind to limit her attendance at this function to the very barest minimum that civil courtesy might demand.

Bending his head over the hand that the new Viscountess was holding out to him, he murmured the accepted polite phrases, barely glancing up at her face as, thrusting out his own hand to the young man at her side, he mumbled, 'Your servant, sir.'

'I doubt that you will remember John, my lord,' came Countess Whitcombe's breathy tones at his shoulder. 'He was probably away at school when you were last…'

'By all that's holy! It's our Mr Wolfe!'

Viscount Bingham's startled ejaculation at once shook Marcus out of his semi-torpid state as, with a perplexed frown, he forced himself to focus his attention on the young man whose hand was still grasping his own. Then, his brain suddenly clearing, realisation hit him in a blinding flash. There in front of him stood the young father-to-be from that godforsaken inn from which all his present problems had sprung! Viscount Bingham and Jack Lucan were one and the same man! *But Lucan? It was hardly possible—his family had known the Lucans for most of his life! How in God's name could he have failed to make so obvious a connection?*

His mind in a state of utter confusion, he found himself being hustled in the direction of a group of guests that had congregated nearby as the young Viscount's voice rang out excitedly, 'Do look, Sophie. You'll never guess who I've got here!'

Sophie?

Marcus's heart stuttered to a standstill as one of the splendidly attired young women turned a questioning face in his direction. 'Sophie!' he stammered in disbelief, as he reached out towards her.

Chapter Sixteen

'My lord.'

Ignoring Helstone's outstretched hand, Sophie lowered her eyes and dipped him a respectful curtsey. Her shock at seeing Marcus descending the stairs some minutes earlier had almost brought her to her knees, with only Egremont's quick thinking preventing her from actually sinking to the ground. And, although her hurriedly concocted tale of having caught her heel in the train of her evening gown had seemed to satisfy her concerned escort, it had very soon come to her that it was simply a matter of time before she would be required to confront the Viscount face-to-face.

As the minutes dragged by, with her every nerve attuned to the looming threat of his approach, she had struggled to keep the rising panic at bay. Eventually, by using every tool at her disposal, she had managed to steel herself to turn and greet him in a relatively calm and dignified manner.

'Your lordship is well, I trust?'

Utterly transfixed by the heart-wrenchingly lovely vision that stood before him, Marcus found himself lost for words. Gone were the prim hairstyle and dowdy grey dress of the one-time governess's previous lifestyle, and in their stead a riotous tumble of shining chestnut curls and a stunning gown of oyster-coloured satin, whose clinging folds seemed to accentuate every single one of its wearer's only too memorable curves, and whose fetchingly low-cut neckline served merely to emphasise the entrancing creamy swell of her shapely bosom.

Conscious of several pairs of eyes upon him, Marcus finally managed to marshal his stunned senses into reciprocating Sophie's curtsey with a polite bow and the standard exchange of courtesies, before forcing himself to stand aside and allow her to return to her friends—whereupon he found himself having to drag in a hefty breath in order to quell his aching awareness of her all too captivating presence barely three feet away from him. Try as he might, he found it difficult to concentrate his attention on the conversation that was going on around him.

'…knowing him as Mr Wolfe, and never having met his lordship before, it simply never occurred to me,' Bingham was explaining to the group. 'Besides which, of course,' he added, shooting his prettily blushing wife an affectionate grin, 'I was more immediately concerned with Elizabeth's problems at the time! Thanks to our dear friend Sophie—or Miss Pendleton-Flint, as I should more properly refer to her—everything turned out just splendidly!'

Amidst the general murmur of laughter and approval that followed these remarks, Lady Susanna turned to her son in some confusion.

'Did he say Pendleton-Flint?' she asked, a bewildered frown furrowing her brow. 'But surely that is the—'

'Not now, Mother, if you please!' muttered Marcus urgently, catching hold of her arm and manoeuvring her firmly out of Sophie's earshot. 'I would prefer that you didn't mention that particular matter just at the moment, if you would be so good.'

'Ah, yes, I remember now,' returned his mother with a perceptive nod. 'You did tell us that your plans in that direction had gone somewhat awry, as I recall.' Her eyes travelled shrewdly towards Sophie who, having returned herself to the safety of her former companions, gave the impression of being fully engrossed in whatever the earnest-looking young man at her side was telling her. 'Such a pity. The girl is rather lovely—as indeed are those diamonds around her neck. The family is quite well-to-do, I imagine?'

'So I believe,' grunted Marcus, eyeing Sophie's eager attendant with some disfavour. His attention having been distracted by rather more emotive issues at the time, any jewellery that Sophie might have been wearing had totally escaped his notice.

'I presume that there is no reason why you may not ask the young woman to dance?' Lady Susanna then enquired of him. 'Even supposing that the two of you have had some sort of a fall-out, I cannot imagine that Miss Pendleton-Flint would be so ill-mannered as to refuse such a request.'

'If you don't mind, I had just as soon...' began her son, but then, after a slight pause, during which his mother seemed to discern some sort of inward tussle taking place, Marcus twisted his lips in a somewhat wry smile. 'Why not, indeed?' he said finally.

Thrusting his way into the circle that had again

surrounded her, Marcus manoeuvred his way to Sophie's side and sketched a brief bow. 'May I crave the pleasure of this next dance, Miss Pendleton-Flint?' he asked, his fingers mentally crossing as he awaited her reply.

'Oh, dear—I'm not certain that—I believe another gentleman...'

Having finally managed to bolster herself sufficiently to perform the customary exchange of courtesies, it had not escaped Sophie's attention that Helstone had lost little time in distancing himself from her. She had done her best to hide the pain this obvious lack of interest on his part had caused her by endeavouring to focus her attention on the words of her nearest companion. But to suddenly discover the Viscount standing there in front of her had the effect of catching her badly off guard and barely able to muster her thoughts.

'For old times' sake, perhaps?' murmured Marcus softly, willing her to meet his gaze as he held out his hand.

Unable to prevent herself, Sophie raised her eyes to his, only to catch her breath as she read the patent appeal therein. Oblivious to the muttered protests that were emanating from several of her followers, and as if in a dream, she found herself laying her hand in Helstone's and allowing him to lead her out on to the dance floor where, as she was soon to discover, a waltz was already in progress, with several other couples energetically engaged in showing off their capabilities.

'I appear to have cramped the style of one of your admirers,' observed Marcus as, executing a nimble side step in order to avoid collision with an over-enthusiastic pair who were about to barge into them, he dextrously swung her into the fast moving mêlée of dancers.

'Lord Murcheson.' Sophie sighed, casting a distracted

look over her shoulder to register the look of simmering fury on the face of the young man from whose side Helstone had just removed her. 'Although I feel obliged to point out that he does have the right to look somewhat disgruntled—this was to be his dance and you have stolen it.'

'Murcheson? His Viscountcy is barely sixty years old,' retorted Marcus with a careless shrug. 'Mine, on the other hand, is well over two hundred—I shall claim seniority of rank.'

Since her nervous system had not entirely recovered from the shock of Helstone's impetuous action, Sophie found herself unable to conjure up an adequately disapproving reply to this somewhat high-handed remark, added to which she could not help reflecting that, despite the apparently imperious manner that he was exhibiting, the Viscount did not seem entirely at ease with himself.

Registering her silence, Marcus, cursing himself for a fool, tried again.

'You certainly look to be enjoying this new life of yours,' he ventured. 'You must be delighted to have been reunited with your father's family.'

'Oh, yes, I am—of course,' she replied, in a somewhat offhand tone of voice. 'Although I must confess that I have not, as yet, had the pleasure of meeting my great-aunt.'

'Oh, you will like her, I am sure,' said Marcus, guiding her adroitly across the floor as he spoke. 'My brother was good enough to introduce the two of us when Miss Pendleton first arrived in the capital—I thought her a most charming lady.'

Feeling duty bound to thank him for the Major's efforts on her family's behalf, Sophie did so, wondering all the while how she might turn the subject to one that was of far more concern to her.

'I was wondering—' she began nervously, as soon as a suitable bout of silence offered itself.

'You must—' blurted out Marcus simultaneously.

Pausing, they both laughed. Then, 'Please go on,' he said.

'No, you first,' she insisted.

Hesitating only briefly, Marcus took a deep breath. 'I dare say you may have been wondering why I have not approached you to beg your pardon for my appalling conduct at our last meeting,' he said.

Sophie's eyes widened in dismay. Having spent a good many sleepless nights castigating herself for her own unseemly behaviour on that unforgettable occasion, she could not allow Helstone to shoulder the entire blame for the event.

'Oh, no, my lord,' she exclaimed in protest. 'Surely it is I who should apologise to you for having vilified you so dreadfully?'

A pensive frown on his face, the Viscount shook his head but, finding himself obliged to direct his attention to the avoidance of yet another maladroit couple in his pathway, it was some few moments before he was able to consider his reply.

'I have little doubt that I deserved every condemnation you threw at me,' he grunted. 'I had every intention of offering you my apologies first thing the following morning—only to discover that you had left the Crayfords.' He paused briefly, before adding, 'I take it that you were asked to leave?'

Sophie gave a perfunctory nod. Mrs Crayford's harsh condemnation of her on that evening was still fresh in her mind. 'I thought it best that I went,' she said diffidently. 'It would have been difficult to remain, given the circumstances.'

Correctly reading the expression on her face, Marcus, heaping mental curses upon her erstwhile employer, tentatively tightened his hold before saying, 'Unfortunately, I was then unable to establish your whereabouts—although my brother did gave me the impression that you had travelled to Harrogate with your family.'

'Oh, no, it was decided that I would do better to remain with the Egremonts for the time being,' replied Sophie, her breath catching as she felt the increased pressure of the Viscount's hand at her waist. 'The family has been extremely kind and generous towards me.'

'No doubt they feel they owe you a debt of gratitude,' acknowledged Marcus, his mouth curving in a mischievous smile. 'It would seem that your intervention at that godforsaken tavern helped to ensure the Whitcombe succession—which must be a matter of great moment, after all!'

An unbidden chuckle escaped Sophie's lips.

'I have the feeling that Mother Nature would have managed very nicely without my assistance,' she replied, her clear blue eyes filling with laughter as she smiled up at him.

His heart seeming to swell within him, Marcus pulled her more closely still. Perhaps all was not lost, after all, he told himself, as he swept her across the floor. If he could just persuade Sophie to overlook his past misdemeanours, he reasoned, perhaps he could set about wooing her in the time-honoured fashion. Given time, and a little help from Lady Luck, it might yet be possible to regain some of the ground that he'd lost.

Her former concerns now fully satisfied, Sophie allowed herself to relax in the Viscount's hold, more than content just to have him shepherd her around the room, their steps perfectly matched to the hypnotic rhythm of the lilting music. Any further conversation was, as far as she was concerned, entirely superfluous; simply to find herself once more in Helstone's arms—for however fleeting an interlude—was, to her, far more than she could ever have hoped or dreamed of. Her whole being deliciously alive to the realisation that Helstone was holding her rather more closely than was generally considered proper, she closed her eyes, tipped back her head, and surrendered herself to the supreme rapture of the moment.

Inevitably, and all too soon, the captivating rhythm drew to its close and, with a sweeping flourish, the final chord rang out across the room, bringing the exhilarated dancers to a laughing, breathless standstill. Marcus, gazing down at the still rapt expression on Sophie's beloved face, found himself wishing that he could just lift her up and spirit her away to some secret hideout, where the pair of them could cloister themselves away from prying eyes and where he would have all the time in the world to demonstrate the true extent of his feelings towards her. The horde of fawning admirers who battled so eagerly for her attention not having escaped his notice, it had very quickly come to him that there was a very real danger of one or other of those toadying dissemblers securing Sophie's hand before he himself was able to conjure up a suitable opportunity to convince her of his sincerity. The sudden ripple of fury that coursed through his veins at the thought of Sophie being pledged in matrimony to any man other than himself was swiftly overtaken by a feeling of sick dread as he was forced to remind himself that his cause was not yet won.

Consequently, and only because there were no other options open to him at that point, it was a very reluctant Marcus who finally returned Sophie to the bosom of her waiting court. His half-hearted attempts to soothe the still somewhat aggrieved Lord Murcheson's ruffled feathers having been grudgingly accepted, it was with a gnawing disappointment that he then discovered that Sophie's dance card was already filled. Her satisfyingly eager suggestion that the Viscount might care to escort her into supper, however, went some way to bolstering Marcus's spirits, but, rather than suffer the indignity of having to stand to one side while a succession of would-be suitors made increasingly outrageous attempts to capture his beloved's attention, he quickly excused himself and went in search of what had become a much-needed drink.

Having procured himself a glass of champagne, Marcus then quit the ballroom and wandered out into the corridor in search of the card room, in the hopes of having his mind distracted from its present preoccupation by means of a few highly concentrated hands of either faro or vingt-et-un.

Even his fervent belief that most of the apparently ardent young bloods who made up Sophie's court were rather more likely to be interested in whatever fortune she might bring with her than they were in her personal charms brought him little solace, since he was sufficiently versed in the ways of the *Ton* to realise that any similar overtures on his part would be regarded in very much the same light. Not that he had ever been particularly concerned as to what the *beau monde* thought of him, as he hastened to remind himself. Sophie's good opinion of him, however, was an entirely different matter, and had suddenly become utterly paramount to his well-being.

On peering into the room designated for card-playing, he was irritated to observe that all the tables were fully occupied, with several other gentlemen already standing by in expectation of taking up any relinquished places. Preferring not to add his name to that number, the Viscount then decided to venture further along the corridor, with a view to ensconcing himself in the library, the quiet comfort of which he had fond memories of having enjoyed back in his youth.

Upon entering the room which, apart from the two wall-sconces at its entrance, was illuminated only by the gently flickering flames that issued from the logs burning in the fireplace, he was pleased to find that, not only did he have the place to himself, little seemed to have changed during his prolonged absence: the high-backed soft leather chairs were still dotted around the room in abundance; the huge map table still graced the wall between the two sets of French windows that opened out on to the terrace, and the faint but unmistakable aroma of musty books coupled with stale cigar smoke still hung in the air.

With an appreciative sniff, Marcus made at once for the carved wooden box that had always stood on the mantelpiece where, to his immense satisfaction, he was to discover that Whitcombe's well-remembered habit of keeping the box replenished with prime Havana cigars had not altered in the intervening years.

Having helped himself to a cigar, he then selected a taper from the nearby receptacle, and was just about to thrust it into the fire when his attention was caught by a soft snuffling noise that seemed to be coming from the far side of the room.

His curiosity aroused, Marcus, setting both cigar and taper down on a side-table, moved quietly across the library floor towards the source of the noise which, he was fairly certain, gave every indication of being the sound of a female in some distress. Not that he had any particular desire to intrude upon the unknown lady's apparent grief, he told himself, but, having inadvertently been made party to it, it was more than he could do to simply stand by and ignore the plaintive whimpering.

Having judged that the sounds were emanating from one of the high-backed armchairs that nestled in a dimly lit corner of the room, he crept towards it and peered over the back of the chair, where he was confronted with the sight of the most piteous looking creature— hardly more than a girl, he concluded—who was doing her utmost to stifle her anguished sobs in the absurdly inadequate handkerchief that she had pressed against her lips.

Finding himself at something of a loss in the face of such overwhelming distress, Marcus was momentarily stopped in his tracks. But then, as commonsense prevailed, he reached down and extracted his own, rather more serviceable handkerchief from his pocket, before stepping round in front of the weeping female and attempting to thrust it into her hand—only to have the panic-stricken girl recoil in fright as she suddenly became aware of his presence.

Struggling to her feet, her tear-drenched eyes wide with apprehension, she raised both hands, as if in self-defence, and backed hurriedly away from him. Sadly, in her frantic haste to flee from the unwelcome intrusion into her wretchedness, she misjudged her step, catching the heel of her slipper in the lace-edged flounce of her gown, and, had not Marcus's reactions been as prompt as they were, would most certainly have tumbled to the ground.

'Do please calm yourself, ma'am,' he begged her, as he steadied the struggling female against his chest. 'I won't harm you, I swear—I am merely trying to be of service. Has someone hurt you? Can you not tell me what has caused you such distress?'

At his soothing words, a fresh bout of tears overcame the girl, sending shivers of apprehension coursing through Marcus's veins.

'Come, please tell me what ails you,' he urged her as, with some difficulty, he managed to pry her violently trembling form away from his own and lower her back into the chair. 'Are you ill? Is there someone I could fetch for you? Will you not allow me to help you in some way?'

More sobs ensued as the girl gave a despairing shake of her head. 'P-please go away, s-sir, I b-beg you!' she choked. 'I am b-beyond help. Beyond both help and h-hope! Oh, how I wish I were d-dead!'

'Oh, come now,' protested Marcus, his original sympathy beginning to evaporate somewhat at the girl's somewhat histrionic outburst. 'I cannot believe that whatever it is that has upset you can be so dreadful as to warrant so desperate an inclination!'

Making a valiant effort to control her sobs, the girl buried her face in Marcus's handkerchief and, after heaving in a shuddering breath, dipped her fingers into her beaded reticule and drew out an expensive-looking pearl choker. 'I have d-damaged the c-clasp.' She gulped nervously. 'It belonged to m-my husband's first wife—when he discovers what I have d-done, I c-cannot begin to imagine w-what he will d-do to me!'

Staring down at the necklace in bewildered astonishment, Marcus found himself unsure whether to burst out laughing or to deliver a sharp lecture to the young woman for having allowed herself to get into such a state over a mere trinket. He rose to his feet, his irritation increasing by the minute. 'Nonsense,' he chided her. 'You are exaggerating, I'm sure. I find it extremely unlikely that any sane man would stoop to punishing his wife over so paltry a matter as a broken necklace.'

'Then it's clear that you do not n-number my h-husband amongst your acquaintances.' The girl sighed, as she dabbed dispiritedly at her damp flushed cheeks.

'Possibly not,' retorted Marcus, who was beginning to regret his impulsive attempt at chivalry and was wishing that he had never involved himself in the foolish creature's absurd problems. 'My name is Marcus Wolfe—Helstone, if you prefer. May I be permitted to know who you are?'

'I am Christabel Sa—I mean Dawlish,' she amended hastily. 'Christabel Dawlish—wife of Sir Randolph.'

Marcus stilled, a frisson of unease trickling through him. Good God, he thought, staring down at the girl's bleak expression in appalled silence. *Randolph Dawlish!* The man was old enough to be the girl's father! Having come up against the elderly baronet on more than one occasion during his own rather too frequent expeditions into the seamier side of London's night-life, he had become sufficiently well acquainted with Dawlish's singularly unpleasant nature to now realise that his young wife's fears in regard to her self-confessed clumsiness might not be entirely without foundation.

'Randolph Dawlish?' he repeated slowly. 'I am slightly acquainted with him, as it happens, but I must confess that I was unaware that he had remarried.' *And his first wife barely cold in her grave,* he thought contemptuously. *Yet how typical of the sadistic swine to*

*find himself another pathetic victim to vent his spite
on so soon!*

Unsuppressed tears gathered in the new Lady Dawlish's eyes. 'Just a l-little over three w-weeks ago,' she
choked, as she hurriedly turned her face away in a futile
attempt to hide her rising distress. 'You have been very
k-kind, sir, but I would be greatly obliged if you would
leave me n-now.'

'No, ma'am, I fear I shall do no such thing,' returned
Marcus, with a determined shake of his head. 'It is clear
that you are in no state to be left here on your own. You
must allow me to escort you as far as the ladies' retiring
room, or to call for assistance at the very least.'

'Oh, no! P-please go, sir, I b-beg of you,' cried
Christabel, her mounting anguish clear to see as she
twisted his soaking wet handkerchief between her fingers. 'I really do not wish to be s-seen by anyone just
at p-present!'

Instinct telling him that it was imperative that he get
the weeping female such help as was humanly possible,
Marcus tried again.

'I really must insist that you come with me now,' he
adjured her, holding out his hand. 'I cannot simply walk
away and leave you here on your own, and you must see
that it would not do for us to be found in here together.'
With more than enough problems of his own to deal
with, he could hardly help being aware that the very last
thing he needed at this juncture was to be discovered
in a dimly lit room in the company of another man's
wife.

Thankfully, the implied threat behind his warning
was enough to bring the clearly petrified Christabel
to her senses. With a frightened gasp she leapt to her
feet and, placing her hand in his still outstretched one,

allowed Marcus to lead her across the room. Upon reaching the doorway, however, she halted and, letting go of his hand, hung back timorously, twisting her fingers together in apprehension before clutching at his arm and whimpering, 'Not past the card room, sir, I beg of you—*please*!'

Biting back a withering retort, Marcus found himself at somewhat of a standstill. Having only just recently observed her husband in the gaming room, he could appreciate the girl's concern, realising that there was every chance the pair of them might well be spotted as they passed by the doorway. Unfortunately, he was also aware that the only way they could possibly reach the relative safety of the ladies' room was by means of the corridor outside.

He stood for a moment, totally nonplussed, as he racked his brains for a solution to the dilemma. And then, in a sudden inspiration, it came to him that if there was anyone who would know exactly what to do in such a situation, it was Sophie! His brow cleared as a simple way out of his predicament at once became obvious. All he had to do was deposit the now softly weeping Christabel back into her chair and go in search of Sophie. Having witnessed the one-time governess's infallibility in the face of the numerous problems with which the marooned group had been beset during that freak snowstorm, he had little doubt that she would be able to come up with some sort of solution to this particular problem. In fact, it would hardly surprise him to learn that Sophie also had at her disposal some fiendishly clever means by which the damaged necklace might be fixed, thus saving the poor misguided Christabel from Dawlish's malicious spite.

Fully convinced that the answer to his current

difficulty was now well within his grasp, Marcus finally persuaded Christabel back into her chair and headed once more towards the door—only to open it and discover that the passageway was now swarming with all manner of people. The absence of music clearly signalled that the supper hour had begun. Within moments hordes of laughing, chattering guests were making their way out of the ballroom into the corridors, out onto the brightly lit terrace and into the gardens, intent upon making the most of the balmy evening air before returning to the supper room to indulge themselves in the sumptuous repast that the Whitcombe cooks had worked so diligently to provide.

Muttering a string of curses, Marcus retraced his steps, grabbed the now violently resisting Christabel's hand and hauled her to her feet, having realised that their only hope of salvation now lay in exiting the library by way of its terrace doors. With luck, they might be able to lose themselves among the thronging crowds.

Just as they were about to step out onto the terrace, however, the library door was suddenly thrust open to reveal none other than Sir Randolph Dawlish himself standing at the threshold! With a terrified yelp, Christabel hurled herself at Marcus and buried her face into his shirtfront, whimpering, 'Save me—oh, I beg of you, don't let him hurt me, sir!'

Sir Randolph, a tall, spare man with thinning grey hair, whose pale and deeply lined face bore testimony to his chosen life of reckless dissipation, stood rigidly in the doorway for some moments, his thin lips twisting in a contemptuous smile as he surveyed the unfortunate scene. Then, striding across the floor with an angry snarl, he reached forward and attempted to wrench his wife away from Marcus who, despite his dismay at the baronet's unexpected appearance, had automatically raised his arms to cocoon the ashen-faced Christabel against his chest.

'So, madam wife!' sneered Dawlish. 'You think to creep off with your lover the minute my back is turned, do you?'

'You are mistaken, sir,' retorted the Viscount, raising his eyebrow in haughty disdain. 'Lady Dawlish appeared to be in some distress when I came upon her. I was just on my way to seek assistance—'

'A likely tale, sir!' Dawlish interrupted, his lip curling in disbelief. '"Tis common knowledge the sort of "assistance" Hellcat Helstone usually has in mind as far as the female of the species is concerned, but this time, my lord, I fear you have met your match, for I refuse to play cuckold to your scheming Lothario! I must insist that you release my wife at once, sir, and do me the courtesy of naming your seconds!'

'Don't talk rot, man!' returned Marcus shortly, while doing his level best to unclasp the disobliging Christabel's hands from the back of his neck. He shot a hurried glance at the growing crowd of curious onlookers who were eagerly converging upon the scene, in the futile hope that one or other of her friends might be among them and come to her rescue. 'I have no intention of meeting you. I assure you that neither your wife nor I have behaved in any way that would require me to do so.'

'Your assurances are worthless, sir!' ground out the now thoroughly enraged baronet, drawing himself up to his full height. 'I doubt that there is a single person here present who is unaware of your dubious history.' He paused, sneering. 'Do I take it that you are refusing to accept my challenge?'

Having finally freed himself from Lady Dawlish's clinging embrace, Marcus now found himself on the horns of a dilemma. Whilst there was no question in his mind that his unlooked-for sojourn with the baronet's young wife had been of an entirely innocent nature, it was not difficult for him to see how such a situation might appear to the average bystander—especially given the highly embellished reputation he had gained over the past few years. Up until about twenty or so minutes ago he would have had no difficulty in accepting Dawlish's challenge, and taken considerable pleasure in wiping the supercilious smirk off the slimy toad's evil visage, but now, having only just succeeded in getting himself back in Sophie's good books, Marcus was not at all happy to find himself embroiled in a scandal that was not of his making. He could only hope and pray that word of this unpleasant event had escaped her ears.

Casting a wary glance over the assembled onlookers, he very soon realised that such optimism was doomed to failure—for there, on the very fringe of the crowd, stood Sophie, her wide blue eyes luminous with unshed tears. The Viscount was beset by a wave of despair, and only just managed to stop himself from howling out his innocence to her. *This is none of my doing, believe me!* his eyes strained to tell her. *This is not what it seems, I swear!*

Having waited for Helstone to return to the ballroom and accompany her into supper, as previously arranged, the somewhat puzzled Sophie had finally made her way out onto the terrace in search of her errant escort. Curious as to the noisy throng of guests surging outside the library doors, she had drifted towards the scene, only to find herself confronted with the appalling sight of Marcus locked in the arms of another man's wife.

Scarcely able to believe her senses, she had stood, almost paralysed with shock, while she listened to Dawlish issue his challenge. It was beyond her understanding that Marcus, who less than half an hour previously had been practically begging her to look favourably on his suit, should have chosen to while away the intervening minutes in a clandestine liaison with some other unsuspecting female—and a married one, at that! Righteous anger began to bubble up inside her chest, and she was just about to turn away from the distasteful scene in shuddering revulsion when she caught sight of the anguished appeal in Helstone's eyes. She froze, as wild seeds of doubt began to plant themselves in her mind, and, unable to prevent herself, took a hesitant step forward—only to find herself being held back by Lord Bingham who, having been notified of the commotion by a diligent manservant, had recently arrived at her side.

'What's going on, Sophie?' he asked, a concerned frown furrowing his brow as he attempted to make sense of the scene unfolding at the library's threshold.

'I'm not absolutely certain, Jack,' she answered him shakily. 'It seems that Sir Randolph discovered Lord Helstone in some sort of compromising situation with Lady Dawlish and has challenged his lordship to a duel!'

'Good Lord!' exclaimed Bingham, casting a nervous look over his shoulder. 'Let's hope my father doesn't get wind of it—a thing like this is enough to put the dampers on the whole proceedings. Ought I to step in and put a stop to it, do you suppose? Wouldn't do to upset the ladies, now, would it?'

Since it was clear that a good many of the gaping bystanders were of the female gender, Sophie could only suppose that the Viscount was attempting to lighten the atmosphere by uttering such a frivolous jest. She herself was unable to find any humour in a situation that might easily lead to Marcus being hurt or, God forbid, *killed*! No matter what he might have done to deserve it, the thought of him losing his life was more than she could bear to contemplate.

'I was under the impression that duelling had been made illegal,' she said worriedly.

'Yes, it has,' returned Bingham distractedly, his eyes still intent upon the interaction between Helstone and Dawlish. 'Still goes on, of course—the participants just have to be careful not to get caught by the authorities. Certain imprisonment, I believe.'

'I insist that you name your seconds, sir!' barked Dawlish, his cheeks purpling with rage as the scowling Viscount continued to refuse to accept his repeated challenge. Then, with a derisive sniff, he turned to face the several other men who had accompanied him into the library, smirking. 'It would appear that the great nonesuch has finally lost his bottle, gentlemen!'

Closing his eyes briefly, as a ripple of frustrated rage ran through his veins, Marcus was finally forced to concede that Dawlish had left him with no choice. Not that he was particularly bothered about having to face up to the man but, having registered Sophie's look of total revulsion, it had become painfully clear to him that any hopes he might once have harboured in that direction were now doomed to failure. Alongside that depressing thought, the possibility of severe injury suddenly seemed of little importance.

But as to the matter of seconds? Marcus was not at all sure that any of his one-time associates would be interested in supporting him, given that he had made a point of shunning all such delinquent company since his recent renaissance. He had no doubt that his brother Giles—after treating him to a severe dressing down for landing himself in such hot water—would have been willing to oblige him, but unfortunately Giles was up to his neck in Home Office affairs and not immediately available.

A pensive frown sifted across his forehead. It was hard to believe that he, with so many friends and acquaintances, should be finding it a problem to drum up a single name.

'Well?' demanded Dawlish belligerently, thrusting his face mere inches from the Viscount's own. 'Are you going to admit you are at fault and apologise immediately or name your seconds—the choice is yours!'

Sophie was beside herself with wretchedness. 'Do something, Jack,' she beseeched Bingham, clutching frantically at his arm. 'I don't think I can bear another minute of this.'

'I'm not altogether sure that there's anything I *can* do now,' returned Bingham, looking somewhat abashed. 'Looks as if Sir Randolph might have a point, after all—messing about with another fellow's wife, you know...' His voice trailed away awkwardly.

But Sophie, having taken a good look at the quietly weeping Christabel, would have none of it. She was finding it impossible to believe that such a little mouse-like creature as the curled-up female on the chair seemed to be would appeal to the Viscount in any way whatsoever. It was becoming increasingly obvious to her that not only was Marcus's supposed transgression distinctly out of character, it would seem that there was a good deal more behind his clear reluctance to accept the baronet's challenge than appearances might suggest. And then, as her mind dwelt upon the decidedly anguished look that had crossed his face when he had spotted her in the crowd, she became immediately convinced that, for some obscure reason or other, he had allowed himself to become a scapegoat.

'You *must* do something about it,' she said stoutly. 'I'm sure that there has been some dreadful mistake. Helstone is not at fault—I would stake my life on it!'

Incensed at Marcus's stubborn refusal to countenance either of his demands, Dawlish suddenly lashed out at the Viscount with both fists. 'Name your seconds, damn you!' he spluttered, becoming almost apoplectic with rage as Marcus, his highly tuned reflexes leaping instantly into action, moved himself well out of the baronet's range.

All at once a ripple of excitement, followed by an expectant hush, ran through the by now utterly spellbound spectators as the young Viscount Bingham shouldered his way through their midst and stepped into the room.

'If you're in want of a second, my lord,' he said, favouring Marcus with a brief smile. 'I would be more than happy to offer my services!'

Chapter Seventeen

'I still don't understand why you just didn't give the fellow my name and have done with it?' exclaimed the exasperated Giles who, when the rapidly spreading rumours concerning Marcus's unfortunate clash with Dawlish had reached his ears, had immediately downed tools and hastened back to Bradfield Hall. 'Surely you must have known that I would support you?'

'I wasn't too sure how to get hold of you,' returned his brother, emitting a weary sigh. 'Quite apart from the fact that I really had no intention of taking up Dawlish's challenge. None of it would have happened had the foul-minded swine been prepared to listen to reason but, no! It was clear from the very start that he was determined to make full capital out of the matter.'

'You think the chap has some sort of a grudge against you, then?'

'Well, it's true that I've managed to relieve him of several thousand pounds over the last year or so,' replied Marcus with a careless shrug. 'And I did catch him

trying to cheat in a poker game a couple of months
ago—not that I mentioned it at the time, but I've always
had the feeling that he knew I'd spotted his careless
gaffe. But to involve that pathetic little scrap of a wife
of his in the way that he did, simply to get back at me,
must surely be the action of the lowest cur on earth! For
that reason alone it would give me the greatest pleasure
to put a bullet through one or other part of his slimy
form!'

Giving a disapproving shake of his head, Giles felt
constrained to point out that Sir Randolph was known
to be a pretty fair shot himself, adding, 'Don't you think
it might be better if we were to try and reach some sort
of compromise? That, after all, is what a good second
is supposed to do in circumstances such as these.'

'Well, I refuse to give him some sort of grovelling
apology, if that's what you're about to suggest,' growled
Marcus, heaving himself up out of his chair and striding
across to the sideboard to replenish his empty glass. 'I've
had more than enough of that particular topic from the
mater.'

'Good Lord, man!' exclaimed Giles, a concerned
frown crossing his face. 'You're not telling me that the
parents have got wind of the affair?'

'Just Ma,' Marcus took pains to assure his brother.
'Luckily, the vast majority of Whitcombe's guests only
learned of it long after it was all over, but naturally, Ma
being Ma, she had to know everything, down to the
last detail. And, since she spent the entire ride home
last evening badgering me, I was finally goaded into
confessing, on the strictest understanding that she kept
it from the old man.'

'Well, thank heaven for small mercies,' breathed the
Major, much relieved.

'I'll have you know that I'm not quite as dicked in the nob as you seem to be implying,' muttered his brother, somewhat affronted. 'I'm well aware that a shock of this sort is enough to bring on another attack—which was yet one more reason why I wasn't too keen to drag you into this affair. I'm perfectly capable of dealing with the matter on my own—it's not as though I haven't had plenty of practice!' he finished dryly.

'Don't be a fool!' retorted Giles, glowering. 'If you're determined to go through with it, then I'm happy to support you all the way—as you well know!' Then, after taking a pensive sip from his glass, he leaned forward again. 'You didn't tell me how Dawlish reacted to Bingham's offer,' he observed. 'I imagine the fellow wasn't best pleased at the thought of Whitcombe's son taking your side?'

'Well, there was quite a bit of teeth gnashing going on, as I recall,' replied Marcus, a faint smile creasing his face. 'Then Dawlish just grabbed hold of his wife's arm, yanked her out of her chair and was about to drag her out of the room when young Lady Bingham intervened and insisted on taking Christabel to the ladies' room to recover from her ordeal—Bingham must have sent his wife some sort of sign, I suppose. Anyway, the long and the short of it is that Dawlish stormed straight out of the building, leaving his wife to God and good neighbours, as it were!'

'Let's hope the poor lass has the sense to remain there until this miserable business is over and done with.' His brother sighed, as he reached for his glass once more. 'Not that I would care to be in her shoes when she finally does put in an appearance.'

Marcus grimaced, his lips twisting slightly, as he replied, 'Oh, I dare say Miss Pendleton-Flint will drum up some sort of solution to that particular problem—as soon as young Christabel recovers sufficiently to unburden herself of her troubles, that is.'

'Miss Pendleton-Flint?' repeated the Major, suddenly alert. 'You didn't mention that she was present at this event.'

'Did I not?' returned Marcus, with a self-deprecating shrug. 'As it happens, our one-time governess was very much present, and had little difficulty in making her feelings on the matter pretty clear, as I recall.'

A curious expression on his face, Giles regarded his brother in silence for some minutes before asking, in a slightly offhand manner, 'Do I take it that you are still carrying a torch for that young lady?'

'Something of the sort,' grunted Marcus, shifting restlessly in his seat. 'Bit pointless, really, since it would seem that this latest escapade of mine has put the final damper on whatever chance I might once have had in that direction. The only husbandry that is likely to affect me in the near future is that which involves crop rotation and milk yields!'

Less than ten miles away, at Whitcombe Abbey, the subject of Helstone's morose introspection was seated at Christabel Dawlish's bedside, endeavouring to piece together that young woman's tearfully stilted version of the previous evening's melodrama.

Although Sophie had no doubt in her mind that the Viscount was innocent of any of the charges that Sir Randolph had flung at him, she had to admit to being distinctly curious as to how the whole distasteful affair had actually come into being. Unfortunately, trying to extract the bones of the matter between the various sniffles, gulps and self-condemnatory tears of the still badly affected Christabel was proving to be no mean task.

Eventually, however, her confidence bolstered by the many sympathetic nods and expressions of commiseration from both Elizabeth and Sophie—not to mention the numerous cups of hot chocolate and soft buttered rolls with which she had been plied throughout the night—Christabel managed to satisfy her listeners that their joint decision to whisk her away from her husband had been well and truly justified.

Having arrived at the scene just in time to witness Bingham offering his services to Helstone, his young wife had demanded to be told what was going on. After hearing Sophie's brief but pithy explanation, Elizabeth had taken one long, lingering look at the wretched-looking creature still cowering in her armchair and had then, after a hurried consultation with her friend, taken it upon herself to waylay Sir Randolph on his exit from the library. Although, to begin with, it had been their intention merely to afford the baronet's wife some sort of temporary respite from the ugly scene that was being played out in front of a score or more of voracious onlookers, neither Sophie nor Elizabeth could find it in themselves to feel a great deal of sorrow upon learning that Dawlish had taken off without Christabel.

A hasty discussion involving both Mrs Egremont and Countess Whitcombe had resulted in Christabel being tucked up in one of the abbey's many guest bedrooms, but, since it had become clear that the girl had suffered too great a shock to allow her to fall asleep, Sophie and Elizabeth had taken turns at keeping her company throughout the night.

'And now,' hiccoughed the girl wretchedly, at the end of her long drawn-out recital, 'the p-poor man is about to get himself k-killed—and all because he tried to h-help me!'

Since Sophie had spent the past several hours endeavouring to rid her mind of such a devastating thought, Christabel's unpleasant reminder was more than enough to send a shudder of dread running through her. Biting her lip, she took a steadying breath and forced herself to concentrate on ridding Christabel of the feelings of remorse that so clearly burdened the grief-stricken girl.

'Come now,' she said soothingly, as she patted Christabel's hand. 'I refuse to believe that it will come to that—Lord Bingham has assured his wife that he intends to take whatever steps are necessary to bring about some sort of conciliation.'

'Sir Randolph is not the sort of man who can be easily appeased.' Christabel sniffed and gave a mournful shake of her head. 'He is so utterly self-centred that the only point of view that has any meaning for him is his own.'

Their eyes meeting across the bed, Elizabeth and Sophie shared a brief moment of compassion for the girl. That there was little love lost between Dawlish and his young wife was very plain to see.

'Forgive my vulgar curiosity, my dear,' ventured the Viscountess tentatively. 'But how came you to marry such an unpleasant man?'

'He had advanced my father a large sum of money for some business venture or other,' Christabel sighed. 'Unfortunately, when the time came to repay the loan, Papa had insufficient means at his disposal and was obliged to ask Sir Randolph for a postponement. Having already learned that the quite substantial amount of money that I was due to inherit from my grandmother on my twenty-first birthday would be paid if I were to marry in advance of that date, Sir Randolph agreed to forego the debt on condition that I married him—otherwise he threatened to haul my father into the debtors' court.' At the memory, her already red-rimmed eyes filled once more with tears as she hid her face in her hands with a choked, 'I couldn't allow that to happen, so I simply went along with it!'

'Dear God!' whispered Sophie, in the certain knowledge that her own father would rather have sold his own soul to the devil than sacrifice his daughter in such a way. Having observed clear signs of bruising on Christabel's arms and back while helping the girl to undress, she could not forbear from adding, 'And, not content with helping himself to your inheritance, it would appear that the horrid fiend beats you, too!'

'It's not the beatings I mind so much,' faltered Christabel, dropping her eyes as her colour mounted. 'It's the—the other ways in which he chooses to punish me that I fear most of all.'

Even though the unspoken meaning behind the young Lady Dawlish's hesitant disclosure was only too clear to her stunned and horrified listeners, both Sophie and Elizabeth were uncomfortably aware that there was little that they could do in regard to that particular aspect of the girl's pitiable existence, other than try to keep her here at the abbey for as long as was humanly possible.

'We'll just have to tell Dawlish that his wife has suffered some sort of mental breakdown and cannot possibly be moved,' whispered Sophie as, with a brief flutter of her eyelids, accompanied by a shuddering sigh, their exhausted patient finally allowed herself to succumb to the sleep that had eluded her.

'Which is hardly a lie, in the circumstances,' returned

Elizabeth fiercely. 'If I were a man, I'd gladly put a bullet into the vile creature myself!'

Her heart seeming to jump into her throat as she was confronted with yet another reminder of the looming threat to Helstone's life, Sophie, clutching at her friend's hand, drew her across the room towards the window, well out of hearing of the now soundly sleeping Christabel.

'Has Jack managed to put a stop to this fiasco yet, do you know?' she asked, her eyes full of concern.

'He was very reluctant to tell me anything at all!' sniffed the Viscountess in disgust, still somewhat piqued that her husband had refused to take her into his confidence. 'However, I did manage to worm out of him that he had spent the better part of the night in consultation with Sir Reginald's seconds—he wouldn't give me their names, of course, but he does seem pretty certain that Dawlish has no intention of pulling out.'

'He didn't say when it would take place, then?'

Elizabeth shook her head. 'Not as such—apart from letting slip that he hoped the Cromptons' ball this evening wasn't going to last all night. So my guess is that the meeting is set for first thing tomorrow morning.'

On hearing Sophie's sudden intake of breath, she paused, regarding her friend with a certain amount of curiosity. 'You seem unduly concerned about Viscount Helstone's safety—I was under the impression that the two of you barely knew one another.'

Unable to prevent the rosy blush that was beginning to flood her cheeks, Sophie turned hurriedly away, simulating a keen interest in a somewhat bland-looking watercolour that hung on the wall nearby. 'We don't,' she replied, with a feigned nonchalance. 'It just doesn't seem fair to me that the poor man should feel obliged to put his life at risk just to satisfy the lunatic ravings of a devil like Dawlish—we both know that his lordship is not at fault, after all!'

Elizabeth, continuing to study the back of Sophie's head, was struck by a sudden thought. 'I was watching the pair of you dancing together last evening,' she said slowly. 'I remember thinking that I had never seen you look so happy—so alive!' Her eyes widening, she took hold of Sophie's arm, spinning her round in order that she might see her friend's face as, in almost breathless fascination, she challenged, 'You love him, don't you?'

Unable to bring herself to deny the charge, Sophie gave a brief nod, her lips quivering with barely suppressed anguish as she blurted out, 'I know it's stupid of me, and I've tried so very hard not to, but I just can't seem to help myself!'

With that, she buried her face in her hands and burst into tears. Elizabeth, thoroughly caught up in her friend's misery, flung her arms around her and, hugging her tightly, murmured, 'Oh, you poor, poor thing—it must be devastating for you not to know what's happening—I swear I'll make Jack tell me if it's the last thing I do!'

Chapter Eighteen

The early-morning mist was still wreathing its diaphanous plumes over the heath's scrubland as Marcus's carriage drew to a halt beside the clump of trees that had been designated for the meeting place. Leaping lightly from the vehicle, his lordship was surprised to note that two other carriages were already in attendance at the scene, despite the fact that the time was still more than fifteen minutes short of the appointed hour.

'Colder than I expected,' remarked Bingham, as he cast a somewhat nervous glance in the direction of Dawlish's waiting group.

Never having been involved in anything of this sort before, he was slightly unsure what to expect. He had heard a good many tales, of course, and had taken pains to acquaint himself with the proper procedure. Since he had already made a thoroughly conscientious attempt at mediation—a second's primary duty, according to his sources—he was reasonably satisfied that he had fulfilled all his requisite obligations. All that remained now, as he understood it, was for one or other of the parties to deal his opponent a relatively harmless injury—a slight nick on the upper arm usually served, it seemed— and justice would be seen to have been done, with neither party having lost face. He had also managed—after some considerable difficulty and the promise of a hefty fee—to persuade his family doctor's junior partner into attending what was, when all was said and done, the sort of activity now punishable by law. But, having observed that Dr Felsham, whose maroon landau Bingham had recognised, had chosen to remain well out of sight at this juncture, the young Viscount could only hope that his father never got to hear of his own part in the illicit proceedings!

Giles, meanwhile, was busily engaged in examining the weapons, which on this occasion had been supplied by Dawlish, whose skill as a crack marksman was common knowledge—not that the Major had any doubts as to his brother's own expertise in the sport, having seen him shoot out a pip at a distance of twenty yards or more.

Having checked the silver-handled duelling pistols to his satisfaction, the Major stood back and watched as one of Sir Randolph's seconds, Captain Dempsey by name, tossed a coin to decide which of the participants should be given first choice of weapon. Dawlish's harsh 'heads' allotted the choice to Marcus, when the coin landed tailside uppermost.

Extracting a battered chronometer from his pocket as the muffled chimes of a distant church clock struck the hour, Dempsey flipped open its case to declare that the time had arrived for Helstone and Dawlish to take their places.

Pistols in hand, the two stood back to back, awaiting the count.

'Time for last prayers, you despicable swine,' grated Dawlish through clenched teeth, his mocking words inaudible to all but the Viscount.

'*One...two...three...*'

His lip curled in derision, Marcus stepped forward. *So the cur actually means to kill me, does he?* he mused, almost unconcernedly. Having spent the better part of the past twenty-four hours putting his affairs in order, including willing all his worldly possessions to his younger brother, he had very little interest in the outcome of this morning's meeting. In fact, once he had registered the look of sheer contempt on Sophie's face after his attempts to signal his plea of innocence to her, the Viscount had discovered that he really had very little interest in anything at all.

'*Four...five...six...*'

His initial anger at Dawlish's accusation had dissipated some hours ago, especially since he had been obliged to face up to the irrefutable fact that, having gone out of his way to acquire the unsavoury reputation with which the name Helstone had become synonymous over the past six years, such a charge had become almost inevitable, given the decidedly incriminating circumstances in which he had been discovered. In fact, it had become depressingly clear to Marcus that it was going to take a darned sight more than a couple of weeks of fixing tenants' roofs and calculating milk yields to cancel out his now deeply regretted history of loose living and self-indulgent profligacy. Unfortunately, as he had also come to realise, without Sophie by his side to help him overcome the stumbling blocks that inevitably lay ahead of him, he was not at all sure that he would be able to summon up either the inclination or the enthusiasm to deal with so momentous a task. In losing Sophie, Marcus was starting to realise that he had lost everything that was truly worth living for.

'*Seven...eight...nine...*'

His brain automatically cutting to the matter in hand, the Viscount tensed, his finger poised to squeeze the trigger on the turn. Just as he was about to take the final step forward, however, he was astounded to find himself staggering to remain upright as the force of Dawlish's bullet ripped through his left coat-sleeve, biting into the tender flesh of his underarm. His shock and anger was so great in that moment that any pain he might have been feeling was thrust immediately from his mind. The treacherous bastard had pre-empted Dempsey's count! Whirling round to confront his assailant, he slowly raised his pistol.

Scarcely able to comprehend that his carefully aimed shot could have missed its intended target, the by now thoroughly shaken Dawlish stood utterly transfixed, his brain refusing to function. Not only had he commit-ted the indefensible offence of discharging his pistol in advance of the call, but he had also failed in his attempt to put a period to his hated enemy's life! But then, as the awful realisation that Helstone was aiming his as yet still loaded weapon in his direction finally captured the horrified baronet's attention, his heart seemed to stop in its tracks and he let out a whimper of despair.

His eyes fixed unwaveringly on Dawlish's panic-stricken face, the Viscount took aim.

'Hold hard, Marcus!' howled Giles, as he leapt across the space that separated him from his brother. 'Lower your weapon, man!'

Temporarily sidetracked by the Major's frantic shout,

Marcus was momentarily diverted from his intention. Seizing his opportunity, Dawlish swung round and, taking to his heels, tore frantically across the grass in an effort to reach the safety of his carriage.

His lips curling in contempt as he watched the baronet haul himself into his waiting carriage, Marcus, lowering his pistol, turned to face his irate brother. 'I wasn't about to kill him, if that's what you were afraid of,' he grunted, somewhat aggrieved at Giles's apparent lack of faith. 'I merely intended to part the swine's hair!'

'You're a damned fool,' retorted the Major, looking suitably shamefaced. 'I can only thank God that the lily-livered cur wasn't as good a shot as he thought he was!'

'Not half bad, though,' muttered Marcus as, suddenly aware of the burning pain in his underarm, he stared down in fascination at the rivulet of blood now dripping from the cuff of his jacket. 'Another inch or so to the right and—'

A wave of blackness swept over him and then... *nothing.*

'What exactly do you mean by "slightly injured",' asked Sophie, eyeing Bingham suspiciously.

'He took a bit of a nick in his arm, that's all,' replied the Viscount with a nervous laugh. 'The doctor didn't seem too worried about it—just a flesh wound, he said.'

Having seen more than enough 'flesh wounds' in her time, Sophie was still not nearly satisfied with Bingham's very sketchy description of Helstone's injury. Having set upon him the moment he had arrived back at the abbey, both she and Elizabeth had proceeded to badger the Viscount until, with the utmost reluctance, he had eventually been browbeaten into divulging the very barest details of that morning's happenings.

'Was his lordship losing a great deal of blood?' she demanded to know.

'Oh, I think we might be spared that sort of detail,' interposed Elizabeth hurriedly, her face paling. 'If Dr Felsham was of the opinion that Helstone's wound wasn't serious, then surely we ought to accept his verdict.'

'Simple flesh wounds have been known to turn very nasty,' Sophie countered in reply but then, having taken note of her friend's rather sickly-looking expression, she swiftly changed the subject to demand of Bingham, 'So, where exactly is his lordship now?'

'Major Wolfe had Felsham accompany them both back to Grosvenor Square,' the Viscount was at pains to assure her. 'Where you can be sure that he will receive the very best of treatment. Anyway, if you ask me, Dawlish is the one we should all be feeling sorry for at this moment!'

'That cur!' retorted Sophie with an angry glare, while Elizabeth merely gave a derisive snort. 'Why on earth you think that anyone would feel a moment's pity for that odious creature is beyond my understanding. After the way he's treated that poor defenceless wife of his, the evil swine deserves everything he gets—not that his punishment for behaving in so outrageous a manner is likely to amount to much more than being blackballed from one or two of his clubs for a couple of weeks,' she added scathingly. 'The brunt of which will be borne by Lady Dawlish, if I'm any judge!'

'And I fear that you would be quite wrong in that assumption,' said Bingham, giving a decisive shake of his head. 'Seems the poor devil suffered some sort of apoplectic seizure not long after climbing into his carriage. Captain Dempsey—one of his seconds—sent a note round to the major indicating that it's highly unlikely that Dawlish will last the night!'

There followed a somewhat awkward silence as Sophie and Elizabeth tried their level best to avoid catching one another's eyes, the guilty remorse on both girls' faces bearing testament to their vociferous and far-reaching condemnation of the baronet earlier.

'I suppose one of us ought to go and break the news to Christabel,' ventured Sophie at last. Not that she was looking forward to imparting such gruesome tidings to Dawlish's young wife, particularly after having spent the best part of the night castigating the man. Added to which, since she was fairly sure that Christabel would immediately assume the mantle of guilt for the whole wretched affair, she had the distinct feeling that the girl's previous display of grief would be as nothing when compared to the one which would erupt upon being informed of her husband's imminent demise.

Having already spent a good many hours at the highly distressed girl's bedside, Sophie was now thoroughly exhausted and would have liked nothing better than to bury her own head in a pillow and devote her thoughts to trying to figure out what might be going on in Grosvenor Square at that moment. As her many years of experience had taught her, even the simplest of flesh wounds had a nasty habit of festering and turning putrid. Tiny threads of fabric could get caught under the skin, setting up an infection. Instruments were often contaminated, and bandages weren't always as clean as they might be—not to mention the very real danger of lead poisoning—all of which might easily lead to amputation and—a violent shudder ran through her as she did her best to suppress the thought that followed—even *death*!

Biting her lip to stop the tears that threatened, Sophie knew that there was no way that she could be satisfied that Helstone's injury was really as trivial as Jack had attempted to imply. She was just going to have to go up to London and discover for herself the actual extent of the damage to his lordship's arm! But first, as she was reluctantly forced to remind herself, there still remained the rather depressing task of dealing with the soon to be widowed Christabel Dawlish. Murmuring a short prayer of absolution, Sophie could not forbear from keeping her fingers tightly crossed as she entered the sleeping girl's room.

'Absolutely not!' Marcus gave a mutinous shake of his head. 'I've already told you! I have no intention of putting in an appearance at Bradfield until this damned arm of mine is on the mend!'

'But if Ma should get to hear of your injury, she'll be pretty offended at you not wanting her at your bedside,' protested his brother. 'You can't have forgotten what she was like when we both went down with scarlet fever that time!'

'There's no reason why she should get to hear of it,' riposted Marcus with a weary sigh, while privately thinking that the only person he really wanted—*needed*—by his bedside at this particular moment was the chestnut-haired, blue-eyed goddess who had so clearly rejected him two nights ago. 'Neither of Dawlish's cohorts is going to want word of their chum's gutless behaviour to get out—especially as the poor sod seems about to cash in his chips, if Dempsey's note is anything to go by. Young Bingham has been doing his damnedest to keep the affair from his father's ears and I certainly don't see Felsham blabbing about it.'

'Well, I'm not entirely happy about leaving you here on your own,' remonstrated Giles. 'You lost a fair amount of blood—you were out for almost half an hour, I'll have you know!'

'So you keep telling me,' retorted his brother dryly. 'However, in case you have failed to notice the fact, I can hardly claim to be on my own, being surrounded by an entire household of highly trained staff whose only desire in life is to pander to my every need. The noble Ferris is on hand to deal with my more personal requirements, and our reluctant medic has promised to drop in at regular intervals to change my dressings. Satisfied?'

'I suppose so.' The Major stood undecided for a moment, before adding, 'But you really do need to rest, if you want that wound to heal properly, so positively *no* visitors allowed—I shall inform Danson on my way out.'

Having spent the better part of the morning suffering the ministrations of the none too happy Dr Felsham, Marcus was feeling decidedly wrung out and only too pleased to comply with his brother's instruction. Particularly in view of the fact that it had been entirely due to the Major's quick response that he had been prevented from falling to the ground when he had collapsed—an achievement that had doubtless saved him from even further injury. Not that the Viscount could recall a great deal of what had followed, other than finding himself back in his own bed being poked and prodded with what he had felt at the time was undue savagery but what he now supposed was quite normal procedure, given the unusual circumstances. Incredibly, and although it had taken off a slice of his skin in the process, the ball from Dawlish's firearm had ripped straight through Marcus's coat sleeve, finally ending its journey at some point on the grass in front of him. And, despite the fact that the surface wound had bled rather profusely at the time, Marcus had been gratified to learn that there had been no damage to the underlying muscle. Felsham had assured the Viscount that a few days' rest and recuperation were all that were needed to return him to full health.

Gradually allowing his eyelids to droop to a close, Marcus was still unable to banish the truly gut-wrenching image of Sophie's horrified face from the forefront of his mind. Would she even care that he had been hurt, should she ever come to hear of it, he wondered, as sleep began to wash over him. Very probably not, was his last distinct thought.

Several hours later, having eventually persuaded Jack to allow her use of a carriage, Sophie, accompanied by one of the abbey's footman, arrived at the front door of Marcus's Grosvenor Square mansion only to find that both bell-pull and knocker had been removed from their housings—the latter a generally accepted signal that the dwelling's occupants were not in residence. Since there were clear sounds of activity issuing from the basement below, with sinking heart Sophie could only assume that Helstone's injuries had been far worse than Jack had been prepared to admit, and that the Viscount must be, at this very moment, lying at death's door!

Ignoring the footman's muttered disapproval, she raised her hand and rapped briskly on one of the door's panels. To her surprise the door, swinging open almost immediately, revealed the odd sight of a rather stately looking individual—the butler, Sophie assumed—who was regarding her with a severe frown on his face while one of his fingers was pressed firmly against his lips.

'If you please, miss,' the man whispered, casting a nervous look towards the highly impressive-looking stairway that stretched away to his right, 'we have illness in the house. I'm afraid I must ask you to state your business and be on your way.'

'But his lordship—' began Sophie, her voice tremulous with apprehension. 'Is he—? That is—I really need to know that he is all right!'

'I'm afraid his lordship is not receiving visitors at the moment, miss,' came the butler's haughty reply. 'If you would care to leave your card?'

Since Sophie had not yet availed herself of the Egremonts' offer to order her a set of visiting cards, she was at something of a loss. A sudden sob rising in her throat, she gave a reluctant shake of her head. 'Just tell your master that Miss Pendleton-Flint called,' she choked and, turning swiftly on her heel, she hurried down the steps, desperate to gain the sanctuary of her borrowed carriage before finally dissolving into the tears that she had succeeded in holding back for the past two days. *If only I had had the courage to accept Helstone's offer,* she found herself thinking, *none of this would ever have happened. Please, God, don't let him die—even if I can't have him, please keep him safe!*

In spite of Danson's determined efforts to achieve absolute silence throughout the building, it was actually the sound of Whitcombe's somewhat aggrieved footman slamming the carriage door rather too vigorously that roused Marcus from his sleep. Feeling much refreshed, he hauled himself up into a sitting position and reached out his hand for the pitcher of water that sat on his bedside table.

'Allow me, your lordship.'

Ferris was there before him, already pouring water into the waiting glass.

'What the devil was that infernal noise outside?' demanded Marcus, as he quaffed back the much needed liquid. 'Sounded like an explosion of some sort.'

'Just a carriage door, sir,' soothed his valet who, having had little else to occupy his time while his master slept, had been standing at the bedroom window aimlessly contemplating the passing traffic. 'The Earl of Whitcombe's, by the look of the door crest.'

'Viscount Bingham, I suppose,' murmured Marcus lazily, allowing his eyes to close once more as he leaned back against his pillows. 'Dare say he'll call again tomorrow.' Having been unable to express his thanks to the young Viscount for his part in that morning's events, Helstone was determined to make sure that Jack was fully aware of how grateful he was for his support.

'No, sir,' returned Ferris, stretching across Marcus to straighten his covers. 'The visitor was a young lady.'

His eyes flying open, Marcus shot up. 'A young lady?' he croaked in disbelief as he flung back the bedclothes and staggered across to the window. Sophie! It just had to be Sophie! Who else but Sophie would be calling on him in one of Whitcombe's carriages?

'Sir, I beg you!' cried Ferris, his face a picture of distress. 'I must insist that you return to your bed immediately.'

Having discovered that Whitcombe's carriage had disappeared from view, Marcus turned on his valet in disgust. 'Rubbish!' he retorted, already engaged in the rather intricate task of trying to remove his nightshirt with only one good hand. 'Stop wittering, man, and get me out of this damned thing.'

'But, sir!' protested his hapless valet. 'Major Wolfe gave specific instructions—'

'No doubt he did,' grated Helstone, doing his utmost to fight off the disturbing sense of weakness that was threatening to overcome his efforts. 'However, unless I am much mistaken, I am still master in this house! So, do as I say and sort me out something to wear—and while you're at it ring for Kimble and tell him that if my curricle isn't round at the front door in ten minutes flat, he can start looking for another position!'

Muttering fierce imprecations under his breath, Ferris felt he had no option but to carry out his master's orders, although he managed to retain sufficient forethought to send down for the brandy decanter while Marcus was engaged in dowsing his head in the basin of cold water that stood on the room's marble-topped washstand.

'Good man!' exclaimed the Viscount when, having dried off his face, his gaze fell on the drinks tray. 'That ought to do the trick!'

Exactly seven minutes and a couple of hefty swigs of brandy later, he was up on the driving seat of his curricle, an anxious Kimble at his side, intent upon chasing after Whitcombe's carriage in the hopes of making some sort of peace with Sophie.

But even as he unhooked the whip from its mounting it became clear to him that, with only one good arm at his disposal, such a task was going to prove well-nigh impossible. A resigned sigh left his lips as, reluctantly passing the reins to his groom, he urged, 'Spring 'em, Kim!'

Having finally cried herself out, Sophie dried her eyes, straightened her bonnet and cast an indifferent look out of the window, simply to ascertain how much further she had to go. As far as she could make out, the carriage was just passing through Chelsea village. As the sudden memory of that magical afternoon flashed into her thoughts, her lips curved in an unbidden smile. Leaning forward, with no clear understanding of what she was doing, she gave a sharp rap on the front window.

'Take the next left, Clifford,' she instructed the coachman. 'I have another call to make.'

Just one little peek, she told herself, as the carriage drew up outside the driveway leading to Marcus's secret hideaway. *I won't even go up to the house. I'll just creep round to the lake and take a quick peek at the view, just to see if it's really as perfect as I remember it!*

Two breathless minutes later and there it all was, exactly as her mind had pictured it…the rose arbour…. the white-painted pavilion…the ducks at the waterside. In a sudden rush, the closely guarded memories of that truly wondrous afternoon came flooding back to her. The scent of the honeysuckle…the warmth of the sun on her face…the succulent taste of the strawberries…the touch of Marcus's hand as he draped the soft woollen shawl over her shoulders…the captivating smell of his cologne…

Countless minutes drifted past as the poignancy of all she had lost threatened to overcome her. She stood silently on the pavilion steps, doing her utmost to ignore the relentless ache in her heart and heaving in deep breaths of the softly scented air, until at last her senses were once more beguiled by the peaceful beauty of her surroundings.

She still had not moved when Marcus rounded the corner of the house. The sight that met his eyes stopped him in his tracks. Whilst he had always considered this vista to be the most attractive of his secret hideaways it seemed to him that, at this moment, Nature had surpassed herself. The exquisite loveliness of the scene now took on a new and more compelling meaning, the fundamental essence of which was Sophie, the captivatingly winsome beauty who had stolen not only his heart but his very soul. How could he ever have imagined that taking her as his mistress would ever satisfy the deep hunger he felt for her? He knew now that, should he live to be a hundred, it would never be possible to have his fill of her.

But what if he was too late? His heart executing a painful somersault at the thought of such a possibility, the Viscount squared his shoulders, took a deep breath and, with no little trepidation, strode purposefully towards her.

Her reverie shattered by the sound of booted footsteps on the gravel path, Sophie, her eyes widening in shock, spun round to face him, a bizarre combination of intense joy coupled with faint apprehension coursing through her body.

'W-what are you doing here?' she gasped, her eyes anxiously raking his body for outward signs of injury.

'I might ask you the same question,' replied Marcus, stepping up into the pavilion and positioning himself directly in front of her, the breadth of his shoulders completely blocking her view of the lake.

Even though his expression was unreadable, Sophie could not prevent her heart from giving a little skip at seeing him standing there before her. 'I just wanted to take one last look—shouldn't you be in bed?'

'Very probably, but that's beside the point at this par-

ticular moment. I believe you came to see me. May I
ask why?'

'I just wanted—needed—to see how you were,' she
said, finding herself incapable of tearing her gaze away
from the penetrating look in his eyes.

'Needed?' Marcus's pulse quickened. 'I rather got the
impression that you had washed your hands of me.'

A puzzled frown crept over Sophie's brow. 'No such
thing. If you really must know, I—'

She stopped, her colour rising rapidly as she struggled
to find the words.

'Yes?' he prompted her. 'I really think I must know,
as it happens.'

'I came to tell you that I had changed my mind,' she
said in a low voice.

Marcus held his breath. 'Changed your mind about—
me?' he asked softly.

Sophie shook her head, the words tumbling out
almost without thought. 'About accepting your offer—
if you still want me!'

Want her! Scarcely able to believe what he was hearing, Marcus stared down at her, his mind in a whirl. *She
couldn't be referring to the* carte blanche *he had offered
her, surely? He had long since dismissed that idea as
being quite out of the question!* Needing to make sense
of what Sophie seemed to be saying, Marcus, passing
his hand across his forehead and uttering a faint groan
of dismay, turned on his heel and made for the water's
edge, his eyes fixed unseeingly on the placid scene
before him.

Having come to realise that she could no longer envisage a future without him, Sophie had already made the
momentous decision that the only way she could have
Helstone in her life was to accept the proposition he had

offered her. But now, as she studied the rigid stance of his body, her heart seemed to shrivel within her. She could only assume that the Viscount was regretting his former offer and no longer desired her. Bitter chagrin swept over her as she watched him turn and retrace his steps to stand, once more, directly in front of her.

Unsure how to begin, Marcus cleared his throat. 'I'm afraid that I am obliged to decline your very generous offer,' he said eventually. 'The truth is that I no longer find myself in the market for a mistress.'

Dropping her eyes, as every vestige of colour drained from her cheeks, Sophie was too shaken to formulate any sort of reply. Her lips trembling, she made to turn away from him—only to have him reach out his hand to catch hold of hers.

'I do have another suggestion that might be of interest to you, however,' he ventured, with just the hint of a smile on his lips. 'But first I have to know what caused you to change your mind.'

Another suggestion! thought Sophie bleakly. *A quick and tawdry dalliance in some out-of-the-way hotel or other,* she could only suppose. But then, she found herself reasoning, if that was all that he was prepared to offer her, could she really find the strength to turn him down, only to live out the rest of her life dreaming of what might have been? Having already thrown the last vestiges of her pride at his mercy, she resigned herself to the realisation that she really had nothing to lose by acquainting him with the true reason for her unexpected *volte face*. Stiffening her shoulders, she raised her chin defiantly and looked him directly in the eye.

'I love you,' she said simply.

Marcus, closing his eyes briefly, felt a surge of exhilaration flooding through his body, temporarily nullifying the throbbing pain in his injured arm. 'Oh, God, Sophie,' he gasped, as he pulled her towards him with his one good hand and buried his face in her hair. 'My dearest, darling girl! You can have no idea how I've yearned to hear you say those words!'

Almost convinced that she must be dreaming, Sophie pulled back and stared up at him, her face full of confusion. 'Are you trying to tell me that—?'

'—that I love you, too,' Marcus interrupted her, as he tightened his hold. 'Utterly and to distraction.'

'You love me?' faltered Sophie in disbelief.

'Now, always and for ever, sweetheart,' Marcus assured her. 'With every fibre of my being and with every breath I take.'

Even as a wild torrent of joy coursed through her veins, Sophie was unable to contain her mystification. 'Then what was the suggestion you were about to make to me?' she challenged him.

The Viscount gave a self-deprecating shrug, a rueful expression crossing his face as he replied. 'I was going to suggest that you might care to take pity on me and do me the honour of marrying me instead. I find that my life seems to make very little sense when you are not part of it.' His eyes darkened as he held her rapt gaze. 'The truth is that I simply didn't recognise that what I felt for you was a good deal more than just unadulterated lust.'

He paused, shooting her one of his lopsided grins. 'Although I am bound to admit that I cannot, in all honesty, claim to have noticed any lessening in that particular area, I've come to realise that I would truly far rather have you as my wife than as my mistress.'

A mischievous smile played about the corners of Sophie's lips. 'I dare say it would be possible to fulfil both duties, if I were to really put my mind to it,' she replied demurely.

Although he was not entirely sure that he had understood her aright, Marcus's eyes lit up as hope flared wildly within him.

'You mean you're prepared to accept my proposal?' he asked, in breathless amazement.

'I accept both of your proposals, my darling!' breathed Sophie, tears of joy filling her summer blue eyes as she flung herself into his waiting arms. But then, as she felt Marcus sag against her, a flicker of alarm ran through her. 'But first, I really do think I ought to get you into bed.'

Pressing his lips against her forehead, Hellcat Helstone—devil to the last—let out a roguish little chuckle. 'Whatever you say, my beloved angel,' he whispered into her ear. 'What man in his right senses could resist so enchanting a suggestion?'

* * * * *